The Churchill Diaries

By

Charles Powell

To Jo,

With love

Charles

10 May, 2010

Copyright © Charles Powell 2007-08-25
Charles Powell asserts the moral right to be identified as the author of this work.

ISBN Number 978-84799-881-1

Dedication

This book is dedicated to all those who seek the real truth about what politicians decide on our behalf and how they decide it.

"The loss of India would be final and fatal to us. It could not fail to be part of a process that would reduce us to the scab of a minor power."

Winston Churchill addressing the House of Commons, February, 1931

"We are going to have worse trouble with Britain after the war than we do with Nazi Germany now."

President Roosevelt writing to an aide about a speech that Winston Churchill had made to Parliament on 10 November, 1942.

"I need not tell you gentlemen that the world situation is very serious. That must be apparent to all intelligent people....."

American Secretary of State George C. Marshall, June 5, 1947

"A book that brilliantly illuminates the difference between what the public thought was going on and what in fact was happening!".

New York Times description of "*Meeting in Potsdam*".

"Lend/Lease involved Britain's surrender of her rights and royalties in a series of British technological achievements. Had Churchill been able to insist on adequate royalties for these inventions our balance of payments would have been very different....   The only solution was to negotiate a huge American loan, the repayment and servicing of which placed a burden on Britain's balance of payments right into the twenty-first century."

Harold Wilson, three times elected Prime Minister of Britain, Memoirs 1986.

Introduction

My grandfather worked directly with Winston Churchill throughout the Second World War. As soon as Winston was appointed to the Cabinet as First Lord of the Admiralty at the outbreak of the war he asked my grandfather to start working for him immediately as a special adviser on military intelligence. Throughout the Second World War he served Winston in that role. Churchill never fully trusted his senior commanders and the intelligence with which he was provided by them. He needed someone who understood the processes of military intelligence but was able to cut through the jargon and mumbo jumbo of one of the most obscure fields of information of all.

My grandfather, Samuel Garbutt, seemed to fit that role perfectly. He was a professional soldier who had served with distinction during the First World War. After the Battle of the Somme he had been transferred from his infantry regiment to lead a small and highly secretive new unit set up to develop new espionage methods which would lead to senior commanders getting much better intelligence about the deployment of enemy troops.

After the war he eventually gravitated to the Indian Army, going on to become Military ADC to the Viceroy. It was a posting that gave him access to a valuable and powerful network throughout the British military establishment. In 1934 he returned to London to command the Army's London District. In that role he was able to extend his personal networks largely through the London social scene. He was a popular dinner party guest and a well known raconteur and after dinner speaker. He first met Winston at a dinner party.

As soon as he joined Churchill at the Admiralty in September 1939 they met together virtually every day for the remainder of the war. He went with Winston on all his overseas trips and was with him at all the great conferences at which the end of the war and the beginnings of peace were planned. Having such close access to Churchill almost on a daily basis gave him one of the closest insights into Churchill's mind as the war unfolded. He was a highly trusted public servant and Churchill did frequently confide in him.

There is no reference to Samuel Garbutt in any official government documents about the Second World War. It is usually that way with intelligence officers. Equally there is no reference to him in any history of that war published up until now. His appointment was never published but there are some photographs taken at the time of the Tehran and Yalta conferences that show him in the same groupings as Churchill.

Somehow in what was a very busy life Samuel (that is what I will always call him in this book because that was the name by which I knew him from my teenage years onwards) did find the time to write his own personal account of his relationship with Churchill and of Churchill's difficult and often strained relationships with Roosevelt and Stalin and with his own senior military people. In that diary there is at least one entry for each day of the war. It is that diary which forms the basis for this book.

He actually started writing the diary when he returned from India but at that time it only included items of special interest to him. He continued writing it after the war but as he was no longer close to Churchill then, again it only contained items of special interest. In the early post war years this was largely a commentary on the performance of the government. He maintained an excellent network of friends after the war and when he retired and this was able to give him interesting insights into what was actually going on in the world.

Samuel always had hopes that someday it would be published but he knew well enough that it would be prevented from publication by the British Government until a very long time after Churchill had died. In his view, and almost certainly rightly, the government was hardly likely to allow publication of any book which would cause the public to question some of the major strategic issues that were involved in conducting the war.

Samuel was always completely loyal to Churchill during the war and he perfectly understood the reasons why what Churchill said and did were different. Publicly there was no way that Churchill was going to indicate any weaknesses in the British position to the British people. But behind closed doors it was very different.

After the war Samuel served initially with the British delegation attached to the Council of Foreign Ministers which was tasked with implementing the peace agreements negotiated between the allies at Potsdam in July 1945. He did not stay there long before he was offered an attractive posting at the British Embassy in Washington where he headed up military intelligence liaison with the Pentagon. He retired in 1950 and died in 1970.

After he retired he bought an attractive Queen Anne house in a village in North Essex. The house faced south and stood close to the large village green. The house had three acres of gardens and throughout his retirement years tending those gardens became his great passion. That area of the country was much favoured by retired military people and that made for an excellent social life for him. He also got to know the local farmers well and that meant it was possible for him to roam the farmlands on long walks. He came to love that countryside and his long walks kept him fit until shortly before his death.

Samuel's only child was my mother. She had been born in 1920 and qualified as a doctor during the war. She spent the rest of the war and many years after it helping to treat people wounded during it. Relieving the suffering gave her little interest in the perpetrators or anything to do with any part of war history. She saw her role as clearing up the human mess it caused.

My father had been a director of a family owned shipping line whose business had been smashed to pieces by the war. He had been much older than my mother and found the work of trying to rebuild that business to be a huge strain. He died while I was quite young. He had no interest in history either.

It was thus to me that Samuel turned in order to try and foster an interest in the diaries and the war. I often used to go and stay with him when I was in my teens and when the time came for me to go to university I chose a course in 20th century history. From then on the project to publish the diaries in some form became a strong interest in my life. It has taken more than 40 years to complete. A major reason why it has taken so long is that I agreed with Samuel that there was little point in seeking publication until such time as German and Russian archives could be thoroughly researched. He was certain that if access ever proved possible then I would find a rich seam of evidence to corroborate his own views about the conduct of the war and about the plans and aspirations of Churchill. In his view that would result in some very different opinions emerging about the true role of Britain. He also hoped that access to the Russian archives in particular would enable what he called "the myth of El Alamein" to be dispelled.

It was not until well after the collapse of the Berlin Wall and the end of the Soviet Union that access to those archives was possible. Not only was I then able to find all the corroborating evidence that I needed but I was also able to find some completely new evidence about the degree of treachery involved by Russia in the way that it handled the flow of information between our two countries in the pre-war years and during the war. In particular I found there the diaries of a British agent who had been a very senior official in the Foreign Office before and during the war. Putting that dairy together with Samuel's proved to be a fascinating experience.

It was while I was staying with him one weekend in February, 1963 that he really whetted my appetite for his story. It was a vile winter that year and every day between Boxing Day and the middle of March the entire countryside of most of Britain was covered by frozen snow. North Essex was worse hit by the blizzards than most other areas and for miles on end the frozen snow was several feet thick. We went out for a long walk after breakfast on the Saturday morning. It was on that walk that he told me about the Battle of Stalingrad and about what he knew about it from Russians with whom he had been dealing at those conferences. It was then that I knew that there was a real story to tell. The Battle of Stalingrad was hardly documented in the West at that time. Few people even knew that there had been a battle there and hardly anyone had any clue how Russia had been able to win it. It was particularly poignant that he should tell me about Stalingrad on such a cold grey morning. The frozen lands of Essex must have looked like the winter steppe west of Stalingrad just before the final stages of that great battle.

In July that year we went out for a similar walk on a hot thundery morning. It was to be the start of a true journey of discovery. It was then that he started to tell me about Kursk and about the impact the great battle there had on the entire remainder of the war and how Stalin brilliantly exploited the result of that battle to set the entire peace agenda. I had never heard of Kursk then but I have hardly gone through a day since without thinking about it. It is a battle that is hardly known about in Britain, even now, but it is the event that enables the mind to focus on the real truth about the end of the war and the Cold War that followed. Winston Churchill was fearful about Kursk before it happened and both obsessed about and terrified by the consequences. Samuel told me about those fears and about the dreadful consequences for Britain.

I was 25 years old when Samuel died. He was buried next to his wife, Rebecca, in that quiet Essex village. He was then truly a man who had found peace in the world and shortly before he died he gave me every encouragement to study and then publish his diaries. He left them to me in his will.

It is more than 35 years now since Samuel died. The research has been done. His version of events has been proved to be correct. Previously unpublished incidents of deceit and intrigue have been uncovered in my researches. I hope that from wherever he is now he approves of this version of his diaries. All direct extracts from those diaries included in this book appear in italics.

The journey of discovery on which I embarked on that July morning proved to be an enlightening and educational experience in every way. It taught me much about Samuel's lifestyle and it was to shape my own life in ways that I could not have imagined as I set out on that walk with him.

There has never been any doubt in my mind since then that he wanted me to enjoy my life as much as he had done. He was truly my mentor, friend and guardian angel all at the same time. But he also taught me how the powerful and famous live. His last words to me shortly before he died were "Enjoy yourself as I have taught you."

The Heads of Government

Samuel worked directly for Winston Churchill throughout the war. During that time he met with Roosevelt and Stalin during the various conferences of the Big Three as they planned for the ending of the war and the ensuing peace. Immediately after the end of the war he worked briefly for Clement Attlee who replaced Churchill after the British General Election in 1945. He told me several times that he wished he had also had the opportunity of meeting Hitler. There was never any prospect of that but how to beat Hitler inevitably dominated much of the thinking of Churchill.

Samuel wrote a thumbnail sketch of each of the Heads of Government who featured in his diary. He believed that they were all flawed people who were dominated by their personal political obsessions.

From the moment that I read those thumbnail sketches I felt that they would make a useful beginning to any published form of his diaries so I set them out here without any editing or changes. I have checked thoroughly to find out whether they are factually accurate and I am fully satisfied that they are. This is what he wrote a couple of years after Churchill's funeral, which he attended.

"May 10, 1967. These are my ideas on potted biographies of the key national leaders involved in the events described in these diaries:

Winston Churchill (born 1874, died 1965). *He was known as a long-serving British politician who became Prime Minister, as leader of a coalition government, on May 10, 1940. As we move further and further away from the times in which the events in this diary took place it becomes more and more evident that Churchill was an imperialist. He was driven by the concept of Empire and that of Imperial power. It is also clear that he supported Hitler and Mussolini, as a matter of policy, until the late 1930's. This was not understood by the public at the time but there can have been little doubt amongst those that knew him well, as I did at that time, that this was indeed the case. It is worth remembering, though, that at that time Winston had no political power.*

He had spent the 1930's in the political wilderness but he was re-appointed to the Cabinet at the outset of the Second World War. His post was First Lord of the Admiralty and he did valuable work in anti-submarine warfare. He was appointed Prime Minister when his predecessor resigned in 1940. After he was appointed Prime Minister, not by any democratic process but on the personal appointment of the King, his main role for the remainder of the Second World War was to direct the war effort. Together with American President Roosevelt he was the architect of The Atlantic Alliance, apparently and as sold to the British people, a declaration of mutual support between Britain and America. In framing it, it was America's intention to cause the break-up of the British Empire. Churchill knew that at the time and had fierce arguments with Roosevelt about the issue. But he told the British people a different story. The Atlantic Alliance does contain commitments that go far beyond the successful completion of The Second World War. Sooner or later the truth will out on this one. Because I know the content of the agreement I know that this pact has limited Britain's freedom to do anything without the specific approval of America ever since.

Churchill's political party, the Tories, was initially popular for its war effort but not popular for its social policies. A general election was called immediately the war finished and the Labour party won a landslide victory. People were completely fed up with Tory policies. A British public grateful for Churchill's wartime leadership, shunted him into political wilderness again. Churchill had been obsessed by military matters since he had been a small child. He served in the British army in two colonial wars. In the First World War, as a government minister, he had conceived the disastrous Dardanelles campaign. He had to resign after that and he went back into the army. He continued his obsession with military affairs right through his long wilderness years and he had many friends in the military who kept him well informed. I was one of those with whom he had good relations before the war.

Clement Attlee (born 1883, died 1967). He had been leader of the Labour party and as such he became Deputy Prime Minister in the coalition government led by Churchill. He became a Member of Parliament in 1922 representing the Limehouse constituency in the east end of London. In that wartime government he was effectively responsible for all domestic matters while Churchill was directing Britain's war effort. Right at the beginning of his premiership Attlee had to represent Britain at the Potsdam conference set up to deal with the division of responsibility for managing Europe after the war. That conference had been planned by Churchill, Roosevelt and Stalin. But before it had even started Roosevelt was dead. Attlee had to take over the British leadership of the conference long after it had started because Churchill had been rejected from office in a British general election. By the time Attlee was taking over Britain's role in the world was already evaporating.

Franklin D. Roosevelt (born 1882, died 1945). Widely regarded as a great American President, Roosevelt was the only one to have been elected to that office four times. He first became President in November, 1932. He had contracted poliomyelitis at the age of 39 and this caused weakness in his legs which he fought largely through vigorous swimming. It was to afflict his health and activity for the remainder of his life. Roosevelt came to power in the depths of the great depression and immediately set about a programme of economic and social reform. One of his earliest and greatest achievements was the creation of the Tennessee Valley Authority. When the war broke out in Europe Roosevelt attempted to keep America strictly neutral, except in respect of Britain to whom he was implacably opposed, primarily because he was opposed to imperialism. When Britain became beleaguered by the combination of the Dunquerque evacuation and the by the air raids in 1940 he agreed to help her through the supply of equipment but at that time he refused all requests for direct military involvement, even though he tried to make America neutral through legislation. His motive was the spread of American power and influence around the world through the support of democratic government everywhere. He sought to help Britain only in order to control her. This was done, initially, through the Lend/Lease of military equipment; ships and aircraft, in particular. After the Japanese attack on Pearl Harbor on December 7, 1941 America entered the war and Roosevelt directed America's global war effort. In order to do that he met several times with Churchill and Stalin. Roosevelt never allowed a British military commander to take overall control of any military activity on any war front in which America was involved, except naval activities on the North Atlantic. Roosevelt died a few weeks before the war in Europe ended. So strong was Roosevelt in American political life that he rarely bothered to consult anyone else about the war. This included his own cabinet.

Harry S Truman (born 1884, died 1972). He was Roosevelt's running mate in the 1944 American Presidential Election. He became President after Roosevelt died on April 12, 1945, a few weeks before the war in Europe was ended. Truman had had a very varied career before he went into politics. He had been a timekeeper for the Santa Fe Railroad, a mail clerk for a local newspaper, a bank clerk, farmer, postmaster, investor in lead mines, an oil investor and then soldier. After he returned to America from military service in France at the end of the First World War he owned a clothing store before he went into politics. In 1935 Truman became the Junior Senator for Missouri. He was lucky enough to become a member of the Interstate Commerce Committee of the Senate. When Truman succeeded to the Presidency he demonstrated ruthlessness, particularly against Britain, that went far beyond anything that the United States had demonstrated before.

Josef Stalin (born 1879, died 1953). *Stalin was born in the small Georgian town of Gori. He had a truly dreadful upbringing. At best it was squalid and brutalized. His father was a failed and drunken cobbler who beat him relentlessly. He suffered from smallpox when he was six; this left him scarred for life. He was saved from this misery by an excellent memory which made him a star pupil at school. It was easy for him to become a revolutionary activist. He robbed banks to fund his revolutionary activities. He was frequently in jail. But he became a very experienced agitator and terrorist. The only thing that mattered to Stalin after that was power. He was widely regarded as vindictive, cruel, rude and oppressive. He trusted no one. He had no problems about using violence under all circumstances. He ruthlessly exploited every opportunity to become leader of his country. He was the driving force behind something called the Second Revolution which was intended to move Russia from being a hopelessly backward state into being a successful and thoroughly modern state within ten years at the most. Literally millions of people were moved around the country to make it all happen. Beatings, torture, transportation and shootings were a normal part of the process. Many who resisted were put into forced labour camps. It was a thoroughly brutal experience for them all. Stalin oversaw the entire Russian war effort and together with Roosevelt, Truman and Churchill shaped the post war world. In that process Stalin achieved most of his ambitions.*

Adolf Hitler (born 1889. died 1945). *It would certainly be right to say that if anyone was brought up in a confused family it was Adolf Hitler. In the families from which he was created intermarriage was common and illegitimacy frequent. He was born and brought up in Austria. When Adolf was born his father was fifty-two years old, his mother just twenty-nine. There is record of bitter and unrelenting struggle between son and father. That struggle may have affected Hitler's school performance which was diabolical. In his teenage years he was remembered as a sickly person given to long periods of brooding and sudden but lengthy periods of hysterical anger. By the age of sixteen he was deeply into hate; hate of the aristocratic monarchies in Europe, particularly Austria, and hate of all non-German races. But at the same time he became fanatically pro-German. His mother died when he was nineteen. The following few years were a time of utter destitution for him. To earn a living he took on completely menial jobs such as shovelling snow, beating carpets, and carrying bags at railway stations. He lived in hostels for the un-employed and fed at soup-kitchens. He eventually left Austria in 1913 and moved to Munich. In 1914 he petitioned King Ludwig III of Bavaria and as a result he was allowed to join the German Army in the First World War. He was gassed in battle by the British at Ypres and invalidided out of the Army as a result. His military record was by no means undistinguished. He was twice decorated for bravery. Soon after the war ended Hitler joined the German Worker's Party. It was there that he learned the science of street politics. It was also there that he learned about propaganda. Under Hitler's guidance that party transformed itself into the Nazi party. Hitler became its natural leader with devastating consequences for the world."*

As I had spoken to Samuel over many years I had detected in his anecdotes a strong wariness about the characters who had led their countries during the war and into peace. This was despite his loyalty to Churchill during the war. Perhaps an over-riding impression I had got of it all was that it had been at best a messy process. I am sure that his brief description of these people was designed to enhance that feeling of messiness. It was perhaps easy for him to write these words when he had achieved peace with the world in his Essex village but I have no doubt that he had experienced much mental strain as he had had to cope with these men and with the way that they were manipulating the world. Finding out the real truth about it all promised to be a fascinating quest.

July, 1963

The morning after that thundery day when Samuel had first spoken to me about Kursk was brilliantly clear and the dark blue cloudless sky heralded a fine summer's day. The weather system that had brought the storms of the previous day had moved through to give us a truly sparkling morning. It was a Thursday and to Samuel every Thursday then was a special occasion for reasons I was soon to learn.

The special nature of Thursdays had everything to do with the fact that it was market day in the local town. Samuel never went to the market but all the local farmers did. They went there to buy and sell animals, meet farm industry traders and share several pints of beer with other farmers in the area.

Samuel had become friends with all the farmers in and around the village. One of those friends was Nigel Hannam. He owned the largest farm in the village. It was called Lake Farm and it stretched over more than two thousand acres. A small area of the farm close to the farmhouse was given over to pigs, poultry, vegetables and fruit. But all the remainder was used almost entirely for growing grain crops. At the northern end of the farm about three miles from the centre of the village there was an area of woodland and a lake, which gave the farm its name. The lake covered about five acres. It provided an abundant source of fresh fish.

Over breakfast that morning Samuel said to me:

"Today we are going to a very special place. It will be a perfect day for what we will be doing. We will be going there for a picnic lunch. We will walk there and that will take us about an hour. Most of the food we will need will be taken by the people we are going to meet there but we will also barbecue some fish from the lake. The girls we will be meeting there have some knowledge about Kursk that I am sure you will find to be very interesting. I will tell you about them on the way there. I will also tell you about much more about that battle. One thing I am absolutely certain about is that your life will change today."

We left Samuel's house soon after nine. Even before we left the house he had started to talk about Kursk.

"For me Kursk was the defining event of the war. It was not possible to say that in advance because we knew so little about what was going on there. We did have information from our spies within the German Armed Forces but we got no information of any sort from within the Russian Government. We could not, therefore, make any accurate judgments as to what was likely to happen. We did know that there was going to be a very big battle and we expected Germany to win it. Indeed, all our planning was based on that assumption. Once Kursk had happened everything changed.

"In the autumn of 1942 Germany and Russia fought at Stalingrad. We know why Germany needed to take that city but we had no idea why Russia chose to make such a valiant stand there. But in the Russian winter they destroyed all the German forces in and around the city. Only a very small number of people managed to escape. Ever since then all the military analysts have concluded that it was the appalling weather that enabled Russia to win that battle. The escapees all said that German tanks and guns could not operate in those temperatures and that it was Russian foot soldiers who won the battle. We did not know how many Russian troops were involved in the battle. It cannot have been many because all the intelligence available to us indicated that Russia had few reserves of men or equipment.

"In the months that followed Germany re-grouped and stabilised the front lines. In doing so they re-took Kharkov against minimal Russian resistance. That was a further sign to us that Russia was nearly at the end of its resources. Indeed there was absolutely no evidence that Russia had any capacity to fight at all. They seemed to have been completely exhausted by Stalingrad. Hence the universal view that Germany would win the final battle at Kursk.

"The prospect of a German win was a scenario that could lead to appalling consequences for Britain. A German win would lead to a prolonged war. The most likely scenario that we had debated was that Kursk would be such an overwhelming German victory that the war in the east would be virtually over.

"Although we had no military information from Russia we did have an endless series of communiqués from Stalin screaming for Britain and America to open a second front in the west so that Germany would be forced to withdraw troops from the east. That was something that was impossible at that time but Stalin repeated the demands at least once a week and he always argued that Russia was being destroyed and that America and Britain were doing nothing to ease his plight. At that time we believed what he was writing but we could do nothing about it. But as Kursk approached we were increasingly facing a doomsday scenario under which Britain might be overwhelmed by German forces in the spring of 1944.

"Although by then President Roosevelt had committed America to a war that could only end with the unconditional surrender of Germany, nobody in Britain then had any idea how or within what timescale that was going to be achieved. There were no promises that could be made to anyone about it. But Winston nevertheless made defiant speeches in the House of Commons. He told me many times that there was no substance to the speeches but he had to make them for morale reasons.

"Winston Churchill knew then that the British public was completely fed up with war. There were strikes taking place almost every week in naval dockyards and in armaments factories. All of them were protests against the war. Keeping news of those strikes out of the papers was in itself a major task. At the time of Dunquerque he was truly a national hero. So he was again after El Alamein. But the slow progress of the allied troops across North Africa and then the uncertain landings in Southern Italy had taken their toll of British morale.

"By then every city, town and village in Britain had lost someone in the war. Every place had their injured. Every week ships were lost in the North Atlantic and the massed bomber raids over Germany resulted in vast losses amongst air crew. It was a situation that Winston could not solve then but more and more people were becoming weary with him and wanted to see a quick end to it all. A German win at Kursk would guarantee renewed fighting in the west and probably five more years of war as America tried to defeat Germany. It was a horrendous prospect that resulted in bouts of severe depression in Winston.

"Winston knew about America's motives for destroying Nazi Germany and he knew that they had nothing to do with providing any sort of lifeline for Britain. He knew that America was fundamentally anti-British but there was no way that he could say that publicly.

"Just twenty years ago everything pointed to a German win and five more years of war while America geared up to defeat the massive German armies. It was a horrible prospect. But it was one that completely dominated our lives.

"But the Russian win at Kursk created a completely new world and a very dangerous one at that. We had no information then and we have had no information since as to how Russia won that staggeringly vast battle. Finding that information will be fascinating. I hope very much that you will be able to find the truth about it all. But given the current state of the cold war with them I doubt that we will ever get the real evidence. What I can tell you is that the

Russian win there transformed Winston's mind from paranoia about a German win to extreme panic about the prospect of Russia taking any active part in the destruction of Germany.

"Winston always had strong ideas and very clear hopes for the future. But they were always based on the notion that Britain would remain the leader of the largest empire that the world had ever known. The Russian win at Kursk destroyed any possibility of Britain being able to maintain that position. That was because even Winston knew that Britain could not possibly go against the strengths of Russia and America at the same time. By July 1943 he knew that neither of them could tolerate any imperial status for Britain. He knew after Kursk that his dreams could never be realised but he went on dreaming them anyway.

"That is enough of Kursk for now. We are going to meet two ladies. One of them is Celina who is the assumed wife of Nigel who owns the farm where we are going. He is at the market today. They have never actually got married. Celina and I meet every Thursday when he is away. She is bringing her friend Nancy. Nancy is the assumed wife of another farmer who lives about five miles from here. They have never married either. That is the way it is around here. Everyone in the villages knows that they are not married. Actually few people here bother to get married. Not having made any marriage vows makes it easy to have relationships with anyone. That is also the way it is here. There are few secrets and that makes for an easy lifestyle. We are going to have fun. Sex is likely to be high on the agenda so prepare yourself for a very exciting day."

I was intrigued that a sixty eight year old man would be going out for a day's sex with two women. It certainly promised to be exciting.

The place to which we went was the lake at the northern end of Nigel Hannam's farm. On three sides the lake was protected by thick woodland and brambles. There was no way that anyone could penetrate that thick undergrowth. That made it a very private place. It was only accessible from the south by a narrow track which led only to Hannam's farmyard and by the path that we had used. Down by the edge of the lake was a grassy strip which had been well mown.

We had only been there for a few minutes when Celina and Nancy arrived. They came up the track in a battered Land Rover. Neither of them was wearing any clothes. Both of them had all-over tans and had obviously spent much time out in the sun in the fine spring that year.

They brought with them a couple of hampers filled with a large picnic, some chilled Champagne and plenty of wine. The Champagne had obviously been pre-arranged for my benefit. Forever afterwards I was very grateful for what Samuel had arranged for me that day. It was certainly the best end to male virginity that could be imagined.

As we sipped the Champagne Celina started to talk:

"Nancy and I joined the RAF on the same day. I came from Devon and she came from Cumbria. The main reason we joined was to get a good social life. There were plenty of brilliant young men in the RAF and we hoped to enjoy that fully.

"We started on the same day and on the same course. Our training course was at South Cerney in the Cotswolds. It was a beautiful place and our social aspirations were fulfilled from the first day. In the first week we had to take some aptitude tests and as a result we were both posted to intelligence work at Stradishall when our basic training course was completed.

"Stradishall is near here and the social life there proved to be absolutely brilliant. The guys on the squadron were great and there were seemingly endless parties in the area. That was how we met our present partners. These days farmers have far more money than RAF pilots so that was the life that we eventually chose. You will see today just how much we enjoy ourselves.

"The squadron based at Stradishall was involved in aerial reconnaissance. When we joined they were flying the Mosquito aircraft. Whenever the weather was good enough they flew along the borders with the Russian controlled areas in the east. The Mosquito could fly well above 40,000 feet and the photographic range from that altitude was well over two hundred miles. They filmed what seemed to be and endless build up of troops and tank armies obviously confronting Western Europe. It was very frightening.

"In 1953 the squadron was re-equipped with the new Canberra jet aircraft. This aircraft was an absolute gem for us. It could fly well above the height at which Russian aircraft and anti-aircraft defences could operate and it had enough range to stay over the target area for several hours. Inevitably, therefore, we started flights over Russia itself.

"My role was to process the film and to interpret what I saw for senior officers. It was the same old story. Wherever we flew we got pictures of a massive build-up of Soviet armed forces.

"The weather over Russia was generally poor and in the first year of the Canberra's service we could only fly ninety missions. But even that number produced very little good film. But what that showed was that deep into Russia there were vast military reserves. In Belarus we found fifty airfields alone, all of them equipped with both fighters and bombers. A direct result of that work was a build-up of American forces in Europe. Within a few miles of here there are several American bases all of them at a high state of readiness. I am sure that they will stay there until such time as there is clear evidence that Russia is scaling down its armed forces.

"Anyway in the summer of 1954 the weather changed over Ukraine. Normally in the summer there it is cloudy and warm with periods of intense thunderstorms. But that summer it was clear for six weeks. It provided us with some superb reconnaissance opportunities.

"On June 10th that year we received some new orders. We were to fly over the area of the Kursk battlefield, try to establish its exact size and try and find out whether it had been cleared of military debris. If not we were to try and count the remnants of guns, tanks and aircraft that might still be there.

"In the weeks that followed we flew more than two hundred missions over that area. I was one of ten people working on the processing and interpretation of the film.

"It was in September that year that all the good film we had was put together for a single presentation to the top military brass in all the services. That presentation covered the entire floor of one of the hangars. I had to go to the presentation to explain the conclusions I had reached about the film that I had processed.

"What we produced clearly stunned the audience. Two things stood out above all else. The first was the sheer size of the battlefield. It was approximately the size of Wales. I remember one general saying that it was by far the largest battlefield ever. The second thing was the vast scale of the Russian defences. It must have taken an enormous amount of time and energy to build them and all the indications were that they were impenetrable to German armour. All the people at that presentation were baffled as to why Germany had attempted to fight there. They concluded, though, that it must have been a severe failure of German intelligence. None of them had any clue as to how Russia had marshalled all the resources needed to create such a battlefield.

"I have no idea of the total count of wrecked equipment that we captured on film. I only know the numbers on those films that I processed. I counted over a thousand aircraft, thousands of guns and at least twelve hundred tanks. It simply had to have been a truly monumental battle there.

"That is really all that I can tell you about it. Now lets us light the barbecue, go and do some fishing, drink some wine and enjoy ourselves. I certainly intend to do so."

We all left that lovely lakeside just before four. On the way back to his house Samuel said to me:

"When I was involved in all that high level security work it soon became obvious that sex was both a binding force between people who trusted each other and a massive potential security risk. What I also learned was that large numbers of people at the highest levels of government had sexual relationships that were well outside any normal marriage limits. Max Beaverbrook who was much trusted by Winston was one of those. He was the owner of the Daily Express newspaper and became Minister for Aircraft Production in the wartime cabinet. He shagged anyone he fancied and it never caused any security problems. His wife knew that that was what he was doing and it did not cause her any problems. There was in any event nothing that she could do about it. He was certainly never any security risk. Winston knew all about his activities and trusted him completely. Max was not liked politically but he got things done. He was a brilliant organiser.

"Louise Harford was one of his girlfriends and she probably had more influence on him than any other person. But she was never any security risk. If you ever find any references to her you will find hers to be an intriguing story. She is certainly the sort of person with whom to share a picnic here. I have indeed done that. Sooner or later I will get her to meet you. You will enjoy it as much as you have enjoyed today. She will be able to give you some information about Russian records which I am sure that you will find invaluable if you are ever able to access them.

"I was certain that Winston never had any such relationships at least in the time that I knew him. He was very devoted to his wife but he did have confidants whom he trusted deeply. One of those who had great influence on him was Alice. You might well be interested in finding out much more about her.

"What I decided to do was join that club. It provided exciting and interesting opportunities. I told Rebecca about it and she and I decided jointly that we would both have other partners. That very much enriched our marriage and she was able to provide me with rich seams of information that she got from people with whom she slept.

"Today was just an extension of the sort of relationships that I have enjoyed for many years. I met Celina on the first day that I moved here. Rebecca knows all about her and all her relationships are well known to the village.

"You will hear from her very soon about just how she wants to carry on with a relationship with you. Please never pass any moral judgments on people like her. She has never hurt anyone and what she does is quite normal. It is the way that the world works. My advice to you is to enjoy it. You will meet some great people and your life will be enriched."

Celina rang me soon after we got back to Samuel's house. She wanted me to go with her to a barbecue that evening at a farm called Sewells which was about a mile outside the village. She said she would collect me in about an hour and that clothes were definitely not required that evening.

At that barbecue there was one of the pilots who had flown those missions over Ukraine. Celina introduced him to me and explained my interest in Kursk. What he had to tell me added some real excitement to what I had already been told

"In the summer of 1954 I flew over Ukraine perhaps twenty times. The Canberra had a crew of two, pilot and navigator. I always flew with the same navigator. We used to leave Stradishall at dawn and stop at Gutersloh in Germany to take on more fuel. Then it was a climb to over 70,000 feet and go straight at the fastest possible speed to Ukraine. The Canberra was a brilliant aircraft and it took just over an hour and a half to get from Gutersloh to Kursk. At that altitude the human eye cannot see anything on the ground at least not in detail so we had no idea at the time what we were filming. But we had to fly precise tracks across the ground to get all the pictures that the boffins back at base needed. The precise flying was controlled by the navigator. We had to criss-cross the territory from north to south and from east to west. Occasionally we would see the jet trails of Russian aircraft far below us. When we did we always headed for Germany immediately.

"It was always fun flying the Canberra. It has superb performance and it handles like the best fighter aircraft. The flights over Russia stopped at the end of July that year when our chiefs got evidence that Russia was introducing into service heat seeking missiles which would have been able to shoot down our aircraft. I was posted onto transport aircraft soon after that but I count my days of flying over Ukraine as the best in my service career."

I met with Celina frequently after that and what she taught me helped me immensely in creating relationships which gave me access to some of the most secret documents in Russian archives. Samuel was right. Sexual chemistry makes things work in the world. It certainly worked for me and helped me find the evidence that made this book possible.

Christmas 1963

It was in October 1963 when Samuel rang me and asked me to spend Christmas at his house. It was an easy invitation to accept. He assured me that there would be some other interesting guests and it was inevitable that I would learn about how to obtain information in Russia. I was intrigued

I arrived in time for lunch on Christmas Eve. It was a cold grey day and there was some indication that it might even turn out to be a White Christmas that year. The weather forecast on the television that morning was certainly optimistic about the prospect.

The sitting room of my grandfather's house had a large fireplace and was always a comfortable place to sit and relax in the winter. There seemed to be an endless supply of good logs to keep the fire burning well.

The other guests were the American general George Patton, his girlfriend Sally Monroe and Louise Harford. They had arrived together just a few minutes before me. Samuel poured us some large gins and explained the arrangements that he had made for Christmas.

"After lunch Rebecca and I will be going to the Christmas Carol service at the American Air Force base at Wethersfield. It is about ten miles from here and we go every year. There are many retired service people around here and it makes for a great reunion for us. We will probably be back around seven this evening. We will have dinner some time after that and go to the midnight mass at our local church. It is after that that I like to start Christmas proper with a few whiskies. Tomorrow we will have our Christmas dinner in the evening but a few friends normally come in for a drink at lunchtime. On Boxing Day we will go to a party in the evening at Celina's house."

As George and Louise had not met Celina before Samuel explained who she was. He did say, though, that it was entirely possible that a party at her house would last all night and that it could well turn out to be very exciting.

Over lunch we talked about the work that Louise and George had done together after the war. Samuel had not previously briefed me about it and I then had no idea either that they had worked together or that their work had been so important.

Immediately after lunch Samuel and Rebecca left to go to Wethersfield. George and Sally decided to go for a long walk through the quiet lanes that surrounded that village. Louise collected a bottle of red wine from the wine rack in the kitchen cupboard and suggested that we go to the sitting room and talk.

Before she sat down she took off all her clothes. As she did so she said:

"I do not like wearing clothes at any time and certainly not when there is the prospect of a good shagging in front of a large log fire like this one. We will be alone of at least a couple of hours so will have plenty of time to enjoy ourselves."

She poured each of us a large glass of wine and then sat down close to the fire.

"When Samuel asked me to come here for Christmas he explained to me that he hoped that it would be possible for me to tell you about obtaining information in Russia. He has explained to me that he hopes that you will be able to uncover some information about the battle at Kursk in 1943. I know absolutely nothing about the detail of that battle but I do know that it caused a complete furore in the relations between Britain and America when it was clear that Russia had won an outstanding victory there. But before I get on to what I know about Russia I will have to tell you something about myself. It is a complex story and I am glad that I will have plenty of time to tell you. We will not spend the entire afternoon talking. Sex features very large in my life and I hope it will between us this afternoon. After a couple of glasses of this excellent wine anything is possible.

"It was while I was at school that I discovered that I had a natural talent for languages. It was a chance encounter that got me my first job as a history researcher. I did two assignments, one in Germany the other in Russia going through endless archives and collecting material for two important new biographies. It was certainly interesting work and I was treated very well by all those that I met.

"But I eventually got fed up with days spent in museums and in numerous private libraries. I wanted to do something far more exciting. Initially I went to work for the Daily Express as a researcher and then I was lucky enough to get into intelligence work. I was trained for that by the army and initially my work was in tracking down terrorists in several British colonies. My work was well regarded and as a result I was posted to the Foreign Office to do political intelligence work. I did three very important assignments in Germany, Russia and America. Today I will tell you about the Russian assignment and about the impact that Kursk had in America. But part of the deal for giving you what I hope will be really useful information is that you should see, whether and when you can get access to and Russian archives, if they have anything on my minder in my early years in the Foreign Office.

"His name is George Ponsonby. He is currently British Ambassador to the Soviet Union. Entirely co-incidentally he has recently bought a house near here for his retirement. I first met him in 1935. He was then in charge of a special unit within the Foreign Office that dealt with political espionage. He seemed to report directly to Anthony Eden, the Foreign Secretary.

"He was and presumably still is a completely committed homosexual. I suspected that he was a deviant who had, how shall I say it, exaggerated tastes. That never gave me any problem because my relationship with him was entirely professional. But I did wonder whether he used his sexual proclivities to set up the quite extraordinary opportunities he created for me to exploit in both Germany and Russia. I will probably never know for certain but if at any stage you find out anything while I am still alive please tell me. It will certainly be interesting.

"Anyway after a deeply disturbing role in Germany when I had more or less unlimited access to military bases which were then under construction George Ponsonby sent me to Russia. I will probably never know how he was able to set it up. But he got me a job working directly for Klimert Voroshilov who was the Defence Minister. I went to Moscow in 1937 and was there until a few days before the war started.

"The thing you have to remember at all times about Russian Government offices is that the processes that they follow are designed to facilitate the work of the secret police operations that are endemic throughout the country. I met Stalin many times and I knew his secret police chief, Beria. Beria's main job was to ensure that nothing happened which threatened Stalin in any way. One of the principal ways of achieving that was through the control of information.

"In every Russian ministry at that time there were two classes of file. The first type was subject based. It did not matter what the subject was there was one file at least for every subject dealt with by that ministry. I dealt with thousands of such files. Everything had to be recorded because every detail of anything could potentially be evidence to use in any witch hunt against possible political enemies of Stalin.

"The second type of file was the personal file of every person in the ministry. Every piece of paper processed by anyone had to be kept in a personal file as well as in the subject file. The amount of paper involved was massive. Files were frequently edited by Beria's police either for political correctness or as evidence to condemn someone to a Gulag. It was a completely horrible system. But it was the way that business was carried out in that country.

"The really interesting thing was that it was also a devious system. No one had any idea how long Stalin would last. No one had any idea when someone might be killed or given promotion and glory. So nothing was destroyed in any file but things were added. Things might be removed from files if they were incriminating but they were all kept safely in another file. So if there is anything you need to look at it will be there. The problem is finding it.

"If you are really going to get into the truth about Kursk you will have to access hundreds of files about the battle itself and you will also have to access the personal files of the key players. There is no centralised control system of files so you will depend on the personal knowledge of the archivist with whom you will have to deal. What you will have to do is find out who the influencers of that battle were and then access their personal files. It will be very much like looking for a needle in a haystack. But what I can promise you is that if you can find a friendly and sexy archivist and then look after her you might be able to find anything.

"Talking about that I cannot possibly go on talking to you before we have a thoroughly good shag together. I am sure that doing it on the rug in front of this fire will be brilliant."

I suppose that it was about half an hour later that she was ready to go on talking about her life.

"Someone who was very important to me then and who is still important to me is Max Beaverbrook. He owns the Daily Express and I met him while I was working there. It was only a few days after I first met him that we became lovers and it has been that way ever since. Max was a close personal friend of Winston's and as a result he was put in charge of aircraft production and transport matters generally. It was Max who eventually extricated me from the devious world of diplomacy and gave me a job supervising the production of Lancaster bombers in America and Canada.. He was also responsible for giving me the job after the war that caused me to work with George Patton.

"At the beginning of the war I went to work in Washington. I have absolutely no way of knowing how George Ponsonby created the opportunity for me to work there. But the work I did there gave me access to some of the greatest secrets in history. Maybe some day I will be able to tell you about them but the one Samuel wants me to tell you about today is the effect that Kursk had on Anglo-American relations.

"In the early war years I had a job which put me in daily touch with the White House. A very enjoyable part of it was my regular meetings with President Roosevelt. They were important meetings and they contributed to the development of Anglo-American relations at a time of huge difficulty for both countries. Being with Roosevelt was always stimulating. He had a very clear focus and knew exactly what he intended to achieve for America. He also knew that most Americans had little interest in Britain and wanted all the political effort in their country to be concentrated on their domestic needs. It was a message that Winston Churchill never accepted.

"My role in the diplomatic processes between the two countries ended a few months after Pearl Harbour and America's commitment to securing the unconditional surrender of Germany. Max then gave me the other job in America effectively managing the production of British bombers over there. But I still maintained regular contact with Roosevelt. When Germany had started its retreat from Kursk he rang me and asked me to visit him urgently.

"To understand how I came to be a confidant of Roosevelt's will take longer to explain than this afternoon and as I have said it will involve discussion about some of the greatest secrets of the war. But I was one of his confidants and because of that he wanted to talk to me about a stormy and impetuous meeting he had had with Winston.

"Immediately the German retreat from Kursk was a clear fact Winston had flown to Washington. No record of that flight will ever be found in any military records because both leaders agreed that all records about it would be destroyed. Roosevelt wanted to forget that the meeting had ever taken place and Winston was absolutely furious that his view of the dangers to Europe following the Russian victory were being ignored. So you will have to accept it from me that a very turgid meeting between them on July 20th, 1943 did take place. I am sure that you will find all sorts of evidence that things changed around that time and that as a result America took over complete control over the war in Western Europe. It was everything that Roosevelt wanted and it set the seal on American domination of the post-war world. But Churchill and his military leaders lost control of military operations in Europe as a result. That is why America now leads NATO permanently.

"Although he was not always right Winston did have a very strong sense of military strategy. He knew that as result of Kursk that Russia was likely to get to Berlin before Britain and America had any chance of doing so. What he wanted to achieve in that July meeting with Roosevelt was a clear commitment that America would do everything possible to prevent any such eventuality. What actually happened was that Roosevelt ordered Eisenhower, his commander in Europe, to ensure that Russia did reach Berlin before the western allies. He did that because he recognised that that could be the final straw for the entire British Empire.

"In exactly the same way that it destroyed German military supremacy Kursk also killed the British Empire. That is what you must look into in your researches. Kursk also created a very strong alliance between Stalin and Roosevelt. I have no way of knowing what the Russian archives will show about it all but I am sure that they will be interesting.

"I am certain that somewhere in the Russian archives you will find the evidence that supports all this. That is if they ever open their files to foreign inspection. It is those files that will prove the biggest drama of the whole war."

Samuel had made Kursk sound important. What Louise had just said about it staggered me.

It was already getting dark by the time she finished talking. We had no idea when George Patton and Sally would return but we had another sex session in front of that log fire as the afternoon light faded away. I knew then that my life had become inextricably linked with the biggest event in the war and with perhaps the biggest story to tell about all the war.

When we left the church after the midnight mass it was starting to snow. When we got back to the house we had several whiskies. I spent the night with Louise and when we were ready to get up in the morning there were several inches of snow on the ground. It made for a magical Christmas but what she had told me changed my life for ever.

About Kursk

Because Samuel and Louise had emphasised the importance of the Battle of Kursk I started my researches by looking into the causes and reasons for that battle. There was really nothing useful available to research until the 1990's when relevant Russian and German archives became available for the first time. In the 1970's detailed accounts of the battle of Stalingrad started to appear but very little was published about Kursk even then. But I was not interested in accounts of those or any other battles. What was more interesting was to find accounts about the planning process for those battles. Who took what decisions and when? If I could find out that information then I might have something which would mirror the diaries of Samuel. I might be able to see exactly, for example, what Stalin was thinking on particular days when Churchill was making big decisions.

In my university course on 20th century history Kursk had not even been mentioned although now there can be no doubt that it was one of the most influential events in all modern history.

When those archives were opened to international research I was staggered by the vast amount of material available. There were literally thousands of documents available of every description. Most of them were about the battle itself. What interested me more was why the battle was fought there. Above all I wanted to find out when and how the battle had first been conceived. It proved to be a fascinating and rewarding quest. What I found was a wealth of personal material about the planning process and the conflicts and friction that it created between the key Russian leaders.

Samuel had known about Kursk because he had been involved in preparing Winston for it. He had been the man who had briefed Winston on all the military intelligence available about the forthcoming battle and its aftermath. Almost all the material he had used for those briefings came from German sources.

Long before I could get access to any German or Russian archives on the subject I read this entry in Samuel's diary. It was just a few weeks after his death in 1970. It was the first time that I had seen anything written about Kursk:

"June 9, 1943 Today has been dominated by a long conference about the forthcoming battle that will in all probability be fought at Kursk quite soon now. We have been getting information both from spies and through radio intercepts about a big German build up around the city of Kursk. From all that we have heard the German build up there is greater than anything they have assembled for a single battle before. Their only intention can be to destroy the Russian fighting capabilities completely. Winston stressed the vital importance of knowing what is going on there and planning for the outcome.

We started with our umpteenth analysis of Stalingrad. We concluded at the time that the Russians had been lucky with the weather and that they were better equipped to fight in those extreme conditions than the Germans. We have been getting very little information from within Russia so we can only really speculate and debate how they won Stalingrad. What we are pretty certain about is that Stalingrad exhausted their reserves and that there is very little left to fight with. Since then the Germans have routed them at Kharkov so all looks set for the final showdown.

We all fully expect Germany to win this one but the implications of that are potentially severe for Britain. Our troops have only recently landed in Sicily and if Germany wins Kursk we can expect them to redeploy large numbers from Russia to the West. They will then certainly reinforce Italy and may well plan for a invasion of Britain. They will certainly try to make it impossible for us make a successful landing in France next year. All in all the strategic implications are severe.

Winston is in a very gloomy mood because it seems inevitable that this war will now drag on for several years. It is something we have talked about many times but there is still no clear future path for us. Kursk might make things easier. It might make them vastly more difficult.

Perhaps Winston's greatest concern is how he will be able to tell the British public, already war weary, just what the implications will be when Germany wins this next battle. It will surely be many more years of deprivation and struggle.

During the meeting he spoke to Roosevelt on the phone. Roosevelt told him to calm down and repeated that America will do all that is necessary to bring about the unconditional surrender of Germany however long it takes. Winston does not like being told what to do by FDR and when he is admonished by him in any way that makes him even more angry and anxious.

We did discuss the prospect of a Russian victory and we all concluded that with her armies in such an exhausted state that must be impossible. As he has done every day for the last few weeks since we have known about the prospect of battle at Kursk Winston sent a signal to Stalin but as he has had no replies from any of them he does not expect to get a reply this time. Whenever Stalin does communicate it is all about the British/American failure to launch a land invasion of France. He thinks it is a deliberate ploy to get Russia to take the brunt of the land fighting. It all makes for very difficult relations between the allies.

One thing we know for certain is that Hitler has travelled to Ukraine today. Our spy in the German HQ there is adamant about that. This must mean that battle is imminent. It looks as if it is all going to get a lot tougher soon."

One of the first things I tried to do when I got access to German archives was see whether Hitler had been to Ukraine on June 9th, 1943. If he had been there, what had been decided? It seemed to me that if Samuel's diary did coincide with German corroboration then there would be immediate enhancement of the credibility of the whole project. What I found was fascinating.

***

Later that same day I looked to see whether there was any reference in the diaries to a visit to Washington on July 20th, 1943 which might corroborate what Louise had told me. There was. Samuel had travelled to Washington with Winston. When I get to that date in the chronology of events I will reproduce that entry in full.

***

In Eastern Ukraine the morning of June 9th, 1943 dawned dark and sultry. Thick clouds kept the humidity level high and there was a constant threat of thunder. Working conditions in the German HQ were very poor. It was even worse for troops out in the open.

North West of the city of Kharkov was the headquarters of German General Erich von Manstein. Von Manstein had led the German invasion of Poland in 1939, the invasion of

France in 1940 and the invasion of Russia in 1941. He was something of a national hero in Germany and he was certainly a national hero amongst all German troops. After the battle of Stalingrad the previous autumn and winter, which had eventually proved so disastrous for Germany, he had been able to stabilise the German lines and re-capture the Ukrainian city of Kharkov.

Von Manstein had commandeered a village for the purpose of creating his headquarters. On the edge of the village was a large farmhouse. In the village there were about a hundred other houses which had formerly been used by farm workers. It was a convenient enough location because it was well served by roads that provided easy access. A nearby level grass field provided for an airstrip which could be used by military passenger planes and fighter aircraft. It was a safe place to locate because it was well away from any Russian artillery but the sporadic battle could be heard in the distance on still days.

On April 11th, 1943, Adolf Hitler had signed the order instructing von Manstein to prepare plans for a major battle designed to destroy the Russian armies that were located around the western side of the city of Kursk. That hot June day he was at von Manstein's headquarters to review the battle plans and decide on a date for the offensive.

Ever since the end of the German military disaster at Stalingrad the previous January Hitler had been lobbied by his generals about the situation in Russia. Some were in favour of fighting a series of tank battles over the summer which would have the effect of destroying what they believed to be the ever weakening Russian armies. Others argued that there was no need to fight any big battles that year. They argued that Germany should consolidate its position in Ukraine and build up defences to make it impregnable from any Russian attacks.

To try and find a way through these arguments Hitler had asked von Manstein to draw up the definitive options. One of these involved fighting a major battle to destroy the Russian armies that were within the Kursk salient. Von Manstein believed that Germany had the overwhelming advantage in manpower and in the availability of tanks and guns and therefore that an attack on the Russian Kursk salient would be successful. If it was, the Russian army would be decimated and that as a consequence the major part of the war in the East would be over. It was the resulting German supremacy which was attractive to Hitler and that was one of the prime reasons why he supported von Manstein's ideas and had instructed him to prepare for the Battle of Kursk.

Hitler had arrived from his lair at Rastenburg in the dripping forests of East Prussia the previous evening. It had been a long flight and he was grateful that the airfield was so close to where von Manstein was based.

It was over a sparse meal that evening that General Heinz Guderian raised for the last time his objections to Kursk. Guderian was Germany's foremost tank commander and had commanded victorious armies in all Germany's campaigns in the war so far. Although he believed the German estimates of Russian manpower and fire power capability he could not accept that it was right to fight at Kursk. Sure, Kursk would have to be taken at some stage but it should be at a time of Germany's choosing. His problem with Kursk was that the battle would be fought on ground of Russia's choosing. What he wanted to achieve was even greater German domination of the battlefield than seemed possible at Kursk. He therefore advised Hitler that one last time to look for another location at which to crush Russia.

Almost all conversations with Hitler were unpleasant experiences. To have dinner with him created a double blow.

Hitler listened and told all those who were dining with him that although the very thought of battle at Kursk 'made his stomach turn over' it was nevertheless essential to win a battle there and do so soon. Hitler said that his reasons for fighting at Kursk were as much political as military. He knew better than any other German that Germany could only retain control of Western Russia if it controlled Ukraine. It did so then and it had to maintain that control. Ukraine was an important agricultural area, indeed, probably the best in Europe. It controlled strategic communications both east/west and north/south and within those communications Kursk was a key centre. Germany had to control the Caucasus oil fields and the Donets industrial basin. Without controlling all these areas all Germany's war aims in the East were pointless. Winning at Kursk was therefore a military and political imperative.

Hitler was not interested in any counter arguments and eventually the talk of any other options died away and they began to prepare for the very detailed discussions that would take up most of the following day.

The big meeting took place in what had been the dining room of that old farmhouse. Despite all the windows being open there was no air moving through the room. It was hot and humid and a very uncomfortable place in which to take the last detailed decisions about the battle.

Hitler's battle conferences were always much the same. The walls of the room were covered with maps and all decisions were taken in front of those maps. Hitler was obsessed with the location of individual military units and always wanted to make the decisions himself about the deployment of those units right down to battalion level. It was hopeless enough in planning phases but completely pointless during a battle because of the lack of accurate data. But Kursk had, at least nominally, to be planned Hitler's way.

All through that hot morning Hitler's generals listened to him postulating about the way individual units should fight. They heard him setting initial objectives for each unit and then what they should all do to consolidate the first day's victories over the following few days. Most bizarrely they heard him plan his victory parade through Kursk for the seventh day after the offensive started.

Mercifully a powerful thunderstorm began in the early afternoon. While there was almost constant thunder and lightning it was impossible for the conference to continue. When the storm had moved on Hitler was no longer interested in talking about the coming battle. All he wanted to do then was return to Rastenburg.

The meeting had been more remarkable for the things that Hitler did not know at that time rather than the things he did know which were mainly about troop deployments.

He did not know that several of the people at the meeting including von Manstein and Guderian were members of a secret group dedicated to his assassination. He could therefore not have known that the next attempt on his life would be made on the flight back to Rastenburg.

He also had no way of knowing that one of the people at the meeting was a Russian spy who would pass all the main details of what was discussed straight through to General Zhukov, the Russian Chief of Staff, within a few hours of Hitler leaving for Germany.

Hitler absolutely did not know that Britain had found a way of breaking most German military codes and that they were passing key data about the German build-up for Kursk to Stalin through an agent who used the code name of Lucy.

Hitler's greatest certainty at that meeting was that his own skilful handling of the retreat from Stalingrad had forced the Russian armies into an indefensible salient at Kursk. He was certain that he had selected a brilliant plan to exploit weaknesses in the Russian position. He was certain that German forces could cut-off that salient and en-circle and destroy several Russian armies. He thought of his direction of that retreat as a masterpiece. It was that that was finally going to win the war in the East for Germany. At least that was what he thought. Although he never explained to any of his generals what made his 'stomach turn over' in his own mind it was the excitement of the coming victory.

He had no way of knowing that Zhukov had persuaded Stalin 18 months earlier that Russia should decoy German armies to Kursk because the land around the city was perfect for large scale tank battles that could irreversibly and seriously weaken the entire German war effort.

Hitler was not worried by German assessments of the likely Russian strength at Kursk. All the German estimates gave Germany an advantage of at least 3:1 in both manpower and armaments. All his generals believed that it was only the Russian winter that had enabled them to gain victory at Stalingrad. They also believed that all the Russian reserves had been exhausted there. He did not know that now in high summer, a time in which there should be a substantial German advantage, that Zhukov had selected Kursk because it was possible to hide vast numbers of men and equipment in the surrounding countryside. Hitler had no way of knowing that the real Russian advantage in numbers was at least 2:1.

Hitler had no way of knowing that the Russians had created at Kursk a deliberate trap which had been made far more effective by the betrayal of German secrets to Stalin and Zhukov.

All British and American war planning had been based on the assumption that Germany would win Kursk decisively. All German planning had been based on the assumption that Germany would win.

In every way Kursk was to change the entire course of the war for Germany, Russia, America and Britain in ways that were completely unpredictable that June day as Hitler left to fly back to Rastenburg.

It had taken many months and the reading of thousands of pages of diaries and official documents to establish all that but there were two things that fascinated me most. One was that Samuel really had known about Hitler's movements on the very day that he was going to that conference. The other was that Hitler apparently believed that he was the architect of the Battle of Kursk. If indeed he was, it meant that his grasp of military strategy was far worse than anyone in Britain could possibly then have imagined.

But from what I had read by then I fully understood why Samuel had attached so much importance to Kursk as being the supreme moment of the war. I looked forward to seeing any equivalent Russian archives.

The Pre-War World Situation

An important part of my university course had been concerned with the pre-war situation in Western Europe. Today Western Europe is as stable, secure and well governed as anywhere. In terms of political stability it is seen as a role model for the world. It was absolutely not that between the two world wars.

My parents had their views about what the world had been like before the war and so did all their friends. My mother's views were coloured by the fact that she was only a teenager in the 1930's. My father's views were much conditioned by his experiences of trying to run a shipping line in the midst of a world trade depression. He talked to me about political weakness at home and about the severe depression in America, which he visited several times in the 1930's.

My university course notes contained a large amount of material on the period. It was generally factual and written without the reflective judgements that historians are able to make as the events they describe recede into the mists of time. One set of notes contained these succinct paragraphs.

"Under the Versailles treaty, which eventually described the end of the First World War and set out the peace conditions to which she should conform, Germany was effectively emasculated and turned into an unstable and powerless state. It did have democratic institutions which were based in the city of Weimar. These were, however, very weak and enjoyed little, if any, public support. They were certainly not up to the job of providing a populous and enterprising nation with any sort of useful government, let alone a government which could lead that nation through political and economic turmoil of an unprecedented savagery. As a result Germany floundered and eventually was decimated by the ravages of hyper-inflation which destroyed all the institutions of the state and almost all personal wealth. Outside Germany few cared. The intentions behind the Versailles treaty were to crush German militarism. To the parties to the treaty that had been achieved.

Inside Germany there were large and sustained grievances against the entire peace process. That was not because people did not want peace but because it was widely believed that Germany had been robbed of any effective part in the peace process long before its armies had been defeated in battle. Eventually those grievances provided some very fertile territory for protesters. The most effective and sustained protesters against the weakened position of Germany were the Nazi party. They started in the streets and beer halls of Munich but by 1932 they had become the largest political party in the country. They were led by Adolf Hitler.

The last two pre-war Chancellors of Germany ruled by decree without any reference to diplomatic institutions of any sort. The last Chancellor, General Kurt von Schleicher had absolutely no interest in democracy and never involved Parliament in any of his decisions. He lasted a mere 57 days before he was sacked at the end of January, 1933. He was replaced by Hitler, solely because he was the leader of the largest elected party in the parliament.

Hitler and the Nazi party then ruled Germany with an increasing disregard for any laws, domestic or international. They also embarked on an aggressive programme of re-armament. The day of Hitler's appointment proved to be a fateful and catastrophic day for the world."

It was easy for me to visit Samuel while I was at university and I did so many times. As we walked together through those fields and as we sat in front of a roaring log fire on winter evenings we spent much talking about the political chaos in Europe in the 1930's. He explained to me that the main reason that he returned to Britain after many happy and successful years in India was because he hoped to find an active role in contributing to the end of that chaos. On his return, he explained, things looked far worse than they had from 5,000 miles away.

In his leisure time he had spent his first few months back in Europe reading up on the developing chaos and visiting France, Germany and Austria. He told me that he would have loved to visit Spain as well but as that country was in the midst of civil war, travelling there seemed all too difficult. He always stressed to me that he had been born in Victorian times and had grown into a man in Edwardian times. Britain was secure and powerful throughout that period of his life. He stressed that what had shattered that security was the First World War. He was certain that that had been such a shattering experience for all those countries involved that almost an entire way of life had been destroyed in all the affected countries.

He was certain that all the evils that had befallen Europe since had been a direct consequence of the disruption caused by that war. He was equally certain that the roots of the American depression lay in America's involvement in that war and in the botched peace, the negotiations for which had been dominated by America. He often described the whole inter-war period to me as a shambles. Nowadays few would disagree with that description.

* * *

My university course was far more objective than the views of a single person and what it taught me was that the 1930's was a period of massive chaos and instability in Europe. That chaos resulted in compromises of every imaginable kind being made by governments and their servants. Espionage was rife, intrigue was rife, elections were suspended and dictators took over the government of several countries. In those circumstances all sorts of people found that they could plot and scheme exactly as they wished. Some of them were successful. But it was a system out of control. Government throughout Europe was weak and politicians who favoured stronger policies that might end the chaos were very much out of favour. Winston Churchill was one of those and he was vocal in public about it. It was certainly a time when flawed and weak people could try almost anything. Some of them succeeded in their personal objectives and seriously compromised their countries at the same time.

At the beginning of that decade things were not much better in America. The Wall Street crash and the subsequent depression caused economic misery throughout that country. The overwhelming view of the American people at that time was that they did not want to have anything to do with the rest of the world. What they wanted to do, as President Abraham Lincoln had once said, was "bind up the nation's wounds." It was President Roosevelt who provided that healing process. He took them right from the brink of despair to being the most powerful nation on earth. They were nowhere near that position when he first took office. No other nation came anywhere near challenging America by the time that The Second World War ended.

Throughout the 1930's there were frequent territorial wars in the Far East involving Russia, China and Japan. Japanese territorial aggression was one of the main causes of these. The only real result of these wars was that Russia was able to secure its Eastern borders. It was to provide important benefits during and after World War Two. Those territorial wars created Russia's greatest military leader, Zhukov.

Those chaotic times led to consequences for Britain and America that could never have been imagined by anyone at the beginning of the 1930's. The post war world could never have been imagined by anyone even at the start of the war in 1939. Several critical international relationships were created out of war itself. One of those was between Britain and America; a relationship largely forged personally by Roosevelt and Churchill. It was a complicated relationship which involved many other people as well. Both of them tried to make it a relationship which could be conducted outside the normal diplomatic protocols. They also tried to make it a relationship which was conducted outside any public scrutiny.

But equally complicated was the relationship that had to develop between Russia and its allies in that war. Russia had started as the friend of Germany; it ended up as being the major reason for Germany's military collapse. The change from being a friend of Germany to becoming its major foe and moving from affection to total hatred was engineered by Stalin and would have been completely unpredictable even as the war began in 1939. But Russia's eventual enmity towards Germany created a strong shared relationship between Russia and America. A shared objective to crush the British Empire was one outcome of that relationship.

The view of my tutor was that the whole situation created a ring of fire that had the capability to consume everything in its path. It certainly did that.

* * *

It is hard now for us to imagine just how powerful Britain was in the world prior to 1939. In the 1920's and 1930's Britain was by far the most powerful nation the world had ever known. It was also the centre of the largest and most powerful Empire in all history. Almost every part of the world was touched in some way by Britain's imperial and industrial power. The Empire covered large parts of Africa, huge swathes of the Middle East, the entire Indian sub-continent, several states and cities in the Far East, all of Australasia, Canada, large parts of the Caribbean, parts of Central and South America and numerous islands in the Pacific.

Britain's role as the largest Imperial Power ever was underpinned by its global trade. Britain provided most of the industrial requirements of the Empire and in return the Empire provided raw materials and food. That trade in turn was underpinned by Sterling which was then the only currency used to finance global trade. The Royal Navy had been developed to provide a protection force for that trade. It was the most powerful navy ever formed.

Great Britain itself was an industrial powerhouse. Its main industries were coal mining, railways, steel, shipbuilding, shipping, cotton milling and agriculture. Each employed more than a million men. Britain exported railways and locomotive power to all parts of the world. Almost every large river in Britain had a string of shipyards. Britain exported industrial machinery to the Empire and other parts of the world and it carried all those goods in British registered ships, thousands of them. All Britain's imports came on British ships. It was a truly dominant trading position.

In addition to all that Britain had gained immense influence in parts of the world that were not within the Empire. For example, it had built and managed all the railways in Argentina; it managed the Chilean Navy even to the point of re-creating a London waterfront in the docks in Valparaiso. It bought vast amounts of cotton from America to provide clothes for the peoples of the Empire. Britain was China's largest trading partner. It was also the largest trading partner of the United States.

At that time America was dominated by internal issues, in particular how to recover from a devastating economic collapse. Russia was dominated by quite different internal considerations. Its leader Stalin was determined both to spread the influence of communism within the country and overhaul and modernise the ramshackle economy.

In the 1930's Continental Europe was in political chaos. Russia, China and Japan were engaged in a series of territorial wars in the Far East.

Britain had no effective competitor over any field of activity across the globe at that time. It was in that world that Samuel had served as soldier and it was in that world in which my parents had grown up. By the time Samuel died in 1970 almost every part of that huge power base for Britain had gone.

The Pre War Years

It is a matter of historical record that after his long career in Government, when he held every important Cabinet post except those of Prime Minister and Foreign Secretary, Winston Churchill initially found his wilderness years, when he was away from government, to be a time of immense frustration and disappointment. He hated to be without political power, he hated to be without the influence over the nation's affairs that that power gave him. Every day included some time when he brooded over that lack of power and influence.

He had first become a junior government minister in 1905. He had then been a member of the Liberal Party. Apart from a short time when he had returned to the Army during the First World War and had served in France, he was continuously in government until 1922. But that year, in a general election, he lost his seat in Parliament. He went back to Parliament in 1924 but this time as a Conservative. The Prime Minister, Stanley Baldwin, offered him the post of Chancellor of the Exchequer. Churchill held this post for five years. It was a difficult period for the British economy. After that he was out on his own, cut off from power, without significant influence.

The only post that would have been of interest to Churchill after that would have been that of Prime Minister. There was no way that Baldwin was going to leave office just to make way for Churchill. In any event Churchill was no friend of Baldwin's and distrusted him personally. So the wilderness years followed. They would last for more than a decade.

To occupy much of his time Churchill retired to his country house in the Kent countryside. It is called Chartwell. Today it is a major visitor attraction. There he took up two hobbies; bricklaying and painting. He built several fine walls through the grounds which have given the whole estate a personal and very distinct character. His painting did well with him producing several good canvasses.

But the main way to use his time was the research, writing and production of several major historical works. The best known is The History of the English Speaking Peoples. But perhaps the greatest was his biography of his ancestor The Duke of Marlborough. There was far too much work to be done on these for him to do it personally so what he did was supervise the work of the several teams that he needed to undertake such a vast task. That work was eventually rewarded by his receiving the Nobel Literary Prize.

Throughout those years he remained a Member of Parliament, and wherever he could he maintained his social contacts with government ministers and with his friends in the armed forces. But all the while he fretted about his exclusion from government. As the years went by he became more and more frustrated about that exclusion and he started to fight the official government line on many issues. In effect he became the leading dissident within the Conservative Party. But until 1938 his opposition to government was without public support and it was without real focus. He was a popular after-dinner speaker in influential circles throughout the land. The government were acutely aware at all times that he had huge capacity to embarrass them on any issue. Churchill was not interested in just any issue, though. He was looking for something that would make him popular throughout the entire nation. He was looking for power.

One of the ideas within the Conservative Party in the 1930's was that India should become self-governing. Then it was regarded in Britain as the most important state in the British Empire, other than Britain itself. It had a much larger population than any other country in the Empire. Churchill was vehemently opposed to that plan and organised almost all the opposition to it. He did so because he passionately believed in the Empire and believed that

Britain gained great strength from its Empire links. But that opposition made it impossible for him to return to any government led by Baldwin or any of Baldwin's associates. Churchill's view of the Empire was eventually to be his greatest weakness. His greatest enemies used that love of Empire to destroy him and to crush British power and influence in the world. It was a supreme vanity leading to a supreme sacrifice.

Things got worse for Churchill in 1936. He was a strong supporter of King Edward VIII, as well as being a personal friend of his. It was the abdication crisis that year that did it for Churchill. He believed that the King should be able to marry the divorced Mrs Wallis Simpson and keep his throne. The government and the Church of England thought otherwise and it was their views that gained very strong public support. As a result Churchill became deeply unpopular. That was something he found very hard to bear. But he did retain sufficient optimism that at some stage he might just get an opportunity to regain his popularity and that he might just find some way to get back into government.

But in 1936 he had no way of knowing how and when that might happen.

* * *

Nov 19, 1936. I met Winston Churchill this evening at a dinner party. The party was given by Lord Beaverbrook and his wife. Before I got there I had no idea that I would meet him. It was an excellent evening and I will be meeting Winston again soon. He did tell me that he had asked Max to invite me because he wanted to meet me.

The party was full of surprises. The principal guest was Joachim von Ribbentrop, the German Ambassador. He was there alone. Also there alone was Louise Harford. I will have to look into why she was there. Maybe she is a close friend of Max Beaverbrook. But that would be surprising given that his wife was there. Whatever, she left with von Ribbentrop. I know Louise's father. He is Head of Military Intelligence in the army, but there is no information available to the public about him and his appointment was never announced.

There have been rumours that Winston has been struggling financially. Perhaps that was why Robin Coutts, the banker, was there. All in all lots to think about.

I spoke with von Ribbentrop before dinner and he told me he hoped that it would be possible for two very senior German army officers to come on an official visit to Britain soon.

Another guest there was Lady Alice Arbuthnot. I had heard of her before but never met her. It was obvious that Winston knew her well. I must find out why.

It was a mild November evening, even positively balmy for the time of year. Winston Churchill decided to walk to the dinner party. The walk took him about fifteen minutes. It was a clear starlit evening with a light southerly breeze, which explained the mild temperatures. That evening he was staying in the Park Lane Hotel at the western end of Piccadilly in London. He had to walk to Eaton Square which is a very smart street in the Belgravia area. He was alone for that walk that evening. His wife, Clemmie, was at their country home, Chartwell.

Winston knew that one of the other guests that evening would be Joachim von Ribbentrop, the newly appointed German Ambassador to London. Winston had met him twice before at diplomatic cocktail parties but this was likely to be the first time that they could have any sort of detailed conversation together.

von Ribbentrop had been appointed to be Ambassador to Britain on 11th August that year. He was known to be very close to Hitler and all the other senior Nazi leaders and as a result there was intense interest in meeting him. In his turn von Ribbentrop was very interested in learning as much as possible about Britain and all those who influenced her future. Von Ribbentrop had become well known to some members of the British Government the previous year. At that time he had had the title of German Minister Plenipotentiary at Large. He had had extensive negotiations with Britain about an agreement which would enable Germany to start building powerful naval ships again. The chief British negotiators had been Sir John Simon, the British Foreign Secretary at that time, and Anthony Eden, who was his junior minister. Von Ribbentrop had attained every objective that Germany had set for those negotiations. He knew that he had thoroughly duped Sir John Simon. He was not sure about Anthony Eden. He was a man that he had to get to know well, after all the previous year he had replaced Simon and was now in charge of Britain's relations with every part of the world except the Empire.

In March 1936 Germany had invaded The Rhineland Zone which had been demilitarized at the end of the First World War. It had formerly been part of Germany. Germany was called to account for that by the League of Nations. It was von Ribbentrop who had addressed that body and had persuaded them to back off from any threatened action against Germany. What the British Government thought about von Ribbentrop was that he was not just Germany's top diplomat but he had great influence back in Germany. What few people in Britain seemed to know was that he was one of the most powerful people in Germany; that he was very close to Hitler, that he had planned and conspired for the invasion of the Rhineland and that he was in reality a very dangerous man.

That such a senior figure in the Nazi party should have been given such an assignment was a proper and fitting reflection of the power that Britain then had in the world. The British Empire was still fully intact. It had grown after the First World War as it had absorbed some former German colonies. It was by far the largest Empire that the world had ever known. But, even more important than that, it covered every continent and Britain had a pervading influence across the entire globe. In Hitler's view, whatever the future direction of Germany, he had to know everything important there was to know about Britain. He had to know everything about the key people in every field of life in Britain. He recognised that it was unlikely that Germany could be a close friend to Britain because he had his own aspirations to develop a powerful German Empire that would inevitably be a rival to Britain. But whatever the future relationship that Britain could have with Germany he needed to have someone who he could trust implicitly to find out everything that there was to know. Hence von Ribbentrop's appointment.

Joachim von Ribbentrop went about acquiring that knowledge by attending every possible event and by meeting as many British people as possible. The traditional diplomatic cocktail party circuit was enormously useful to him. He got invitations to at least fifteen events a week and he went to almost all of them. To start with he went to meet people so that he could determine their real value to him. That took about three months. Thereafter his meetings became more and more selective but they also became more important. In those first three months he was easily able to learn about who the most influential people were, about their views and about what were likely to be the policies acceptable to the British people.

The results of all that were deeply disturbing. His first conclusion was that the British nation believed that they were invincible. Every British national that he had met had told him that. The second was that he found that the British believed that their Empire would last for a very long time, that it was successful and that Britain had done a very good job for its colonies. He had met several representatives from different parts of the Empire. They all expressed strong emotional attachment to Britain. Australia, New Zealand and Canada were very loyal to Britain. It was perfectly obvious that India was not. It wanted independence as soon as possible. Ribbentrop was fascinated by the idea that the most populous country in the British empire strongly wanted independence. He wondered whether it was any indication that the Empire was far weaker than British people supposed.

His third conclusion was that Britain was actually very weak economically. While the people thought that Britain was strong the reality was that it was becoming very weak. Britain's pretence to the world had been that it was very strong and powerful. It had been a surprise to von Ribbentrop when he learned that things were actually very different. But perhaps the biggest surprise to him had been about the divisions between the top and the bottom of the country. He had researched that extensively and he had found most of the establishment to be complacent and largely living in the past. But he had also found a huge undercurrent of dissatisfaction at other levels in society. The economic depression was taking its toll of morale and confidence, of that he was certain.

By the time he had to leave for that dinner party with Lord Beaverbrook, von Ribbentrop had decided that he needed to get much more into the detail of individual views and he needed to start to explore a wide range of future scenarios. He sensed that Britain might actually be approaching a position of considerable instability, whatever the establishment might be thinking, and he therefore needed to understand both the opportunities and threats that might follow from that. A whole range of intriguing possibilities seemed to be emerging. As Churchill was seen to be emerging as a voice of dissent, talking with him was as good as any person with whom to start.

It was going to be an interesting evening. This was possibly going to be the first evening since he had been in London when he might start to put together a brief for Hitler that found a possible way for Germany to navigate its way through the opportunities and threats that Britain presented.

Lady Alice Arbuthnot was a long-standing friend of Churchill's. Her husband had died a couple of year's earlier in a car accident. He had been a professor of classics at Oxford University. Beaverbrook knew that she had been a close friend and confidant of Churchill's for many years. He was very happy to encourage that relationship in return for future favours from Churchill himself. He was equally clear that the relationship between the two of them was entirely intellectual. Beaverbrook believed that Churchill would return to government one day and he wanted to do everything to ensure that he personally benefited from that. Inviting Winston and his confidant to the same dinner party was the very least that he could do.

Von Ribbentrop spoke to Alice at length while the cocktails were served before dinner. He was impressed by her links with the academic world in Britain. He already knew that the academic world was a very important part of the British establishment and he was very grateful to meet Alice. He was sure that she would enable him to develop and strengthen his contacts in that area. He would certainly use any links that he could exploit through her in the future.

He also found time to talk with my grandfather before the meal began. He was the most senior British Army officer whom he had yet met. It was an important contact. But he was by no means the most senior British officer that von Ribbentrop had met. When he had negotiated the Anglo-German Naval Agreement in 1935 he had met the most senior officers who were managing the Royal Navy. Extending his military network into the Army and later into the Royal Air Force were important objectives for von Ribbentrop. He hoped that any connections he could develop would help him assess the true military capabilities of Britain.

But Louise Harford was something completely different. Several years earlier she had been a researcher on Beaverbrook's staff. He then did fancy her and he still did fancy her. She had been and was still a very exciting part of his life. They were regular sleeping partners and had been ever since she had first worked for him. It was a very enjoyable relationship for both of them. Louise liked men who were significantly older than herself. She had usually found that that created a non-threatening relationship. She also liked the style that wealth and prosperity brought to older men. In any event they both enjoyed their sex together.

Beaverbrook was certain that his wife never knew of his relationship with Louise. Even if she had known he would not have cared because he always did his own thing. But Louise did come to their house for dinner parties from time to time. This was one of those times. Those times always arose when there was a single man coming to the party. Louise usually left with that single man. This night she was going to leave with von Ribbentrop.

After she left The Daily Express, Louise went to work for the British Government as a spy. She was trained by them to extract the highest level of secrets from senior foreign government ministers and officials. That was what she was going to do that night. Beaverbrook had no clue that that was what she was now doing, neither had any other person at that party. In addition to getting information for the Foreign Office Louise also used to provide Beaverbrook with very useful stories from time to time. He hoped that he would soon get one about von Ribbentrop. But what she learned that night was going to be crucial to the future conduct of British foreign policy. That night she would get the measure of the German Ambassador. The British Government often worked like that.

Lady Beaverbrook sat at one end of the table. Winston Churchill was on her left; von Ribbentrop was on her right. Sitting next to Churchill was my grandmother, Rebecca. Sitting next to von Ribbentrop was Louise. The table was narrow and that made for easy conversation and close eye contact. The conversation was lively, interesting and intense.

It was when the main part of the meal was over that Churchill and von Ribbentrop could be alone together. They went with their brandies to a corner of the sitting room. Churchill took not only a large glass of brandy but a decanter full of the stuff as well.

Not only was Churchill not in government, he had not been in government for many years. He was actually seriously distrusted by most of the senior politicians in the British Government. He had no access then to any sort of real government secrets. But he craved to know all those secrets; he craved to be back in power. In 1936 that prospect looked very remote. Britain at that time was simply not interested in anything that he had to offer.

But he was briefed by some of his remaining friends who still had political influence. Those friends included Anthony Eden, the Foreign Secretary. Those briefings certainly helped him to develop opinions and policies but those briefings and his subsequent ideas were by no means comprehensive. In talking to Churchill, therefore, von Ribbentrop had no expectations that Churchill would give him any insights into what the government might or might not be doing. What he did want and what he was going to get were straight opinions from the most obvious dissident in the land. He actually thought that Churchill probably did not have any useful policies at that time. But he did suspect that sooner or later Churchill would find some sort of platform around which those dissident views could blossom and flourish. He was determined to find out what those views might be. He was determined to make a judgement as to whether Churchill was a friend of Germany or a foe.

The conversation that evening was almost entirely about Churchill's views. Von Ribbentrop offered nothing. But it was a real chance for Churchill to tell a senior foreign dignitary exactly what he thought of Britain and what it had to do in the continuing world depression. Churchill's argument started from the position of Britain's greatness as the world's largest imperial power. He argued that that was good for the world, good for peace, and good in fact for everyone. But he did deplore the weak political leadership in Britain at that time, under

Prime Minister Stanley Baldwin. He argued that Britain had squandered an opportunity to lead the world out of recession. He claimed that if he had been Prime Minister different policies would have been followed which would have averted the worst of the problems. But they did not talk about the detail of any of those ideas that evening.

The only question that von Ribbentrop asked him was about armaments in Europe. Did Churchill envisage that Britain should remain the dominant military power in Europe? The answer was convoluted and complex. Churchill referred to earlier times in Europe when there had been several imperial powers. He referred to the world order that had been established by the Congress of Vienna at the end of the Napoleonic wars. He reminded von Ribbentrop that it was an alliance then between Prussia and Britain that had made that possible. That Congress had forged a peace that had effectively lasted a whole century. It was the longest period of peace ever known in Europe. Germany had gained an empire; Austria had been able to spread its influence. The power of France had been crushed. Britain had had peace, at least in Europe. Good times had resulted. It had been a political model that had brought many successes. It should be the basis of future peace in Europe.

Over dinner von Ribbentrop had invited Louise to spend the night with him. She had readily accepted and he was getting anxious about spending as much time with her as possible that night. After about an hour he was becoming weary with Churchill's accounts of British greatness. But he did want the conversation to continue. He needed to understand what drove this man, why the obsession with empire, why he was not in government pursuing all those ideas about which he had talked. So they agreed to meet again. It was actually Churchill who suggested the next meeting and it was Churchill who suggested the location. Von Ribbentrop was invited to spend a weekend at Chartwell. They agreed that it would be the first weekend in February. There they could talk for many long hours. It would be von Ribbentrop's first weekend at an English country house.

* * *

That same evening Anthony Eden was at a dinner party of a very different sort. As Foreign Secretary he was feeling overwhelmed by the endless succession of crises in Europe and the increasing Japanese aggression in the Far East. Like most politicians Eden was arrogant. He believed his love of secrecy and intrigue to be a strength. He trusted his own ability to make political decisions even though that same process would eventually lead to his political end.

Since he had become initially a junior minister in the Foreign Office and, more recently Foreign Secretary, he had had to deal with more crises than would be reasonable in any lifetime. There had been that diabolical crisis in France in 1933 when the business empire of Sergei Stavisky had collapsed dragging into it numerous government ministers and senior officials. The result had been racism and social strife on a spectacular scale. What that crisis had exposed was political weakness, corruption, parliamentary irresponsibility and ineptitude. It led to extremist attacks on the basic institutions of the state. Many European countries were plagued by similar problems in the 1920's and 1930's.

Then there was the crisis in Austria. The authoritarian Chancellor there, Engelbert Dollfuss, suspended constitutional government in 1933 and then started a war against his left-wing rivals which eliminated any early prospect of a return to parliamentary democracy.

And then there were the Nazis who had no regard whatsoever for political conventions or the rule of law. In June 1934 Hitler and his henchmen undertook a bloody purge of their rivals. Hundreds of people were killed in a single day. No country took any stand against those brutalities. Britain certainly did nothing. Then there was the Italian dictator, Mussolini, rampaging away in Africa trying to create some useless kind of Empire by slaughtering primitive tribes.

After all that came a string of Stalinist purges in Russia. It was all turning out to be a decade of complete disintegration of everything. Class animosities were rampant, racism was rampant, politicians were utterly corrupt; the interests of the general public were ignored.

Eden was well aware that it was an utterly sick world in which he operated. But he was equally well aware that there was no will in Britain at that time to do anything about it. Britain had no effective military capability at that time other than the Royal Navy. The depression in the early part of the 1930's had robbed the country of any capability to finance any sort of armaments programme. So, really all that he could do in the Foreign Office was watch the ever developing chaos as it spread its cancer throughout Europe and the world.

He also knew that the great mass of the British public did not care about any of those things at that time. To them Germany was a distant land with fundamentally different interests. Russia was even more distant. Hardly anyone in Britain even knew then where Italy was. France was regarded as Britain's traditional enemy, even though there were strong common interests between Britain and France. They had, after all, both taken huge pain together as allies during the First World War.

Eden was also concerned that evening about the attitude of his Prime Minister about it all. Stanley Baldwin was popular but he did not seem to have any grasp of, or interest in international affairs. So Eden felt lonely and isolated. In those circumstances he was going to do his own thing.

One thing that Eden had realised was that normal diplomatic processes were incapable of producing the truth. If another government set out to obscure any sort of truth and instead rely entirely on propaganda how was it possible to know what was really going on? Eden knew that Britain needed to get deep into the real truth of what was going on throughout Europe to have any hope of influencing events. So he secretly set up a small group within the Foreign Office just to find out that truth. That unit was led by George Ponsonby. And he was having dinner with him that evening. George Ponsonby was an Assistant Under-Secretary in the Foreign Office. He was a brilliant linguist and widely regarded as a high-flying diplomat.

The dinner took place at Eden's London home in Rochester Row, just a few minutes walk from the House of Commons. Some months earlier Eden had selected Ponsonby to lead a new political intelligence section within the Foreign Office largely because he liked the intellect of the man. Eden needed lots of time with George Ponsonby to plan a political espionage programme which might just yield useful information to Britain about what seemed to be ever mounting dangers throughout Europe.

For Eden it was a very successful evening. He authorised a large increase in the political espionage activities. Ponsonby was going to manage those. In particular Ponsonby was going to have to find some way of penetrating the innermost secrets of both Germany and Russia. It did not matter what it cost; it just had to be done. Considerable progress had already been made; Eden just wanted a lot more of it. Eden passionately believed that he could not do his job effectively unless he could get better knowledge of what was going in both those countries. It was impossible to make useful judgements about whether either of them was likely to be a friend or enemy unless he had more information about their real intentions.

A plan was agreed between them. More people would get sucked into the espionage trap. Someone that Eden particularly wanted to join the team was Guy Burgess, a BBC journalist. He never explained to George Ponsonby why he was interested in him but he did tell him that he would have to find a way of recruiting him into the Foreign Office and he would have to find a way of usefully occupying his talents.

* * *

Every politician has to make decisions about his or her advisers. It is not possible to be active in politics and be in isolation. The choice of advisers is usually crucial to political success. Issues such as personal networks and contacts are an important part of the selection process. Winston's closest political associate was Anthony Eden. They had been close friends for many years. Their friendship had been maintained through all the years when Churchill had been deeply unpopular within his political party and more widely in the country. The two men met regularly and Eden was always prepared to brief Churchill on matters that did not fall within official secrecy. Eden was Churchill's best contact in government at that time.

But it is not possible to be in politics and maintain any narrow source of information. So Churchill had had to develop his own network of contacts who could keep him informed and who could shape his own opinions and policies. He developed a network of influential constituents, senior members of the armed forces with whom he remained popular, some business leaders, foreign diplomats and some very loyal personal friends.

His wife, Clementine usually called Clemmie, was very strong in her support for him at all times and she was always very forthright in passing on to him any views that she had heard. That included frequent and regular criticism of him by other politicians. The most regular charges against him were that he was arrogant, rough, sarcastic and over-bearing. Clemmie told him that many times but it never seemed to make any difference. Winston was Winston and advice was not something that he liked, but sometimes he did listen. But he only listened when he needed some guidance as to how he could increase support for himself in any way.

Churchill's relationship with Clemmie was strong and loving. But it never escaped his arrogant approach to most things. Churchill did whatever he wanted to do. Clemmie and Alice complemented each other in the advice and guidance they each gave him. Clemmie's advice was usually about dealing with people and trying both to encourage his aspirations and to find better ways of getting his views across to others. Alice's advice was always about affairs of state. Clemmie's advice was practical; Alice's advice was intellectual. Winston often accepted but did not always respect both sources of advice.

What he usually did when he was away from home was write to Clemmie. She kept all those letters and through the entire duration of their marriage she kept about 1,600 letters from him. One of those letters was sent the morning after that dinner party with von Ribbentrop. It read:

Dearest Clemmie,

Last evening I went to a dinner party hosted by Max Beaverbrook. His principal guest was Joachim von Ribbentrop, the German Ambassador in London. I am sure that if I were Foreign Secretary or Prime Minister I could do a deal with him which fully protected Britain's interests around the world. He seems to have an enormous respect for what we have achieved in creating and maintaining our Empire. I am sure that good and enduring relations with Germany could be established provided that we each respect the other's imperial aspirations.

W

* * *

When Winston went back to his hotel with Lady Alice Arbuthnot the first thing on his mind was that he needed to share some serious anxieties with her. Lady Alice was someone that he trusted implicitly although he did not always take her advice. She was about fifteen years younger than him and they had known each other since he had first been appointed as First Lord of the Admiralty in 1911. She had originally lived in his constituency and Winston had known her parents well. She had then gone to work for him in the Admiralty as his social secretary. She had the task of organising his diary and all the events that were inevitably required in such a high profile job.

They sat in a corner of the lounge and ordered a decanter of brandy and two glasses. Winston planned to debate current affairs with Alice for at least a couple of hours.

That evening Churchill was concerned about the developing chaos across seemingly all of Europe. True, the symptoms were different in different countries, but there was chaos, nevertheless, virtually everywhere; more concerning to him than the chaos was the fact that no one seemed to be interested in doing anything about it.

"Alice, if you follow international affairs, as I do, it is impossible to escape the conclusion that large parts of Europe are degenerating into chaos. But there seems to be very little about it in our newspapers and there also seems to be a total lack of interest in it in our government. At this time I can only foresee that it will all get worse. If nobody is really trying to solve the crisis then logic says it must get worse. I do not say that because I know every detail of what is happening in France, Germany, Austria, Russia or anywhere else. I do say it because indifference to problems seems to be endemic throughout the continent.

"In all that chaos it does seem as if Germany is interested in expanding its territorial control, maybe by creating some sort of Empire. Italy is certainly already doing that in Africa. I have no quarrel with that. Our Empire has been one of the greatest successes in history. Following our example might just be a way of reducing the chaos in Europe.

"Here at home our government seems to be completely uninterested in international affairs. Such minute interest as they have seems only to be about preserving the fragile peace in Europe. They are doing nothing to strengthen any resolve to solve any problems.

"In Britain there is long running economic recession. They have not succeeded in doing anything about it. They keep on talking about India and they seem to want to get rid of one of our greatest imperial assets. For me it creates a condition of great despair. I am certain that I can contribute massively to solving these problems but they do not want to have anything to do with me.

"One of the issues that has caused me the greatest personal despair was the total lack of any government interest in my views about the abdication crisis. King Edward was and is a personal friend of mine. I believe that he was entitled to personal happiness and as a friend I will always be loyal to him. So for the government to reject my views which were based on loyalty to me friend the King was particularly hard for me.

"Alice there are so many things whirling around in my mind at this time that it is hard to make sense of them. Just go into a bit more detail about what is going on in Europe. Fascism is proving curiously popular in some countries. It is certainly restoring higher levels of employment in Germany. It may even be restoring national pride there. In Italy it is providing a strong focus on central government for the first time. But there, by way of contrast, there is a huge rise in Marxist-Communist ideas. They are very opposing doctrines so these presently popular ideas may provide further conflict. America showed huge interest in Europe in the later stages of the Great War and in the early years of peace but it now seems to have shut out any interest in Britain and Europe.

"I have to get back into government and I am sure that I have to find some way of doing that which has popular appeal. But what does the public want in these indifferent times?"

Alice knew exactly how to handle him in situations like that. They talked gently for a couple of hours. After she had listened to him going through it all with obviously increasing frustration she said:

"Look Winston, you cannot solve all of those problems. You cannot do anything about what is happening elsewhere in the world until you have a power base here. You do not have that at the moment. You will only have two ways of getting back that powerbase. The first is by exploiting weaknesses in the existing leadership. Currently Baldwin is popular but he has been around for a long time. Who can tell how long he might last? The other thing that you can do is develop something completely new: some new idea or position or policy; maybe some way of countering some threat. But you will need powerful allies. My guess is that you will only find those after things get much worse."

It was not something that Winston wanted to hear. He wanted support for some kind of immediate action to bring his frustrations to an end. But he also knew that Alice would always provide him with wise counsel.

* * *

Louise spoke German as fluently as her native English. It was therefore easy for her to talk with von Ribbentrop. She had several different conversations with him in German during that dinner. In the first she explained why she was there. She had worked with Beaverbrook some years earlier and he still gave her occasional work commissions. Her family had been friends with Beaverbrook for many years.

In the second conversation they talked about her work;

"I am a researcher attached to London University. Some of the research I do is commissioned by government, some by industry, some by newspapers, but most of the work that I do is commissioned by academics and historians. There are vast university libraries all over Europe which had hardly been touched for centuries. Every time a writer thinks of a new book on some aspect of history they need to find some new material to make the book more interesting and to introduce new features. Finding that material is what I do. In addition to the university libraries there are the British National Library and numerous important collections at large country houses throughout Britain and Europe. I learned German and Russian so that I could research libraries there.

"I did some extensive research work in Germany a year or two back that enabled Sir Charles Petrie to write a new biography of Bismarck. I have recently returned from Leningrad where I have been doing some work on Catherine the Great."

Von Ribbentrop had no interest in any of that. To him academics were just part of the way to get influence. He did not care what they actually did.

Very little of that actually applied to her but it gave an excellent cover for the work that she did do. She was employed by the Foreign Office to act as a political espionage agent and a military spy. She did her work both in Europe and America. She had been trained for that job by British military intelligence and she had been thoroughly trained by the British army in all matters related to self protection and survival. She was a tough operative in a murky world. She was at that dinner in order to try and understand the character of Joachim von Ribbentrop. To do that she was going to attempt to sleep with him that night. She knew from sheer experience that sleeping with someone was an excellent way to understand any differences there might be between the declared public position of someone and what they were really like.

It was about midnight when she left with von Ribbentrop to go in his car to his official residence on Prince Albert Road, just north of Regent's Park It was just two doors down from the home of Joseph Kennedy, the American Ambassador. Von Ribbentrop had twice been to Kennedy's house for cocktail parties.

Von Ribbentrop's bedroom was on the southern side of the house. If it had been properly decorated it would have been a very attractive room. But it was not attractively decorated. The dominant colours were black and red. There was a swastika flag on one wall. There were several tables around the room seemingly covered with framed photographs. There were no women in any of those photographs. They were all of political events or military activities of several different kinds; training exercises, parades, award ceremonies, inspections of armaments factories. Working on the assumption that bedroom photographs were only likely to be ones of great personal importance Louise concluded that women were utterly unimportant to von Ribbentrop and that he was both master and servant of the Nazi regime. This man could not possibly be the polished diplomat he so tried to be in public. This man was a complete Hitlerite; the nine photographs in that grisly bedroom of them together were more than adequate testament to that. Louise was not looking forward to the night, but she had come fully prepared for anything. She just wondered how much of a deviant this man might be.

On the last table she looked at there were two decanters of whisky and two glasses. Also on that table was a document. She would read what she could of it whenever she got the chance.

Immediately he arrived in the room he poured himself a complete tumbler of the whisky and gave her a much smaller amount. He then started to talk about the personal opportunities the Third Reich presented to the people of Germany. He talked about how it had changed people's lives for the better all across Germany. He explained that other peoples in Europe were looking forward to the same sort of opportunities. It was a chilling message.

When he had finished that first tumbler of whisky he poured himself another and took a sip of it. He then started to remove his clothes. He told her to do the same and instructed her to put on some ghastly military garment that covered the top part of her body. She hated wearing any sort of clothes in bed and here he was already insisting on some kind of clothes fetish session. In her experience all forms of fetish and deviation fantasy indicated abnormal and unpleasant behaviour. This session was likely to get a lot worse before she could bring it under control. He then put on some form of medieval armour again on the top part of his body. He also put on some chain mail leggings that came up to mid thigh height. He carried her to the bed and tied her wrists to the bed head and her ankles to the foot of the bed. Her legs were well spread apart. He never touched her with his bare hands but used some kind of wooden device to insert into her. He hit her constantly with gloved hands. The gloves were thick and harsh.

When he got bored with that he untied her, took off his armour and gave her a whip with which to hit him. She was very happy to do that. Initially he lay on the bed on his front but later he rolled over on to his back and he demanded that she whip him all across the lower part of his body.

Louise always carried the means to deal with people who behaved like that. When he got bored with the whippings and was preparing to put on some frightful new piece of clothing she went to her handbag, took out a sedative pill and slipped it into his whisky. She then made him drink deeply. He liked doing that anyway and he knew that the drink would make him wilder. The sedative was very strong and he was asleep in seconds. She put him on the bed and then read that document, dressed and left the house. The same servant who had let them in also let her out. It was obviously quite normal. The effects of the drink and the pill would last for at least six hours. She doubted he would realise what had happened to him. That type of sedative had a strong amnesiac effect. He probably would not even be able to remember the last part of the dinner party. If he tried to finish the drink in the morning he would certainly go back to sleep again. That way he would remember even less.

* * *

She went to see her minder in the Foreign Office later that morning. It was always that way after important encounters in London.

She knew that she would be looked after wherever she went. She was an important agent who had already produced much valuable information. They would always go out of their way to protect their best. As she left von Ribbentrop's residence she walked towards a taxi that was parked at a taxi rank about a hundred yards down the road. She knew that it would be waiting for her there. When she went out for the night on official business there was always a plan for getting home safely. It was always that taxi. It was always close by when she needed it. It was always the same driver. He always called her "Ma'am". She always called him "Sid". She had no idea what his real name was but she knew that he was a much trusted operative in military intelligence. She knew that her father had arranged for him to look after her.

Equally there was always a plan for protecting unwanted access to her. Occasionally she wanted people to contact her. To them she always gave a discrete number. It was a number allocated to the Putney phone exchange in southwest London. She lived in a very different part of London. It was always answered by the secretary to her mentor. Sometimes, and only when she was in the office, she was then put straight through to the caller. Sometimes Louise called back. Sometimes people she had been with tried to contact her through whatever institution she claimed to be associated with. In all cases the response was that a message would be left for her to call back; but the caller was always told that she worked in all sorts of different places and they could not predict when she might be able to collect the message. They did not have a private phone number for her. In all cases a message was passed immediately to her mentor's secretary again on a different discrete line that was only used for such purposes.

She went home, had a deep hot bath, covered her bruises in Arnica, that was said to be good for such conditions and then went to sleep. It started as a very troubled sleep but she got fed up with that and took a sleeping pill. That certainly did the trick and she then slept soundly until well after nine. She had another bath, dressed her bruises again, grilled some bacon for breakfast, made some hot coffee and then rang her mentor at the Foreign Office. They arranged to meet at eleven at their usual location.

She normally worked in a small obscure office close to Horseguards Hotel in Whitehall Place. It was in reality a safe office for the Foreign Office to meet with some of their most highly valued people. It was connected by underground tunnels to several key government buildings. It could also be accessed from Horseguards Hotel through a room on the first floor there that they rented permanently. The brass plate on the street door to the office read: London Academic Research Ltd, Marketing Office. She travelled on the Underground and got off at Embankment Station. It was just a short walk from there.

Her mentor and minder in the Foreign Office was George Ponsonby. At that time he was an Assistant Under-Secretary but he was widely regarded as a high flyer and as a consequence he had been given some large responsibilities. At that time his main role was to develop as much information as he could about all the key leaders in both Germany and Russia. Eden, the Foreign Secretary had given him an additional and personal brief about establishing and managing a political espionage unit within the Foreign Office. He had explained at the time that he did not think he could rely on military and police intelligence alone.

It was impossible to tell at that time whether each or either of Germany and Russia represented either a threat or an opportunity for Britain. It was a time of great instability and things could go any way. People in both countries were disappearing from government almost every day and new people were coming into powerful positions. The world order established at the Versailles conference at the end of the First World War was being challenged in every sense. How it would develop seemed to depend entirely on the senior people in both Russia and Germany. Von Ribbentrop was certainly one of those very senior people. Everything was known about what he had said in public but nothing was known about his private life, if any. Louise had been briefed to start that investigation. Little was known about the actual strength of his position in Germany.

George Ponsonby was definitely gay. That was not a matter of any material interest to Louise. He was her boss and that was that but she did like working with him. The impossibility of any sort of emotional relationship made it a very safe working arrangement. It was all entirely professional.

George Ponsonby did eventually go on to much higher things in British diplomacy. He was knighted and his last posting was as British Ambassador to Moscow at some of the tensest times of the Cold War. He retired in the 1960's and went to live with a diplomatic service friend of his at a small but very attractive country house in North Essex. That friend was Sir Michael Curtis, another gay, who had been British Ambassador to Germany in the early 1960's. Both of them were involved in the same intelligence work in the years leading to the Second World War and indeed right up to the time they retired.

But that November morning the issue clearly on Ponsonby's mind was building up an accurate picture of von Ribbentrop. Although little was known about any detail of his background he was believed not to be just German Ambassador to London, but effectively Hitler's free roving ambassador and therefore effectively in charge of the Foreign Ministry. If that were so it had to be proved. He was not thought to be in London for any innocent reasons. That was why Ponsonby had the job of finding everything about him and reporting to his masters accordingly. Louise was his best agent and he knew he would get both accurate opinions and accurate facts from her.

His first words to her were:

"Von Ribbentrop's secretary has tried to contact you at London University this morning. He wanted to say how pleased he was to see you last evening and that he was sorry that you could not spend time together afterwards.

"Apparently he wants to invite you to a cocktail party at his residence on Friday week. Sometime nearer the time I will get my secretary to respond to it. What answer we give will depend on what you have to tell me."

The pleased Louise because it meant that the sedative had had its intended effect to make him forget the last parts of the evening. But given the time of her meeting with Ponsonby it also meant that he had not consumed any more of that drink after he had woken up.

When he had poured the coffee for Louise she started to talk:

"His conversation at dinner last evening was obviously intended to be charming and informative but he also wanted to listen. He was a dignified dinner guest and had he not been who he is he would probably have enjoyed the occasion. He listened intently to both Beaverbrook and Churchill in particular. But he also had a quiet chat with General Garbutt before the dinner started. I could hear something of all those chats.

"The one with General Garbutt was quite short. Von Ribbentrop informed him that Germany believed that the new Naval Pact was likely to prove very good for both countries and in his view it was likely to lead to much more friendly relations between the two countries. Accordingly it was likely that some senior German Army officers would be interested in visiting Britain sometime in the next few months. It would certainly be interesting for them to meet with some of their British counterparts. Garbutt replied that any such meetings would have to be officially sanctioned through diplomatic channels. If they were sanctioned he would probably be involved at least socially."

George replied:

"That is very interesting. We have not heard anything like that from Berlin. It probably would be sanctioned if it was requested. The government here is interested in anything that might preserve peace in a very dangerous world. If that is the way Ribbentrop is thinking just now we should hear something within the next two weeks or so. It will be interesting to see what report Garbutt puts in."

Louise went on:

"The conversation with Beaverbrook was obviously intended as a way to use a private meeting to spread German propaganda. Basically what Ribbentrop was saying was that Germany would be happy to give The Daily Express exclusive opportunities to visit Germany so that they could see the great progress being made by the German people under the Nazi government. Beaverbrook was certainly interested in the idea but he pointed out that there would have to be complete editorial freedom for his paper. No agreement was reached between them but they did agree to meet again to talk about it all. Ribbentrop was talking very enthusiastically about the whole situation in Germany. I got the strong impression that he feels confident enough about the British position to feel that launching a propaganda war would now be both possible and appropriate. I was not able to hear the end of the conversation but I will be seeing Max Beaverbrook again soon and I will find out from him exactly what then transpired. I will see you again after that to let you know about it all.

"After dinner von Ribbentrop and Churchill went to sit in the corner. They both had large brandies and Churchill took a decanter with him as well. I went with the ladies and we were within hearing distance of them. I was the nearest to them and listened intently to what they were saying. I missed a few things because I had to answer questions from the others.

"Their talk was largely about the importance to Britain of its Empire. Churchill explained that the Empire was far more important to Britain than anything in Europe. The whole purpose of

British Naval might, for example, was to support and defend the empire and all the trade routes associated with it. He said that if Britain had a choice it would choose Empire rather than Europe.

"But in a wider sense it was obvious that there was broad agreement between them on many issues. Ribbentrop was talking about German aspirations to link very closely with its ethnic neighbours, particularly Austria and the Sudetenland. He envisaged that they would inevitably become part of Germany and portrayed that as the will of the people there. Ribbentrop believed there were strong parallels between German aspirations in the eastern parts of Europe with Britain's colonial policies. Indeed there seemed to be a strong common interest.

"They did agree to meet again. Their next definitive meeting will be when von Ribbentrop goes to stay at Chartwell, probably in February. He will be going there for a weekend."

George Ponsonby said:

"Hmmm. We are all sure that Winston will do anything to get back into power. Maybe he is exploring a possible powerbase that would unite a significant part of the Tory party around some kind of alliance or, as a minimum, a no objection position in relation to what Germany might do. Recognition of imperial aspirations might be part of that. At the moment almost anything might succeed in the chaos we have in this country. Britain has very little military capability at this time. The aftermath of the First World War saw to that. Economic chaos has drained the nation of much of its wealth. So the opportunity clearly exists for some new ideas to emerge. I am sure that Churchill is examining how he can bring that about. We have known for some time that we are going to have to watch him closely. I will look into how we can infiltrate that meeting. Tell me now about Ribbentrop."

She thought before starting on that one:

"It was easy enough for me to fix to go back to his residence with him. It was impossible for me to tell in advance just how awful it would be. In the car he talked about how powerful he was in Germany. He described how he had been involved in the very foundations of the Nazi party and how he was one of Hitler's most trusted aides. Hitler never did anything in connection with any other nation without consulting him. Without the Nazi party he would never have been able to reach such a position of power and influence. It was certainly the talk of a very arrogant man and a man very proud of what he has achieved under Hitler's patronage.

"When we got to the house we went straight to his bedroom. It was truly a ghastly place; pictures of Hitler and military activities everywhere. The whole room was decorated in red and black. It was exceptionally nasty and unwelcoming. He had loads of whisky in the room and poured himself a whole tumbler. He gave me a smaller one. He ranted on about the wonders of the new Germany for about half an hour. While he had been pouring the whisky I noticed that there was a document on the table where the whisky was.

"What followed was the most horrendous and abusive sex session I have ever encountered or heard of. To say that he is perverted would be a gross understatement. He was exceptionally cruel. My bruises from the beating he gave me will last for ages. He also wanted me to whip him on the lower parts of his body. He must have been very used to it because he had whip marks all over him and he hardly flinched when I hit his balls with the whip. He wore bizarre garments at various stages including some mediaeval armour.

"Anyway as soon as I could I gave him some more whisky into which I had put a strong sedative and I made him drink it, promising some more bizarre antics. He drank a lot of that whisky and within seconds was fast asleep. As soon as he was, I read that document. It was a hand written account of a meeting with Hitler just a few days before he left Berlin to come to London. The substance of that meeting was that it was all about their shared view that the current weak British leadership was unlikely to survive. Sooner or later someone new would come along who would start to address Britain's real issues. Ribbentrop had to find those people and influence them in favour of German policies. He also had to find ways of neutralising anti-German feelings in Britain. Proving that Nazi policies were doing wonders for Germany was all part of that.

"After that I left. Other people must have similar states of disgust because the man on the door was in no way surprised to see me go. It is self-evident that I will not go near the pervert ever again. He is completely evil and in my view a man who is that nasty must have nasty policies as well. We are clearly going to have to step up our efforts in Germany to find out exactly what is going on."

"Louise, thanks for that. Obviously I could not have known in advance just how awful it would be. But I will ensure that he is told that you will not be in London then. I cannot imagine that you will want to meet with him again.

"I am preparing a new mission for you. It will be a very important one in Germany. The details are currently being finalised and when we next few within a few days I will tell you about it.

* * *

November 24, 1936 I met with Ronnie Harford today. I had not met him since I returned from India. I told him that I really wanted just to make contact again and that I could never know in advance when I might need either information or advice from him. He seemed pleased with the fact that I had been to see him. As I left I mentioned that I had met his daughter at a social event, but I had not been able to find out what she was doing these days. He told me that she was a researcher who worked both for historians and newspapers. To me that sort of explained the link with Max Beaverbrook but it seemed an odd sort of role to justify her being at such a dinner party. I suspect that she has a much more important job and that she was there to find out more about von Ribbentrop. I must try and find out more. I wonder if Winston knows anything about her.

* * *

A few days later Louise was asked to meet with George Ponsonby again. They met at her office. During a long and detailed meeting he gave her all the details of the work she would be doing in Germany.

Ponsonby started the meeting by saying:

"Louise, we have a very interesting informant in Germany who has been providing us with some very important information. I cannot tell you who he is or how he has been able to provide us with any sort of information. But what I can tell you is that he told us about three months ago that it was getting too risky to give us any further information. He might be able to do so at some stage but there could be no guarantee. It would be best to proceed on the basis that he could provide nothing. But what he did offer was to set up a way of us putting our own agent into Germany under the right conditions so that we could continue to get the information that he would have provided and probably much more as well.

"Since then we have had to research the option he suggested and prove to ourselves that it would be at least as safe for us as any other option. That research was very important because potentially the information that we could obtain is very valuable.

"We have now decided that everything is in place to enable us to take up his suggestions in a way that will not compromise British security policies or any person involved in implementing them. We now want you to go to Germany and get us that information. We are satisfied that there is no other way that it could be obtained efficiently. That you can do it I have no doubt. I am also satisfied that it will be as safe as any spying mission can ever be. It is a very well structured plan and the opportunities to gather excellent information are likely to be numerous. One day I might tell you how it was all done.

"We have been able to create a new identity for you in Germany. Under that you will be working as an administrator for a company called Achtgrenze, which is a large construction company based in Düsseldorf specialising in military contracts. While there you are to find out as much as possible about the military build up in Germany, what bases are being constructed, where and which units will be using them."

He told her where she would be living and about how she could communicate with him. She was to stay in Germany until she had mined the whole seam of information available to her. She would be leaving for Germany the following weekend.

"While you are there you will be adopting the identity of a girl called Sabina Heyer. She looks almost identical to you and it is she who has actually been appointed to the job you will be taking up. Tomorrow you will be fully briefed on her, the role you will be taking on and the apartment that you will be using. We have found a new future for her with which she is very happy."

* * *

As soon as she got home that evening she rang her father. She arranged to have lunch with him at home on the Saturday. Her mother was always at charity meetings on Saturdays so they could talk freely.

Louise told him where she was going and what she was going to do. Her father knew that such a mission was being planned by the Foreign Office but he had no idea that she would be involved. In his view it was a well planned and very important mission that had every chance of success but as always it carried considerable risks. He told her that he would arrange for her to be watched over by someone who could look after her if the need aCurtis.

He also told her that he would arrange to be informed of all that she had discovered in Germany because, as he said, you can never trust any of those diplomats.

They agreed that they would meet up as soon as she had returned from Germany.

* * *

December 10, 1936. I have been to spend a couple of days with Winston at Chartwell. It was a thoroughly enjoyable time and I was entertained in great style. Winston was most interested in my experiences in India and how Britain was viewed in India. We agreed that we would meet regularly in the future. On the last evening I was there we were joined by Anthony Eden. It was the first time I had met our Foreign Secretary. I got the very strong impression that he was feeling overwhelmed by the seemingly endless series of crises in Europe and by the Japanese aggression in the Far East.

Although Winston is seen a very much of a pariah in government circles he maintains excellent relations with Eden. It was not possible for Eden to be completely candid with Winston because of the strong dislike of him in government but nevertheless I got the strong impression that Eden was very frustrated by the lack of interest in all these complicated issues by the Prime Minister. I have only met Stanley Baldwin once and it was difficult for me to form an impression of him at the very formal event involved so I do not know what to make of him. Winston is very sore at the continued popularity of the PM in the country.

One particularly interesting conversation with Winston was after dinner on the first evening. I told him I had been very distant from what had been going on in Europe for several years. In coming back to London I had become confused as to what had actually been happening and where the strengths and weaknesses of it all really were. I asked him for his assessment of it. In reply he said:

"Samuel, in this country we have two serious problems. The first is the weakness of our economy. We have had recession, low investment, high unemployment and serious industrial unrest. I have frequently said that these problems are not being addressed by Baldwin and his government. Given these problems I do not understand why he remains popular. Our second problem is the weakness of our armed forces. True, there was much public clamour after the last war for there to be disarmament and Britain responded by cutting our forces dramatically. They are now at a level where we can hardly do anything. If we faced a serious threat we would be in serious trouble. Investment in our armed forces would help the economy dramatically.

"There are many problems in Europe but they are largely of a domestic nature in each country. They are presently of little interest to the country at large but they are of concern to our Foreign Office as Anthony Eden will tell you tomorrow. Despite some of the problems there are encouraging signs. In the last three years or so Hitler has transformed the German economy. The currency has been stabilised, unemployment has fallen and there seems to be investment in all sectors of the economy.

"From what I can see Hitler seems to have imperial aspirations. If he achieves these without threatening Britain the German economy will improve still further. I have supported some of the things that Germany has done and I see, for example, great strength in the Naval Agreement that was agreed recently. That should enable Germany to develop its armed forces but in a manner in which they will always be much weaker than Britain. It is very much in our interests to have a Europe which is stable from a military point of view. Russia is a great unknown at this time and could very well threaten us at any time. We know virtually nothing about what is going on in that country. In such circumstances it makes sense to have Germany as an effective buffer between us.

"I have no doubt that Germany has imperial aspirations; Hitler has made this very clear. It is an aim that I support. The British Empire has proved that empires are good for the stability of the world. The control of that Empire is one of our greatest strengths. There is no prospect of Germany being able to put together any empire which even remotely challenges ours and therefore I do not see any threat to our own empire from that source. I have made speeches supporting some modest imperial aspirations for them. There is no point in having Europe made up of pathetically weak states. Germany became that after the Versailles treaty. What matters, though, is that we in Britain are able to control their military aspirations in particular. That is why the new Naval Agreement is so important. I am sure that it will provide a good governing framework for several decades to come.

"I have been criticised by many for showing any support for Germany. There are many people in Britain who see her only as an enemy. But you only have to look at what has been achieved there in the last three years or so to see that there are lessons that we can learn that would benefit our country. The quickest way to restore economic growth, for example, would be to expand our armed forces.

"I have to say that I am more critical of our own government for doing nothing than I am of any European government. We have to do something here quickly to reduce unemployment and improve our financial strength.

"I know enough about history, though, to know that the real judgments about what was right and wrong will be made in many years time when the complete perspective is known. But I have no doubt that when the real histories of our present time are written Baldwin's government will be judged as being very lacking. It is that rather than anything that is happening in Germany or anywhere else in Europe that is the cause of my immense frustration at this time."

* * *

It was less than a week after Louise had taken up her job with Achtgrenze in Düsseldorf that she first communicated back to George Ponsonby. The agreed procedure was to drop a letter through the letter box of another apartment in the block in which she lived. The letter was retrieved within a few minutes of her depositing it. It was taken to London by courier by the first possible train. It was read by George Ponsonby the next day. A copy of it was read that morning by her father as well. Ponsonby never knew that her letters to him were being read by General Harford.

On the morning after she had deposited that letter for it to be taken to London Louise saw Sid across the street as she walked to work. She was pleased that her father had sent him to Germany to look after her. She also knew then just how her father would know all about the contents of her letters.

* * *

The contents of that first letter were to be the focus for a meeting that was to set in train a process of diplomatic intrigue and deceit that was to prevail through the next several decades. She never knew that neither did her father.

Louise met her first employer when she was head girl at her school. It was the occasion of the annual sports day and prize-giving. At lunch that day she sat next to Sir Charles Petrie who was an eminent historian and a governor of the school. Louise was a gifted language student and Sir Charles knew that. At lunch that day he offered her a job as a researcher on his team. He wrote numerous books and needed to research masses of documentation to make them both interesting and informative. He was about to start work on a biography of Bismarck, the first German Chancellor and needed people with good German language skills to read through thousands of documents in German libraries and private houses. She took the job and provided him with much interesting material for the book. He subsequently used her to do research work in Russia on Catherine the Great because she also spoke Russian.

Louise never knew that Sir Charles had founded an organisation called Royalist International. Whether she would have ever approved of its role is not known. The public claim of Royalist

International was that it was to campaign for the restoration of royal power anywhere, but particularly in Greece. In reality it was to provide cover for clandestine diplomatic activities.

The meetings of Royalist International took place once a month in as unlikely a place for diplomatic activity as it was possible to imagine. In the 1930's Evensong was a very popular church service. Churches were generally full on Sunday evenings. St. Mary's Church in Graham Street in the West End of London was a fashionable church and it had been chosen as the meeting place of Royalist International. It met there one Sunday evening each month. The members of the group would go there to meet one another as they prayed.

One of the members of Royalist International was Michael Curtis who was George Ponsonby's assistant. The Sunday after Louise's letter was received was scheduled as a meeting of Royalist International and Michael Curtis went to the church that evening to meet with Otto von Papen. Otto was a second and very much loved cousin of Franz von Papen, who had been German Vice-Chancellor and was now German Ambassador to Austria. Otto was a medium ranking official in the German Embassy in London then. Franz von Papen was a very senior and influential member of the Nazi party, but he also had strong leanings towards Britain. He had developed a taste for the British way of life when he had been sent to Washington in 1914 as German military attaché to the United States. Over there he had met many British diplomats and that was where secret diplomacy between the two countries had taken place. It was Franz von Papen who had paved the way for Louise to go to Achtgrenze.

As they knelt together before the service began Michael Curtis told Otto von Papen that the mission seemed to be getting off to a very good start. They would talk again in four week's time.

On the way out of church Michael Curtis walked next to Igor Molotov, the Russian Trade Attaché, based in London. They agreed to kneel together before evensong the following Sunday evening.

* * *

The following Sunday evening Michael Curtis and Igor Molotov went to the back of the church. They got there early so that there would be space round them. That way no one else could hear what they were saying. They knelt seemingly in prayer for ten minutes but during those ten minutes they were starting a process of spying, disinformation, double dealing, deceit and treachery that was to dominate diplomatic contact between Britain and Russia for many decades.

For Michael Curtis it was a very important meeting. He well knew who Igor Molotov was. He was the result of one of the serial womanising sessions of his father, Vyasceslav Mikhailovich Molotov, the Russian Foreign Minister. Igor was publicly known to be his father's child and the only one he had by any woman other than his wife with whom he kept in touch. They had a special and close relationship. It was much easier to deal with Molotov through his son than through Ambassadors in either country. Igor had been at the inaugural meeting of Royalist International by invitation. That had been after he had arrived in London as Trade Attaché.

That evening Igor Molotov told Michael Curtis that it would be in Britain's interest to send a senior diplomat on a secret mission to Moscow. Russia was becoming increasingly concerned about Japanese and American military activity in the Far East. There might well be some benefits to both Britain and Russia from sharing some of the intelligence that they both must have on this subject. It was surely in the interests of both countries that there should be a continuing peace in the Far East. After all, Britain's colonial interest relied on peace being maintained.

Michael Curtis said that he would ensure that a suitably qualified and experienced person would go to Moscow but he would need to know how the Russians could guarantee the secrecy of the mission and when it should take place. Igor responded that they should meet again next Sunday evening in the church and if a suitable name was then forthcoming he would describe the travel and security arrangements.

They did meet the following Sunday evening and they agreed that George Ponsonby would go to Moscow. He would take a week's holiday with the intention of visiting Amsterdam. He would go there by train and ferry, and check into a hotel from where he would be collected by a Russian diplomat. He would then be taken to Amsterdam airport from where he would be flown to Moscow. While in Moscow he would be staying in a safe hotel controlled by the government. Similar arrangements would apply for the return trip. He would be flown back to Amsterdam from where he could return to London in his own time. He would be in Moscow for three days.

* * *

December 23, 1936. I went to a cocktail party this evening at the Foreign Office. Anthony Eden was there and I spoke to him for a few minutes. He gave a gracious speech and wished that we all had a very good Christmas.

I had a long chat with George Ponsonby who seemed very knowledgeable on military matters, possibly because he had served in the Great War. He did tell me his rank but not what his responsibilities were although I asked him several times. In my assessment he seemed to be a homosexual. At the beginning of the party he had what looked like a very intense discussion with Eden. It is a common military view that there are all sorts of funny people in the Foreign Office who cannot be trusted. I wonder if he is one of those.

* * *

Louise's job allowed her to go and visit Achtgrenze construction sites all round Germany. She worked in the Contract Monitoring Office at the company's head office and the only way to produce accurate reports for senior management was to go and see all the different projects. It provided a wonderful opportunity to gather vast amounts of information. Her manager regularly told her that the work that she did in the improving the management of their contracts was much appreciated.

Her first visit had been to Dresden where she had seen a new Luftwaffe base being built. Then she went to future Luftwaffe airfields up the eastern side of Germany. After that she went down the west side of the country. She was utterly and totally appalled by the sheer scale of what was going on. Every time she got back to Düsseldorf she sent a letter to George Ponsonby. Every time she did so she got an acknowledgement pushed through her own letter box by the time she got back after her next trip. In those acknowledgements there were always words of encouragement about the excellent work that she was doing.

When she reckoned that she had finished with Luftwaffe sites she started on the Army, the Wehrmacht. With all the confidence that the company, the Nazi Party and the armed forces had in her it was not in any way difficult to arrange anything. Sleeping around with senior military personnel also helped. She was delighted that none of them behaved in any unpleasant way towards her. There was no repetition of anything that she had experienced with that ghastly Ribbentrop creature. But they all gave her useful information about the military build-up in Germany.

She was both appalled and amazed to discover that the Wehrmacht was building barracks for 36 divisions of troops. That was far beyond anything that had even been imagined in the rest of Europe by any government. The implications of everything that she was learning went far into the realms of horror.

Throughout those months she sent regular reports back to London through that letter box arrangement. They were all acknowledged.

And then she started on the navy. Before she had left England she had learned that the terms of the Anglo-German Naval Agreement negotiated in 1935 by Sir John Simon, the then Foreign Secretary, and Anthony Eden had meant that Germany had accepted that it could build up to thirty-five percent of the capacity of the Royal Navy and that no vessel that they built could be more than 10,000 tons in size. Submarine construction was specifically prohibited. But she went round submarine construction yards where at least thirty submarines were being built.

Then she went to a shipyard in Kiel to find that two 26,000 tonne battle cruisers were under construction. These had been given the provisional names of Gneisenau and Scharnhorst. They were later to prove to be very fearsome weapons. That was quite enough for her. She was sure that she had discovered far more than could have ever been contemplated by anyone back in London. It was far worse than anything she had read about the Naval Agreement. If things were that bad already how much worse were they going to get?

She travelled by the diabolical train service back to Düsseldorf and the next morning she told her manager that she wanted and needed at least a week off. She wanted a holiday to try and rest after the intense work of the last few months. She said she planned to go down to Bodensee, a large lake down in the south of the country near the Swiss border, for about a week. It was a very popular place for holidays. He agreed that that was right and told her that she had done some excellent work. He told her that there would be plenty more work when she returned.

The following morning she took the first train to Holland. Later that day she took the ferry from Hoek Van Holland to Harwich. It was an overnight ferry and she arrived back in London in the middle of the following morning. As soon as she got to her flat she rang George Ponsonby's secretary and said she needed an appointment to see him. They met at three that afternoon. She had been away from Britain for five months.

At that time Louise wondered whether she would ever return to Germany. She could not have known at that time that she would return again nearly a decade later under completely different circumstances.

* * *

June 8, 1956. Louise Harford came to stay over the weekend. Since I got to know who she really was we have met regularly to talk over old times and the work we were both doing then. This time we were talking about her work for the Foreign Office in 1937 when she was in Germany. I quizzed her about what had happened to all the information that she had gathered and why she thought it had not been used to help Britain prepare for war. She told me that she was in no doubt that it had been suppressed by the Prime Minister, Stanley

Baldwin, who found it all very unappealing. He was not interested in anything to do with armaments and they interfered with his agenda, which was purely domestic. We speculated on the role that Anthony Eden had played in the Naval Agreement negotiations but we simply did not have enough information about whether his role was honourable or duplicitous. We suspected the latter. Whatever his role it was obvious that Britain had been thoroughly duped into accepting an agreement that Germany had no intention of honouring. The German negotiator had been von Ribbentrop.

* * *

I had been intrigued by the reference in Samuel's diary to George Ponsonby. Samuel had certainly not mentioned him to me. It was not a name I recognised from any British history covering either the pre-war period or the war itself. But his name did appear in the British Diplomatic List and he appeared to have a distinguished career. He was knighted for his service to Britain. His last diplomatic post was as Ambassador to Russia. Samuel never mentioned him to me which was probably because he had no real idea of what the man was doing. It was only when I was able to get access to Russian archives that I found reference to him and to his initial contacts with the highest levels of the Russian Government in 1937 that I was able to put together an account of what he had actually been doing.

Those archives included the minutes of the meetings that Molotov had with Ponsonby and the reports put in by the other people described here. From all those reports it is possible to describe in detail exactly how Ponsonby became an agent of the Soviet Union. It appears to have been very simple to exploit his weaknesses. Those same notes show how simple it was for the Soviet authorities to make Guy Burgess one of their agents as well, with the willing assistance of Britain.

* * *

A few weeks after Louise had gone to Germany George Ponsonby had gone on that secret mission to Moscow. He, too, had taken the train ferry via Harwich. In Amsterdam he had checked into the Delft Hotel on Herengracht, a quiet street very close to the city centre. He had never been to Amsterdam before and he found it to be a very attractive city. He decided that as soon as he returned from Moscow there were several attractions in the city that he would visit before he returned to London. The gay clubs were certainly of interest to him. There seemed to be plenty of them.

He had arrived in Amsterdam in the morning. He had no idea when he would be contacted about his flight to Moscow. It was a tense time for him not only because he was dealing with the unknown but also because he had never been in an aeroplane before. He had no idea how long it would take to fly to Moscow and he had no idea what perils there might be along the way.

He did not have to wait long before he was contacted. It was actually only half an hour after he had checked into his hotel. There was a knock on his door and after he had opened it he was spoken to by a tall young man who introduced himself as Yuri Butkov. He said he worked for the Russian Foreign Ministry. He would be taking him to Moscow the following morning. They would be leaving on a Dutch KLM flight at eight in the morning. That meant they would have to leave the hotel a little before seven. The flight would take all day. They would have to stop twice on the way to refuel at Hamburg and St Petersburg.

He thought that the whole flight was a thoroughly miserable, cold and noisy experience. The only benefit of it was that he was able to get to Moscow within a single day, something that would have been completely impossible then by any other means of transport.

They were met at they airport by a Foreign Ministry car and taken to their hotel right in the centre of the city. That evening over dinner in the hotel Butkov told Ponsonby that he would be meeting Vyascelav Molotov, the Foreign Minister the following morning. The main purpose of the meeting would be to see whether it would be possible to set up some completely secret processes under which the British and Russian governments could communicate over matters of mutual interest. The current tension in the Far East would be a good example of just that.

It was around ten in the morning that Ponsonby was driven to the Kremlin. To him it looked as if the whole place exuded formidable power. He could not imagine how it could ever be possible to create such a massive place in a country like Britain. It was completely and utterly extraordinary.

But he was made welcome there and on that first morning of his in Moscow he was shown into Molotov's office, deep in the heart of the whole Kremlin complex.

It was a huge office and at one end of it there was a very comfortable seating area with a large low coffee table between the sofas and chairs. On that table were both coffee and vodka. Molotov made it clear that he was going to use both and he recommended that Ponsonby did the same.

Molotov then went straight into the agenda that interested him:

"Comrade, I am pleased that you were able to come to Moscow to meet with me. I am particularly pleased that someone as senior as you in the British Foreign Ministry has been able to spend the time to come and meet with me. We have been studying for some months now how we can establish much more secure communications channels with Britain. In our experience normal diplomatic channels are neither quick nor secure. I have come to be very suspicious about the normal protocols associated with the service I am sure there is a need to bypass all normal communications routines in the diplomatic service. There have to be processes which are based on trust and competence. I am tired of purging Russian officials who have probably been leaking sensitive information to completely unauthorised people. What they have been doing is weaken political control of governments and that has to be wrong. Russia needs close and reliable links with other countries and has to achieve those in one way or another. All of us here are sure that Britain has the same need.

"The world is a very dangerous place and is becoming more dangerous. Russia has a huge domestic reform programme that we are carrying out. It will strongly benefit international trade when it is completed.

"Russia also believes that states should be secure within their own borders. There seem to be many parallels with Britain in those policies. To make them work, though, there has to be the highest trust in the communications systems that apply between governments. In particular there has to be quick communication. What I want to achieve is a situation in which there will be a British official in Moscow who is not attached to the British Embassy with whom I can communicate at any time. I would put into London someone with similar status. My son Igor had assessed that something along those lines should be achievable. I would like you to think about it all and come back in a couple of days to talk it all through in more detail."

They both knew that this was just diplomatic mumbo jumbo for the simple phrase "We would like you to work for us." Ponsonby was grateful that he had been given time to make his fateful decision. Nothing would change his mind but there were implications about current work that needed to be thought through.

They then went on to talk about the threat of war in the Far East. Molotov was increasingly concerned that Japan was using its presence on the Chinese mainland to threaten the border with Russia. The border was a very rough and isolated area and was potentially vulnerable to any sort of massed Japanese attack. He hoped that it would be possible to get some of that pressure relieved by Britain using some of its naval might in the Far East to undertake some potentially demonstrative manoeuvres in that general area. It was an interesting discussion that they had and it added completely new dimensions to the sort of world problems that were being continuously evaluated by the British Foreign Office. But it was something way outside Ponsonby's normal remit and it was an issued that he should never have discussed. Issues of that sort would normally only be discussed at Ambassador or Government Minister level.

That evening Ponsonby was taken off by Butkov to a gay club in the Lyublino district of the city. It was around half an hour's drive from the hotel. It was a bitter cold evening and there was virtually no one about in the streets. There just seemed to be endless piles of snow everywhere.

But the club itself proved to be a very warm and welcoming place. It was a bit like a London gentleman's club with lots of leather sofas everywhere. Waiters cruised around taking drinks orders. Ponsonby seemed to have been on vodka for most of that day so he stayed on it. It was while they were on their second drinks that Butkov introduced Ponsonby to two young men whom he said were emerging as bright stars in the Russian military. They had both been awarded with high achievement medals just a year before, and they were well known members of the club.

They all agreed to have dinner together. After that Butkov left and the two men took Ponsonby off to the nude dance hall at the back of the establishment. It was there that night that he agreed to become a spy for Russia. They took him back to his hotel at about dawn. But in the hours that he had been in that club with them he had had the most sensational gay sex of his life. Provided that one or both of them came to London he would set up that deal for Molotov.

The following morning Molotov knew that Ponsonby was trapped. He was very pleased that he had been able to get the services of such a senior diplomat so easily. But then he knew the man's weaknesses. He had the photographs at that club the previous night to prove it.

But Ponsonby was nothing if not a devious man. He had to set it all up in such a way that he could get Guy Burgess into Russia freely and as often as necessary. He had to find information of his own which he could use to gain power and influence in the Foreign Office. Guy Burgess could be and he hoped would be that prime contact for which Molotov was looking. He would get Guy Burgess to provide that essential communications link. That would please Anthony Eden.

But he had no way of knowing whether he could trust Guy Burgess. The man might or might not get access to the right information. But he knew that if, somehow, he could get Louise into Russia she would produce real quality information.

That morning he started to explore the city on his own. He was pretty certain that he was being followed. That meant that he could not talk to anyone about any serious issue. The authorities would almost certainly find out exactly what he had said to anyone whom he had met. But he was not looking for conversations, he was looking for ideas. Ideas about how he could get Louise into Russia at some stage in the near future. He needed to do that so that he would have his own source of information about what was going on in Russia.

For a year or so British Intelligence agents had been seeking to find someone who worked in a key Russian ministry who looked very much like Louise; someone who had no family would be even better. Just before he had left London he had been told by them that they had found a girl called Ludmilla Tereshkova who worked as a junior conference administrator in Josef Stalin's office. She met the requirement fully. Her appearance in terms of weight, height and features was to all intents identical. Her only relative was her mother who lived in Irkutsk in Central Asia. It was an untravellably vast distance away by train and they had not seen each other since Ludmilla had left home to go to Moscow on a government scholarship several years earlier. What the intelligence agents had also found out was that Ludmilla was due to be transferred to the office of the Soviet Defence Commissar, Klimert Voroshilov, in a few weeks time when she had finished her outstanding work. On her move she would gain substantial promotion. In her new role she would be close to the commissar and would be organising all his important meetings. It looked like an ideal solution but the problem was how to bring it about.

As George Ponsonby tramped the streets that morning he was seeking inspiration about how it could all be achieved. He did get that inspiration. But before he could put his ideas into effect he would have to go back to London and talk with Anthony Eden, although he would never be able to give Eden the reason why it was essential for him to approve the murky deal he intended to do with Molotov when he saw him the next day.

Yes, that was how he would do it. But it would be cunning, deceitful and a straight lie to his own boss. But he knew enough about diplomacy to know that the best deals were done that way.

Ponsonby went back to see Molotov, as agreed.

"Comrade, what you have proposed to me can be achieved. I will, however, need a few days after my return to London to put in place the necessary details. It will need the approval of my minister but as what you have proposed is in accordance with his own thinking I am sure that he will give it his approval. As soon as he has agreed we will arrange for someone to come to Moscow to be the link with you. I have someone in mind but I cannot give you his name until he has been given the assignment.

"The issue of the naval exercises in the Far East is more complex because that will require wider approval from within our government. But I fully understand the issues you put to me and I am hopeful that approval for them will be forthcoming rapidly.

The evening after I last met you I met with two young officers at a club. They would be welcome in London at any time."

Molotov's answer was short:

"Thank you and welcome"

That was the way that Ponsonby and Burgess became spies for Russia.

Molotov was a man who knew how to exploit weakness. He knew that whoever Ponsonby sent to Moscow would be just as pliable as Ponsonby himself had been.

He smiled to himself as Ponsonby left his office full of vodka.

* * *

One of the documents that I found in the Russian archives in 1994 was the diary of Ponsonby. It was in several volumes and it gave an account of his dealings with America, Russia and with British governments. It was easy for me to establish that I was the first person to study his diaries. So far as I am aware no one has since looked at them; certainly until now nothing in them has been published. Only the archivist whom I befriended and who helped me find the revealing documents that I have used in this book knows where they are now filed.

One entry reads:

"February 2, 1937. Since I have returned from Moscow I have had plenty of time to reflect on the decision that I made there to become the most important informer available to them in the British civil service. It is a decision that I made in principal many months ago as I came under increasing pressure from Anthony Eden to manage a growing network of British spies operating around the world. It was strongly reinforced by the high quality of information that I was receiving from my agent in Germany. I have enjoyed both the intrigue and the danger of the espionage business. It gives me thrills and excitements that I have never found elsewhere. But I have known for months that I would have to make a choice as to where my loyalty should lie. The very fact that I needed to make a choice meant that it could not be Britain. By working for Britain I could not get real excitement. I like working with Eden but most of the others were not to my liking at all. I despair about the negativism of British life today.

Loyalty to America would be impossible for me. I do not like its material culture and I never feel happy dealing with Americans. This trip to Russia left me in no doubt that I would be very welcome to them. They made it clear that I would be treated as a hero there if I was able to provide them with key inside information about Britain and its policies and intentions. The way that I was treated when I was there made the decision very easy. I have never been treated as well before. In order that my position and work are not compromised I shall have to find a way of handing over my other responsibilities so that I can concentrate on serving my Russian masters. It will be an exciting time."

* * *

February 12, 1937. I got a call from Winston this morning. He wanted to see me in London for dinner this evening. He wanted to tell me about a fascinating weekend he had spent with von Ribbentrop.

It was while Ponsonby was away that von Ribbentrop had gone to Chartwell. It was a cold weekend and the weather was generally dreadful. It had been snowing lightly in London early on the Friday afternoon but there had not been enough to disrupt von Ribbentrop's journey down by car, at least initially. He arrived soon after six. In the last fifteen minutes of the drive it had started to snow heavily. The driver was dreading going back to London in those conditions. A servant took von Ribbentrop to his room and told him that drinks would be served in the lounge in half an hour.

When he went down to the lounge only Winston was there. He immediately poured whiskies for them both. Winston said that his wife would join them for dinner in about an hour. The following day, depending on the weather, they could wander though the grounds and generally talk. A dinner party had been arranged for the Saturday evening and von Ribbentrop would be welcome to stay until after lunch on the Sunday.

They sat in front of the roaring log fire. Churchill had been editing one of his books all day and was bored with reading endless pages of typed script. Von Ribbentrop had had a tough day dealing with a mass of detailed documents about the risks associated with a possible invasion of Austria. One of those risks was what Britain's reaction might be. He had not yet been able to assess that, although he had been in London for many months.

Since he had last met Churchill he had studied the man in meticulous detail. But he had by no means come to any final conclusions about what his report to Hitler would say about him. Over this weekend he needed to open up the conversation, he needed to find out what the man's bottom line might be. Everything that he had heard was that Churchill was well and truly out of power now but could very quickly get back in if the public mood changed. He needed to assess what those circumstances might be.

For his part Churchill was still looking to see whether Germany presented a threat or an opportunity. Von Ribbentrop started to talk almost immediately:

"Winston, I probably do not have to teach you anything about German history. But there are lessons from our history which are very important at this time. As you know, until the latter part of the last century Germany was not a unified country. It was a succession of small states largely ruled by separate but inter-related royal families. It was not a formula which provided any great strength nor was it one which brought together numerous peoples who shared the same culture, the same language and broadly the same aspirations. The largest of those states was Prussia which had a very strong alliance with Britain during the Napoleonic wars. It was an alliance that worked.

"The unification of Germany created great pride in our country. That unification was an important event for the vast majority of the population. It created a pride in our nation. That pride was destroyed as a result of The First World War. Our nation was smaller, and dramatically weaker as a result of that war. Sure, Germany fought hard in that war but it did not cause that war. Fundamentally that war was caused by effete royalty trying to bully their own relatives without regard to the consequences; a bit like a family row on a world scale. What most Germans want to do is to forget all that and the diabolical consequences that flowed from the disastrous peace settlement and get back to where we were in 1914. Most Germans also believe that it is an aspiration that deserves the support of the rest of the world. It will be achieved sooner or later.

"What has happened in Germany in recent years is that there has been a huge resurgence of national pride. We have got rid of that terrible inflation of our currency. We have started to talk to other nations, including Britain, as equals. The feeling that we were being suppressed is going. In an economic sense we are currently doing better than almost any other country in Europe.

"That is what I would like you to understand as the starting position of our friendly talks this weekend. I look forward to hearing more of what you want to tell me."

Just before Clemmie came down for dinner Winston and von Ribbentrop looked out of the window at the floodlit gardens. It was snowing heavily.

After dinner they talked at great length over numerous brandies. What Winston said was largely a repetition of what he had said the previous November. This time, however, von Ribbentrop spoke of the triumphs of the Nazi regime so far. In particular he spoke of the huge increases in the morale and confidence of the German people following the stabilisation of the currency. Von Ribbentrop told Winston how that increase in national confidence was going to be used to restore Germany's greatness.

Before they went to bed they looked out again. It was still snowing.

Churchill woke several times during the night. His mind was in turmoil. He did not know what parts of von Ribbentrop's story to believe, if any. He liked many of the things he was hearing but he could not be sure that they were not threatening to Britain. Since the end of the Great War Britain had been the only major power in the world, let alone Europe. It was a position he would have given his life to maintain. So few people in Britain then had any idea what was happening in Germany. He was one of them. Sooner or later he would have to make up his mind on the issue.

He probably had not had enough brandy before he went to bed. But each time he woke up he felt deeply frustrated that the only contact he could have with von Ribbentrop was informal. They could talk about anything they liked but at best they could share information and come to opinions about the other. But they had no power to make any deal with the other. That Churchill felt to be intensely frustrating. He would have loved to be in the thick of any international negotiations at that time.

The next day was a beautiful sunny clear morning. It was also bitterly cold with a light northerly wind. After breakfast Winston and von Ribbentrop went out for a walk through the grounds. While they did so von Ribbentrop told Churchill that he would be submitting a formal request for two German Army generals to visit Britain in the near future. They were von Manstein and Guderian. He hoped Winston would be able to meet them. Winston was very happy to do that.

The thick snow was crunchy underfoot. Winston showed him what he had achieved with the building of the garden walls and then they went in to look at Winston's paintings and books. They talked about what Winston had achieved there as they toured the grounds. Von Ribbentrop had no interest in any of that. As a result they soon started again on political talk. Winston's main point remained, as it had been in London, about the Empire. Winston told him:

"The main political issue facing our country is the preservation of the Empire, not giving India independence as is being advocated by the government. If Britain gets on with dealing with that issue rather than trying to deal with other irrelevancies, Europe will start to become an easier place in which to live."

That was his view and he put it over forcefully. That was the point he really wanted to make after his night's turmoil.

Then they went on to talk about Mussolini. Von Ribbentrop explained that Germany had not offered or provided any physical support for the Italy's imperial adventures in Africa. But they did support his aims. It had been greatly regretted in Germany that she had had to give up the African colonies at the end of the First World War. Churchill agreed about the moral support for Italy. He was certain that Italy was doing the right thing in trying to create some sort of empire.

By the time von Ribbentrop left on the Sunday afternoon they had perhaps had fourteen hours of conversation together, with no one else being involved. Von Ribbentrop knew that he was unlikely to have any other opportunity that great to talk to any other British politician. But he was shortly going to have to give Hitler advice based on precisely what he had heard from all the British politicians that he had met. He found it very hard to judge Churchill. He just did not know where he stood. But what he felt strongly was that the values of peace and Empire that had been espoused by most of them were probably the true British values at that time.

It was to prove to be a mistake that would cost Germany very dearly. But eventually it would be far more costly to Britain, because neither of those values of peace nor Empire were sustainable.

* * *

Samuel had often talked to me about the fractious relationship between Winston and President Roosevelt. It was much easier to research Roosevelt because large numbers of American war records became available during the 1970's and 1980's. By and large these confirmed the views in Samuel's diary about the relationship between the two men. They also confirmed very definitely the views that Samuel had expressed to me about the way Roosevelt managed the American Government and the American war effort. Those same views came through clearly in many entries in the diary.

All the American records that I studied before 1988 were official records released by the American Government. But in 1988 I was in Washington for a business conference. I had time away from the conference one morning and I decided to go and look round a bookshop in the Washington district of Georgetown. It was there that I saw a copy of recently published book called The Memoirs of Sally Monroe. I remembered meeting her at Samuel's house a quarter of a century earlier. The book had been published about a year after her death. The jacket described the book. In it I found an account of a meeting she had with President Roosevelt the very day that von Ribbentrop was walking the grounds of Chartwell with Winston Churchill.

* * *

That weekend in Washington the weather was far worse than it was in Britain. It had snowed for most of Thursday and Friday and on Friday afternoon a howling wind right out of the north had got up. The temperature was extremely cold by the Saturday morning and the wind chill factor made conditions outside any building almost unbearable. Travel was virtually impossible. All railroad and bus systems were completely shut down; so was the minimal air transport that operated in those days. Journeys were possible by taxi only where the streets were clear. Thick, warm clothing was essential for any journey.

President Franklin D. Roosevelt was at the White House. His wife, Eleanor, was at the Presidential retreat at Camp David, out in the Maryland woods and cut off from Washington by that snow storm. That suited Roosevelt just fine. He did not even think that it might be possible to speak to her by telephone. He certainly had no intention of doing so. It was actually his first real day of peace since the inauguration of his second term as President. When he got up that morning he planned to use the day for reflection about his first term and to think through just how he might pursue some of his personal ambitions in his second term. Uppermost in his mind was that if he could not start to implement those personal ambitions in the next two years he might never be able to do so.

Roosevelt had a very personal style of government. It was based on his taking sole control of all matters that he regarded as important and leaving the rest alone. He spent little time with any members of his cabinet, even Henry Morgenthau who was a long term family friend and Treasury Secretary. To Roosevelt, Cabinet meetings were trivial affairs and not an important part of government. What he did do, though, was keep track of the pulse of government through a system of personal informants. He had at least one in every important ministry and they kept him well informed about what was going on. With the information that they provided he was able to intervene in the affairs of any ministry at any relevant moment. It was a system that exasperated his cabinet colleagues but it had proved effective throughout his first term in office.

The American people had clearly thought so too because they had given him a very strong level of support in the national elections the previous November. The real basis of his support in the country was his implementation of the New Deal which was his personal programme to lead the nation out of the diabolical depression it had suffered early in the decade. He had organised the New Deal himself with scant regard for any other members of the cabinet. It had been a complete success so far and the nation was returning to economic stability and prosperity. The majority of the voters knew that it was Roosevelt personally who had led them back from the abyss. They were very grateful to him, but all they really wanted was more of the same thing. They wanted more stability, more prosperity and much more of what they called "normalcy": that was Bible belt, small town America living in harmony and prosperity undisturbed by anything else in the world.

But Roosevelt knew that that dream was impossible. He knew that the world was becoming a much more dangerous place. Everyday he got reports from around the world about German, Italian or Japanese aggression. He knew that sooner or later America was at risk of becoming engulfed by those external problems. His job was to prepare America for whatever intervention was necessary but he also recognised that the American people were completely against any involvement in anything outside America's shores. His own ambitions were very much in relation to the wider world. He knew very well that he could not pursue them without domestic support. He knew he had no solution to that conundrum at that time but he knew he had to plan and prepare.

What he decided to do that day was spend the morning thinking and then meet with two of his key informants in top ministries. What he did after that would depend on what they might have to tell him. With his wife snow-bound in Maryland he was free to do whatever he wanted. It was going to be a day in which he would identify some future opportunities and he hoped that it would be a day which would eventually lead to rapid and radical change in the world.

One of his informants at that time was Mandy Douglass. He had first met her when she was the wife of the mayor of a small town in Tennessee. Roosevelt had been there to open the first stage of the Tennessee Valley Authority public works programme that had done so much to re-invigorate that part of America after the great depression. He invited her to Washington and arranged for her to get a job in the State Department, as personal assistant to an Assistant Secretary of State. Mandy never went back to Tennessee. She was divorced from her husband within six months of her arriving in Washington.

Mandy spent some time alone with Roosevelt every week. She kept him informed as best she could about what was going on in State Department. It was an important if informal role for her to brief the President because at that time State Department was very much under the influence of the British Foreign Office. That was one of the benefits that Britain enjoyed because of its vast global influence. But it meant that Roosevelt was not able to trust State Department and he took little notice of the formal briefings he got from them. His view of Britain was certainly not theirs. Roosevelt's relationship with Mandy was purely intellectual. It was about discussion and debate. But he always felt it to be a very relaxing one that he much enjoyed. He was delighted that she was forming a very close friendship with a senior

Democrat senator whose wife had died about a year earlier. That enabled him to maintain close contact with that senator on domestic political issues. Having an inside track on communications was always useful.

Another much trusted informant was Sally Monroe. She was a beautiful black girl, the daughter of a civil rights activist. Her father had spent many years in jail because of his campaigning in the Southern States. But he had been pardoned by Roosevelt and had come to Washington to thank him personally for that action. He had brought Sally with him. Roosevelt found Sally employment in the Defense Department. She was a brilliant mathematician and she quickly gained great credibility in that department for the development of military communications codes. She proved to be a very good employee. She had a important boyfriend. He had recently been American military attaché at the embassy in London. His name was George Patton. He was later to prove to be one of the most effective American military leaders in The Second World War.

What he thought first thing that morning was that he would ask them both to come to lunch with him. There would be no difficulties about them getting to the White House despite the snow. They both knew each other because he had introduced them at a White House reception. They both had apartments within half a mile of the White House. The snow was always cleared first around that area of Washington. They could easily get there.

With no work to do he started to think. To think about the state of the nation and about how he could go about achieving his greatest ambition, which was the destruction of the British Empire. But he had never mentioned anything of the kind to any member of his cabinet nor had there been any such issue raised in the election campaign. That had all been about the continuation of the New Deal. The American nation was mending well from the great depression. His New Deal policies had achieved that. But there was no interest in America in international issues. Americans just wanted to look after themselves at that time. Roosevelt had wider ambitions and he was determined to achieve them but he had no idea then of how he could convince the American electorate that that was the right thing for them.

As he looked out on those huge piles of snow he thought deeply about the developing chaos in the rest of the world. His only real conclusion that morning was that if things really did get any worse America might be in a strong position to deal with any issues that aCurtis. But it would be a difficult battle to convince the American people.

Roosevelt did not give any thought that morning to Winston Churchill. Although he had heard of him he thought he was a failure and a man of no importance. But he did give lots of thought to all the other things he had been hearing from London.

After the girls arrived they talked about what was happening in both the State and Defense departments. State was coming under enormous pressure from Britain who wished to contain any possible expansion of American interest outside American soil. Defense was trying to work out with State a policy under which America could retreat from any involvement in the problems gathering elsewhere in the world.

After that they talked for many hours about the sort of influence that he would like America to have in the world. He told them why he had sent Joseph Kennedy to London, as America's Ambassador. That was because he needed to find out the real truth about Britain; what it stood for and what it could and could not do. He told them of his frustrations about the advice he was receiving on international issues from the State Department. It was all very different from anything in the election campaign but Roosevelt had been given a free mandate and provided he pursued his New Deal policies it was his view that he was free to do whatever he wanted. He would exercise that freedom as soon as a suitable opportunity arose. Not even he was in any position to predict the circumstances under which he would secure that freedom.

Mandy and Sally were giving him all the ammunition he would need to intervene in the affairs of State and Defense Departments at just the right time. But that time had not yet come.

Although Roosevelt never indicated to any of them exactly what was going through his mind it nevertheless proved to be a very useful occasion. By the end of the day Roosevelt was convinced that he might well be able to achieve that great ambition of his. All the reports he was getting from Kennedy in London were that Britain was very weak financially and that the chaos in Europe was spreading. Out of that there just had to be some opportunities that he could exploit.

* * *

It was immediately after that weekend at Chartwell that von Ribbentrop submitted a formal request to the Foreign Office that Generals von Manstein and Guderian wished to visit Britain in order to build on the goodwill that had been generated by the Anglo-German Naval Agreement. They proposed a visit lasting not more than five days sometime during the spring. A reciprocal visit by equivalent British officers would be welcome at a later date. The request contained minimal biographies of the two generals. von Manstein was simply described as the Commander of the German Army. Guderian was described as the Commander of Mechanised Troops.

It took nearly ten days to formulate a reply. Prime Minister Baldwin was in favour of the visit. Eden was doubtful. He wondered what the real purpose might be as there was nothing to negotiate with Germany on military matters and there could be little goodwill after the German invasion of the Saar and the Rhineland just a year before. Eventually Eden did agree to the visit but on strict terms.

So the Foreign Office replied that the visit would be welcome but as there was no formal agenda and nothing to negotiate it should be treated as completely informal. The officers and up to two immediate staff for each should plan to arrive at Croydon airport by nine in the morning on the last Monday in April. They should plan to leave the same airport on the Friday morning. The Foreign Office and the German Embassy would work out an appropriate itinerary under which they could meet their counterparts and other senior officials and politicians.

As it was to be an informal visit it would be necessary for the visitors to wear civilian clothes at all times. All British officers that they met would be similarly dressed unless they were being visited on a military base.

Those terms were acceptable to von Ribbentrop. What mattered more to him was that officers of that seniority had access to Britain and could come and see at least see some of the military facilities for themselves.

* * *

Two days after Ribbentrop had left Chartwell Winston had another guest. This time it was Guy Burgess. He had been there several times before, each time to interview Churchill on a topical issue. Burgess was still working for the BBC as a journalist and he wanted to interview Churchill about the latest Parliamentary skirmish on the subject of India. The day before the Prime Minister had been asked some ferocious questions about a possible date for Indian Independence. There had been no useful answer but in the supplementaries there had been some very strong views expressed about the folly of any such idea. Winston had been one of those to speak in the strongest possible terms against any such independence. He had described the whole idea as destroying the soul of every proud Briton.

Over lunch at Chartwell Burgess had got some excellent quotes from Churchill which would all be repeated in a radio programme on the subject to be broadcast a few days later.

It was towards the end of the lunch that Burgess said that he hoped to be leaving the BBC soon;

"I have enjoyed my time there but I have been discussing a much more interesting job with a very different organisation. I will know about it very soon now."

* * *

One of the intriguing things about the Russian archives was that although they contained a very detailed account of what George Ponsonby did for them, there was no mention of Ludmilla Tereshkova or how she was replaced by them. Ponsonby's diary contains no mention of her but Louise told me in the 1950's what she knew.

This suggested to me that throughout all of his dealings with the Russian Government Ponsonby was playing an exceptionally devious game. Guy Burgess turned out to be a very dangerous spy for Russia and passed many of Britain's greatest state secrets to them. It was Ponsonby who got him into Russia in the first place. We know that Ponsonby was given a brief from Anthony Eden which resulted in Louise going to Russia. As soon as I was able to get deeply into those Russian archives I found Ponsonby's role to be fascinating. So far as it is possible to tell he was never investigated by the British counter-espionage authorities. Indeed he went on to become British Ambassador to Russia at the height of the Cold War. I have often wondered whether he was involved in matters that go far beyond the scope of this book. There are several references to him in Samuel's diary but not a single one after the start of the war. His full role will therefore remain an intriguing mystery. The only useful records about Ponsonby are those he wrote himself, now in the Russian archives.

I never did meet George Ponsonby although he moved to a house only about three miles from where Samuel lived. Samuel must have met him in the local social circuit but he never mentioned him to me.

* * *

When George Ponsonby got back from Moscow he went to meet with Anthony Eden again. There were two things he needed to discuss with him. The first was those naval exercises in the Far East that Molotov had requested. They were actually nothing to do with Ponsonby; even discussing them with anyone was outside his normal remit. He should have handed the task over to the man responsible for the Russia desk. But he needed those exercises to take place and soon, certainly within a few weeks. He knew that there were several powerful Royal Navy ships in Hong Kong and he was certain that they could be used for his purposes. It did not take him long to persuade Anthony Eden to have orders issued that would have several of them steaming to the Sea of Japan within a month. It would be heralded as an important illustration of Russian and British solidarity in the face of increasing tension in the Far East. Eden agreed with Ponsonby that those ships should be seen off Japan and although it took him several meetings with the First Lord of the Admiralty to get it organised, it did happen. Those naval exercises were never discussed with the Prime Minister nor were they ever mentioned in the British press.

The other was to talk about Guy Burgess. All he told him about that was that he thought it was possible for Guy Burgess to do some work for them in Moscow that would be very valuable in providing fast track communications between the Russian leadership and the British government. There had been some informal contacts with the Russians over the last few months over the issue and they were interested. The really new thing was that Burgess had impeccable credentials and appropriate cover to do that job. The Russians would allocate a suitable person to come to London in order that, if necessary, they could have direct and secret communications with the Foreign Secretary.

Eden was pleased with all that. The role in Moscow for Burgess rewarded him for past services which Eden had appreciated. He smile whimsically as Ponsonby left his office.

Ponsonby still had a vast amount of work to do in order to get Louise that safe cover in Russia. But by the time she had returned from Germany that work was complete.

Guy Burgess first went to Moscow about three months later, he did meet Molotov and he regularly communicated back to London exactly what Molotov wanted London to hear.

On his first trip there Burgess was taken to that same stylish gay club that Ponsonby had visited there. From that evening onwards he always provided Russian intelligence with reliable information about what was going on in Britain. But what the Russians never knew was that he had become an acquaintance of Winston Churchill's. That was a secret that Burgess chose to retain for himself so that he would have more information power. It was to prove to be very valuable when he eventually returned to Britain to take up a post in the Foreign Office in London.

* * *

When Louise met George Ponsonby at three in the afternoon of the day that she got back from Germany she had rather assumed that she was just going to be de-briefed on everything that she had done in Germany. That afternoon she was with him for five hours and she was by no means finished with giving him the detail of all that she had seen. He had started by telling her what had happened to all the information that she had already sent back via the courier system. It had all been evaluated by military intelligence who were appalled at the scale of military developments in Germany. Senior military commanders who had been briefed about it were absolutely clear that Britain had no way of countering such a threat and they advised ministers accordingly. Summarised versions of it had been sent to the Prime Minister who dismissed it all as scare mongering. After that she told him of many things about Achtgrenze and the Nazi party which she had not included in her messages to London.

But before they parted that evening he told her that he had a far more dangerous mission that he would like her to start within a few weeks. This time it would be to Russia.

The next two days were all German de-briefing, but the following morning he told her of his diabolical plan. She was to go to Russia to replace Ludmilla Tereshkova who worked in Stalin's office but was soon to be promoted to the office of Klimert Voroshilov, the Defence Minister. He told her about how it was being arranged and what she was to do while she was there.

In the meantime she was able to have plenty of time off in London and to spend several very enjoyable evenings and nights with Max Beaverbrook.

* * *

Louise went to meet with her father the day after the briefing for her trip to Russia had been completed. She had no way of knowing whether he had received all her despatches from Düsseldorf or not. It did not matter to her. What did matter was that she should pass on her personal feelings about the horrors of the war machine that she had been able to see over the last few months.

Before she had even had any chance to speak he said;

"Louise my dear, I have read every one of your despatches. In Military Intelligence we have made maps of it all and these are in a secure place. The cumulative effect of everything that you have discovered is the certainty that Germany is preparing for war. There can be no other explanation. Almost all of it is in defiance of international treaties and agreements. The implication of that is that Germany cannot be bothered with such things. It all makes Europe a very dangerous place.

"The problem now is not about the knowledge that you have provided but what we do with that knowledge. It has been passed on in summary form to the Prime Minister but he has personally ordered it all to be suppressed. He will not allow the armed forces to do any planning based on any of it nor will he allow any of it to be passed on to any other ministers. So far as he is concerned what matters is that Britain is a force for peace in the world and will not be going to war with Germany or anyone else in Europe. In any event he argued that the British Empire is far too powerful to be a target for any nation like Germany. He also told his officials that he thought that it was all a complete fabrication because he had been assured by von Ribbentrop that their intentions were purely peaceful.

"And that is exactly where it stands today."

She was appalled by what he told her, but he assured her that it was not possible to do anything about it given the Prime Minister's instruction. Nevertheless he assured her that it was all in a safe place and could be used by military commanders as and when necessary.

She told him that she was going to Moscow and what she was going to be doing there. He promised her that he would arrange for her to be looked after there.

* * *

It was three weeks later that she travelled to Moscow. She went by train. It was a miserable and very lengthy journey. Long before she had even got to Russia she was numbed by the entire experience.

On the way she had plenty of time to think about what Ponsonby had told her about Ludmilla. Ludmilla was to be secreted out of Russia the day after she was due to arrive. Louise wondered how it was possible that George Ponsonby was able to arrange such things. But what she was certain about was that there was a spying world that was far murkier than anything in which she had been involved so far. If a way could be found to place her in a high government office in a foreign country then there just had to be a very large amount of deceit and intrigue about. She was just grateful that she had been trained so well in survival techniques. She wondered what Ponsonby's real role might be but she knew better than to enquire into anything like that.

When she did eventually arrive at Moscow's main railway station she was met by a grey haired man who told her that he would take her to a safe house for that night. The following evening he would take her to Ludmilla's apartment where she would be living for the rest of her stay in Moscow. She reckoned that he must be some kind of real expert in clandestine operations. She just assumed that he was British, but she had no real idea. He seemed to be very good at speaking Russian and he looked as if he could have been Russian. He only spoke to her in Russian. He said his name was Konstantin Millerovo. Whatever he was, he always seemed to be available to help her whenever she needed help while she was in Moscow. George Ponsonby had briefed her about him and he had told her that he was completely reliable.

* * *

In the Russian archives I found many references to the Naval exercises in the Far East that had been organised on the instructions of Anthony Eden. They included many compliments about the impact they would have and about the speed with which it had been organised.

* * *

It was the evening after Louise had arrived in Moscow that the British Embassy held a cocktail party to celebrate that naval co-operation off Japan. Anthony Eden flew to Moscow to be the official host and his presence guaranteed that a strong Russian delegation attended. As was customary the entire private offices of the Russian ministers involved were invited. This included Ludmilla Tereshkova who had only started work for Voroshilov that day. She had hardly got time to meet anyone in that ministry and her work that day had been entirely concerned with administrative matters.

It was about half an hour after she had arrived that the Head of Chancery at the Embassy offered to take her on a tour of the building. She never returned from it. She left Russia that night on a chartered plane to Denmark and then on to Britain. When she got there she was brainwashed, given a new identity and then shipped to a distant part of the Empire with enough money to get settled.

Louise took her place at the party wearing exactly the same clothes as the real Ludmilla had been wearing. She had the keys to Ludmilla's apartment in her handbag. She had taken on Ludmilla's complete identity. To all intents and purposes she was now Ludmilla.

* * *

Guy Burgess had first met Winston Churchill when he was a BBC reporter. He had gone to interview him in his room in the House of Commons. The interview was to be included in a radio programme about the state of the nation as seen through the eyes of people who had influence but not power. Burgess was a highly educated man and he admired the sheer intellectual effort that Winston Churchill had been putting into writing his books. He knew full well that it was no ordinary task. That was one of the reasons that he had wanted to interview him. He wanted to get Churchill's historical perspective on the state of the nation.

What he also got was an invitation to go down to Chartwell to talk about it all in much more detail. He judged, correctly, that Churchill was interested in almost any audience for his views as that there were few people interested in listening to him at that time.

Churchill provided him with insights to the British character of which he was not previously aware. He also judged that Churchill was depressed by the complete failure of Britain to be able to do anything at that time. But he was not able to work out what Churchill would do if he had the power. He was concerned about all that talk about the Empire. He felt sure that Churchill was not living in the past but that talk of the Empire made him look like a relic.

It was a view that he passed back to Moscow and it was a view that his masters in Moscow would have many opportunities to test in the future.

* * *

It was a bleak February afternoon in Berlin in 1994 when I came across a letter from von Ribbentrop to Hitler. It was a chance discovery. At the time I had been studying files dealing with the German invasion of Austria. This letter had been misfiled probably because it had the same date as a letter about von Ribbentrop's views on Austria which was the next document in the same file.

It was February 1937 when Ribbentrop wrote to Hitler. It was a long and detailed letter. It was the first thing he did when he got back to London after the weekend at Chartwell. The letter started:

```
Mein Fuehrer,
Ich wollte dir nachts mitteilen uber solche wichtige
Sachen bis ich die Fuhrer der verschiedenen Grupen der
britischen Gessellschaft gut kennengelernt hatte; aber
jetzt habe ich Sie kennen gelernt und kann ich dir einen
verstandnisvollen Reportage geben.    Es ist interessant
und wichtig.  Es werde unsere politischer Grundsatz fur
viele Jahre ordnen.
```

Translated that reads:

"I did not want to communicate with you about such important matters until I had met widely with the leaders of the different groups in British society; but I have now done that and I can give you a comprehensive report. It is both interesting and important. It will shape our policies for many years to come. I believe that Britain has been effectively neutralised by its own weaknesses."

It went on:

"Everything I have heard proves this to me. I have consulted widely amongst all types of people that make up the British establishment. I have also tried to find revolutionaries in this country but in reality there are no effective ones at this time. Britain is dominated by two things. They are retaining its place in the world and in ensuring that there is a continuing peace."

He went on to analyse the British political, military and industrial leadership. He could find no great strengths in any of it. He then looked at Britain's military capabilities. His view was that the navy was powerful, indeed it was undoubtedly the most powerful navy that the world had ever seen. But he also concluded that it was there to protect trade routes. He judged that Britain's naval capabilities were centred around heavy capital ships only. There seemed to be very little anti-submarine capability. Its primary purpose was defensive and not hostile. It was therefore a relic of empire trade rather than an instrument of war.

He wrote that Britain had deep financial weaknesses and was therefore unlikely to be able to fund any expanded military effort without great sacrifices being made by the people. There seemed to be no taste for any such sacrifices.

He then went on to analyse the views and positions of people prominent in public life. That included all government ministers. Baldwin, Chamberlain, Eden and others were on that list. He was certain that there was no will amongst any of them to adopt any sort of hostile line against Germany or any other country. National policy was, in his view, all about peace.

Then he went on to analyse the dissident voices in Britain. Churchill was one of the people on that list. Of Churchill he wrote:

"He is dangerous, turbulent, tempestuous and unpredictable but he is obsessed with empire. He is much more like us than any other political leaders in Europe. I do not think there is any realistic chance of his gaining political power in Britain again. Even if I did I do not believe that he is any threat to Germany. If he were to become a threat to Germany it could only be because he fundamentally changed his attitude to almost anything. But I do not think there is any likelihood of his opposing Nazi power and expansion. He has told me that he is sympathetic to it."

In writing that letter he had fundamentally underestimated Churchill's craving for political power. He had failed to understand that Churchill would do anything to regain political power and glory. It was to prove to be an expensive but utterly unpredictable misjudgement.

* * *

Samuel discussed the world situation many times with Winston during the late 1930's, usually when they were dining together. A typical diary entry reads;

"March 17, 1937. Had dinner with Winston this evening at the Army and Navy Club. He was in an expansive mood and very much wanted to talk about his dream for the future of Britain. He has said many times in Parliament and in other public places that he regards the maintenance of the Empire and India in particular as being of supreme importance to the whole future success of Britain. Tonight he said all that and more. What he told me is that he feels very tempted to do a long tour of the main parts of the Empire with a view to establishing himself as the unquestioned leader of the pro-imperialists in Britain. He is desperate to get back into real political power and currently feels that unquestioned alliance to Empire interests is the best way to do this. But he also said that he would hate to be away from Britain if there is any prospect of a crisis hitting the National Government that he might be able to exploit. He hates the Prime Minister for his weak attitude to the Empire and India in particular. He probed me again extensively about my experiences in India."

* * *

The first reference to Guy Burgess in any Russian archives was dated December, 1937. It described how he had been supervised by Yuri Butkov on his first visit to Moscow and how he had been sexually seduced into the Russian espionage services.

* * *

It was late in 1937 that Guy Burgess first went to Moscow. He was met when he arrived at the railway station by Yuri Butkov. He was taken to the Novodny Hotel where he would be staying for the two or three days that he would be there.

The following day he was taken on a tour of the Russian Foreign Ministry, again by Butkov. There was a reception at lunch time for a visiting delegation from Finland. Butkov took Burgess along to that. Just before the formal lunch began Butkov introduced him to Molotov.

When the Finnish delegation had left Burgess was invited to go to Molotov's office. Although Molotov was a serial womaniser he recognised that gays had their uses; principally that they could be bought. If the British government were going to put up this man to be the principal communications lackey between himself, Molotov, and the highest levels of the British government then he, Molotov, would buy the man. They talked for about half an hour. After that Burgess was asked to wait in an ante-room while Molotov and Butkov talked together.

Butkov was given his instructions;

"Butkov, you must make this man a spy for Russia. We must use him to get whatever we can out of Britain. I do not care what it costs. He can, for example, have an apartment here in Moscow. He must travel freely between London and Moscow and each time he comes here I will see him and give him some sort of message to take back. You will have the job of debriefing him on everything that is going on in London. Just get him on our side as soon as possible and then send him back to England. Set up some first rate communications with him there. It was a good idea bringing Ponsonby over here and getting him laid in that gay club. He has done us proud as a result. Well done."

That was exactly how it was set up. Burgess was taken to the same club that they had used to seduce Ponsonby. It took just one night of extreme gay sex to ensure his complete commitment to spy for Russia and betray high level British secrets. No nation ever paid so much for sodomy as Britain did for the pleasures for Guy Burgess.

* * *

April 27, 1937. Today I met with German Generals von Manstein and Guderian. We had an enjoyable lunch together. But by any standards it cannot have given them much insight into our military capabilities.

* * *

It was a fine clear morning when the Lufthansa Fokker Tri-Motor carrying Erich von Manstein and Heinz Guderian arrived at Croydon. They each had one male and one female staff officer with them. They were met by von Ribbentrop, a senior official from the Foreign Office and Brigadier James Walton. He commanded an Infantry Brigade and spoke fluent German. He had had a background in military intelligence and was to be their minder.

They would be staying at von Ribbentrop's residence at least for some of the time that they would be in England. James Walton would be with them at all times except when they were in the German Embassy or residency or on any private British property. There would only be one of those: Chartwell.

An interesting, if not very informative tour had been arranged for them. The first visit was to be to Wellington barracks, close to Buckingham Palace in central London, later that morning. The first battalion of the Coldstream Guards was based there and they were on ceremonial duties in London for that month. The visitors would watch the preparations for the Changing of the Guard, they would watch that ceremony and then they would go to the Tower of London for a lunch to be hosted by General Garbutt, the commander of London District.

Both von Manstein and Guderian were of Prussian aristocratic origin. They both appreciated the formalities and dignity of armed service and the ceremonies that they had seen that morning had very much impressed them. Over lunch the conversations were very much about military history. They re-lived the Battle of Waterloo where Britain and Prussia had jointly defeated Napoleon and his French armies. It was very much an enjoyable lunch for all of them.

That afternoon they went down to the Woolwich Arsenal, which was where shells and ammunition for both the Army and Navy were manufactured. They were not allowed to see much of it but they did note that it was a very large factory. It seemed to have huge capacity. That was why they had been taken there.

On the Tuesday they left early in the morning to go to Aldershot, which describes itself as the Home of the British Army. In reality it is not and never has been, but it is a nice title. When they got there they were given a presentation by the Officer Commanding on the overall role and deployment of the British Army. No accurate figures were included in the presentation but the role of the British Army operating on a global basis was. It was explained to the visitors that Britain had never had to defend its own home territory since 1066. All of its subsequent wars had been fought on other people's territory. Most of the presentation was about the Empire. The information was of little use to the German generals.

After a lengthy and very social lunch they went on a tour of some of the infantry training facilities in the area. There was a lot going on but neither of the two German generals was impressed. What was happening was good but it did not replicate battle field conditions in any way. Their own training facilities were on a much larger scale and much more demanding.

Later on that Tuesday they were driven down to Salisbury Plain which was the main tank training area in Britain. They stayed that night at the senior officer's mess at Bulford Barracks. It was in a large and very comfortable house just on the edge of Bulford village. The senior officer there had been a tank commander at the first ever tank battle at Cambrai in 1917. He had been one of the pioneers of tanks and had seen them move from being crude weapons into the most sophisticated land battle machines that were available.

Heinz Guderian was a radical and an innovator. He had never met anyone before who had been a tank pioneer. He loved the debates and arguments that evening. The British officer with whom he was verbally jousting was Major General Ernald Pearce. They relived those final tank battles in World War One and debated what it all meant for future warfare. Early in the morning they did reach agreement that the role of the tank was as a highly flexible, fast and manoeuvrable weapon. It was not a substitute for a field gun. But it did need huge logistics support. Rather than being a single weapon it was part of a weapons system. It was probably the first weapon to achieve that status.

On Wednesday they watched tank manoeuvres taking place on Salisbury Plain. Von Manstein and Guderian thought the training ground to be tough and highly varied. It certainly simulated some very tough European conditions. They liked what they saw, but they guessed correctly that almost all the tanks in the British army were out that day. Their joint view was that British tank operations might be good but they were likely to be very small scale.

Thursday was lunch with Winston at Chartwell. Both generals were delighted to meet a descendent of the Duke of Marlborough. They knew much about the victor of the battles of Blenheim, Ramillies, Oudenarde and Malpalquet in the early eighteenth century. That alone was enough for one conversation with Churchill, but he wanted to talk about something completely different. He wanted to talk about modern warfare in the twentieth century. He wanted to talk about getting away from anything like the endless and pointless attrition in the trenches of the Great War.

So they explained to him the concept of Blitzkrieg. It had been written about by Bismarck but Germany had not been industrially powerful enough to apply it on any front in the Great War. In recent years of the twentieth century it had become re-defined as the concept of total war which started with aerial bombardment which was followed by overwhelming force on the ground.

It was a long lunch and they all enjoyed it. The only thing that Winston knew for certain at the end of it was that Britain was not in any position to mount anything like Blitzkrieg against anybody at that time. The country was far too weak militarily to do anything except undertake skirmishing. He had no idea what the true military capabilities of Germany were. But he did conclude that Germany would not go to war unless it could conduct Blitzkrieg.

* * *

May 10, 1937. I had lunch with Winston and Max Beaverbrook today. Max had been working on a plan to send a team of journalists to Germany at the invitation of von Ribbentrop. It had apparently been mooted at that dinner party when I had first met him last November. He was really hoping that he would be able to get some really good news stories but he also feared that the German Government would use it entirely for propaganda purposes.

* * *

Lord Beaverbrook did take up Ribbentrop's offer to provide facilities and access for Daily Express journalists to visit Germany and examine in detail the improvements in daily life that had been brought about by the Nazis. It took a long while to sort out the details and in any event Beaverbrook was in no hurry to send them. It was late June before their itinerary had been agreed and they were able to travel to Germany. He sent a team of 10 on that propaganda trip. They all travelled out to Germany together. The team leader was one of the deputy editors. They first went to Berlin for detailed briefings by the British Embassy and the German ministries. Altogether they were in Germany for a month. They visited Nuremberg, Dresden, Munich, Stuttgart, Frankfurt, Dortmund, and Bremen. They saw factories, road building programmes, agricultural projects, sports facilities, schools, universities and hospitals. It was all a very boring exercise. They went to three political rallies. They saw nothing military. They were very well looked after. They thought the commitment to factories, sports facilities and road building to be very impressive.

Beaverbrook also sent another ten journalists secretly to Germany at the same time. They all went as tourists. They all entered Germany by separate border crossings and all followed separate itineraries. Between them they covered the whole of the country over a six week period. They were able to stay in ordinary hotels and talk to whomever they liked. They detected mixed views on almost everything.

After they had returned each was asked to write up his trip, not just in terms of what they saw and heard but in respect of impressions as well.

They all wrote of huge contrasts as compared with what was going on in Britain at that time. They also all wrote that there was a great sense within Germany that something very big was going to happen. No one knew exactly what it might be but there was a mixture of hope and dread about it all.

The ten journalists who travelled independently inevitably found a much wider range of views than did the other group. The one real thing that they got which the others did not get was the general appreciation of the work that had become available. It did not matter to them that it was work in armaments factories and on the construction of military facilities. It was work and it was well paid work. It was a huge and much appreciated contrast to those miserable years of Germany's economic collapse during the Weimar Republic.

Everyone singled out the building of the autobahns as being of great interest and significance. They were the first high capacity, long-distance roads to be built in Europe. They would undoubtedly have to be copied elsewhere in Europe.

When they had finished their writings the deputy editor turned them all into what was effectively a book. They would in due course publish that book. In the meantime Beaverbrook decided to start serialising it in The Daily Express starting towards the end of September.

It proved to be a popular serialisation. It told of rapidly growing German confidence, widespread support for what Hitler had done to improve ordinary lives, and growing expectations that Germany would be well positioned to embark on some major new achievements. The overall British reaction was that it was a chilling message. The paper was inundated with letters about it all. Most of them were critical of the British government for underestimating what was going on in Germany.

von Ribbentrop rang Beaverbrook after the articles had been running for several weeks. He thanked him for publishing them but he made no comment about the contents.

Churchill and Beaverbrook discussed the articles several times through the autumn of 1937. Those conversations certainly helped Churchill make up his mind what he wanted to do. They were by no means the decisive factor but they did point him more firmly in a new direction.

* * *

The most important occasion for change in Britain in 1937 was not one of the cataclysmic political or military events that were the scourge of Europe at that time. It was an event intended to signify stability and tradition. It was the coronation of King George VI.

It was an opportunity for the nation to celebrate and forget. There was a lot to forget. This was the first coronation in Britain since 1910. There was the First World War to forget, when everyone in the country lost at least one friend or relative. There was the depression to forget, with the devastating impact that it had had on the economic life of the nation. There was a period of long industrial strife to forget. And perhaps finally there was the pain of the abdication the previous year.

Every single person in the land had something to forget. With a new King there came a coronation and with that coronation there came hope.

That was how the people saw it on May 12, 1937 when King George VI was crowned in Westminster Abbey. Everyone in the country had at least one great hope. Peace and stability were by far the most popular.

* * *

June 16, 1937. Winston called me this morning and suggested that we have lunch together. He hoped that Max Beaverbrook would be able to come as well. He told me on the phone that he wanted to talk about the changed political landscape since Baldwin had resigned.

Max was there and Winston suggested that the three of us met regularly. It is obvious that his friendship with Max is very important to him. Max, in turn, seems to find a way to publish almost everything that Winston tells him. It certainly provides the Daily Express with strong leading articles.

Winston said he wanted some military input from me each time we met. No secrets, of course, but a military interpretation of what was going on. That did not give me a problem and anyway having a meal with the two of them was always a pleasure. So we agreed to meet regularly in the future.

Winston was somewhat baffled about what seemed to be a complete change of direction within the PM's office. Baldwin had been only concerned about domestic issues but had done very little about them. Chamberlain seemed only to be concerned about peace in Europe. Winston had no problem with a peace agenda but he wondered why it was more important than the very pressing domestic issues which remained in a state of chaos.

* * *

In May Baldwin had resigned and had been replaced by Neville Chamberlain as Prime Minister. Chamberlain immediately started a long campaign to preserve peace in Europe under the threat of Nazi German aggression. The very last thing that Britain wanted at that time was any further war in Europe. But the government was strong, at least in terms of votes in the House of Commons, and popular.

The only thing that really changed with the change of Prime Minister was that Chamberlain regarded his first task to be the achievement of peace in Europe. Diplomatic contact with Germany was stepped up. Von Ribbentrop found himself to be in a very influential but amusing position. He played as duplicitous a role as can be imagined. He was a war monger handling peace overtures.

It was just a week after his appointment that Chamberlain met von Ribbentrop for the first time. The meeting took place at Chamberlain's request at 10, Downing Street. At it Chamberlain made it clear that his first objective was to secure continued and lasting peace in Europe. He asked for assurances from von Ribbentrop that that was an objective shared by Germany. Von Ribbentrop assured him that Germany's objective was also peace and that as soon as it was practicable to do so there should be a meeting between Chamberlain and Hitler to sign an agreement to that effect. But he went on to explain that for such an agreement to be effective it would be necessary for German rights to be restored and some of the provisions of the Versailles treaty would need to be rescinded. These provisions included allowing the Saar to be a permanent part of Germany and allowing an extension of the recent Naval Agreement with Britain to cover other military matters as well.

Chamberlain agreed that the two countries would work together towards such an agreement but without any pre-conditions about the outcome other than lasting peace.

As he was driven away from that meeting von Ribbentrop was well satisfied. The diplomacy work that would be needed over the next year would certainly keep Britain at bay. In the meantime Germany would continue to advance its war preparations.

* * *

In 1997 I was reading through the private diary of Voroshilov. I found an entry dated 27th July, 1937. It read:

"The management of my office has improved in recent weeks and I put this down to a new girl who has been transferred to me from Stalin's office. The improvement is such that I can now get much more done each day. There is so much to do that her contribution is appreciated. I spoke to her this evening to try and get to know her better. Maybe she will be my next mistress."

* * *

Louise was not surprised to see Sid on the tram one morning a few days after she had arrived in Moscow. She was very comforted to find out that he was there to look after her. She knew that if anything went wrong he would find a way of getting her to safety.

It was about a month after she had started to work in Voroshilov's office that she was alone with him for the first time. She had planned the conversation that she wanted to have with him over the previous weeks. She had had to work out exactly how she could work best for Britain while she was working in his office.

Her largely administrative work had proved to be of the highest quality. Before she had gone to Moscow Ludmilla had been carefully briefed on the work that her counterpart had been due to do. She fulfilled that role exactly in her early weeks there but she felt she could do more. Her work involved setting up meetings and taking minutes, and typing and distributing instructions and memoranda from Voroshilov.

She found him to be a very hard and ruthless man. She was not sure whether he enjoyed power. She knew that some people did. But she thought it rather more likely that he exercised such ruthless power because he feared that if he did not someone else would want to dominate him. She did not like him, but he was always around and he was clearly in control. He had also established control at all levels of Russian military life. He had set up all the necessary apparatus to ensure that that was the case. That included a savage purge of the officer ranks.

It was a fact of life that everyone in Russia at that time seemed to be under some kind of surveillance. The secret police were everywhere. She knew that she had been followed to and from work on a number of occasions. If there had been a problem they would have wanted to haul her off to a Gulag. Of that she had no doubt. She had been to many meetings at which decisions had been taken to send people off to the wastes of Siberia. She knew the form.

It was early one evening. He had just finished a lengthy meeting on the planning for hostilities in the Far East. She had not been involved in that one. She was just one of eight people who organised the meetings in his office. It was a huge workload to progress any meeting through from first conception to the distribution of the minutes. She found that she could handle the planning of three meetings simultaneously but she, along with all the others, could only handle one set of minutes at a time.

Voroshilov clearly wanted to chat and she was an attractive girl. He said to her:

"Comrade, how do you find the work here?"

She replied:

"Comrade, I cannot remember exactly how long I have worked here now, but I enjoy the work and I believe that I am very good at it. It is important work. I would not be allowed to do it unless my work was trusted. Many times I have been told that my work is very accurate and that it makes the work of delegates to your meetings more efficient. I do have ambitions to move to other positions within the government and I hope that that will be possible. But in the meantime my main ambition is to work for you on your most important meetings. I am sure that you will benefit from having one person allocated to those rather than just using one of the team as you do now. But whatever happens I will continue to do excellent work."

"Yes, that may well be possible. I have been given good comments about your work. Now tell me what is going on in the streets of Moscow. I do not get the chance to leave this office very often. It seems to be a very busy time for us all."

"I do not get the chance to see the whole city. I work six days a week and I live by myself in an apartment a few stops on the tram from here. On a fine evening it is pleasant to walk home. I do not need to buy many things so I only use the shops in my area, mainly to buy food. I have a few friends and we mostly meet up for lunch on Sundays. They all have administrative jobs in government. They are people very much like me. Two of them have young families.

"We live in a quiet area of the city but what we hear is that there are many people moving into the city because of the economic reforms. There are new factories opening round the edge of the city but they still do not provide enough work for all those people. So there are many people in some parts of the city who have no work to do. It is causing unrest in some areas, although I have never seen any of it."

"Thank you, Comrade. I only hear what my usual informants tell me. It is always interesting to hear a different view. Next Saturday, please take the day to visit one of those areas about which you have spoken. When you next see me after that you must tell me what you saw."

It was not the conversation that she had intended to have with him but she had got exactly the right result. She would be able to go to his most important meetings more often and she had the cover she needed to look around Moscow more widely.

* * *

Both von Ribbentrop's own diary and the official German archives include many references to what he did immediately he had returned to Berlin. He became Foreign Minister and met with Hitler every day to plan the next great international moves for the Nazi state.

I had first started to read von Ribbentrop's diaries during the summer of 1993. As the work of a man who had denied any involvement in the founding of the Nazi party in the Nuremberg trials they were completely astonishing. There cannot have been any doubt from his diaries that von Ribbentrop was perhaps the strongest thinker in the whole Nazi party. He probably had as much influence on Hitler as anyone. He may even have been the greatest influence on that man.

What perhaps influenced me most was the blatant way he described the desirability of war against both Russia and Britain. He judged both to be weak and incapable of challenging the might of Germany. It was in that tone that he wrote in his diary a paraphrase of what he recommended to Hitler immediately after he returned from London to Berlin to take up his post of Foreign Minister.

He started with a frank assessment of all the strategic options open to Germany:

"Our main objectives for some while now have been about creating lebensraum in the east for our people. We have long recognised that that means we have to take control of Austria, at least some parts of Czechoslovakia, and most of Poland. There are increasingly good reasons why we might also want to move into Hungary and into several parts of Russia, particularly Ukraine and Belarus.

"It is impossible to imagine that Britain will not take some sort of exception to that. I do not know when and where they might make a stand against such large scale invasions. At the moment they are weak financially and they have very weak armed forces at home, except, of course, for the Navy. That remains as formidable as ever. But the air force is weak and the army is mostly deployed in the Empire.

"The overwhelming mood of the British people at this time is for peace. It does not matter who you talk to in the government or in business or in the academic world. Peace is their priority. There are dissidents, of course, but they have very little political platform and they are short on arguments because of the general weakness of the British economy and because of the weakness of the armed forces at home.

"The second thing that they all seem to want is to retain their empire. That is far more important to them than any kind of political activity in Europe. You have to remember that the main purpose of the Royal Navy is to protect the empire trade routes.

"Britain is by far the most densely populated country in Europe and it does not therefore offer much opportunity to give us more lebensraum. In any event physically it is a small country.

"I do not think we should plan any invasion of Britain at this time. But if they take hostile steps towards German territory then we should consider then what we do about them. In the meantime I think we should take a decision that says that if

Britain does declare war on us for whatever reason then we should seek to blockade the country immediately with our U-Boats. That will effectively cut them off from their empire. It should completely neutralise them because they will quickly run out of food and raw materials. They are completely dependent on imports from the Empire for their survival.

"What I think we should now do is advance our plans in the east and keep stringing Britain along with a promise of peace.

"A far bigger issue that we must address is that of Russia. We need to ensure that Russia does not side with any of our eastern neighbours and above all does not see us as any sort of enemy. We might even see whether we can agree with them to carve up Poland together.

"One thing that we must also remember is that Russia is also weak. The debilitating effect of the purges on the armed forces has weakened their military capability. The uncompleted economic reforms have severely weakened their economy in the short term. In the long term they will be stronger, but for the next few years they will remain weak."

After another two hours discussion that was exactly what they agreed to do. The die for war was cast in that room in the Reich's Chancellery that afternoon. Von Ribbentrop was authorised to keep both Britain and Russia at bay until such time as Germany had sufficient advantage to wage war against them.

* * *

November 30th, 1937. Winston rang me this morning and asked me whether I would like to buy him lunch. He said he had something very important to tell me and there was certainly something to celebrate in it all. He assured me that Max would be there as well. We went to the Army and Navy Club. I booked a private room there. As soon as Winston came into that room it was obvious that he was very excited. He went on to tell me that he had finally made up his mind on exactly what position he was going to take in the developing political crisis that was engulfing the whole of Europe. I listened intently to all that he had to say........

Underneath that entry and in a different coloured ink was another which simply read; *"See also the entry for June 14, 1957."* It had obviously been written as he had read through his diaries during his retirement years.

The entry for that June day in 1957 read:

"I have known Lady Alice Arbuthnot for many years. I first met her at the same dinner party at which I met Winston back in 1936. I used to meet her occasionally during the war and since then we have maintained a regular correspondence with occasional phone calls. Last week she invited me to go and have lunch with her in London.

At that lunch we were reminiscing about Winston and I told her of my lunch with him that day in November, 1937 and about how enthusiastic he had been. I also told her that in the light of subsequent events it seemed as if something had happened the previous day which had been a turning point in his life. Alice quizzed me as to the exact date of that lunch and as I remembered it very clearly I told her. She then told me about her dinner with Winston the evening before he had that lunch with me."

Looking over those diary entries it seems that it was Winston's evening with Alice that enabled him to crystallise his political thinking around the ideas and policies that would eventually lead to his becoming Prime Minister.

Samuel's diary for June, 1957 included the words:

"I was certain Winston Churchill decided to change his mind that evening they were together in November, 1937. I am certain she was the catalyst."

I read over those two entries many times. I also discussed them with Alice on at least three occasions. The more I read them and the more I talked with her about them the more I realised just how important the events were about which I was reading. I realised just how important was that meeting on November 29, 1937 with Alice. It was surely that evening that made him into a Prime Minister.

Samuel's diary was not even known to exist by any other historian. That meant that no one else studying Winston's life and times could possibly have had any insight into the events that led to his change of mind, his adoption of a completely new political position and the impact that all that had on his eventually becoming Prime Minister. These sections of Samuel's diary were all about why Winston became the man he did. This was information to which only I had access.

I checked it all against all the other sources of Winston information known to me and I could not find reference to Alice in any of them. I could find information about Alice. There was plenty of that in press files and numerous other public documents. But I could not find anything that connected her with Winston. It was when I learned from Louise that she had met them together at a dinner party in 1936 I realised that I and I alone had the key to Winston's transformation from a political pariah into a leader in waiting. It was then that I truly understood the tortuous agonies that he had gone through as he sought to find a way back to power as the chaos swamped Europe in the late 1930's. I realised then the importance of Alice in his life.

* * *

Alice had moved from Oxford to London and she had bought herself a small house in Eaton Mews. Winston used to go there a couple of evenings a week after the business in the House of Commons was finished. They usually spoke for a couple of hours before he went to a hotel.

After Neville Chamberlain had become Prime Minister the pace and direction of government had changed. Tensions were beginning to emerge in the National Government team about the real direction of policy. Everyone agreed that peace was a desirable aim in it is own right. The tensions were about whether Britain was approaching the problem from a position of strength or because it was pathetically weak and had no real alternative to look for peace because it could not possibly fund any other future.

As the autumn of 1937 wore on the arguments became more vocal and more public. The choice seemed to be very stark. Appease Hitler or confront him. Confrontation was only possible through strength. Almost everyone agreed that Britain did not have that strength in Europe at that time.

Winston Churchill became more and more confused about what he could do to help and clarify the situation. Even more than that he fretted about how he could get real power so that he could influence things right from the centre. He hated appeasement but he loved the Empire. No one in Britain was talking about the Empire anymore. All the talk was about Europe and about the choices that Britain had there. There was no potential threat from the Empire. There was a potential huge threat from Europe, although no one had any idea how to quantify it.

It was certainly one night in late November, 1937 that Winston's thought started to crystallise. It had been bitterly cold that evening and as he drove in the taxi from the Commons to Eaton Mews there were strong snow showers. He longed to be inside that cosy little house. He arrived there about eleven and let himself in with the key that Alice had given him.

It had been a busy day for him. He had had lunch with Anthony Eden. That had proved to be a highly fortuitous occasion. Eden had wanted to talk and he had certainly wanted to share some of his anxieties:

"Winston, I am very much in a dilemma and I will soon have to make a decision as to what I do about it. The probability is that I will have to leave the government in protest about their useless foreign policies. I am Foreign Secretary but increasingly I feel that my views are being completely ignored by the Prime Minister.

"I have access to large amounts of hard intelligence information coming out of Germany. I cannot tell you how we get it but what I can say is that it all points to a military build-up far beyond anything that has ever been published in this country. It is horrifyingly vast and in respect of their navy it goes far beyond the new naval agreement that we have with them. Indeed there is now evidence that at the time we reached that agreement with them they had already exceeded their entitlement. It is entirely clear to me that Germany is preparing for a war despite the assurances that we have had to the contrary from von Ribbentrop on numerous occasions. We have almost continuous discussions with the German government about the issue but the only common ground that can be reached is about just how much re-armament can be tolerated. That is simply appeasement and appeasement is always wrong. It will never contain any potential enemy.

"We are also getting some good information from within Russia. It has been very difficult to find out really what is going on there but just now we are lucky enough to have some really good information. What it shows is that they are deeply into a domestic reform programme which will take years to complete. While they are doing that they have virtually no interest in anything else. They certainly do not see Germany as a threat to them but they are talking with Germany about how they might jointly carve up Poland.

"I have said all this to Chamberlain but he rejects it all and tells me that he accepts German assurances that there are no hostile intentions there.

"It is all a complete madhouse. It certainly cannot go on.

"I have been thinking that I must resign because I simply cannot go on with this charade. But what can I do if I resign? I know too much to be quiet. But if I say anything the Prime minister will rubbish everything that I talk about. So what will my position be if I resign?

"What I have been thinking about more than anything else is whether I can be part of a focus on re-armament in this country. There is no doubt in my mind now that we are going to have to go to war against Germany at some stage. The occasion will undoubtedly be a German invasion of Poland. I have no idea when that will be but I am certain that it will happen.

"Re-armament will be deeply unpopular in this country but it will inevitably happen. What I really want to know, I suppose, is whether you are prepared to commit yourself unreservedly to that course. If you are I will resign and join you. We can then fight the government together. Winston, can you do that?"

Winston sat back, lit a cigar, took a couple of sips of brandy and closed his eyes before he replied:

"Anthony, what you have said sounds very attractive but there is no way that I can give you an immediate answer. But what I can promise you is that you will have an answer from me tomorrow. I do not see any point in appeasement, I think it very likely that we will have to re-arm, and I think it likely that there will be war in which we will be involved. But what I have to think through is the impact that that will have on the British public. It will certainly not be popular. I also have to consider whether it is the issue on which I can re-enter the mainstream of politics. But answer I will have for you tomorrow."

Eden said that he would be in the Commons then and they could speak briefly there if necessary.

The work of the Commons that day had been boring and tedious. It was about the licensing of bus services. The government had proposed to bring in a whole string of new regulations to control an industry that had seemingly been doing rather well. There was no practical necessity for it. It was simply a bit of political dogma inflicted on Parliament by the Labour members of the National Government. It was a price that the Tories had to pay for continued national unity. It all seemed so pointless. Winston had opposed it and had made a passionate speech about government intrusion into commerce. But it was all so boring. All he wanted to do now was talk to Alice.

After he arrived Alice immediately opened a bottle of Gevrey-Chambertin and a few minutes later some giant bacon rolls were ready. He told her both about his talk with Eden and about all that boring rubbish in the Commons.

She had some things to say as well and she had decided that she would lead the conversations. She had been thinking about his dilemma for a long while now and she thought she had found a way of leading him out of it. His account of his conversation with Anthony Eden, in her mind, provided a powerful catalyst for change in his political life. When they had finished the bacon rolls she said:

"Winston, there is no point in your fretting about wanting to gain political power again. Just fretting will get you nowhere. What you have to do is find a problem and then offer yourself as the solution to that problem. When you talk publicly at the moment you talk about imperial power and the need to maintain the integrity of the Empire.

"About this time last year we went to that dinner party that Max gave for that German Ambassador. Your talk was all about the Empire. But that really is not important to most people. They recognise that the Empire is there. They do not see it as being threatened. They therefore do not see it as a problem. They are not therefore looking to anyone to come along and offer them a solution to that non-existent problem. There are no votes in that direction. There are certainly no votes in opposing the independence of India. That independence is going to happen sooner or later.

"No, what we have to think through is what your alternative line should be. Find the problem and even more difficult find the solution to that problem. Convince people that both the problem and the solution are right and you will feel the groundswell of public opinion supporting you. But it is not going to be easy.

"Look at the current situation in Britain. All the people want is peace and stability. The coronation provided a huge focus for public support along those lines. Nothing else matters just now. So if you want power your arguments have to be about those issues and those issues alone. My own view probably accords with that of Anthony. I have met von Ribbentrop, just as you have. My view is that he is a very devious and nasty man. I cannot trust him. But he is the German Ambassador and Britain therefore has to deal with him.

"Anthony is doing just that now. He is obviously finding it be a most unsatisfactory process otherwise he would not have talked to you in that way. So let us look and see whether appeasement is a sufficiently big issue for you and whether it might form the basis of a political comeback for you. Let us also look at what the alternative is to appeasement. If there is an alternative it might provide you with the right platform. One thought I have been having as we have talked so far tonight is that it is not so much what can be done while appeasement is the policy but what happens when appeasement fails. What I suspect is that because peace is such a popular objective for all of Britain appeasement might also be a popular policy. It certainly would be if it succeeded. But what if it fails? What happens then?

"You see, Winston, it is not about criticising what is happening now. It is all about solutions. What is your solution if appeasement fails? Because if it does fail, and it surely will, the British people will immediately ask "What happens now?" If appeasement is doomed you must be able to answer that question."

They talked for a couple of hours and at the end of it they agreed that anti-appeasement would be the cause. Re-armament would be the solution. At the end of it all he told her that he would be relentless in his opposition to the government and he would never give up on his demands that Britain urgently re-arm. It would not be popular, at least at the beginning, but he was sure that as more and more of the truth emerged the British people would see that there was no other way. Before he went to bed that night he wrote to Clemmie.

Dearest Clemmie,

I will be home in a couple of days. When I am there I will explain some major changes in my thinking. But I believe that I have now found the cause on which I can build a return to top level politics. It will certainly be controversial but it has a real prospect of success. What I am certain about is that I will not be alone in this new cause.

W

There was just one last thing he had told Alice before he left and that was that he wanted to talk it over with Max and Samuel. Max because he would need the support of at least one influential newspaper and Samuel because he needed to understand the military implications of it all.

Samuel's diary said it all:

"Our lunch that day endorsed his ideas and from that day on a new Winston was born."

From then on Winston never wavered from that course.

* * *

Eden did resign a few weeks later citing as the reason his inability to continue to support any policy which appeased any dictator, particularly Hitler and Mussolini. From that moment onwards Churchill and Eden were firm political allies. It was a very firm beginning to a very firm comeback by Churchill. But there was still a long way to go.

A few weeks later Guy Burgess sought a meeting with him, really for old time's sake. At it Winston explained to Burgess exactly why he was now completely committed to an anti-appeasement policy and why it would be right for Britain. Every word was passed back to Moscow.

In March Churchill invited both Eden and Beaverbrook to a weekend at Chartwell. From that moment onwards The Daily Express came out strongly against Chamberlain and in favour of strengthening Britain's armed forces so that any dealings with Hitler could be undertaken from a position of strength.

Churchill publicly criticised everything that Chamberlain said and did. It was a risky policy because Chamberlain and his policies were popular in the country. There was a general dread of anything but peace.

* * *

One of the most dramatic events that took place in the whole of 1938 was the German annexation of Austria. It was perhaps the event that showed Britain at its weakest throughout those years of crisis; the level of the crisis being seriously underestimated by the British government.

By then von Ribbentrop had formally left his post as German Ambassador to Britain. He had gone back to Germany and had reported to Hitler. The two of them had then formulated their detailed future strategy towards Britain.

In March 1938 von Ribbentrop returned to London for a few days in order to complete his handover at the embassy and have a few last meetings with the most senior people in Britain. One of those meetings was with King George VI at Buckingham Palace. It was apparently very friendly.

On Friday March 11th his final meeting in Britain was to be over lunch at 10 Downing Street with Chamberlain and Lord Halifax, the Foreign Secretary who had replaced Eden. The agenda was to talk about peace. During that lunch Chamberlain received a telegram from the British Ambassador to Austria reporting that the annexation of Austria was already taking place and that tanks were already rolling through the streets of Vienna. There was no significant or organised resistance reported in the telegram.

Halifax was apparently apoplectic with rage about the whole incident but von Ribbentrop assured him that the reports were most unlikely to be true. Halifax accepted that explanation and calmed down. It was certainly a bizarre event and showed just how gullible British government ministers were. The telegram from the ambassador had told the truth.

My examination of von Ribbentrop's diary in the German archives showed that he had planned to be in London that day just so that he could see the reaction of Chamberlain and Halifax as the tanks rolled through the streets of Vienna. He recorded in that diary:

"We will have no trouble with this British Government."

On Monday March 14th Hitler made his triumphal entry into Austria and his triumphal drive around the streets of Vienna. It was the first time he had been back to his homeland since he had left to do all those menial jobs in Germany.

Britain and indeed anyone else for that matter had not been able to do anything about it. Even after that Britain continued with its policies of appeasement. Yet more nations were to suffer in order that the imperial cravings of Hitler and his disciples could be satisfied. The killing spree was about to start on a huge scale.

* * *

In the latter part of the winter of 1938/9 Germany had been becoming increasingly hostile towards Poland, seeking essentially to restore their pre-1914 frontier. That meant a large increase in German territory at Poland's expense.

Throughout that period of turmoil Poland sought allies, particularly France and Britain, with whom she could conduct consultations in the event of any threat from Germany materialising.

In Britain the peace-hungry Chamberlain was facing pressure for a public statement on what he would do to help Poland. All the Poles had wanted was a friend with whom they could conduct consultations. But Chamberlain was in the mood for something different. He had shied away from any simple moves to prevent Hitler from invading Austria and Czechoslovakia. It was actually far worse than that. He had put the entire strategy of his government at risk by actually helping Hitler to get what he wanted in those countries.

The pressure was building up on him to make a statement to the House of Commons on March 31st. He had to answer a parliamentary question about Poland that day. The statement he did make was utterly astonishing. He said: "Britain and France would lend Poland all support in their power if Poland were attacked."

Chamberlain had made that statement without regard to any aspect of the potential military situation. Germany already had thirty five divisions in place. Britain had just two divisions in the UK. It was therefore an impossible and deceitful promise to Poland. It was greeted with incredulity in Britain.

* * *

Then came Munich. All that diplomacy which had started with Chamberlain's appointment the previous year had finally culminated in a summit meeting between Hitler and Chamberlain. It took place in Munich. It was Chamberlain's assessment that he had to get a peace deal. All the intelligence that he had received about what was going on in Germany suggested to him that things were getting more dangerous with each passing day. Until Eden had resigned the information he had been getting had seemed to be of very high quality but with Eden gone the quality and frequency of the information had deteriorated; he had no idea why. He did not know of Eden's relationship with Ponsonby. Nor did he know anything about the information he had been able to provide. But there was no reason to believe that Germany was not a threat. He simply had to prevent the British people being dragged into another European war.

For his part Hitler accepted the von Ribbentrop view that peace and the Empire were all that mattered to Britain. He was very confident that they would not actively start nor provoke a war and therefore they could be dealt with as non-threatening neighbours. Hence a peace deal was entirely possible. But there was no way that Germany would allow any such deal to constrain their own thinking or actions. They wanted to get Britain out of the way.

Chamberlain flew to Munich to meet Hitler in September 1938. A deal was agreed that essentially allowed Germany to invade Czechoslovakia. It accepted the legality of the earlier invasion of Austria. It allegedly guaranteed peace for Britain.

When Chamberlain stepped off the plane back from Munich on September 30th and had returned to Downing Street he read a statement that he had agreed with Hitler:

"We, the German Fuhrer and Chancellor, and the British Prime Minister, have had a further meeting today and are agreed in recognizing that the question of Anglo-German relations is of the first importance for our two countries and for Europe. We regard the agreement signed last night and the Anglo-German Naval Agreement as symbolic of the desire of our two peoples never to go to war with one another again. We are resolved that the method of consultation shall be the method adopted to deal with any other questions that may concern our two countries, and we are determined to continue our efforts to remove possible sources of difference, and thus to contribute to assure the peace of Europe."

After that Chamberlain added his own words:

"My good friends, for the second time in our history, a British Prime Minister has returned from Germany bringing peace with honour. I believe it is peace for our time… Go home and have a nice quiet sleep."

Someone who did not sleep well that night was Winston Churchill. He had been outside Downing Street to hear the announcement. Immediately he had heard it he took at taxi to Eaton Mews. He needed to rehearse his strategy with Alice. He would be meeting Eden in the morning.

Before Chamberlain went to bed that evening he read a letter from King George VI which read:

"I am sending this letter to meet you on your return, as I had no opportunity of telling you before you left how much I admired your courage and wisdom in going to see Hitler in person. You must have been pleased by the universal approval with which your action was approved. I am naturally very anxious to hear the results of your talk and to be assured that there is a prospect of a peaceful solution on terms which admit of general acceptance. Please come to Buckingham Palace as soon as you can so that I can express to you my heartfelt congratulations on your success in Munich.

In the meantime this letter brings the warmest of welcomes to one who by his patience and determination has earned the lasting gratitude of his fellow countrymen throughout the Empire."

* * *

When Roosevelt heard about Munich he immediately instructed Joseph Kennedy, the American Ambassador in Britain, to draw up a state of the British nation statement so that he would be able fully to address American policy towards Britain. At the end of his letter to Kennedy he wrote: "I need to know which way the British cookie will crumble."

Kennedy's reply proved to Roosevelt that Britain was bankrupt, had little capability of going to war and was essentially trying to buy peace at any price. He added that Chamberlain's policies were very popular in Britain but were coming under increasing attack from a consortium of dissidents led by Winston Churchill.

* * *

After that Britain and Europe slid inexorably into war. The government knew that but was not prepared to tell the truth. Austria and Czechoslovakia had been annexed by Hitler and no nation came to their defence. But the British government did take some steps to prepare for a possible war. But they were not very visible steps. They agreed to acquire more fighter aircraft, particularly Hurricanes and Spitfires. The order was very limited and was never announced publicly, at least not at that time. They also agreed to acquire some additional ships, called corvettes, which might be suitable as convoy escorts. The number they agreed to acquire over a two year period was just fifty ships each of about a thousand tons. In reality they were just glorified trawlers. The relevant cabinet papers prove that they were intended to be just a small insurance policy.

* * *

The biggest political event of the summer of 1939 was the one last piece of the jigsaw that Germany needed to put in place before they started an all-out war. At the time the only knowledge that Britain had about what was going on came from the information that Louise was able to pass back to George Ponsonby. Because Eden had left the Foreign Office Ponsonby did not pass the information to anyone. He did not know that copies had gone via Sid to Ronnie Harford. Neither Chamberlain nor Halifax had access to what was being negotiated between Germany and Russia. It probably would not have made any difference if they had.

But it concerned a series of meetings between von Ribbentrop and Molotov. Louise had been to some of the meetings. They were about finding a peace treaty between Russia and Germany which included a jointly agreed invasion of Poland. She reported back to London on them regularly. But those communications never went to politicians. The army and air force chiefs were aware of them thanks to Ronnie Harford but they had no authority nor any resources to plan for the defence of Poland.

Right at the outset of those talks George Ponsonby realised that Louise would have to be extracted from Russia as soon as and immediately after such an agreement was reached. He was canny enough to know from his own experience that any such agreement would be followed quickly by action. He worked tirelessly to put in place such a rescue.

Eventually an agreement was put in place on August 23rd, 1939. It was a warm and very humid day in Moscow. It had started with torrential thunder storms and the skies remained grey for the rest of the day although the clouds seemed to get higher and higher as the day wore on.

Russia had two overwhelming priorities at that time. The first was to protect its borders in the Far East. The second was to complete the domestic reforms which were taking far longer than anticipated. Reducing and eliminating any German threat would enable them to concentrate on those two. Participating in the invasion of Poland and gaining territory in the east of that country was a small price to pay for peace with Germany.

The agreement between von Ribbentrop and Molotov was signed in the late morning. It was followed by a celebration lunch. All the staff involved in the work needed to achieve that agreement were allowed the rest of the day off. Louise had been one of those and she had been allowed to leave. Louise left the Kremlin at around three.

When she got to the tram stop she was immediately joined by Konstantin Millerovo. He told her that she should not go back to her apartment. They would both be going to a different tram stop and when they got there she should stay reasonably close to him as they made their way to a vehicle. He would get in it first and she should get in on the other side after him. It would be the first stage of her journey out of Russia. It could not wait. It had to be done that evening.

The tram went into an area of Moscow that she had never visited before. Eventually after about forty minutes they reached a stop just by a church. The church seemed to be the only substantial building in what seemed to be a run down area. Konstantin got off the tram and walked quickly to the north side of the church. She was about ten metres behind him. There was a large black saloon car waiting there for them. Immediately she was inside they sped off out of the city. She had noticed that it had government registration plates. That probably meant that it would not be stopped at any road blocks that seemed to proliferate at that time.

They drove for an hour and came to an airfield. Apart from one aircraft on the ground the place was deserted. The car took them straight to the plane. Its twin engines were already running. Konstantin told her that she would be on that plane going to Helsinki. She would be met there. He would not be going with her.

The plane took off within a minute and immediately flew off to the North West. Soon after take-off the Finnish captain came and spoke to her. He spoke reasonable English and told her that the flight was likely to last 2 ½ hours and it would be getting dark when they got there.

It was an uneventful flight, even if it was noisy. When the aircraft arrived at the terminal in Helsinki she was met by George Ponsonby. She was very pleased to see him. He took her immediately to a luxury hotel where he had booked a room for her for the night. He had brought over some of her clothes from Britain, so that at least she would have something to change into and he had arranged a private dining room in which they could have dinner that evening. Finally he told her that they would be going to London in the morning.

* * *

Over dinner the talk was all about what she had been able to achieve in Moscow. At the end of the meal he told her that she would be going on to Washington after a few days in London. She desperately wanted that time in London. Louise needed to see Max Beaverbrook again.

* * *

Louise did spend the following evening with Max Beaverbrook. It had been nearly two years since they had last been together. They met at the Savoy, had Champagne and then went to a concert. This one was entirely appropriate for them that evening. It was at the Royal Albert Hall. The orchestra was the BBC Symphony Orchestra and the two main works were Rachmaninov's Second Piano Concerto and Tchaikovsky's First Piano Concerto; very romantic music for such a reunion.

Afterwards they again had dinner at the Savoy Grill. It was over dinner that Louise started to talk seriously; there were tears in her eyes as she started to speak:

"Max, going to that concert this evening made it as perfect a return to London and to you as it could possibly be. It has already been a perfect Friday evening. I cannot tell you where I have been, at least not yet. But the work I have been doing has proved interesting and valuable. That particular assignment is now finished and I think it is unlikely that I will go back there again.

"I have a new and potentially very exciting assignment coming up. I am not going to be in London for long. I do not know whether it will be two or three days, probably not more. It may be possible for me to tell you this time where I am going, in which case it should be possible for us to keep in touch. I will know that on Monday. In the meantime I suggest that we spend tomorrow evening and night together.

"Something I simply have to share with you tonight is that war is going to start within a few days from now, definitely no later than next Friday. I know many people are expecting it to start soon and I am certain that British intelligence sources know that it is going to start imminently. But the exact date can only be known to very few people. But I know for certain that it will start next Friday morning. I know that Chamberlain and his cronies have other views. They believe, for example that that ridiculous Munich pact will prevent war and protect Britain. I can assure you that those who have planned this war have not taken the slightest notice of Chamberlain or anything that he has done.

"It is already Friday August 25th. It will be deeply shocking to Britain when war comes. I cannot tell you how I have gained this information. I probably never will be able to tell you but you must accept it from me that it is correct. It is not information that you can use in any ordinary sense of the word. But you can certainly try and get your friend Winston to step up his attacks on the folly of our Prime Minister. If you had your journalists in Germany at this time they would be telling you of a great sense of excitement and tension. No, don't try and guess where I have been."

She looked into his eyes and held his hand:

"Max, I have thought many times about you over these last two years. I would dearly love to spend more time with you. But my commitment to my work is very high and I am very good at it. This evening, tonight and tomorrow are going to be a very special island of peace for me in what is a very turbulent world. So let us not talk anymore about war. There is nothing that we can do about that. Let us enjoy ourselves. Can we spend some time together during the day tomorrow? I would like you to take me somewhere outside London. In this fine weather the countryside will look superb. Please find somewhere we can go to for a very peaceful lunch."

He thought while she still held his hand.

"Louise, let us go to Brighton. I will book a room in the Grand Hotel there for tomorrow evening. We can go down by train in the morning. It will only take an hour from Victoria station. I will send my driver down in advance and he will meet us at the station and take us wherever we want to go. There is bound to be a good play or concert on. We can come back on Sunday afternoon."

Louise was very happy with all that.

They travelled on the Brighton Belle Pullman that left Victoria at eleven on the Saturday morning. The room he had booked was a top floor suite with a sea view. Lunch was in a small open air restaurant at the bottom of The Lanes; just a few minutes walk from the hotel. In the afternoon his driver took them to the great cliffs of Beachy Head near Eastbourne. They walked over the downs there for a couple of hours. The evening was spent at Glyndebourne. The opera there that evening was Verdi's Nabucco. It was the first time that Louise had heard the Chorus of the Hebrew Slaves. She wondered just how many more slaves there would be within just a week from now as the Germans rounded up the Jewish population in Poland.

Louise had spent all day Monday being briefed by George Ponsonby. He told her all about her travel to America, the arrival plans there, communications procedures, and an outline of the work she would have to do. The detail would depend on exactly what could be achieved within the White House environment. He also told her that she would have yet another new identity for her stay there. Her name would be Angela Smith. It was actually the name of someone who had been in the British diplomatic service until recently. Louise resembled her. Angela had died in a car crash. But more important was that no one in the British Embassy in Washington had ever served with Angela, so no one there knew what the real Angela was like. But Louise was getting used to changes of identity and what they meant in practical terms. She knew well that she had to live her new identity in every way.

Louise left Southampton on the Tuesday morning on the *Queen Mary*. By the time she got to New York the war had started.

* * *

On the Monday Winston and Max Beaverbrook met for lunch. That Monday, August 28th, they went to Martinaez Restaurant in Swallow Street near Piccadilly. Beaverbrook was in sombre mood. Since he had last seen Louise the previous afternoon he had both missed her and he had been reflecting on what she had said about war. He had no way of knowing where she had got that information but he had every reason to trust her. He could not think why she should have told him about it unless she had absolute knowledge on the subject. For him the only thing to look forward to that day was the call he was expecting from her later in which she would be telling him when she was going and hopefully where to.

So he started immediately on Winston:

"Winston, I have heard from a very reliable source that war will start on Friday. I cannot tell you the source but I am told that if I had the right person on the ground in Germany it would be easy to put two and two together. I believe my source and as a result I am sure now that that is exactly what is going to happen. It is probably inevitable. But what concerns me even more than that is that Chamberlain is still sticking to that ridiculous bit of paper he brought back from Munich. I suppose Poland will be where it all happens. And that makes it even worse because of the treaty he entered into with Poland. Britain has never had any possibility whatsoever of physically defending Poland in any way. But that is exactly what he agreed to do.

"There is no doubt in my mind that he had a clear mandate from the British people for peace. I think we would both agree that has always been the most desirable objective. But to attain it you have to start from a position of strength. Chamberlain has always negotiated from a position of weakness; not only him, Baldwin was no better. He wasn't even the vaguest bit interested in foreign affairs.

"Winston I want to run a major front page article on Wednesday. I want the headline to be *The Brink of War*. I intend it to be a complete castigation of everything that Chamberlain has been doing. But I also want it to be a platform for you. If war really is now going to happen there simply will have to be new policies to replace those that have failed.

"What I would like you to do is pen something which purports to be an address you will have made to an imaginary private meeting tomorrow evening. I will quote it in full in Wednesday's paper."

It did not take Winston long to gather his thoughts. As he did so he picked at the garlic prawns that he had selected as his starter.

"Max, what you have said does not surprise me. We have not been given the truth about Germany by the government for a long while now. It is possible that they do not know the full truth. If that is so they are being very reckless because it means that they are trying to sell a peace policy to our country when they do not have the slightest idea what is going on. If they do know the truth and war does break out this week it means that they are lying. Either way it is an impossible position for them.

"If war does break out then some radical new policies will have to be introduced immediately. Britain is currently far too weak to engage in any major fight, except that is, at sea in a traditional set piece naval battle. Britain would win that but it probably would not win anything else.

"Yes, run that article on Wednesday and I will pen you something before tomorrow evening.

"Max, I have been getting ever more strident over the last few months. That is because that not only have I thought war to be inevitable but I believe that it is the only way to contain and eliminate these bloody dictators who have afflicted our continent in so many evil ways. But they have become very powerful people and it will take a long and difficult struggle to overcome them.

"Over the last few weeks I have been reading all about Abraham Lincoln. He was truly a great war leader. He was not trying to defeat a despotic dictator; he was trying to overcome the institution of slavery. But the issues that he had to face are exactly those that our government will have to face over the weeks, months and years ahead. The issues are all about acquiring the right levels of skill and the right volume of resources to achieve final victory. As he found on top of that it was necessary to gain and then maintain public confidence in the war effort. We will have exactly the same tasks in the years ahead.

"Max, I do not see how even Chamberlain can keep me out of government if the war does start. I am sure that as soon as the truth becomes clear the public will expect to see me there. The support that I have had over the last few months since I unequivocally came down against the aggressors has been growing all the time. I am sure your paper on Wednesday will help it all along."

* * *

August 28, 1939. Winston rang me this evening to tell me of his talk with Max over lunch. Max and Winston have been good friends for many years now and I do not know what

Winston would have done without Max's support and encouragement. I told him that he certainly had my support for what was going to go in that article. I agreed with his diagnosis of the state of our armed forces. I am only too pleased that Britain will not be the first in line for invasion. At this time it would be impossible to resist a major invasion force. The conversation was a long one and towards the end I wished Winston luck for the next few days. I am very confident that he will be back in government very soon now.

* * *

Louise rang Max on the Monday evening. He was in his office at the time. She said she would ring at six. She did exactly that. It was a warm, bright evening. The phone call was short and simple:

"Max, my darling, I am going away tomorrow. I am going to Washington. I have no idea how long I will be there or indeed how I will get back with the war on. But I will deal with those issues as and when they arise. I am sure that I will be safe in Washington, but I will miss you. I will try to keep in touch and will try to work out how I can do that after I arrive there. Good luck, my darling and best wishes."

She did not allow him to say anything. She just put down the phone.

* * *

That evening Louise had dinner in London with her father, Ronnie. They went to the Army and Navy Club where he had booked a quiet table in one of the several alcoves that were around the sides of the large dining room. It was well out of earshot of other tables and it would certainly be possible for them to talk there. She told him about her new assignment and what was expected of her while she was in Washington.

"Dad, before I went to Moscow I had no real idea what to expect. The job that had been assigned to the girl that I replaced was certainly an interesting one and I believe that I was able to pass back a lot of valuable information to London. Voroshilov's office was a very busy place. He had a lot of meetings with Stalin and an outcome of each one was that there was more work to do. A lot of it was about using the army as a sort of police unit enforcing the mass movement of people around the country. There was absolutely no humanity in all of that. It was simply a matter of having the right number of people in the right places to fulfil the economic plan. There was also a lot of work associated with crushing rebel groups in the Southern Republics. Border incursions were another big issue.

"I met Stalin many times but always at meetings. In my view the most important thing of all about him is that no one should ever underestimate his supreme power and capability. He may be ruthless, sadistic, rude and barbaric but that fiercesome exterior hides a cunning and very capable leader who is determined to make Russia successful. He was very pleased that he had been able to neutralise Germany and although he never actually trusted anyone he did feel that it would be incredibly difficult for Germany to renege on the new pact that had been drawn up by Molotov and von Ribbentrop. He was sure that it would provide Russia with a secure border to the west. He was very concerned about that while there were risks that he had to eliminate so that he could get on with his main idea which was economic reform at home.

"He did not trust the armed forces for one minute but Voroshilov was an effective barrier between him and them. After Stalin had conducted all those purges the situation had stabilised but it was an uneasy peace.

"Voroshilov's office was very busy. There were constant comings and goings of senior officers all of whom were given political objectives to fulfil. Most of them regarded his office as a hostile place but there were one or two who knew how to manage the system. I am sure that the one to watch is Zhukov. He did a brilliant job in Manchuria earlier this year. In many ways what he achieved there bucked the system. He took no notice of bureaucracy or entrenched military opinions. He just got on with it. A good example is that when he arrived there the headquarters unit was about 100 kilometres from the front. He went straight to the front personally and directed the troops from there. In the end the only thing Stalin cared about was the result."

Ronnie asked her what would happen if at any time Hitler did renege on the deal with Russia, after all he had reneged on every other deal he had done.

She replied;

"Hell hath no fury when compared to Stalin scorned. I would expect him to do everything in order to protect Russia. But he is not planning anything at the moment. He is absolutely focused on modernising the entire country. He certainly sees no need to do anything else at this time."

Towards the end of their meal Ronnie said to her:

"I did keep a close eye on all that you were sending from Germany and Russia. It was all valuable information. But it was of little interest to our politicians. Baldwin suppressed most of the stuff you sent from Germany because it did not fit his agenda. What that really means is that the truth was too inconvenient for him. It was the same when you were in Russia. What you were sending about the von Ribbentrop-Molotov pact had strong similarities with what was going on between us and Germany. Chamberlain saw that as vindication of what he was doing and not an indication of a future threat. Anyway, now everything is going to collapse. Those senseless policies will now be condemned forever.

"Your mission to Washington is not going to be dangerous physically. It is a peaceful country and visitors to Washington are well respected. It will be very different from both Germany and Moscow. But it will not be an easy mission. Chamberlain attracts virtually no respect in America. He is not seen to stand for anything and he hardly communicates with them about anything. Roosevelt is strangely anti-British although that is a view that the Foreign Office does not accept. They believe that they have a very good grip on State Department and that is sufficient to ensure that America is a friend of Britain. We warn them about it from time to time but they take no notice.

"Politically you will find that America is almost totally focused on domestic issues. No one seems to want to have anything to do with Europe or indeed any other part of the world at this time. That will mean that the messages with which you have to deal may well be difficult ones.

"You will certainly enjoy the lifestyle over there. I suspect that things are going to get very tough over here very soon. If only Chamberlain was living in the real world we might have been able to do some useful planning but nothing has been thought through at all. Good luck. I knew some while ago that you would be going to Washington. I have arranged for you to be looked after as always."

* * *

The Daily Express article caused a ferocious storm in the country and in government. Chamberlain even made a statement in the House of Commons in which he said that the imminence of war was wrong in fact, and wrong in likelihood. Britain, he said, was going to rely on the Munich agreement in which consultation processes had been put in place. Those would be strong enough to deal with any threat to Poland. He also went on to say that the commitment to use the British armed services to help Poland should be a sufficient deterrent for any potential aggressor to that country.

* * *

One of the last things that Hitler did before the invasion of Poland was to send a telegram to the Duke of Windsor. He had briefly been the uncrowned King of England before the abdication. He was a personal friend of Winston Churchill and Churchill had lost considerable public support by taking his side through the abdication crisis.

The telegram read:

"I thank you for your telegram of August 27. You may rest assured that my attitude to Britain and my desire to avoid another war between our peoples remain unchanged. It depends on Britain, however, whether my wishes for the future development of German-British relations can be realized."

It is interesting that no such telegram went to Chamberlain. Many years later and after German archives had been sequestrated long after the war had ended it became clear that the Duke of Windsor was central to German plans for the government of Britain should a German invasion be necessary.

It was also interesting that the Duke of Windsor and Winston Churchill had remained close personal friends before, through, and after the war. The Duke of Windsor passed the contents of that telegram on to Churchill. He was saddened that his friend had been dragged into senseless diplomacy. He was even more saddened that Hitler might have thought that the Duke had any influence in Britain. That was impossible after the abdication.

But what Churchill knew that that telegram meant was that Hitler had no intention of maintaining any kind of peace in Europe.

The Early War Years

September 1st, 1939. Today has been tense and chaotic. Germany did invade Poland this morning as I knew they would. The information that Max had given us earlier in the week proved to be absolutely right. It is a tragic day for the government because it shows that the peace policies that they have pursued have been useless. Where it all leaves Chamberlain I have no idea. As a minimum his credibility has been shot to pieces.

All day long the troops under my command have been on exercises throughout the capital preparing anti-aircraft guns, barrage balloons and searchlights. No one knows whether there will be any direct threat to Britain but it makes senses to take precautions just in case. We have practised our air raid precautions in the last few weeks but never on this scale before. A lot of work needs to be done to get all the troops up to an acceptable level of performance but they will get there.

I would have loved to be able to talk to Winston today but I have been far too busy in my headquarters and touring several sites. He has been on the radio several times criticising the government for having no plans to deal with the failure of the diplomatic processes. Chamberlain has also spoken, telling the people that Germany must cease its invasion of Poland and enter into meaningful consultations with Britain and France about the whole matter. I cannot imagine that consultations with Britain are anywhere near Hitler's mind at this time. I am sure that we will be formally at war within a few days. May God help us then.

* * *

Poland was invaded by Germany that Friday morning. It was the world's first major Blitzkrieg attack. The overall German commander was von Manstein and the commander of the German armour was Guderian. In less than a month Poland was completely defeated and divided into three government areas. In the east the Russians took complete control. The western part of the country was completely subsumed into Germany. In the centre there was a jointly governed area. It was all written into the Molotov/Ribbentrop agreement; it was all a complete stitch-up. If Chamberlain had read the intelligence available from Russia about that agreement he would have realised that Poland was going to be destroyed within days. If he had read information that was readily available to him but which he had suppressed he would have known that Hitler never had any intention of honouring any agreement with him.

Britain did not lift a finger to help Poland despite Chamberlain's promises to Parliament nor did it have any capability of doing so. Its commitment to Poland had been a charade designed to hide the illusion of peace. But having said it would defend Poland Britain had no option but to declare war on Germany. It was all a tragic failure of bad politics and bad diplomacy made worse by false promises.

When I read George Ponsonby's diary in 1994 I found an entry relating to the information that Louise had given him about that agreement. He wrote that he kept all the information that she had given him about it to himself. He never briefed Halifax or Chamberlain about it. He was already into the business of deception and deceit. He was already editing the intelligence and only providing Britain with what <u>he</u> wanted the government to know.

* * *

September 2, 1939. Chamberlain made a broadcast this morning to say that Britain has asked Germany to cease its hostilities in Poland with immediate effect. He has also given Germany an ultimatum that unless hostilities cease within 24 hours Britain will be at war with Germany.

I was not able to speak to Winston yesterday as I was fully engaged in preparing additional plans for the defence of London. There is a lot to be done but the troops are in good spirit and readily accept their new responsibilities for the active defence of the capital. It is all rather different now with war being imminent. In peacetime it was largely theoretical.

* * *

September 3, 1939. I did speak with Winston today. He fully supports Chamberlain's broadcast and believes that we will be at war with Germany tomorrow. There have been strong demands in the newspapers and on the radio for him to be given an important role in government. I am sure that will happen very soon now.

* * *

One thing that Chamberlain did soon after the invasion of Poland was invite Churchill into his government. There was huge public clamour for such a move and it would have been impossible for him to resist it.

Churchill became First Lord of the Admiralty. The morning he was called to Downing Street to be given his appointment he had a lengthy meeting with Chamberlain who clearly did not have a clue what he should do about war priorities. So Churchill suggested his own agenda:

"Mr Prime Minister, We face immediate threats from German U-Boats. I do not know just how many of them are already at sea blockading these islands but whatever the number; every one of them is a threat. It is my most urgent task to counter that threat. The first essential step is to impose a convoy system on all merchant ships departing from or arriving at UK ports. Any such convoys need to be defended and at the moment our resources to do that are minimal. I must therefore immediately authorise the building of many more escort vessels. That will have to include destroyers and frigates of far greater capability than the puny corvettes that have so far been ordered.

"Any convoy system will impose severe restrictions on the supply of goods and materials to this country. War supplies have to be the priority. There will inevitably be restrictions on the supply of food and fuel and that means that we must introduce a rationing system immediately. It will not be popular but it is the only way of ensuring continuity of supply.

"The second way to counter the threat is to authorise a big research programme into anti-submarine warfare. Powerful methods have to be found quickly to equip the Royal Navy with whatever new technologies can be found to give them a leading opportunity to destroy the threat. There will also have to be a big increase in the training capabilities of the Royal Navy. It will not be easy but it has to be done."

His final statement was that it was essential that the production of fighter aircraft was expanded immediately. If there was any threat other than a naval one it would first come from the air. Britain had to be prepared for that. That would mean that more fighter aircraft would have to be produced.

Chamberlain's view was entirely political. The British public had forced him to take Churchill into his government. It was that article in The Daily Express that had finally done it. Much as he loathed him, he could not get rid of him. He also knew that if Churchill could not get his way in government he would make sure that the people knew about it. Chamberlain did not have any alternative but to do what Churchill had said.

* * *

September 4th, 1939. Late this morning I got a call from Winston. He told me of his appointment to the Admiralty. He wanted to see me as soon as possible at his office there. He said he had important military matters to discuss. Nothing could really have prepared me for wanted he had to say to me. I will try to write as accurately as possible everything he said to me then. It was a conversation that would have profound effects about the conduct of the entire war.

When I got there he started to talk immediately. What he said was:

"Samuel, as I told you over the phone I am now back in Cabinet. It is a much smaller role than I would have liked but it is an important one and I shall endeavour to do it well. I have already put several demands to Chamberlain about convoys, rationing, more convoy escorts and some substantial additional capacity for the Royal Air Force. He has agreed to implement them all.

"Later today I will start the work of finding out the actual fighting capabilities of our navy. I fear that in the key areas of convoy protection and anti-submarine warfare they are not good. Germany was not allowed to build any submarines under our pact with them but initial intelligence available to me suggests that they could already have more than 50, possibly already at sea. The effect on our merchant shipping could be devastating.

"When the First Sea Lord told me about these submarines an hour or so ago I was appalled. But apparently the information about them has been around for a couple of years. When the construction programme was first discovered Baldwin was told about it but he chose to suppress the information. His cabinet was not even told. What was even worse was that nothing was done to prepare us to meet such a threat. Chamberlain apparently refused to consider any such intelligence as having any validity. He was certain that his negotiations with Hitler could be trusted.

"That all leaves us in a mess. Those submarines will start to attack us immediately and we will lose valuable ships as a result. It will be a tough time. We have no effective means of response just now. The British people will inevitably hear of and be affected by those submarine attacks. They will wonder why, with the greatest navy in the world, we could not prevent them. It may take us years to get mastery of the U-Boat menace. But it is something that we have to achieve.

"That brings me on to the real point of this meeting. I cannot be an effective minister if I am going to have to rely on completely useless intelligence information. I therefore am appointing you to be my military intelligence advisor. You will retain your current rank and all privileges associated with that. You will hand over your current responsibilities immediately. I will be arranging a replacement for you with the War Minister. You will work in an office close to me here and your job will be to give me the best possible briefings on the whole military intelligence front. You must use all of your excellent contacts throughout all our armed forces and intelligence services to ensure that I am always told the truth."

I did take up that post and started work with Winston that afternoon. Immediately after I had accepted the appointment I went to see the First Sea Lord, Sir Dudley Pound. I have got to know him well over the last couple of years. He welcomed my appointment and said that anything that caused ministers to take military intelligence seriously was to be welcomed. He made it clear that he looked forward to working with me but he also warned me that the starting position for the war was very bad. He welcomed any contribution that I could make to improving things. While I was with him he received a phone call to say that the passenger liner Athenia had just been sunk by a torpedo off the Irish coast.

Within minutes of my moving into my new office there was a much more detailed briefing from the First Sea Lord than anything he had said to Winston or me in the morning.

We met in a large map room underneath the Admiralty building at 4 o'clock. Winston was there, so were the Permanent Secretary and several senior officials. Winston was already in a foul mood because of the loss of the Athenia. It seemed that he was taking that loss personally.

Dudley Pound was accompanied by the heads of his divisions, all of them Admirals. The meeting was intended to be a brief to Winston and me about the current state of the navy, its preparedness for war and the priorities that needed to be pursued. It was a very detailed presentation. It all told a grim story. There were four parts to it.

He started with the Home Fleet. This he described as being ready for immediate battle. It was by far the largest battle fleet in the world and had the potential to destroy any other fleet. It was mostly anchored at Scapa Flow in the Orkney Islands. Intelligence available about German resources indicated that there were six ships there which posed a significant threat. They were Bismarck, Tirpitz, Graf Spee, Deutschland, Scharnhorst and Gneisenau. They were all currently in different ports in North Germany. There were spies keeping each of them under observation and it was certain that Britain would know of their movements within 12 hours of their moving. The destination would probably not be known. He said that the Home Fleet was fully prepared to eliminate any or all of them.

Then he dealt with the defence of UK ports. Since the war had started, work had commenced on mining the approaches and entrances to all naval ports and the Dover Strait. There were hundreds of ports and priority had been given to those on the east coast. Because of a lack of capacity it would be many months before the work was complete.

Then he described the deployment of ships around the Empire. He claimed to be happy with the capabilities of squadrons in South Africa, India and Singapore. The Australian and Canadian navies had competent but limited fleets available to counter any immediate threat to them.

Finally he came to merchant shipping and the formation of convoys for their protection. This he said was a major problem. There were probably 400 ships at sea headed for Britain and probably another 400 due to leave Britain within the next week. The exact numbers of ships were not known. Most of these ships had no sort of long range radio equipment and the positions of the arriving ships were not known. Most of them would probably not know that war had started. A system of convoys was being started for all ships leaving Britain but it would be at least six weeks before all arriving ships could be covered. The maximum number of escorts available for departing convoys was likely to be no more than 2 per convoy. This would only provide minimal protection. A major problem was that most merchant ships were very slow. Convoy speeds were unlikely to exceed 7 knots which was below the speed at which submarines could travel below the surface. What was needed was a huge escort building programme, massive recruitment and a big increase in research about new weapons systems. This all might take 2 or 3 years to achieve. In the meantime all merchant shipping would be vulnerable. There were known to be at least 57 German U-Boats. Only 27 of these were ocean-going types and it was believed that 17 of them were at sea. Because of the long and difficult passage from North German ports to likely target areas off the west of Britain it could not presently be predicted just how many U-Boats posed an imminent threat to shipping. But he did expect more sinking of our merchant ships to take place almost immediately. It was a grim picture. He thought that naval ships were well protected.

Winston made some immediate decisions about a faster programme to protect all British ports from any enemy naval activity and about building more convoy escorts of a much higher capability than the corvettes under construction then. He wanted detailed plans for it all within a week. He then rang Chamberlain and asked for an immediate meeting of the cabinet war committee.

At that emergency meeting, the War Cabinet endorsed a proposal from Chamberlain that the government step up still further the acquisition of fighter aircraft and that Churchill be authorised to lead a major build-up of Britain's capability in anti-submarine warfare.

They also authorised the despatch of two army divisions to France to help in the defence of that country should that be needed. They were almost the entire home based British army. That deployment was an inevitable consequence of the reckless and joint guarantees that Britain and France had given to Poland. How moving two divisions to France had any prospect of helping Poland was anybody's guess.

After he returned from that meeting Winston told me that he had an idea which would help the convoy escort problem but he was not even going to tell me about it until progress had been made. He was certainly not going to tell the Prime Minister about it.

* * *

September 5, 1939. Winston was absent from the office for most of the morning. When he got back he would not say where he had been. But judging by his mood it was obviously a most important event for him.

* * *

Winston went to see Joseph Kennedy, the American Ambassador, at his residence. The two men had met several times before but only on the cocktail party circuit. This was the first time they had met for any formal meeting. Churchill had been delighted that it was possible to see him at such short notice.

Winston went straight into the details reasons for the meeting;

"Ambassador, whilst I see this as an exploratory meeting there are nevertheless some important business issues that we need to discuss and progress. At this time my primary tasks are to protect the country's merchant shipping and to prevent any naval attack on Britain or on British capital ships. Britain has a fine navy but it is woefully lacking in convoy escort ships. I will be doing a review of the exact impact of that later today but in the meantime I have been wondering whether America has any destroyers or similar ships that could be leased or borrowed by Britain. If there are, they could provide an important and immediate improvement in our naval capabilities."

Kennedy made no comment but said that he would pass the enquiry back to Washington and he would do so urgently. But he did say that such an enquiry could not be handled as any sort of normal trade transaction. It would have to start with the President. It was all political. He reminded Churchill that America had a policy of strict neutrality in relation to any conflicts not on its own borders and that naturally included all of Europe.

Winston was happy with that first meeting. So was Kennedy.

* * *

September 6, 1939. I went to see Ronnie Harford today. My purpose in doing so was to put together a plan as to how I was going to work with the various intelligence agencies in order to support Winston. It proved to be a very important meeting. Ronnie was very critical of the way that intelligence had been used by ministers over the last few years, the last couple of years in particular. He gave me two examples. The first concerned the placement in Germany of a very capable and effective agent. That agent had provided high quality data about the build-up of German armed forces and about the facilities that were being constructed for them. There was no possible doubt from what had been provided that Germany was creating armed forces on a scale unimagined in Britain. The only possible use of those forces was invasion of other countries; Austria, Czechoslovakia and now Poland. Where next? Britain, possibly? Of especial interest was that that agent had actually seen the construction of more than 50 U-Boats in direct contravention of the Naval Agreement. But Baldwin and then Chamberlain had dismissed such intelligence as irrelevant. They had actually suppressed it because it did not fit their view of the world and because it did not meet their expectations of what they could achieve in negotiations with Germany. All they had wanted was to pursue their peace agendas. If anything got in the way of that it would have to be suppressed.

Ronnie also told me that an agent of the British Government had been present in Russia when the von Ribbentrop-Molotov pact had been agreed. In it were precise plans for the invasion of Poland, with dates and specific military objectives. Ronnie knew that this information had been passed to London but he was pretty sure that it had not even been handed on to ministers. He had no idea why it had not been passed on but he was certain that even if it had it would have been rejected completely by Chamberlain anyway.

His message on this one was about politicians failing to face up to the truth of what was actually going on in the world and just believing their own rhetoric. It made Europe a very dangerous area.

When we got on to what we could do together he was very positive. He held out particular promise for an agent whom they had recently recruited in America who seemed to have very close access to the White House. It remained to be seen just what information would be obtained but there was every reason to believe that it might be possible to get information directly from Roosevelt himself. He went on:

"What we do not have is anyone of real calibre in Russia at this time. I wish we did. It would be very interesting to know exactly what is going on now. We did have someone there until about ten days ago but that person had to be withdrawn. It was far too dangerous for them to stay with war soon to start. Russia is very secretive. For example there is very little radio traffic for us to monitor. You normally get heavy volumes of radio traffic before a training exercise let alone just before a military invasion But with their invasion of the eastern part of Poland there was virtually no Russian radio traffic. They must communicate by some other methods.

"We know something of the secrecy with which Stalin and his ministers operate, particularly the Defence Ministry. Until ten days ago we had very good information about that. It is certainly my view that they operate with secrecy that is unprecedented. They are obsessive

about it. All the indications are that this emanates directly from Stalin himself. It is something that we will have to deal with. We cannot possibly have a nation that large so close to us which operates with such secrecy. If we cannot break it down we will never know whether they are a threat to us or not. We are going to have to penetrate Russian secrets somehow.

"Germany is an altogether different proposition. We have several good agents on the ground there. We are getting what we regard as high quality information from most of them. We also have access to several Germans who are feeding us with what seems to be useful information. In some circles in Germany it seems that there is intense hatred of the regime and an equally strong disloyalty to it. That is why we have been able to get so much help. The Germans also use radio traffic very widely. In the recent Polish campaign we were able to track the locations of most German units entirely through radio intercepts. The problem we have, though, with them is that they are using a very sophisticated code system. We have no idea how they are doing it but we are going to have to find a way of cracking it. Until we do we will only know that they are sending messages. We have no idea of the detailed contents.

"To find solutions to such problems I have been looking at the priorities for the future.

"We have to know the intentions of any enemies. We have to know their planned military deployments. We have to know the effect of battle on their forces, what damage they have suffered. We have to know the real intentions of our allies, whether indeed they are friendly. What about the French, for example? All of them will communicate in code so we will have to break those codes.

"The biggest priority in my mind is to try and crack those German codes. I have asked the politicians several times for the necessary resources to do so. But what it will require is that the finest mathematicians and language experts will have to be taken from our universities and put into a secure location where they do nothing else apart from code breaking. So far all those requests have been refused. But it does occur to me that Winston could set up such an operation just within the navy. He would not need to go to Cabinet about it. All he needs to do is buy a country house somewhere and then send call-up notices to all those brains that we will need. If you can persuade him to do just that it will be a very valuable service.

"The next thing I have to do is find a way of getting some really good people into Russia. That looks to be really difficult and I do not have any proposals let alone answers at this time.

"The whole thing is so vast that we cannot possibly cover it all. So we have to decide just what we can do.

Over the following hours we did develop a plan. Within it I would talk to Winston about the code breaking need, I would also talk to him about the need to get some good people into Russia. But before I talked to Winston I needed to get detailed briefings from the heads of Naval and RAF intelligence.

* * *

September 7th, 1939. I went to see Admiral Max Horton this morning. He is temporarily in charge of naval intelligence. He told me that all the German capital ships were known to be in German ports. That was the good news. The bad news was that all those ports were heavily mined and had been for months. The only conceivable threat to those ports came from the Royal Navy. He had personally briefed Chamberlain about it back in May but he had been told by him to stop scare-mongering. He had been told by Chamberlain that his discussions with Hitler were strong enough to deal with any threat.

He went on to say that the U-Boat threat was very serious. Each evening at 6 o'clock German time all the U-Boats surfaced so that they could receive an update to their orders. It was not possible to interpret those orders because of the complexity of the codes used but it was possible to locate the U-Boats. The previous evening there had been 17 U-Boats in the Atlantic. Under the Naval Agreement there were not supposed to be any. 5 of those ships were to the southwest of Ireland, the remainder were stretched across the great circle shipping routes between Scotland and Greenland. There were another 10 in the North Sea. They all posed a very dangerous threat to British shipping. He expected to hear within hours of the destruction of the first British cargo ship of the war. He did not think that it was improving intelligence that was going to win the naval war for Britain but much improved equipment and much improved tactics. Britain had to be smart to win. But he did think that cracking the German naval codes would make an important contribution.

Later on I went to meet with Air Vice-Marshal Arthur Harris who manages RAF intelligence work. I do not think that I have ever met anyone as aggressive as him. Winston will probably love the man. He offered me nothing in the way of real information. He was certain that there was no present threat to Britain from the air. He said they had all sorts of information about the number of German Luftwaffe units and their capability but they all seemed to be tied up in Poland then. But he did say that they were worried about the codes the Germans were using. He would certainly support efforts to break them.

* * *

September 8th, 1939. When Winston returned from the Cabinet this afternoon I was able to brief him on what I had learned from the Service Intelligence Chiefs. He readily agreed to set up the code breaking service suggested by Ronnie Harford and he instructed his private secretary to get on with finding somewhere for them to start work immediately. He called in Dudley Pound and instructed him to arrange for the issue of call-up notices to the people who would be needed to start it all.

Again, there was a footnote. Dated June 3, 1965 it read:

The British public has still not heard of all the work that was done at Bletchley Park. It is already more than 20 years since the war ended. Obviously someone thinks that it should still remain a major secret. I know that what Winston set up that afternoon eventually provided some very important information that undoubtedly helped our war efforts in many ways. I am sure the public will be very excited when they do learn what was going on.

* * *

September 9, 1939. It was around noon today that Winston heard about the loss of the first cargo ship. I was with him at the time. It had been carrying iron ore from Canada to Liverpool. Winston seemed to take the loss of the ship personally.

There was a footnote to the diary entry for that day. It read:

February 16, 1961. I have been re-reading the diaries over these last few weeks. What has struck me very strongly is what a major impact the submarine war in the North Atlantic had *on our lives then. As you will see as you read on it completely changed the lifestyle of Winston and it dominated every facet of life in Britain. It constrained almost every aspect of the conduct of the war until such time as Britain was able to eradicate the U-Boat menace. Those first sinkings were horrible portends of terrible things to come. Winston was right to concentrate on the North Atlantic right at the beginning of the war. But with every new horror arising it became obvious just how far Britain's anti-submarine defences had been allowed to decline in the years before the war. I go to church every Sunday now and when there I pray for the souls of all those people who lost their lives in those ships as a result of that negligence. Most of them were civilians. What a waste.*

* * *

October 14, 1939 Winston was in deep despair today. Last night the Battleship Royal Oak was sunk in a submarine attack. So far 30 merchant ships have been lost at sea including 3 yesterday. Britain has already lost a quarter of a million tons of supplies.

* * *

Germany was clearly not ready to start war on Britain immediately. They were clearly not in a position to engage in any land battles in the west because of their commitments in Poland. There was initially no British Army to fight on Continental soil. They were also in no position to engage in any aerial warfare with Britain. Their forces were too heavily engaged in Poland for there to be any possibility of that. But what they were in a position to do was attack Britain by sea. It was exactly as had been foreseen by Hitler and von Ribbentrop when they met after the latter had returned from London.

U-Boat attacks on lone vessels approaching the British Isles began almost immediately. On October 13 one U-Boat commanded by Kapitänleutnant Gunther Prien actually breached the defences of the Scapa Flow naval anchorage in the Orkney Islands. Three large naval ships, including the Battleship Royal Oak, were sunk. The U-Boat escaped.

But it was out in the Atlantic that the battle really raged. It was there that Hitler had decided to create a stranglehold on the Empire trade routes. It was there that the U-Boats were stationed. Each month the lost shipping tonnage increased despite the operation of a convoy system right from the outset of war for all but the fastest ships. Inbound ships continued to arrive independently until the end of October, 1939. They were very vulnerable. Many were sunk.

* * *

The *Queen Mary* docked in New York early on the Sunday morning. In the last few hours they had deliberately slowed down so that they would pass the Statue of Liberty after dawn. It was a clear warm September morning. Louise had been briefed by George Ponsonby that she would be met on the pier by Gerry Taswell. He would take her on the train to Washington. Gerry was from the Embassy in Washington and he was responsible for the practical management of all staff postings there. She had travelled under her new name of Angela Smith. She had got used to new names by then and being called Miss Smith by the crew did not cause her any problems.

On the voyage she thought many times about her new role. She had been briefed by Ponsonby that she was to be responsible within the Embassy for relations with the White House. There were numerous officials there who were important to Britain. Improving relations with them was very much a diplomatic objective for the British Ambassador in the United States at that time. The Embassy had good relations with State Department but relations with the White House had been frosty for several years. She was to work under the direction of the Ambassador and was to tell him what she had learned and achieved in her dealings with White House officials. But what Ponsonby had also told her was that she was to find ways of meeting privately with Roosevelt and when she had achieved that she was to become a direct liaison between him and the Foreign Office. She was not to tell the Ambassador that she had any such contacts. This was especially important because he rarely had any opportunity to meet with the President. The Foreign Office or rather George Ponsonby himself intended that this personal liaison with the President should be one of the great secrets of diplomacy. He loved the intrigue associated with it all.

One of the most important things Ponsonby had said to her was that any information she passed back from her personal meetings with Roosevelt would be attributed to an American source. She would always be described in British Government circles as an American informer. She was even given an American male codename. In the British Government in London her dispatches would always be attributed to Bradman. The name was selected because there was no one working anywhere in the Federal Government with that name.

To enable her to do her job in Washington Louise had been given a senior diplomatic rank. That meant that she had been able to have a first class cabin on the Queen Mary. That made both for a comfortable voyage and an excellent social life on board. It also meant that she would be able to have a first class seat on the train to Washington. Most of the people Taswell escorted were very much more junior than her. He had never accompanied a female diplomat before and he was looking forward to it.

After she had seen the Statue of Liberty and the New York skyline she had breakfast and then went down to the pier. She was followed by her steward bringing her luggage. Ronnie was exactly where George Ponsonby said he would be. They took a taxi to Penn Central station. As the train was not due to leave until eleven, Gerry got the driver to take them on a tour of New York on them way. They stopped in Greenwich Village for a coffee in a little Italian coffee shop.

They got to Penn Station about fifteen minutes before the train was due to leave and went to their reserved seats. While they were waiting Gerry told her that a welcome cocktail party had been arranged for her at six that evening at the Ambassador's residence, which adjoined the Embassy. When they got to Washington Gerry would take her to her apartment and would then collect her in time to take her to the Embassy. After that the next appointment she would have would be with the Ambassador the following morning for breakfast. Thereafter she would join him for his regular morning meeting with his senior staff at nine each weekday morning. He went on:

"You know, of course, that you will have a car here with your own driver. He will meet us at the railway station in Washington. He will be available to you at all times."

Angela knew all that. She had been briefed on it by Ponsonby. She knew the driver and he would be the conduit for secret messages that she might need to send and receive.

Privately Gerry was certain that she would cause a sensation in Washington. She was a very attractive young lady and she would be in a city which had virtually no female diplomats.

At Washington station she was delighted to see Sid once again. He was to be her driver. To him she was very special. He knew that she was on an important mission to Washington. He would look after her at any time. When she saw him she said to him;

"Sid, why am I not surprised to see you here?"

* * *

Angela's meeting with the Ambassador on the Monday morning was very important. She had the title of First Secretary. He needed to brief her about the White House officials with whom she would be dealing.

But before he got on with that he briefed her on the changes in the government that had taken place over the weekend, particularly about Churchill's new appointment. The Ambassador said he was very supportive of her role. It had not been done before because they had all been confident that the excellent relationships that everyone in the Embassy had with State Department would meet all Britain's requirements. But recently there had been some telling signs that Roosevelt was consulting State Department less and less. In such circumstances it was necessary to find someone new who could take a direct approach with the White House. He was pleased that London had supported the idea and he was very pleased that she had been sent to Washington to do it. He was sure that she would be popular with White House officials. They had been told of her appointment and welcomed it. A cocktail party had been arranged in the residency for that evening to which several of them had been invited. All those invited would be coming and that included the Chief of Staff.

The Chief of Staff was called James Westfield. He spent half an hour with Angela that evening but more importantly he invited her to visit him in the White House the following afternoon. It was to be an auspicious day.

* * *

At the daily Embassy meeting the following morning she told the Ambassador that she would be visiting the White House that afternoon. He was very keen to hear what went on so he asked her to come to supper at the residence that evening. He had to go out earlier to two functions but he expected to be back by nine.

Angela arrived at the White House in good time for the three o'clock meeting. She was immediately shown into Westfield's office. He had an office close to the President's in the west wing. It looked out towards the towering Washington Memorial. In winter, when the leaves were off the trees, it was also possible to see the Lincoln Memorial off to the west and the Jefferson Memorial across the still ponds and the lawns of the Washington Mall. It was a most attractive spot. She envied anyone who could have an office like that.

"Welcome, Angela. I am sure we will meet many times in the future but I did want your first visit to these offices to be a memorable one. I will take you on a quick tour of the place; then I will explain how we are organised. After that the President would like to meet you. He will be back from a meeting at the Senate sometime between five and six."

Roosevelt phoned through to say that he was ready to see her a few minutes before six. They met in the Oval Office. She went alone to see him. He immediately put her at ease by saying:

"I am sorry if I have been a few minutes late. I do have to meet with our Senators from time to time. They are a powerful group of men and it is essential to keep open the communications lines with them all the time. Today was about their wish that we introduce more schemes like the Tennessee Valley Authority scheme. That was a very successful scheme that I conceived down in the south to re-generate the Tennessee valley which had become a dust bowl during the agricultural recession. What I set up there was a vast tree planting programme which employed many people but it also allowed the land to be returned to normal agricultural use within about five years. I am entirely sympathetic to their arguments but that scheme was specifically tailored for that area. We left it that I would consider tailor made schemes for other areas of our country.

"Your Ambassador told me a couple of weeks ago that London wanted to set up the post that you have come here to take up. I was very intrigued when I heard about it but the more I thought about it the more I thought that it might prove to be a very useful function. I can well imagine that he is frustrated by communications between us at this time. Whether things can improve will largely depend on what you personally can achieve. The problem is that there is a very cosy relationship between my State Department and your Foreign Office. It is a relationship that has to change and until it does things will get more strained between our governments. How you can help, I will explain to you shortly.

"I have a very fine Ambassador in London but he has found it very difficult to get access to the highest levels of government. Your Prime Minister, Chamberlain, seems to be ploughing a very narrow furrow at this time. He does not seem interested in hearing any views other than his own. The result of all that is that communications between our two governments seem to have become very formal and frankly rather moribund. If there is anyway your new job can help to improve that situation it will be very welcome.

"At this time of the afternoon I usually have a dry martini cocktail. I always mix them myself. Would you like one?"

She said she would like that. After he had poured them he went on:

"I gather you only arrived in this country on Sunday. That means you will have left London before Britain's war started. I am sure that you will have been advised of the changes in the government there since then.

"There is one very interesting development of which I am pretty certain that you are not aware. I will tell you about it. It will also be a very interesting test as to whether there can be a viable extra diplomatic post in your embassy which effectively by-passes the normal diplomatic protocols. If you can deal with it, it will prove that I can trust you. If you cannot, you will not be welcome here. It is as simple as that.

"Normally if Britain wanted something from America it would send any such request through the Foreign Office in London, who would then pass it through to the embassy here in Washington. It would then be passed to the relevant American department. If America wanted anything from Britain it would do the same thing in reverse, getting its own embassy in London to make the local contacts. You will, of course know about these things.

"Last week Winston Churchill visited my Ambassador in London and put an idea to him about how America could help Britain in this war. The message was clearly intended for me personally. It was also clearly intended to be sent outside the normal diplomatic channels. I would be very surprised if you knew what it was about because it could not possibly have been conceived until Winston had his new ministerial appointment. I will not tell you now what it was about. It was, however, very intriguing and will take a lot of thought before any reply can be formulated. Like most diplomatic notes it contains both opportunities and problems.

"I would like to have someone who is close to the White House within the British Embassy here. It would be nice to have someone who we can trust. I am certainly very happy to give you the chance to prove that you can be in that position. But it is essential that whoever it is I am going to trust can develop communications with London that by-pass all the normal embassy channels. That is what you have got to do. I will know when I hear from you again whether you have achieved that because I am certain that Churchill only went to see my ambassador because he wanted to make sure that his Foreign Office and the embassy here did not know what he was doing. If you get the right information for me I will know that you have ways of by-passing the normal diplomatic channels.

"What I would like you to do is to find out what that message from Winston was all about. As soon as you have found out contact James and he will fix for you to see me at the earliest possible opportunity. If you have not come back within a week I will assume that you do not have access to the highest levels in government in Britain and that therefore your role is invalid. So can you do that?"

Angela had been looking straight into his eyes as he had been speaking. When he had finished she took a small sip of her martini and looked straight at him again:

"Mr. President, it is now Tuesday evening in Washington. It is late at night back home. I have no doubt that I will be able to meet your request. But I cannot predict exactly when I will be able to come back to you. I hope it will be before the weekend but if it takes a little longer will it be possible for us to meet over the weekend?"

"Yes, Angela, that will always be possible. Now enjoy your drink and tell me more about yourself."

"Mr. President, I already know the drink is excellent. I will certainly enjoy the rest of it. As for me, I cannot talk about the previous postings that I have had. But what I can say about them is that they have been extremely interesting. I have gained a reputation for working in difficult circumstances. The results of my work have always been excellent. I am strongly motivated by doing the best for Britain. It is a very tough world in which I have to do that. I am sure that you will get to understand the quality and reliability of my work.

"Last evening I met several people from your government. I am sure that James has told you about them. They have made me very welcome here. I am sure that my time here is going to be just fine."

After that they went on to talk about the scene in Washington and some of the things that he had done as President. He mixed more drinks. A little later he asked James to join them and he mixed a third drink for each of them. James preferred whisky.

When Angela came to leave Sid was waiting outside with his car. Once they were on the move she asked him to take her to her apartment and to pick her up from there in time to be at the Ambassador's residence by nine. She said she would give him a message then that she wanted sent that evening to London. In the briefing she had had with George Ponsonby they had agreed that Sid would pass all the secret messages between them. That was the main reason he was going to be in Washington; that and ensuring her safety. But this message was not going to go to George Ponsonby. It was far too important for that.

* * *

On the way to the embassy Angela said to Sid:

"Sid, I will leave a message on the car seat that I want sent to General Harford immediately. There will be no copies sent to anyone else. When there is a reply to it I want you to bring it to me as soon as possible. There is another message that must go to George Ponsonby. We certainly live in interesting times. Thanks."

Her father received her message immediately he went into the office on the Wednesday morning. It was in code so that no one else could understand it. He then rang Samuel and arranged for them to meet within the hour.

The message to George Ponsonby simply said that she had had her first meeting at the White House. It was just about getting to know James Westfield. She had remembered well what her father had told her about the information she provided not getting through to the right people. She had remembered his warnings about diplomats and she was not going to send anything to Ponsonby which might be really important or sensitive.

Immediately Samuel had sat down Ronnie started:

"Samuel, I told you the other day that we had high hopes of an American we had recently recruited. It now transpires that all is not quite what it seemed to be. The person concerned, who goes under the code name of Bradman, was selected by the White House to be a go-between with the British Government. We had no idea about that when we recruited him but it does now seem to be a fact of life. What I have heard from him this morning is that Roosevelt wants to use him actively in the process of communicating directly with key people in the British Government. I have no problem with that. The man's credentials are excellent and he does work in the White House. There is no reason to believe that what he passes to us is anything other than the true word of Roosevelt. If the system works we will be able to get information directly from Roosevelt which by-passes the normal diplomatic processes. I am completely in favour of that. Our experiences in recent years of what happens to high grade information when it reaches our Foreign Office are not encouraging.

"Yesterday Roosevelt gave that operative a challenge. That challenge is for him to find out the content of the message Winston sent to him last weekend via Ambassador Kennedy. It is obvious that Roosevelt wants to know whether Bradman really does have access to the highest levels in our government. If he gets the correct information we will have someone spying for us in the White House and we will have an ultra secret and secure communications channel with Roosevelt. I did not know that Winston had met Ambassador Kennedy and I have no idea what they might have discussed. However, I think that we have no option but to find out. If our man can go back with the correct information then we have an open channel to Roosevelt. If he can't go back with that information his entire credibility is shot to pieces. What I need you to do is to talk it over with Winston."

To Samuel it seemed obvious that Winston would agree to use this new channel for communications. If he had already met with Kennedy in secret it must have been because he did not want his colleagues and the Foreign Office to know what he was doing. He probably did not even want the Prime Minister to know. Samuel had no problem with that and readily agreed that he would discuss it all with Winston.

His diary read:

I explained it all to Winston and he readily understood the significance of it. He questioned me intently about who this Bradman was but other than telling him that he was an American I could not give him anything more. I am sure that Ronnie knows exactly who the operative is but he is not going to let me know. What is much more important is that the quality of information is good. Winston did tell me what he had discussed with Kennedy and I went to see Ronnie again to tell him.

As soon as Sid received a signal from Ronnie on the Wednesday afternoon he went to see Angela. After she had read it she contacted James and asked him for a short meeting. She met him later that day and explained that she needed to have a private meeting with the President as soon as possible. Roosevelt was in Philadelphia that day and was not expected back until the following morning. Nevertheless James rang his tour manager there with a request that he be allowed to speak with Roosevelt as soon as possible. He gave the code word they had agreed to cover any possible meeting with Angela. Roosevelt rang back within half an hour and told James that she should be at the White House for lunch at twelve on the Thursday. He said it might be a long meeting.

* * *

Roosevelt had no doubt that Angela would come back with the required information. There could be no other basis for her wanting to see him urgently. But in his mind once he had validated the situation that she actually did have access directly to Churchill there was no need to rush things. His main objective in wanting to see her that day was to get to know a very attractive girl very much better.

The lunch took place in his private sitting room which was on the first floor just above the Oval Office. There was a small dining area at the western end of the room.

They started by having gins and tonic. Initially they stood to look at the view but as he could not stand for long because of the damage caused to his legs by polio many years earlier they soon went over to the sitting area.

"Angela, please tell me about the message that Winston sent me."

So she told him about the idea of trying to acquire surplus American ships that would be suitable for convoy escort duties. He was entirely satisfied with that. But he then went on to tell her why it was not a simple decision, why he simply could not just say yes to a friendly nation which was clearly going to need those resources.

"Angela, if you go round this country you will find that the majority of the people have a friendly, if old-fashioned, attitude to Britain. Very few of them have been there so they do not know what it is like. But all of this nation, at this time have a dread of going into another European war. The end of that last one was very messy, the peace was even worse. America led those peace negotiations and made a shambles of it. That shambles in turn became the disastrous depression through which we have all been. My country would not allow me to risk anything like that again.

"What that all means is that it is not possible for me to come to an immediate decision. I have spent a great deal of time thinking it all through and I am nowhere near a conclusion. But very much in my mind is trying to see whether there is a way to help Britain with Winston's request. We certainly have the ships available. If and when I find a way through what is a very complex jungle I will let you know because I am sure that you will be involved in any implementation. Now let us talk about different things. Tell me about yourself. Tell me a bit more this time."

"I started life as a researcher. I worked for a couple of newspapers doing that. It was well paid but not mentally stimulating. So I went into academic research, mainly history. There are large numbers of libraries in Europe which have hardly been looked into for centuries. They contain masses of unpublished material which is proving to be of great interest to historians. That was certainly stimulating work mentally. My brain used to ache at the end of each day. Then a friend introduced me to a senior diplomat and he suggested that I try to get into the diplomatic service. I had to take an exam, which I passed with flying colours. I speak German and Russian and that helped. Since then I have been lucky. I have had several good assignments and I have been very effective in all of them. Quick promotion followed, which is why I am at my current rank at a young age. I think this current posting must be some kind of reward for the work I have been doing recently. That is about it really."

He went on to describe his own background. She thoroughly enjoyed talking with him. He had a very sharp mind and a wide range of interests. She particularly liked his view of American history. She had not been aware of any of the detail of that before. Long before the time came to go she started to look forward to other opportunities to meet him like this. She found him to be a very exciting companion. It was all so different from those fanatical Nazis and those boring terrified people who worked in the Defence Ministry in Russia and in the Kremlin.

* * *

A couple of weeks later she was called by James Westfield on the Thursday morning. Could she meet the President the next day? He could not see her earlier because he was meeting with some members of his cabinet out at Camp David and he would not be back in Washington until sometime the following morning, Friday

Again, she arrived at the White House at about twelve. She was very pleased with what she was wearing. Low cut white blouse, loose and very light pale blue jacket, tight fitting navy skirt, no stockings and navy loafer shoes.

The gins were being poured as she walked into the room. As soon as the servant had left Roosevelt kissed her on the cheek and took her over to the sofa.

"Angela, let me tell you the basis on which I am going to reply to Churchill. It will not be possible for you to convey the reply to him. Because he put the request through our Ambassador in London, the reply must go that way. What you can tell him, though, is that a favourable reply will be on its way soon through that channel."

He outlined the reply to her and said much work would be needed to turn it into practice. He hoped that she would be involved in that work. Because of all the contracts that would be involved the work would have to be done through the Embassy but as it would be led by the White House he assumed that it would fall within her work remit.

He then went on to tell her of an idea that he was going to implement:

"Angela, I like the idea of your government having someone here who specifically looks after the relationship with my office. I am going to send someone to London who will do much the same sort of job for me there. That person will be leaving for Britain soon. I haven't yet finalised that appointment but I will do so this evening. When it is all in place both governments will have communications processes of their own that are outside the normal diplomatic channels. That will be good for security and will mean that only me and whoever it is I deal with in London has the overall picture. Any contacts between our two governments will be much better for that. It will also mean that I will get unfiltered information.

"But one thing does concern me greatly and it is that your Prime Minister is currently engaged in what seems to me to be a completely unrealistic approach to almost everything. I do not understand why he went out of his way to tolerate Hitler's European invasions; I do not understand why he offered to protect Poland when Britain was clearly not in a position to do any such thing. I do not get any communications from him directly. Everything goes through the diplomatic channels and is therefore filtered by someone or other. I would personally be very surprised if he were to last long as Prime Minister. I do not see how a man who has had a peace policy which has become seriously discredited can possibly now conduct a war policy against the same man with whom he had that peace policy. We seem to have a much simpler view of the world over here.

"That American view is very clear. We are not going to war with anyone unless we are attacked or someone declares war against us. We have and we will continue to make that very obvious.

"I do understand what Winston Churchill has requested. It is not an easy request but it makes sense for Britain to ask it and if we can agree to it it will help Britain. If we do find a way of helping Britain that same solution will apply to anyone else who makes a similar request.

"Because Churchill seems very clear in the requirement he put to Kennedy I will deal only through that channel for the time being. In saying that I am not taking sides about who I should be dealing with. The fact is that the only direct approach from any British minister at the moment is from Churchill."

* * *

It was early in October that Kennedy called Winston to say that he had had a reply from Roosevelt and they needed to discuss it urgently. Churchill went immediately to the residence on Prince Albert Road. He had been invited for lunch. He thought that that was probably a good omen, because it meant that they would have at least a couple of hours together. He had been encouraged by the optimistic report from the agent in Washington.

He arrived soon after twelve and was shown into the same sitting room in which they had met before. Kennedy arrived a couple of minutes later and immediately asked Winston if he would like a drink. The both chose whiskies. The autumn sun was streaming into the room and they sat in one of the large window bays.

Kennedy started the conversation immediately:

"Winston. I have to tell you that your idea has been thoroughly looked into by Washington. In giving you their reply I have been asked to convey a personal message from the President to you. It is actually a message to the whole British government and will be conveyed to them should our talks today lead to anything. Any conversations we have today are still at the informal stage. Whether they proceed to anything else depends entirely what we decide to do when I have given you the President's response to what you asked.

"The President and all his government are adamant that America does not want war and will do nothing that any enemy might use to start a conflict. Public opinion in America is very much focused on domestic issues at this time. The depression hurt badly and there is still a long way to go to recover from that. The President is very popular because of the way that he has handled that issue.

"Something that you and everyone else have to remember about America is that although we speak English we are not a British nation. There have been more direct immigrants from Germany, Russia and Poland than there have from Britain. A higher proportion of the Scandinavian communities have migrated to America than the proportion from any other part of the world. Millions of Italians and Spanish people have come to our country. All of those people are American voters and they all have views about war and whether America should be fighting one. They also all have relatives back in those countries. Members of Congress and the Senate have immense powers and they have to take account of local interests in their states. There is no way that those local interests can be ignored by any President. A fine example of it all is that voters in America of German origin do not want to go to war with Germany under any circumstances.

"The more that you learn about America, the more you will realise that it is a very complex society. On every major decision the President has to steer his way through all those community interests and views. He also has to steer his way through Congress and the Senate. Ultimately they can stop him doing anything.

"You were right to approach me informally with your idea. Any formal approach by the British government would have had to be rejected, because of all those domestic considerations and because of the need to keep out of war. America will defend itself but cannot be seen to lead any war campaign at this time.

"What your informal approach has permitted is a review by Roosevelt not so much about any principles that lie behind what I have just said but about what the detail means. If the discussions remain at the level of principle they will fail.

"Our President is a very clever man and he has devoted a large amount of time into thinking through the implications of the proposition that you put to me. He fully appreciates that you will have wanted an urgent and fully supportive response to your request. But there is no way that that could ever have been possible. Domestic considerations mean that America cannot at this time support the war aims of any other country. He has to say that publicly and he has to show that publicly.

"If you ask him whether he has personal support for one side in a European war rather than another you will get exactly the same reply.

"So you have to ask altogether different questions. I will not go through all the analysis through which he has been but I will illustrate all of it by illustrating just one question.

"Suppose you had asked whether the American government would grant an export licence to a commercial company for the export of some redundant military equipment that was going to be scrapped after it arrived at its destination the answer to the question would almost certainly be yes. It happens all the time.

"If you ask the question about whether America might have some old naval vessels that could possibly be suitable convoy escorts the answer is yes.

"So what we have to do is go down the road of asking some very specific questions the answer to which might be yes. When enough questions have been asked and enough answers have been given to provide the content of a possible contract then all those questions can be asked of the President at the same time. That is the process to get round his dilemma and your requirements. Let us talk more about it over lunch."

* * *

November 29, 1939. I went with Winston to Liverpool today. He wanted to meet the first of the American destroyers to arrive in Britain. He made a speech which included the sentence;

"Driven from the gun to the torpedo and from the torpedo to the mine, U-Boats have now reached the acme of villainy." It certainly reflected his very strong feelings on the subject.

The conversations between Winston and Ambassador Kennedy led directly to Britain leasing fifty V & W class destroyers from an American scrap metal company. They were old ships, having been built towards the end of The Great War. All the ships had to be collected from America by British crews. All the ships had to be re-named. Payment would be made over a fifty year period. They provided much needed convoy escort capacity. The first of them was in service by mid-November and she was the only escort for a convoy from Halifax, Newfoundland to Liverpool that sailed on 19th November. She was named *Vagrant*. They joined up with another escort 200 miles west of Liverpool. Two weeks later three more of those old destroyers joined the Royal Navy. They were called *Valentine, Valkyrie and Value*. Over the following three months another 46 ships joined the fleet from that source. They were all completely worn out within three years. But by then, Britain had developed enough ship building capacity to be able to produce sufficient high quality convoy escorts on its own.

Those old destroyers formed the basis of many deals which were to erode the sovereignty of the British nation.

Angela was involved at every stage of drafting all the agreements.

* * *

November 30th, 1939. Winston was in a very pensive mood today. He started by asking me why I thought Roosevelt had taken so long to respond to his simple request for destroyers. As I had no idea why the President did what he did I told him that he would have to talk to the President about it directly when they first met. Winston then remarked that although he would like to meet him, he thought it very unlikely that he would be able to do so in the near future. He certainly would not be able to go to America and he thought it to be extremely unlikely that Roosevelt would come to Britain while it was at war.

But he went on to say that he suspected that there could be any number of reasons why it should take Roosevelt so many weeks to agree to a scrap yard selling some old ships to Britain. It had eventually proved to be such a simple deal that it could have only taken a few minutes to agree to it.

But what he was really trying to do was develop a set of rational and cohesive arguments as to why America should come to Britain's aid in a big and very public way immediately As we spoke he developed a list of reasons varying from historical ties to ethnic connections. He felt certain that bringing America into the war would be a huge achievement which would be popular with the British public. If he could bring it about he might be seen as the saviour in Britain's hour of need.

I pointed out to him that he was probably biased because he was half American and I tried to point out to him that all the intelligence we were getting from Washington was very clear and it demonstrated that America had no intention of getting into any war unless it was attacked directly. I tried to tell him that he should listen to what was coming from America and deal with the world as it really was. There was no point, I told him, in engaging in wishful thinking. But he was not listening to me. He went on about it being the duty of America to come to the assistance of the most powerful country in the world.

At the end of this entry there was a footnote referring to a discussion Samuel had with Alice in 1959. It read:

July 22nd, 1959. Another very hot day in this fine summer that we are having. Alice came to spend the weekend here. Winston had spoken to her many times during the early days of the war and as he was getting into the real issues in the Admiralty. She told me that she had found him very difficult to manage then. He was always difficult, she had told me, but he was especially difficult whenever he was dealing with Roosevelt. She told me that he had paced up and down in anger in front of her as he fretted about why Roosevelt did whatever he did. She said that he had no option but to believe the briefings he was given but he always found them to be so irrelevant to Britain's real needs. He really could not understand why Roosevelt could not accept his point of view. Alice attributed it to great stubbornness on Winston's part but also to immense determination on his part to get it right for Britain. It wasn't until later in the war that she knew that Winston was not going to win and that is why she then put a lot of effort into getting him to accept realities. It was by no means a battle that she won. But equally she knew that the effect on him of not getting his own way would eventually become very brutal.

* * *

Roosevelt had not needed that month or any other period of time to think through and authorise that deal over the destroyers. It was actually a very simple deal but it had to be disguised. What he really needed time to think through his entire strategy towards Britain.

He decided that he would not consult anyone about it. Certainly not State Department; they were still a vassal of British foreign policy. Neither would he consult the Treasury. He certainly would not consult Henry Morgenthau Jr. who was Treasury Secretary, although he was an old family friend. His thought processes were very inflexible. That would have made it impossible for Roosevelt to talk to him about any long term strategy towards what was a friendly nation, Britain; particularly as that strategy might have to be very threatening.

But by the end of the month that he allowed himself Roosevelt had worked out what he wanted the American end-game to be. He could not work out all the steps on the way because they would have to be led by opportunity. But he did decide that he would use every opportunity presented to him to push all the players closer and closer to the achievement of that end game in which America would be the ultimate winner. Every single request from Britain for more help would be used as an opportunity to push the argument along one extra bit.

The briefing he had got from Kennedy on the state of Britain's finances and its real political objectives in the world were an essential and very useful starting point for Roosevelt's thinking processes. In Kennedy's assessment Britain was all about pretending that it was strong and dreaming about permanent imperial status. Kennedy was not and never had been a friend to Britain. That was why he was in London.

Roosevelt developed a consistent and increasingly strident message that he would pass to the British government through Angela, his private attaché in London and through all the official channels as well. It had become Roosevelt's personal agenda, whatever else were the circumstances were of war in Europe, to destroy the British Empire. The leasing of a few destroyers was just the first step in that process. What delighted Roosevelt about it all was that one of his protagonists was Churchill who was probably the Empire's firmest friend. In Roosevelt's mind it all made for a delicious cocktail of political intrigue at the highest levels.

* * *

The person Roosevelt sent to London as his personal attaché was Sally Monroe. There were several reasons for her selection. The first was that he liked her. The second was that she was very good at secure communications procedures. The third was that her close friend George Patton had been military attaché in London; he would be able both to help her and to enable her to understand the British culture. But above all Sally Monroe was controversial. As the daughter of an imprisoned black civil rights activist she would inevitably be controversial in Britain at that time. Although Britain had an empire in which lived hundreds of millions of non-white people, very few of those people had gone to live in Britain. To have a high-ranking black diplomat in London with a very special job would be an absolutely delicious way of creating tension. Roosevelt would aggravate that tension by passing some of his most secret messages to the British government through Sally. If they wanted to deal with America they would have to deal with her at least part of the time. It was to be an altogether different role from the one Angela was performing in Washington. Sally would be there to taunt Churchill. She would be there to aggravate. She would be there to slow down his demands. She would be there to help Kennedy to impose American supremacy on Britain. Her principal task would to ensure that he, Roosevelt, achieved his political ambitions in respect of Britain.

He did not tell Angela who he would be sending to London. He thought about it, and decided that he probably would tell her at some stage but he would need to know her a lot better before he would do so.

Sally left for London a couple of mornings after she had been given her instructions by Roosevelt. She travelled on a US Air Force plane that was taking diplomatic supplies to the London embassy. The plane was a C54 Skymaster. It would be a long and noisy journey across the Atlantic. It had to stop twice on the way at Gander and Prestwick. Before she left, Roosevelt did send a telegram to Kennedy saying that she would be coming to London. She would have the rank of First Secretary and she would be given personal assignments directly by the White House. She had full diplomatic status and she would have to have a suitable office in the Embassy. She was to be fully integrated into the Embassy team. She was there to keep watch on the British Cabinet.

Soon after she arrived in London she went to the House of Commons to meet Winston as she had been directed to do by Roosevelt. She went in the late morning. To make that feasible Roosevelt had passed one message through Angela to say that he would be contacted in that way. She was asked to send a message to Winston that the contact would be a surprise and the first conversation would be about destroyers. Sally was easily able to get into the central lobby of the House of Commons with her diplomatic papers. She asked the policeman there whether Winston Churchill was available.

Winston was in his office in the Commons that morning. As soon as he got the call from the policeman he came down to the lobby. When he came up to the desk she turned to him and said;

"Mr Churchill, President Roosevelt has asked me to come and talk to you about destroyers."

He looked at her in complete astonishment. So that was what Roosevelt had meant about it being a surprise. Winston had never spoken to a young black girl before even though his first posting as an army officer had been to Africa. That alone told an important story about how the Empire was governed.

* * *

November 27, 1939. Winston told me today that Roosevelt has appointed a personal attaché to work in the American Embassy here. The role of this diplomat appears to be to act as a go-between with Winston and Winston alone. It is a curious role but Winston seems happy with the idea but he told me that he is not happy with the messages he is getting from the President. He said that the messages he was getting were very strongly about American detachment from the issues surrounding the war in Europe. Winston cannot work out why that is and he believes that Roosevelt is entirely wrong. To Winston, American involvement in the war is exactly the right thing for them to do. He regards it as their duty to help protect Britain and its Empire.

* * *

It was around mid December that Max Beaverbrook received a letter from Louise for the first time since she had arrived in Washington. She knew that there was going to be a special plane to London before Christmas and she knew that it was going to carry public mail for the British citizens in Washington. It was not a letter that she could send through the diplomatic mail. She knew she could rely on Sid to get her letter onto that plane. The letter read:

My Darling Max,

I hope this letter reaches you in time for Christmas. If it does, it comes with all my best wishes to you and to your family for a very enjoyable time. I cannot imagine what a Christmas will be like in conditions both of blackout and stern food and fuel rationing, but I am sure you will find a way to make the best of it. Here in Washington we have no such restrictions and all those with whom I am in contact are looking forward to a couple of day's break from all the hard work we have to do.

I live in an attractive and comfortable apartment which is in a quiet tree lined street. The social life here is very good indeed and I have met many new friends. My work is enjoyable and important. It is quite different from my last couple of assignments.

Public opinion here is very sympathetic to Britain's plight but there is overwhelming opposition to any active American military involvement in the war. The public take the view that it is Roosevelt's role to build on his domestic successes and restore America to economic health. Everything else is a distraction to them. Winston's pleas for more American help are reported here but nobody wants to listen. The subject comes up frequently at social events to which I go and all British views are usually contested with the phrase "Why should we?"

I cannot imagine that it will be possible for you to come to Washington at any time while the war is on but if you do come please write to me before you come at PO Box 17981, Washington DC and tell me where you can be contacted. There are many nice places we could visit together.

You are often in my thoughts,

Dearest Love, Louise.

She did get a reply about a month later. In it he said that it was unlikely that he would get any chance to go to Washington. Things were hectic in Britain as his newspaper needed to cover whatever it could about the unfolding war story and its impact on ordinary people in the country. He wrote that Christmas had been enjoyable despite the lack of so many of the usual festive items. He hoped she was still enjoying herself and he finished by saying that he always missed her.

* * *

Apart from the loss of *Royal Oak,* three other large naval ships and the mounting convoy losses the war got off to a quiet start so far as Britain was concerned. There were no land engagements in Europe. There was no enemy aerial activity over Britain and there was no military activity in any part of the Empire.

But every night there was a compulsory blackout throughout Britain. Food rationing started immediately after war began because of fears that the convoys would not be able to deliver the food supplies from the Empire on which Britain depended. At that time almost all of the sugar consumed in Britain came from the Caribbean. Most of the wheat required for the milling of flour came from Canada. Large quantities of beef and lamb came from Australia. Tea and coffee came from sub-tropical colonial countries. Clothes rationing was introduced soon after that, largely because of the difficulties of transporting cotton from the colonies and America. The failings of British farming that led to such colonial dependence were to remain un-corrected both during and for many years after the war.

The deprivations then being suffered by the British people were to get far worse as the war years proceeded. But few people could then imagine how things could possibly get worse than they were in January 1940. The weather then was utterly diabolical throughout Britain. There were intense blizzards followed by severe frosts. That January the Thames froze over in London for the only time in the 20th century. When the thaw came there was severe flooding. Moving about became almost impossible that month. Factories were closed because it was impossible for workers to get to them. Moving supplies around the country was impossible for at least two weeks. In that month another 200,000 tons of shipping were lost in the North Atlantic.

Those early months of the war were called The Phoney War. Apart from the deprivations and the shipping losses nothing seemed to be happening.

* * *

But one thing that was happening was that the views of the British people were changing. They no longer regarded peace as being a realistic option and sooner or later they expected Germany to attack Britain because of its apparent support for Poland. Increasingly it was being thought that Germany might have planned to attack Britain anyway. The consequence of all that was that there were ever more strident demands being made on the government for there to be much more visible action that Britain was preparing to defend itself and then preparing to bring the German menace to an end. There were all the usual calls for a short sharp war. "Give the enemy a bloody nose" was a common rallying cry.

The truth was that few people in Britain had any idea of the sheer military power of Germany at that time. The assumption was widely made that Austria, Poland and Czechoslovakia were weak countries militarily and that any country would be able to beat them. One of the most frequent assertions made was that British Naval strength would be able to bring down Germany at any time. Why was it not being used? But all the while these arguments were going on political pressure was mounting on the government. The government in turn was offering no more action other than what it had already authorised, which was a major expansion both in fighter aircraft and in convoy escorts.

It all came to a head in May. It became obvious that Chamberlain no longer commanded the support of his own party, let alone the support of the government as a whole. In those days it fell to the King to appoint a successor. His own choice was Lord Halifax, the Foreign Secretary, and he consulted very narrowly about whether such an appointment would be possible. Halifax was very much Chamberlain's choice and the choice of senior Tories. But over the last few months Churchill had been becoming ever more strident in his demands for large scale preparations so that the enemy could be beaten. At the same time he was managing the only active war front that Britain had at that time, the North Atlantic convoy routes. The news from there was getting worse and worse. It did not seem to matter how many convoy escorts were commissioned; more and more U-Boats were able to travel much farther west and loiter there for far longer periods of time. What Churchill really wanted then was for the American navy to take over escort duties halfway across the Atlantic. Canada was helping but it had very few suitable escorts. All Churchill's requests were refused by Roosevelt, and each refusal was explained to Angela. Each time Churchill met with Sally Monroe he explained his view to her. Each time it made no difference. America was not at war so could not risk its ships in war zones and could not be seen to be putting its peoples at risk in any military engagements.

Eventually the political pressure in Britain became so great that the King finally had to act. As Halifax was not acceptable to the Labour members of the governing coalition the only choice he could make was Churchill. It was well known at the time that the King, though, was definitely not in favour of Churchill. Privately he hoped that he would fail. But Winston became Prime Minister on 10th May, 1940, the day that Germany launched its invasion of France.

He immediately undertook some small changes in the Cabinet and redistributed the responsibilities of some members of the government. He, personally, took charge of the entire war effort and delegated domestic and colonial matters to Clement Attlee, the Deputy Prime Minister. Eden re-joined the Cabinet as Foreign Secretary and Beaverbrook joined the Cabinet as Minister of Aircraft Production. Churchill not only wanted more fighters, he wanted large numbers of powerful bombers so that he could take the fight to the enemy's homeland.

* * *

May 10, 1940. When Winston left Buckingham Palace after his audience with the King he drove straight to Downing Street. Within minutes of his getting there the Cabinet Secretary phoned me and instructed that I should go there as soon as possible. When I went into the Cabinet Room it was obvious that Winston was absolutely thrilled to have got the most difficult post of them all. When I had sat down he said to me:

"Samuel, I have now got the job of running this entire war. It would be nice to have a party to celebrate it but that will not be possible given the situation in France. I want you to be my

military intelligence adviser here. So that you have seniority over all the other intelligence chiefs I will arrange for you to be promoted. . Excellent intelligence and being able to break into all the enemy's codes will be vital parts of our success. That place you found at Bletchley Park must be expanded as rapidly as possible. Cost is immaterial. All I want are results. So a task for you is to get that organised. You must appoint the very best people to manage it all.

"I will also need a daily briefing from you about any new key intelligence. Our experience is that moist of the attacks on the convoys take place at night so I will be up then to ensure that I know what damage is being inflicted on us. Every ship lost will be a wound in my soul. Damn those bloody people for letting our country get into this mess. You will have to change your life so that you can be with me in the bunkers every night. I am sure that it will be a tough time for us all.

"But far more important than any of that is what is happening in France today. I am getting confused messages from our commanders. What seems to be clear is that they are being driven back by overwhelming German force. So get in touch with them personally if you can and find out what is really going on. Report back to me at least every hour. I shall be calling the service chiefs to a meeting in about an hour from now. We have to work out a plan to help our people in France. I shall want you there. In the meantime I am going to send another message to Roosevelt. He has simply got to help us now".

* * *

It was two hours later that Angela was contacted by Sid. He went to her apartment to give her the message from Winston. It was still early in the morning in Washington. He said to her:

"Ma'am, The Prime Minister has sent you an urgent message. He requires immediate action. I am sure when you read it you will agree. I will be in the car outside to take you to the White House."

Angela read the message that she had to take to Roosevelt. It read:

"I am sure that you will have heard that our forces in France are now under attack from large German armies. I have no idea how long we will be able to resist them but if the German force becomes overwhelming my concern will be for the safety of our people and that will mean that we may have to evacuate our forces to Britain. Britain itself might then come under direct attack.

This is a new crisis for us and it opens a new and very dangerous phase in this war. I have no doubt that the British Empire will prevail over Germany in the end, but equally I am in no doubt that we are going to need help. I have every reason to believe that America will stand behind its long trusted friend and provide that help in our hour of need. That hour of need is now.

I look forward to your commitment that we will immediately see that support."

She rang James Westfield and asked for an immediate meeting with the President. She was asked to come over straight away and was told that the President would give her breakfast. James told her that FDR had thought it likely that she would need to meet him at short notice that morning.

Roosevelt was, as always, not in any sort of hurry. He was in his study when she arrived and the table had been laid for breakfast for the two of them. After her pressured times in Germany and Moscow she had come to enjoy his relaxed style of life and she knew that whatever the outcome of their meeting she would enjoy being with him.

He would not allow her to talk serious business until after they had finished breakfast. As it was being cleared away he said to her:

"Angela, I know what Germany has done to attack your forces in France and I assume that you have come to me with another demand about that from Winston. I will hear from you what he has to say. Do not give me a piece of paper but read to me what he has written. He has a wonderful way with words and I am sure that he will not have understated his case this time. So please tell me what he has to say."

"Mr. President, Britain is my country and it is bleeding right now. Winston Churchill is the leader of the government there and there cannot be anyone who has a greater passion for Britain than he does. In reading to you what he has written I will try my best to convey the emotion and passion of the British people at this time.

"What he has written is a cry from the heart of every Briton for help now."

She read the letter and emphasised that the hour of need was now. When she had finished she looked directly at him as she had done so many times now and said:

"Mr. President, there is no Briton who does not wish passionately that America was already helping Britain in every possible way. There is no Briton who does not believe that Winston is the best possible man to ensure that that help is received from America. A tear will be shed by every Briton tonight if you cannot intervene directly in this terrible war. The deprivations and hardships are affecting everyone and they will surely get worse. If you offer the hand of friendship now you will find eternal friends over there. I would dearly wish that I can reply to Winston that you will honour his request."

FDR thought for 10 minutes or so before he gave his answer;

"Angela, I would be grateful if you could send a message to Winston on precisely the lines that I am going to outline to you now. It is not a reply that he will like. So I will explain it to you more fully. He has already been told by Ambassador Kennedy why America cannot support Britain in any military sense at this time. He simply has to respect that situation.

"It is the widely held view of Americans that we paid a huge price in the Great War, and we got no return for that. We came in at the end of the war, fought hard, many of our people were killed and we got involved in what has turned out to be a disastrous peace process. We have more Germans than British ethnics in this country and they are appalled at any idea that we might go to war against their families. We have millions of people of Polish origin in this country and they want their country to be liberated. They don't tell us how we can do that but they are determined that that liberation will not be the cause of the deaths of their relatives. We have millions of Italians over here and they make very clear their views that there should be no violence against their relatives.

"America is not a sibling of Britain. It is a completely free standing and independent country. It was created by people who wanted democracy and wanted to get away from the old values in Europe. Most Americans see Europe as the past.

"We have a Presidential election in America this November. Although I have already been President for two terms my party wants me to stand again in view of the crises around the world. They want to see stability in America at this time. They also want to see the continuation of the domestic programmes that I initiated and which have been so successful. If any candidate at those elections suggested that we should go to war in Europe they would surely fail to win any significant number of votes. It is as certain as that.

"If I was to seek re-election on the basis that I wanted America to go to war to help Britain and for no other reason I would certainly lose. There is no one in this country that will tell you otherwise.

"If Churchill wants American support now I can assure you that it will be rejected by the American electorate later this year. On that basis there is nothing that I can do to provide what seems to be a request that America should go to war with Germany now. That is simply not possible.

"If Churchill wants an extension of the Lend/Lease programmes that is always possible. It depends on the need and the availability of equipment. Aircraft, guns, vehicles, ammunition are all possibilities. But people are not. Nor is any direct investment in Britain. But we cannot commit our forces at this time. It does not matter how many times he asks me. It does not matter how many speeches he makes in Britain. It does not matter what the expectations of the British people are. The answer will always be the same. The situation will only change if America itself is threatened. But we see no likelihood of that at this time.

"So that is what you have got to tell him. I know it is a tough message. We have an election in this country in November. Sure, I understand what Churchill wants but he is not going to get it from me unless and until America is attacked. I have to say that I see no likelihood of that happening."

Angela knew that there was no way that such a reply would ever be accepted by Churchill. From what she knew about him she thought it unlikely that he would even listen to such a reply. All he wanted was an unconditional yes. But she would pass on anything FDR had said to her.

* * *

It was on the evening of May 10th, and as the British divisions in France were already being forced back towards the coast that Churchill called Eden to an urgent meeting. It was to impart instructions about an issue over which he had thought for several months and which he was determined to implement immediately if he became Prime Minister. Chamberlain's obsession with trying to achieve an unreal peace would have made it very difficult for him to implement even if he had thought it to be a good idea.

But Churchill had no illusions about the prospects for peace in the short term. There were none. He knew that peace could only come now if Germany was well and truly beaten as a result of war. His few months in government since the invasion of Poland had taught him that Britain was woefully inadequately prepared for almost any military offensives at that time. Whatever he was going to have to say in public in order to boost public morale and give a confident message to the enemy would have to be a smokescreen until such time as Britain had built up the resources to defeat Germany.

Never in his lifetime would he learn the extent to which Hitler had considered a wide range of options about the expansion of Germany. Nor would he ever see the detailed papers that pointed to the fact that Hitler's worst fear was of a strong alliance between Britain and Russia. Churchill can never have known the part that that fear played in Hitler's eventual decision to invade Russia.

If Churchill had known that on May 10th, 1940 he might have made a different decision. That can only be the subject of speculation. He might have chosen to start a diplomatic initiative to create an alliance with Russia then. But he did not. He took the Molotov-Ribbentrop pact at face value and took account of the intelligence coming out of Russia that Russia then was only concerned with domestic issues. He had no reliable information on the size of Russia's armed forces nor did he have any information on Russia's industrial capabilities.

In particular he did not know that the information coming from Russia was being filtered by communist agents like George Ponsonby who had senior positions in the Foreign Office.

But what he chose to do was what he had planned to do and to him it was the only option. Britain could not win a war against Germany on its own, so it had to have a strong and willing ally. To him the only one available was the United States. It was America which had made the difference in the later stages of the Great War. He was sure that they would be able to do so again. It did not matter that he was getting messages from Roosevelt that offered no support for his position at all. He therefore said to Eden;

"Anthony. It is my assessment that the only nation capable of leading the fight against Germany is Britain. But we have no prospect of beating Germany at this time. Their armies are so much vastly bigger than ours that we could not succeed. But we have to build up our capability to defeat them. That, I believe, we can only do with the help of America. Roosevelt is very reluctant to give us much help at this time. It must therefore be your top priority to do whatever is necessary to eliminate any American objections to active support for us in our quest to defeat Germany. We will, of course, have the support of the entire Empire throughout this war and we will find other allies as well. I very much hope that France will support us strongly at all times. But the highest objective must always be America. All your people in Washington must stop being kind the Americans, they must start pressing them into active support for us."

Eden knew that he was being asked to do was unreal at that time but he said he would direct the Ambassador to stiffen up all approaches to the US Government.

* * *

On May 11th Eden had his first private meeting with George Ponsonby since he had been re-appointed Foreign Secretary. It was a private dinner at his house in London. The two of them agreed soon after the war started that it would be impossible for them to meet unless and until they could do so in an official capacity. Ponsonby could not take any risks that he might be seen meeting with a senior focal point of opposition to the government's policies. His own security might be severely prejudiced if he were seen to be doing so.

It was George Ponsonby who had requested the meeting. When he rang Eden in his office within the Foreign Office building he had said that he needed to tell him something very important.

Eden had been extremely busy all day catching up with all the significant things that were happening in the world of diplomacy. He was particularly concerned about relations with America. The Ambassador there still had warm relations with all the senior people in State Department but he was concerned that the government overall was not more friendly to Britain. He had hoped that America would have been prepared to be more open about support for Britain. It was clearly something that Eden was going to have to address. The instructions he had had from Winston the previous evening made the whole situation both more urgent and more difficult. He found it impossible to imagine what the way forward might be.

His other problem was France, where the government did not seem to be very staunch in its support for strong opposition to Hitler. Hitler must know that too. It made for a very unstable relationship between Britain and France. It also made for a very uncertain future for the two divisions of British troops in Eastern France. It was a matter that was going to have to be addressed urgently. He was not even sure whether France had any stomach for a vigorous defence of its entire country or even any part of the country against German aggression. The next few days would tell. It probably all depended on the rate of any German advance into France. He was going to spend all of Saturday with Churchill. They could debate the issue then and try and find some way forward.

They started by reviewing the information that Guy Burgess was getting from Moscow. Russia was then very much into introspection. Stalin believed that the Molotov-Ribbentrop pact had ensured that there would be no threat from Germany. All Russian effort was on the second reform plan. When that had been achieved Russia would be able to look at some wider picture of events in the world. Despite the importance of the plan, militarism was still an important part of Russian life. There was some build-up in the armed forces, particularly the army, but the main purpose of that was to provide a force to control the civilian population if ever the need arose.

Neither of them had any idea at that time that Burgess was providing Russia with much higher grade information about Britain and its weakened state. It was information that Stalin was never to forget.

Then Ponsonby got on with the issue that he really wanted to talk about:

"You will doubtless recall exactly what you said to me when you asked me to set up that secret diplomatic intelligence unit. Well it did provide us with some very important information from within both Germany and Russia. Since then we have used it to gain some new insights into Japan, France and Italy. Ministers have been fed the key parts of it as part of the normal briefings. Halifax was not told about the unit nor where some of the information he was given had come from. That was because I did not want there to be any change in the status of the unit. If there had been, one of our operatives, in particular, would have been seriously compromised.

"We have been able to recruit an American with very close access to Roosevelt to be our informant in the White House. He goes by the code name of Bradman. The Ambassador in Washington knows about the access. But he does not know about the information that is being gained nor does he know in detail how it is being gained. We have every reason to believe that the information is of the highest quality, some of it coming directly from private meetings with Roosevelt himself.

"The message that we are getting from our operative is not good news for Britain. What it shows is that Roosevelt intends to be a much stronger participant in the foreign policy field. The independence of State Department is going to weaken. In the meantime the President is determined that Britain should respect the extreme reluctance of both the American government and the American people to get drawn into a war. Practical help such as the provision of some more old ships will always be considered in order to provide help to a friend, but beyond that everything becomes very difficult.

"I can brief our operative to say whatever we like to Roosevelt and I believe that under all circumstances we must maintain that link because it is giving us a different perspective from that provided by the Embassy. Their information is much softer, but this might just be because we have such good links with them.

"What we must do this evening is decide how we are going to handle it all in the future."

Eden had thought many times about the consequences of there being a secret communications channel right to the top of the White House. Getting that access had been one of the objectives he had originally given to Ponsonby. no two secret channels, the other one being direct to Churchill. He had known for a long time what he would decide as and when he might be Foreign Secretary again.

"George, Thank you for telling me all that. What you must do as soon as possible and certainly within the next twenty four hours is redirect all communications with that operative to me. No one else must be able to see a single word that comes from or goes to that source. If anyone else does get into that communications chain it will be the subject of immediate dismissal and a certain trial and sentence."

Ponsonby agreed to do that. It meant that he would no longer see any of the material from Washington. In his mind anyway what he was receiving from Moscow was much more rewarding and his personal relationship with Guy Burgess was getting very much stronger. By not seeing the Washington communications his position would no longer be compromised, particularly as he had passed all the information there was to know about Lend/Lease to Guy Burgess who in turn had passed it to Molotov. That information was to prove a useful negotiating lever for Stalin to use in his negotiations with Roosevelt in later years.

* * *

Immediately Angela read in a diplomatic telegram about the government changes in Britain she wrote again to Max:

My Darling Max,

Very many congratulations on your new appointment. I am sure that it is well deserved and that you will do well at it. It sounds like a very important appointment at this time.

It also sounds to me quite possible that such a job might bring you to Washington. If it does at any time it will be easy enough for me to find because I have a friend who works in the British Embassy here and he will know if you are visiting from London. If you do come it would be nice to go away for a couple of days to some quiet retreat and enjoy ourselves.

Dearest Love, Louise

* * *

The plan for Germany to invade Holland, Belgium, Luxembourg and France was prepared by von Manstein and Guderian. Manstein had devised the plan, Guderian was to be the principal general with responsibility to carry it out. They had fought hard and long for it to be accepted by Hitler as **the** plan under which those countries would be overrun quickly.

More senior generals did not like it, believing that it contained unacceptable risks for Germany even though the German forces available for it massively overwhelmed anything that Britain and France could throw against them. As a consequence, just before the plan was due to be implemented Hitler moved von Manstein from his command in the west so that he could be put in charge of an infantry corps in East Prussia. Hitler had fought in that area of France during the Great War and he was very concerned that there might be some repeat of the trench warfare. But above all he was certain that his generalship would eliminate any risks associated with the invasion plans.

On the morning of May 10th when the blitzkrieg attack was launched Germany had 135 divisions massed along its borders with those countries. Britain had a mere 2 divisions in France. The fact that the German campaign so nearly failed was entirely due to Hitler's wish to control the battlefield and nothing to do with the plan. All the decisions made by Hitler had the effect of slowing down the German advances towards the French channel ports. Each time Hitler slowed down something there was a greater chance of escape from France by the British forces.

On the evening of May 9th, just a few hours before the attack against France was launched Guderian went to the top of a steep hill at the very western end of the Ardennes. From it he could see the still peaceful forest that rolled all the way westwards to the French frontier. In the morning he would be commanding the 19th Panzer corps as it skirted round the northern edge of the French defences called the Maginot line. He would then lead them due west until they reached Abbeville. Then they would turn north towards Calais and the French ports. There they would destroy the British Expeditionary forces. But the whole plan depended on speed.

Hitler was not only not keen on speed; he was terrified that Germany might have to face a re-run of the Flanders battles of the First World War. It was an odd decision considering that it was speed that had enabled Germany to overrun Poland so quickly. But Hitler was adamant. He was determined that Germany should not get bogged down into some kind of fixed battle. Therefore he ordered that some of Guderian's troops be placed into reserve on May 19th. It was that order that slowed down the whole campaign and enabled the bulk of the British troops to be evacuated across the channel from Dunkirk. Fierce fighting by the RAF had pinned down the German armies until 26th May, by when almost all the British land forces had been able to escape.

Hitler's timidity in relation to the battlefield had allowed the British armies to escape. Equally German aggression against France had made any kind of peace with Britain impossible at that time.

But what Hitler had gained by mid June was unlimited access to the French Atlantic ports. That would solve the problem of getting U-Boats onto their operational stations much more quickly. It would also mean that they could spend far more time at sea. The North Atlantic convoy war was about to get very much more tough, very quickly.

* * *

May 13, 1940. Ever since I was appointed to advise Winston on military intelligence matters I have given him a frank account of the information available to me. As he was so busy with naval matters most of the material I gave him was about naval issues. But I also kept him abreast of Army and RAF key material as well. This included information about the deployment of the German armies. Included in my briefings to him was information about the huge build-up of German forces in the last couple of months. Each time I had briefed him he had thanked me for the information. I was therefore somewhat stunned by a meeting he called this morning. He wanted to give both Eden and Ronnie Harford a blasting for their failure to give him warning of the German advance into France. Ronnie gave as good as he got.

* * *

The German advance into France was the first crisis with which Churchill had to deal as Prime Minister. An attack by Germany into France had been expected but nothing on that scale had been imagined or contemplated. Churchill was both alarmed and appalled by what had happened. But equally he and all the British high command were delighted at the way that the RAF had been able to contain the German forces, albeit for only a few days, and by the sheer luck that they had encountered in getting the British forces off the beaches at Dunkirk.

It was on the third morning after the German attack had started that Churchill called in Anthony Eden and Ronnie Harford, the Head of Military Intelligence. Overnight he had felt that if Britain had better intelligence about the German armies it would have been better prepared to deal with the onslaught. He was determined to deal with that issue and prevent any repetition.

He could not blame Eden because he had only just re-appointed him as Foreign Secretary but he was determined to take it out on Harford and on Eden's department.

Winston started the meeting by saying to Ronnie:

"Our forces are being overwhelmed in France. There was no warning that anything on this scale might happen. So why did we not get any warning from you? After all it is your job to provide the government with intelligence information of the highest quality."

Harford replied:

"Prime Minister we did have accurate information about the size of the German forces and I believe that we had accurate information about their locations. I am sure that Samuel will have given you the main details regularly over recent months. The fact that we had such information stemmed from decisions made by Anthony Eden when he was Foreign Secretary back in 1936. The size of the German forces and their locations have been tracked since then. I have regularly advised your predecessors of exactly what was happening. When Eden was previously Foreign Secretary he and I used to discuss the whole issue regularly.

"We started an intensive investigation into what was happening to the German armed forces late in 1936. We were lucky enough to get some superb information then about exactly what was going on. I personally briefed Mr. Baldwin on the matter but he instructed me to cease and desist from any further investigation into the matter. He said that he did not believe my reports and poured ridicule that any nation could have as many troops as Germany was alleged to have.

"He instructed me not to discuss the matter with any other government minister but I did continue to discuss the matter with Anthony Eden. Jointly we set in place some ways to keep our information up to date. Those measures remain in place today and they give us accurate information.

"When Mr Chamberlain was appointed Prime Minister I requested a meeting with him to explain my anxieties as to what was happening in Germany. He agreed to meet with me and he listened to what I had to say. But it was not a good meeting and he ended it by saying that Britain was not interested in knowing about the state of the armed forces in Germany. All that mattered was finding a formula for peace. He went on to instruct me not to meet with him again on the issue and not to discuss the matter with anyone else. He instructed me to disband any surveillance of German forces.

"I do not normally disobey orders but on that occasion I did. I did not take any steps to disband anything. I went on receiving high quality information which I passed on to the highest levels in our forces. I spoke with the commanders in the Navy, Army and RAF regularly about it all and they told me that they, too, had been instructed that it was irrelevant to Britain's interests.

"After Chamberlain had given me those instructions I nevertheless asked to see him on two subsequent occasions. The first was about a week before the invasion of Poland. I warned him that such an event was likely. He categorically refuted that and said that his agreement with Hitler was strong enough to prevent any such occurrence.

"The second occasion was only last week when I warned about the imminence of a German invasion of France. He rejected that as being a highly unlikely event.

"I do not accept and will not accept that military intelligence failed in any way. I am not responsible for the development of political policies but I am accountable to those who are. I personally believe that much more effort is going to have to be put into military intelligence but there will be no point in that unless the politicians, including yourself are prepared to listen."

Eden explained in greater detail than he had ever done before what he had authorised when he was previously Foreign Secretary. Churchill claimed that he had not heard any of it before from either of them. He was appalled that successive Prime Ministers had effectively suppressed accurate information about the state of German war preparations. Although he agreed that he had had regular briefs since he had been at the Admiralty he claimed to have no idea that Germany had amassed forces on such a huge scale. What appalled him even more was that it was known about but never actioned in Britain. Churchill asked them whether there was anything more that he ought to know. It was Ronnie Harford who spoke:

"Yes, there is. It has long been rumoured that Hitler is planning an invasion of Britain. All the information available to us suggests that he is planning to do that next June, that is June 1941. The information that we have about it just now is that it will be a simultaneous series of landings by troops and tanks on beaches in several parts of Southern Britain, particularly Kent, Sussex and Dorset. That will be preceded by a massive bombing raid on London and the landing of parachute troops at various sites around London. New information is coming in all the time but we cannot be certain about it yet. The plans keep changing and there is some indication that an invasion of Britain is only one of the options available to Germany for next year.

"Although I did not personally speak to Chamberlain about this I know that he was given the information. He said that it would never happen because of the agreement that he had with Hitler."

* * *

May 13, 1940 (contd). After they had gone Winston told me that he felt angry at the way Britain had become so dreadfully exposed to the risks of the destruction of our armed forces, our merchant marine and to invasion. Although he had vented his anger on Eden and Harford he was nevertheless in a depressed mood. He said to me "Samuel, the Germans have 135 divisions advancing through France and we have 2 that are retreating to the Channel ports. How can the greatest nation on Earth ever have got into such a situation?"

I could only remind him that the dismemberment of our armed forces had been brought about by government which believed it had to offer peace to the nation. I told him that I thought they had achieved a very shallow peace with no security. We could not continue the conversation as he had to chair a meeting of the War Cabinet. I cannot imagine that it can have been a happy meeting.

* * *

May 22, 1940. Winston often goes to the Commons in the early afternoon. Today was no exception. I do not know what happened there but he came back in the foulest mood.

That morning Winston had received a message that Sally wanted to meet with him urgently. She had a message for him from Roosevelt. Winston did not wish to be seen in public with her so he arranged to have access to a committee room for the meeting. All the committee rooms have more than one entrance. That meant that he could go to the room without being seen with her and without having to use the same door.

If he had been seen with her his explosive anger would have interested anyone. He was not prepared to run that risk.

It was what Sally had to say to him that angered him more even than talking to her, a black girl, at all.

"Mr. Prime Minister, President Roosevelt has asked me to talk to you urgently. The message he wants me to pass on to you is very important and he hopes that you will take notice of it. Indeed, he has asked me to tell you that if you do not take notice of it the future terms and conditions about any co-operation between Britain and America in this war will get tougher. What he wants you to do is to stop making any demands on America. He cannot deliver what you want and he is getting very put off by what he sees as endless demands by Britain. As the American people know, he is a man of his word. He just wants you to accept that.

"But he does regard it as both inevitable and desirable that you should meet eventually but it is his assessment that such a meeting is unlikely to take place this year. He judges the situation in Europe at this time to be too critical for there to be any possibility of you travelling to America during the next few months. He is certain that you will meet and when you do the future shape of relations between the two countries will become clear. But he does want me to make it clear to you that future relations do depend on your toning down your demands on him.

"I know that this is a tough message for you to accept and the President knows that better than anyone else. But as he has instructed me even in politics reality overcomes everything else sooner or later. He just wants you to accept that reality."

Winston then stormed out of the room, rang Alice and said that he had to meet with her that day.

* * *

September 9, 1963. I met with Alice for lunch today. We went to a new restaurant down by the river near Blackfriars Bridge. It was a lovely day and we were able to sit outside. It is a very relaxing place and should do well. Alice told me about that day in 1940 when Winston had been given that roasting by the black girl that Roosevelt had sent to London. Alice said it was a day that she would always remember because she had never seen Winston in such a foul temper before, indeed it was the only time she had ever seen him like that.

Winston had arrived at her house within half an hour of his meeting with Sally. He had stormed about cursing Roosevelt and his damned arrogance, as he called it. He also cursed Roosevelt for sending the black girl to London. If he had to send anyone, why not send a proper diplomat? He even questioned how it was possible for Roosevelt to know such people.

Alice said to me; "Rational speech with him that day was impossible until he had calmed down. The only way I could do that quickly was to give him a large brandy. After about half an hour he did sit down but he then said he was hungry. Bacon sandwiches were always his favourite snack and I always had the ingredients for them. After a couple of those and another large brandy he started to talk in a more rational way. What he said to me was:

"Alice, the situation we face in these islands is one of the gravest despair. We know of German plans for an invasion next year. We know the strength of the German forces. We know that there is no way that we can match that armoured might. From everything that I see Germany now has the potential to bring the British nation to an end and the potential to destroy our empire. Why cannot Roosevelt see that? Why cannot he see that what we have created must be preserved? Why should the people of Britain suffer so much just because he will not give us more help? How else can I win the war and return Britain to a normal state of life? How else can Britain retain its domination of the world?"

"I told him that there was no point in asking questions to which there was no answer. I certainly could not answer any of them. I understood why he asked them and I knew from long experience that he was always asking himself questions like that. But it all seemed so pointless.

"We had to go back to exactly the same issue that I had discussed with him in his wilderness years. It was the same issue that had eventually brought him back to power. It was that he had to find the problem to which he was the solution. He had to offer the British public a solution, not just an endless series of unanswerable questions. It was then that I asked him who he thought he was fighting. His answer then was that he seemed to be fighting Roosevelt. He said he ought to have an easy relationship with him but it certainly didn't seem like that.

"I had to tell him that any idea of fighting Roosevelt was nonsense. America was not at war with Britain and it probably never would be. So we went over the matter of who the real enemy was and how that enemy could be fought. Britain only had one significant enemy in the world at that time and that was Germany. Italy was allied with Germany but constituted far less of a threat. Of course he accepted that Germany was the enemy but he still felt that he had to fight Roosevelt in order to get more American involvement in the war.

"The argument raged between us for a couple of hours before he started to think. I managed to get him to concentrate his thought on a single enemy, Germany and then on to Britain being the sole country that could defy Germany. I think that he had been thinking that way for sometime but with all the other problems with which he had to deal his thoughts had not properly crystallised before.

"By the late afternoon he had decided to position himself as the sole defender of freedom in Europe and as the sole leader who would defeat Hitler. He had decided that would be the way he would lead Britain in the months and years to come.

"Before he left me that afternoon he had started to work out how he could convince the British public that that was the right course of action. What we had done was identify the right problem, which was about defiance of Germany. In doing so we had identified him as the British bulldog defying the German might. It was an image that he liked. It was then that he started to work out those fine speeches of defiance that he would make to the Commons and the country. All that stuff about fighting them in the air and on the beaches was born in my house that afternoon.

"But we did go back to talking about Roosevelt again. He accepted from me that he had no real influence on the man but that it was probable that at some stage America would enter the war. He agreed that he would keep all his options open with respect to America. As he left he told me that that would include bullying Sally from time to time. He thought he would enjoy that."

As I sat on the train home this afternoon I thought about that turbulent afternoon she must have had with Winston that day. It was clearly a turning point in his role as Prime Minister and in the way that he led the country. It certainly led to his gaining an immense reputation as an inspirational war leader. What he said to the nation as a result of those discussions inspired millions to renewed and very vigorous efforts in the defence of their homes. I remembered my own reaction at the time. It was that Winston had become great. It was when I first heard that speech of defiance that I knew that we would win the war. I did not know how but I knew that we would.

* * *

As Winston was driven back to Whitehall after his afternoon with Alice he knew that she was right about how he should position himself with the country and Parliament. He knew that he had to be the symbolic leader of a defiant Britain. That would be how he would position himself for the remainder of the war, however long it lasted.

But he knew, perhaps better than any other person on earth, just how inadequately prepared Britain was to win that war and just how vulnerable it was to a large scale German invasion. That was why, whatever the difficulties, he had to get American support that went far beyond anything they had offered to date. To try and achieve that he decided that he would not take heed of Alice's advice. He would be the usual headstrong Winston. He would bully Sally and Bradman to ensure that they got his message across to Roosevelt and he would barrage Roosevelt with signals about Britain's peril and about help in the country's hour of need.

But above all else he resolved that he would never give any indication to the British people just how desperate Britain's situation was.

* * *

September 14, 1953. I meet up regularly with Ronnie Harford, usually for weekends together. When he comes here we stroll through the countryside. When I visit him we play golf. He has retired to Sandwich in Kent where he has bought a house in the middle of the town. He has become a member of Royal St. George's Golf Club. The course there is reputed to be one of the best in the country. It is very attractive, set, as it is down close to the shores of Sandwich Bay. It has very fine views but it always seems to be windy. We usually play a couple of rounds over the weekend. It is a very demanding course, well above my usual standard, but it makes for two very good days out.

We often talk about old times and the numerous crises through which we went together during the war. This last weekend our talk was dominated by the planned invasion of Britain by Germany. At the time we were getting large amounts of what we believed to be high grade intelligence from our spies, German informers and radio intercepts. Almost all of this information was about the German armies. There was virtually nothing about what was happening within the Luftwaffe.

Always when we talk about those events we speculate on what will be found in German archives if they are ever released for historical research. They are currently in Russian hands so we might never see them, but we do know from previous wars that German archives are of very high quality. If they can ever be found they will certainly be very interesting.

At the time of the planned invasion we had to make decisions about the value of the information that we received. One decision we did make was to assume that there was a 40% risk that the information might be false. It was a decision that proved to be invaluable when we came to planning our own invasion of Europe, then expected in 1943. But when Ronnie and I were talking at the weekend we were only concerned with knowing what the German archives might contain and how much of what we knew back in 1940 and early 1941 was accurate.

* * *

I was first able to get access to the German archives covering the early war years in 1993. I was able to see some papers which had not even been looked at by other researchers. I was fascinated by those that covered the invasion of Britain that had been considered by Hitler for 1941. Samuel's diaries detailed a long series of meeting that considered the intelligence that was coming from British agents and informers throughout the planning period for this invasion. It was uncanny to read in the German documents that every major decision made by Hitler or any of his military staff about this planned invasion was communicated directly to senior British people within 24 hours. The German documents make it clear exactly when each decision was made. Samuel's diaries record when he received the information.

One of the fascinating aspects of the German records was that they included reports from von Manstein and Guderian following their visit to Britain in 1937. In those records there is a detailed account of what they saw and what they discussed. There is a long account of their meeting with Churchill and their assessment that he would not fight German aggression against other countries. But crucially their reports were very clear in their assessments that Britain did not have the capability to deter any large scale invasion.

After the German invasion of France those records had been updated. Both generals had been asked by Hitler for their current views on the capabilities of the British. They both wrote that in the planning for the invasion of France they had underestimated the capabilities of the RAF but they fundamentally believed that the British Army had no power to resist a much superior German force.

Samuel's diaries also record that Britain was virtually powerless to do anything about an invasion on the scale being planned by Hitler. At least 100 divisions would have been launched against Britain within the first month. The naval invasion would have been preceded by air raids employing at least 3,000 aircraft. The scale of it all was truly enormous.

Samuel records that Britain might have been able to provide trained manpower for around 15 divisions in that time scale but they would have been without tanks and any sort of effective transport vehicles. Perhaps that all explains Winston's desperate attempts to get the Americans involved.

The German archives did reveal that the Luftwaffe had been instructed by Hitler early in 1940 to plan for bombing raids on some British cities which were to be scheduled for the summer and autumn of that year. Of particular interest in the records was those entries that dealt with Hitler's reactions to events as they unfolded in the bombing campaign. As Ronnie and Samuel had expected there was evidence that the Luftwaffe was deliberately not using radio communications in order to fool Britain.

* * *

May 29, 1940. Winston has been in a foul mood all morning. For days I have been telling him that Germany will very quickly be able to base its U-Boats in North West France at ports like Lorient. This will be mean that they do not have to make the long transit passage between Germany and the open Atlantic. It will make things very much more difficult for our shipping. The U-Boats will be at sea for much longer periods of the year. I know that he has been fretting about the problem but there is nothing he can do in the short term.

So when he came in this morning he said to me:

"Samuel, So far this year U-Boats have sunk 150 of our ships. Our merchant fleet is a million tons smaller than it was this time last year. We cannot build ships fast enough to cope with the attrition rate. It is no comfort to me that you have been telling me that things are going to get far worse.

"But what you have also been telling me is about the large numbers of German aircraft that are now based very close to our shores. The other day when Ronnie Harford was here he was talking about a possible German invasion next year. Supposing they come this year? What I want you to do is to step up the intelligence gathering.

"This afternoon there is a War cabinet meeting and we are going to authorise a big increase in fighter aircraft production. Max Beaverbrook is good at organising programmes like that. Apparently they can build Hurricanes and Spitfires in just a few days. I feel certain that we are going to need as many as they can produce. I just wish that we could do something about getting more convoy escorts quickly. I think I will have to get Max working on that as well."

* * *

It was two weeks later that she got a letter from Max. It read:

"My Darling Louise,

"Winston has given me a new responsibility. I am now to deal with ship production as well as aircraft production. Britain's needs are such that we must find more of everything very quickly. The production rate of fighter aircraft is being increased immediately. No one knows whether there is an imminent threat to our country or not. But what is certain is that there are very large numbers of German aircraft based within striking distance of us.

Losses of ships at sea have far outstripped our capacity to build more. As a consequence the hardships in Britain are going to get much worse. Rationing is being tightened. The requirement for new ships is so great that I might have to come to America to see what I can find there. It will not be in the next three months or so because there is so much to do here. But I will come as soon as I can.

I am longing to see you again.

Love, Max

* * *

In 1993 I was able to look at the Russian archives for the same period. I needed to verify that Russia was really maintaining a policy of such secrecy that it was to all intents and purposes impossible for Britain to obtain any useful, information from within that country. There were three types of relevant information that I found.

The first dealt with the risk assessments that Russia had done about the impact of information leaks to Britain. The Stalinist view in 1940 was overwhelmingly that Britain was a potentially hostile power and that all possible steps had to be taken to prevent the leak of any serious information to her. The mitigation of that risk was done through fear and bullying.

The second concerned the plans to programme both Burgess and Ponsonby so that the only information to go to senior British people was only that given to them in pursuit of a policy of deliberate disinformation. In other words Burgess and Ponsonby were only to be able to handle manufactured information from Russia. Neither of them knew it but they were in the business of passing on lies and complete information fabrications. There was massive evidence in the files that Russia took considerable steps to reinforce this flow of bogus information. Those steps included radio blackouts amongst the armed forces so that Britain had no idea what was really gong on in the country.

And finally there were hundreds of pages of documents about what Ponsonby had provided to Russia about Britain and its policies. Through what Ponsonby had provided Stalin had access to almost all Treasury files on the performance of the British economy. He had access to numerous Foreign Office policy studies including all those on Russia. It was truly a mine of valuable information that showed exactly what the most senior people in government were thinking and what they were planning to do. Up until May,1940 it showed the deepening divisions between Britain and America.

It took me several years to find and read it all but the picture that was presented to me was one in which almost all of Britain's secrets were available to Stalin. In retrospect it was truly horrifying to know that Russia was in a position to exploit it all.

* * *

In 1940 Hitler had no plans to launch any kind of large scale ground attack on Britain that year. He was preparing plans for a general invasion of Britain the following year under the codename Operation Sea Lion. But he did have plans to run a bombing campaign against Britain. It was to be solely on provincial cities and towns and he had specifically ordered that London should not be bombed. That bombing campaign started on July 10th. It was not any great strategic plan that caused him to change his mind and expand that into a general bombing campaign and include London in it. It was sheer and complete apoplectic rage.

That rage was caused by something very simple. One night in the second half of August, one hot still night when Berlin was sweltering in a heat wave and real sleep was almost impossible for its residents, a small number of British bomber aircraft flew over Berlin just before midnight. They had not been detected as they flew over Holland and Germany. All they did was drop a few incendiary bombs of no real military significance. The damage was minimal to property and people. But Hitler simply could not believe that Churchill might have sanctioned such a raid.

Early in the morning of August 29th the British bombers struck Berlin again. It was then that Hitler went insane with rage. He ordered that the Luftwaffe should start attacking London by day as soon as possible. By September 4th he had ordered that night bombing should also take place. Those orders turned some spasmodic bombing raids into the Battle of Britain.

* * *

July 10, 1941. In mid-afternoon Winston called a crisis meeting of the war Cabinet. I was also called to it and so were the three Chiefs of Staff. Several British cities were being bombed at the time and Winston needed to work out an action plan for the civil emergencies that it was causing and he wanted to boost our defences against future attacks.

* * *

What is now called the Battle of Britain was later deemed to have started the day those provincial bombing raids had commenced on Wednesday July 10th, 1940. It was a typical summery showery day over southern England and the Channel. There were German bomber raids on Swansea, Falmouth and in Suffolk. 6 British and 13 German aircraft were destroyed that day. One of the primary targets in those early days was shipping in the Channel and in the North Sea. The bombings continued on an almost daily basis. In July British aircraft losses were 73 and German losses were 157.

From 8th August onwards the German attacks increased in severity. Thursday August 15th was a fine day over the whole of the country. As a result there were heavy air attacks over the south of the country and some small attacks elsewhere. Bristol, Birmingham, Southampton, Boston, Harwich, Swansea, Crewe and Beverley were all bombed that day. In all 30 British and 75 German aircraft were shot down that day.

It was on Saturday August 24th that the first bombs fell on London; although London had not been targeted and there was no doubt that they had been dropped in error.

The first bombs commanded by Hitler fell on London on Thursday September 5th. Liverpool, Manchester and 40 other cities and towns were bombed that day. After that London was bombed almost every day and night until October 31st when the Battle is officially assumed to have come to an end. Throughout the campaign Britain had lost 930 aircraft and Germany had lost 1623. It was a bloody price to pay for no German military advantage. For Britain it was just as well that all those additional fighter aircraft had been ordered before the war had began. But it all brought the immediacy and horror of war to every part of Britain.

Churchill had sent telegrams to Roosevelt at least three times every week throughout the bombings. He had instructed Bradman to talk to Roosevelt as often as possible and he had bullied and harangued Sally every day. Not one of those approaches got a positive response.

Roosevelt never responded to any of the telegrams directly. But he did call Angela in for lunch on Monday September 9th. The previous day 412 Londoners had been killed in the bombings and 747 injured. He told her that nothing would change. America could not commit troops to any war in Europe at this time. It simply did not matter what the plight of Britain might be, the American people simply would not allow it. She duly passed all that on to an increasingly fretful Churchill. He felt as if the whole world was coming down on him. It had all got a lot worse because he felt as if democracy itself was being threatened. He could not understand why America did not see it that way.

* * *

Roosevelt's own diaries show that he decided to change the way that he dealt with Britain early in November, 1940. His diary for November 8 reads;

"The barrage of requests that I have been getting from Churchill is becoming very boring and will have absolutely no impact on American opinion. But I have to consider what I will do after the election to implement my own plans for Britain and its empire."

* * *

On November 10th, Roosevelt asked Angela to lunch again. It did not matter to him what message he was going to give her. Each time they met it was a pleasant social occasion even if they were dealing with matters of supreme importance to both America and Britain.

"You know, Angela, one thing has baffled me very much in the recent blizzard of messages that I have been getting from your Prime Minister is that he believes that the recent bombing raids on Britain are threatening democracy itself. I well understand that the British people are undergoing severe hardships at this time. Every possible source of information I have tells me that. I get regular and comprehensive reports from Joseph Kennedy that tell me just that. There is no doubt in my mind about any of that. I fully understand that things are going to get worse, probably very much worse.

"I also understand that if Britain is invaded then it will be very difficult for the German forces to be contained and destroyed. Britain may well get overrun and become part of Germany. In various ways I have told Winston that I cannot help him other than through the Lend/Lease programmes. I am bored with reading all that repetitive stuff he sends me. Things will not be any different after the election. The only circumstances in which the Congress will allow me to go to war will be if America is attacked in any significant way. We do not believe that Germany has any capability to do that and we do not see any other significant enemies out there at this time. So war for us is impossible. We will not commit American forces to any theatre of war outside our own shores at this time. There is no point in is talking any more about that. From now on I am not even going to read what Winston sends me directly. If he has anything genuinely new to say to me then he only has to send you here and you will get my attention immediately.

"But let us go back to what he has said about democracy. His comments rather stunned me. In this country we fought against Britain in order to establish our democracy. We have fought a bloody and lengthy civil war in order to ensure that all those who live in this country have their freedom. Upholding democracy is fundamental to the American constitution. We had a democracy here long before you did in Britain. We intend to protect our democratic institutions from any threat. If American democracy is threatened from any quarter we will fight anyone to protect it. That will be popular in this country. But no such threat exists at this time.

"We have our election soon and all the indications are that I will be elected President again. When I am I will be making my State of the Union address in January. I can promise you that that will all be about democratic rights and about how America sees the extension of those rights all around the world. On the day of my inauguration I will want you to send a copy of my speech to Winston. It would be a very good idea for him to read it closely because it will make it very clear what we mean by democracy and what sort of democracy it is that we will defend at all costs.

"Some time after my inauguration it will be essential for your Prime Minister and me to meet. Given the problems of the war I have no idea where we will to able to do that safely. But we will have to meet and we will have to talk directly about what can and cannot be achieved together. It will certainly be an occasion to which I will look forward. At the heart of our discussions then will be democracy. It will certainly be an interesting time. Please tell him all this."

* * *

November 16, 1940. Last night was another long slog down in the bunker with Winston. There was a ferocious convoy battle during the night in which four large merchant ships were lost. Winston reminded me several times that already this year we have lost 380 ships. He is haunted by the view that Britain's lifeblood is draining away with each sinking.

* * *

From the end of the Battle of Britain onwards Winston's working days got longer and longer. A large part of his work was done in the Cabinet War Rooms deep under Whitehall. In particular he spent almost every night down there when he was in London. He always required his key staff to be with him when he was there at night and that made for some harrowing lifestyles.

After the height of the Battle of Britain, night bombing raids had started across the entire United Kingdom whenever the weather was clear enough. These usually started at about nine at night in the eastern part of the country. Almost all of the convoy battles took place at night. Initially they were within a thousand miles of UK land but they gradually moved westwards. Midnight UK time in winter, later in summer was a typical time for the torpedoes to start running. Winston liked to get immediate reports on the scale and intensity of these battles. Sometimes they lasted a few minutes, sometimes they lasted all night. Winston never went to bed until things had quietened down. But every night while he was waiting for attack reports he nursed a bottle of brandy until it was healthily empty.

He continued to have regular meetings with Alice. Evenings with her now were impossible because of his duties but he did meet her at her little house for regular lunchtime sessions. He found her to be a real source of strength to him as the war conditions got more and more difficult.

* * *

November 22, 1940. Winston has been in a much better mood these last few days. He has had reports from General Wavell, our commander in the Middle East that there is a very good prospect of being able to defeat 6 Italian divisions that occupy Libya. Winston has now authorised him to begin an offensive against them as soon as possible. He is satisfied that there are good chances of success and he is very anxious to tell the British people some good news at last.

* * *

North Africa had the only active land theatre for Britain since the fall of France in May. The primary role of the British Army in that theatre was the defence of Egypt and the Suez Canal. There had been constant skirmishes between the British and Italian armies for months. But early in November British intelligence officers were noticing that the Italian armies were withdrawing from their frontline positions. British patrols were not meeting any resistance. In December the British Eighth Army began an offensive against the Italian armies that had been in Western Egypt and Libya. By early February, 1941 all the Italian armies in the desert had been destroyed. It was for Churchill a very enjoyable respite in a very difficult period. It gave him a superb opportunity to tell the people of a great victory in the desert.

* * *

In November 1940 during a visit by Molotov to Berlin Hitler had asked him to take back a message to Stalin effectively asking him to join in the dismemberment of the British Empire. Hitler had already asked Italy and Japan to join in the same process. It was all a direct result of the information that von Ribbentrop had gathered whilst he was in London. Stalin was interested but only provided that Russia could take over British interests in the Persian Gulf (as it was then called) and in the Indian Ocean. At that time that was more than Hitler could envisage and the idea was dropped but it was not to be the last approach that Stalin was to receive about the British Empire. The next serious one would be from an altogether different source and it would be taken more seriously.

* * *

January 7, 1941. Winston was sent a copy of Roosevelt's State of the Union address yesterday. Apparently be had been promised it a couple of months ago. It is obvious from his mood that he does not like it at all. He told me that it looks like a threat to the British Empire. He also told me today that he has received a proposal from Roosevelt that the two of them should meet. In my opinion such a meeting is long overdue and I much encouraged him to go ahead with it.

I have read Roosevelt's speech and it is very strong on principles but there is no detail of how America could possibly implement such principles.

Winston had been up all the night because there was another ferocious convoy battle and he needed to keep up with the news coming in from Egypt. Things have been going very well there. He left to go to a meeting in the Commons.

* * *

When Winston had re-read that speech many times he decided that it was time to bully Sally about it. His meeting with her at the Commons was terse and difficult.

"Sally, I have received a copy of your President's State of the Union address. I am very unclear as to whom it was really addressed. It says nothing about the state of the Union but just sets out some principles of democracy. In doing that it seems to seek to impose American democratic standards on the rest of the world. I do not think that any such approach is desirable or necessary. Britain is the biggest democracy in the world and we do not need to be taught about how the principles of democracy should be applied across the globe. You can certainly tell him that if it is directed at us it is unwelcome."

Sally knew all about civil rights and freedoms in America. It was something deep in her because of what had happened to her father. His freedoms and hers had depended on what Roosevelt had been able to do for him. She was never going to forget that nor was she ever going to forget how much Roosevelt's pardoning of her father had meant to the family. So she said to Winston:

"Mr. Prime Minister, I have read that speech and I can assure you that it well describes the passions that Americans have for democracy. Most Americans left Europe in order to live in a free and democratic society. I am only here because of our President's respect for all democratic principles. I can assure you that when you meet him he will impress upon you for the principles that he has outlined in his speech to be at the centre of any expanded relationship between Britain and America. You have told me many times that you want an expanded relationship. He has told me that he is ready to meet with you and that it is very much in your interest that such a meeting should happen. He would like you to suggest a time and a place. But whenever it does take place his democratic principles will not have changed."

* * *

March 22, 1941. Winston told me this afternoon that he was going to Chartwell for the night and the following day he would be holding a meeting that was going to reach decisions about a huge build-up in our capabilities for destroying U-Boats. He feels safe about going there today because there are no indications that there are going to be any U-Boats near our convoys tonight. There is no bombing threat either because the weather forecast is for very bad flying conditions.

* * *

March 23, 1941. Anthony Eden rang me early this morning. He wanted to share some very important information he had just received from a contact of his in Germany and he needed to agree a joint approach to Winston about it.

* * *

It was in March 1941 that Churchill detected a shift in the emphasis of the war. It was not something that he had authorised or planned that caused it. Rather it was the combined work both of British military intelligence and of the spy network that Eden had established that brought new information to him about a completely new direction that the war might be taking.

From his discussions with von Ribbentrop back in the winter of 1936/7 Churchill might have been able to glean the true intent behind German ambitions towards getting more lebensraum for her citizens. But he, like almost all other politicians at that time, simply did not have the imagination or suspicion to realise just how vast the scale of German aspirations might be. It was impossible for him and many others to work out just how devious and cunning the minds of Hitler and von Ribbentrop might have been.

Winston had thought that the conquest of Czechoslovakia, Austria, parts of Poland and some Baltic states might satisfy German ambitions but it was that intelligence information that started to come through in March of 1941 that convinced him that there might be a much bigger plan for the expansion of the German Empire.

He first got to hear of it all one bleak, grey and very wet day morning. Anthony Eden had phoned him that morning to say that he had information that he needed to share. He had had a conversation with Samuel a little earlier and they both needed to meet him together that day.

It was potentially very important information and they needed to deal with it urgently. It was a time of huge problems for Churchill. He was particularly concerned about the battles for the safety of the convoys in the North Atlantic. It was only a few weeks after he had forecast an ever increasing struggle in the North Atlantic in a speech in which he had used the words:

"We must therefore expect that Herr Hitler will do his utmost to prey upon our shipping and to reduce the volume of American supplies entering these islands. Having conquered France and Norway, his clutching fingers reach out on both sides of us into the ocean."

That day Winston had arranged to have lunch at Chartwell with Admiral Sir Percy Noble who had just been appointed as Royal Navy Commander-in-Chief. Nothing was more important then than trying to find a solution to the U-Boat problem. The things had to be destroyed and Percy Noble had to lead that effort every hour of the day and night. Churchill knew that Britain would be ruined and probably annihilated unless he had both American support and the U-Boat menace was eliminated. Large scale American support was proving elusive so he had to find some way of getting the Royal Navy to solve the U-Boat problem. 3 million tons of shipping capacity had been lost in 1940 and the same level of loss was continuing into 1941. The implications of a loss rate anything like that continuing were horrendous.

When Eden had rung him to say that they needed to meet urgently because he had some very important new war intelligence Churchill was initially dismissive. Eden had nothing whatsoever to do with the problems in the North Atlantic and at a War Cabinet meeting only a couple of days earlier Churchill had got complete cabinet support for more effort in the war at sea. Nothing else had been discussed in cabinet that day. He was actually somewhat annoyed that Eden had rung him early that morning to demand an urgent meeting.

Over lunch Churchill did agree with Percy Noble on some large increases in the plans for the protection of the convoys. There were several strands to what they agreed. The first was to make an appointment for the command of what they called the Western Approaches. The person proposed by Admiral Noble was Admiral Max Horton. He was a distinguished anti-submarine officer and was personally well regarded by the crews of the convoy escorts. The principal reason why he was selected was that he had a very good record of giving good officers their freedom to develop tactics and experiment about the best ways of destroying a relentless and unforgiving enemy. Churchill liked that approach and it was to serve Britain well.

The second thing on which they agreed was to develop long range aircraft. It was the only way to keep the U-Boats under the surface and it was the only quick way to attack them as well. Admiral Noble explained to Churchill that there had to be aircraft patrols covering the entire middle of the North Atlantic in all daylight hours during all suitable weather conditions. At that time it was almost technically impossible to achieve and in any event large numbers of aircraft would be required. Churchill agreed to talk with Roosevelt about how America might help. He also agreed to get Max Beaverbrook on to the task immediately.

The third thing on which they agreed was the formation of what they called Escort Support Groups. These would be fast warships which would not necessarily sail with the convoys but would be based in mid-Atlantic to support any convoy as it passed through the areas of the greatest danger. Admiral Pound was authorised to get on with it all irrespective of the cost.

The only thing that concerned Churchill that day was winning what was looking like an increasingly difficult battle.

* * *

Eden and Samuel arrived at Chartwell at around four in the afternoon. Churchill was very enthusiastic about what he had agreed with Admiral Noble and spent the first few minutes of the discussion telling them about it.

But what they had to tell him was vastly more important than that. They had been intercepting German radio traffic continuously since the war began and they had had some success in breaking German codes. There was still much of the traffic that they could not understand and the volume of traffic had increased so markedly in recent weeks that even the enhanced intelligence staff simply could not read it all. But the sampling that they had done pointed very strongly to the large scale movement of troops from Central Germany and France towards the borders with Russia. The troop movements had started about a week earlier on a small scale but had been increasing steadily since then. Eden explained that in 1937 they had been able to get some brilliant information about the construction of military bases throughout Germany. They were both barracks and airbases. There were many in the eastern part of the country. These were now being filled with personnel being moved in from other areas of the country. All these movements were now taking place on an enormous scale.

They had also had reports from numerous personnel on the ground about train movements, vehicle convoys moving east, aircraft movements and gossip from railway stations and bars. The consensus of those who had access to the consolidated information was that Germany was preparing for some kind of attack on Russia. There was no other logical explanation of what was happening.

Samuel explained that until the previous week they had seen a build up of German forces along the North Sea coasts that would be consistent with the preparation of an invasion of Britain. But that had all changed and in some cases units that had only recently arrived in France, Belgium and Holland were being moved east.

There were really only two explanations for what was going on. It could be a gigantic attempt to confuse and deceive Britain. By moving forces away from the Channel and North Sea coasts it could easily look like a manoeuvre designed just to confuse. It they could be moved away quickly they could be returned just as quickly. But either way that meant that a surface attack on Britain was not imminent. Or it could be the start of a campaign against Russia.

Whatever it all meant there was clearly something very important going on. Churchill was absolutely delighted by what he had been told. He was certain that the information pointed very strongly to the likelihood of a German invasion of Russia. To him that meant that the pressure was off Britain to some extent. But he was more concerned not so much about the information but what they did about it.

It was very late by the time that they had agreed an action plan. Eden was authorised to step up diplomatic contacts with Russia, partly to warn that country of the danger and partly to explore what co-operation might be possible. Samuel was authorised to increase still further the resources needed to maintain accurate and reliable surveillance activities. Churchill, himself undertook to contact Roosevelt on the matter.

That evening Churchill went to bed with a sense of elation. It was the first time since the war began that he had seen even the prospect of good news apart from those early victories over

Italy in North Africa. What really caused him that elation was that he thought that Germany would probably defeat Russia and in doing so its pursuit of lebensraum would be satisfied. If all that happened Britain might be safe and the war could be ended quickly with some kind of treaty with Germany within which the two countries respected each other's imperial aspirations. That was what Churchill dreamt about that night and that was what he thought to be the best option.

That same night Hitler had exactly the same thoughts. von Ribbentrop had truly achieved a meeting of two very important minds.

* * *

But it was not to be. Churchill did send a message Roosevelt via Bradman and he spoke with Sally the following afternoon. Essentially the message he passed through both of them was that Germany seemed to be developing hostile intentions towards Russia. That created an opportunity for America to provide much enhanced aid to Britain so that plans could be advanced for a British invasion of continental Europe. In that way the German problem could be solved quickly.

When Angela got her instructions from Churchill she immediately requested a meeting with Roosevelt. She was not entirely clear what she was required to try and achieve with him. The plea from Churchill had seemed to be more demanding than anything that she had seen before. But as always she would give it a try.

What Roosevelt told her when they met was that it did not matter whether Germany was attacking Russia or any other nation. The only circumstances under which America would take up hostilities with Germany would be if Germany or any of its allies attacked America.

Roosevelt expressed some frustration to her that Churchill did not seem to understand the American message. He added that the only way forward was for him to meet with Churchill and then when they had reached agreement on diplomatic institutions they could pave the way for more American aid.

The message that Sally passed on to Winston a couple of days later was more specific about a meeting. She told him that the sooner it took place the better.

* * *

March 28, 1941. Winston wanted to chat to me about the proposed meeting with Roosevelt. He said he had talked to some of the members of the War cabinet about it as well. He told me that it was something he had to do even though he had the gravest doubts about entering into any discussion with Roosevelt about democracy. All he wanted to do was talk about how America was going to help with the war. But he knew that Roosevelt would always want to bring up the democracy issue but he could not imagine what he wanted to say which went beyond what had already been said in that State of the Union speech. What he wanted my ideas about was when he should arrange the meeting. He needed a view as to when would be a suitable time for him to be away from Whitehall and that depended on military intelligence. The view that I gave him was that he should wait and see exactly what Germany was up to. If they were going to attack Russia in contravention of their treaty, that was when he should go because it would mean that Britain was not then going to be attacked.

He told me he thought that that was right. He was very concerned about how long he would have to be away for such a meeting. He assumed that he would have to travel across the

Atlantic and that meant that he could easily be away for 2 weeks. It was a daunting prospect but it would have to be done. He instructed me that I would be going with him.

* * *

What did work at that time was that George Ponsonby was able to use the contacts he had developed in Russia to develop further communication between the two countries. It was that enhanced communication that led directly to the two countries becoming obvious allies for the first time. The Russian Government gave their ambassador in London, Ivan Maisky, instructions as to what he should say when he was asked to a meeting at the Foreign Office.

* * *

May 20, 1941. While we were in a review meeting with Winston we got the terrible news that the German battleship Bismarck had left port and had sailed into the Baltic. We presumed that it was bound for the Atlantic. Churchill was apoplectic about it. He called in Percy Noble immediately and instructed him that Bismarck had to be destroyed. A ship of that power free to roam through the Atlantic could do untold damage to anything within its path. He told the Admiral that if necessary the entire resources of the Royal Navy had to be deployed to destroy her. Cost in men and materials were not important. It was the first time that I had ever heard such an order. Nothing mattered to Churchill that afternoon except the destruction of Bismarck.

Admiral Noble accepted those orders and invited us to move to the Admiralty tactical room in fifteen minutes. He would explain the situation to us all then. That room was just a few doors down the corridor.

When we got there, Admiral Noble gave us a full briefing. He explained the deployment of the fleet and the orders that had already been sent out. The battleships Hood and Prince of Wales would be sailing by midnight, the cruisers Norfolk and Suffolk were already at sea patrolling the Denmark Strait through which Bismarck would have to pass. The cruisers Manchester and Birmingham would be sailing within the hour and the aircraft carrier Victorious was being withdrawn from an extreme high priority convoy to provide some sort of air cover out in the Atlantic. She was a fast ship and could go wherever Bismarck went, but her aircraft were very slow even if they could carry a single torpedo each.

While we were there we heard a report that Bismarck had been seen by a reconnaissance Spitfire aircraft. Its course and speed had been confirmed. All the ships being sent to destroy Bismarck were warned to expect action within 48 hours.

* * *

May 23, 1941. More battleships have been ordered to join the force hunting the Bismarck. Ramillies and Revenge have been taken off convoy duties to help sink this beast.

* * *

May 27, 1941. Bismarck was finally sunk this morning. It took a fleet of 19 capital ships to stop her. Winston immediately went to the Commons to announce the victory. After he returned he was in a state of massive relief. He said to me: "Samuel. We have the biggest navy in the world, but we have been unable to provide a proper escort service for our convoys. It took all those powerful ships to sink Bismarck and in the process we lost Hood, the fastest ship we had. We had to strip convoys of their meagre escorts and while we were hunting Bismarck we lost another 21 ships in convoy. I did instruct that it had to be done without regard for cost. We now know what that meant. America has a large navy and they will not even use a single ship to help us. What a war."

He had been completely exhausted by the Bismarck battle during which he had not slept for a single minute. But he slept then. I left him to his dreams while he slept in that dreadful office chair he used.

* * *

June 22, 1941. The whole of Winston's team was in the bunker last night as we waited for news of the German invasion of Russia. Winston was very excited about it all. He saw it as excellent news for Britain.

* * *

To all intents and purposes Britain and Russia became allies on 10th June, 1941, just twelve days before Germany launched its invasion of Russia that it called Barbarossa.

At that time there were obvious German preparations for war. Long after the war had ended it was possible to understand the scale of what was going on but in the spring of 1941 only partial information was available but it suggested that something very hideous was about to happen. When the full figures became available it was easy to see that three million men and thousands of aircraft had been massed along all the borders with Russia. All the bases that Louise had seen back in 1937 were fully occupied. For months Germany had been making statements that the troop movements were merely training exercises. Russia accepted that explanation and refused to believe that Germany had any war intentions. Stalin still had other and far different priorities. But Britain knew that the German intentions were all about occupying vast areas of Russia to create more lebensraum for its people and to enslave all the Slav people. The German agenda was as horrible as any in the 20th century or at any other time in history. Britain knew a lot about what was going on because it was able to break some of the German military codes. In any event the sheer scale of military radio traffic was so great that something dramatic must have been about to happen.

Samuel Garbutt and Eden had kept Churchill fully informed and the more he learned about it the more relieved he became. He was certain that the pressure was off in the west. It did not mean peace but it meant that there was no likelihood of an imminent invasion of Britain. He continued to inform Roosevelt about what was happening.

In early June Churchill authorised the Foreign Office to meet with the Russian Ambassador in London in order to share some of the information that they had with him. Churchill chose to do that because he was certain that an attack on Russia was imminent and he had information from German sources that Russia was making no plans to deal with it.

Therefore the Under Secretary for Foreign Affairs, Sir Alexander Cadogan, asked the Russian Ambassador in Britain, Ivan Maisky, to visit him on 10th June. It was a meeting that lasted just over two hours. Maisky was given a very detailed account of some of the German forces were said to be finalising preparations for war. Unit names, numbers of troops, aircraft and guns and planned initial targets were all included in the lists that were given to Maisky.

Exactly as Britain had described Germany invaded Russia at dawn on June 22nd, 1941. Again exactly as Britain had described their armies consisted of 153 army divisions; that is more than three million men, 3,500 tanks and 2,700 aircraft.

* * *

In the early days after the German invasion Stalin was in a severe state of shock. Fundamentally he could not believe that he had been outsmarted by someone more cunning than himself. His initial moves were all about trying to restore peace with Germany. Those quickly proved to be pointless. But when Stalin was convinced that there was no prospect of any peace with Germany he authorised Molotov to begin discussions with Britain. At that stage all he had in mind was exploring whether Britain was prepared at that time to open up a land front with Germany so that German troops would have to be withdrawn from Russia. So Maisky went back to see Cadogan again.

Maisky's message was quickly passed up to Eden and Churchill. It had not come at an easy time for Britain. It was only a year after the appalling humiliation of Dunkirk. Britain's supply lines were becoming severely restricted by U-Boats. Shipping losses, both of merchant ships and escorts had escalated since the U-Boats had access to French ports. Transit times for them were shorter, journeys much safer for them and they could stay at sea for longer. They now operated in large numbers right across all possible convoy routes in Mid-Atlantic. The bomber raids on Britain by the Luftwaffe continued relentlessly whenever the weather was clear enough.

In those circumstances it was Churchill's conclusion that there was no way that a credible second front could be opened up anywhere in Western Europe at that time. All the coastlines under German control were heavily defended and it was known that Germany had vastly larger numbers of troops in the west than Britain and its allies could possibly muster even after allowance was made for those that had gone to Russia. So what Maisky was told was that Britain would open up a second front when it was strong enough to do so. It could not be predicted when that would be but it would certainly not be in 1941. But Cadogan was asked to put a further point to Maisky. It was all about Britain and Russia establishing some kind of communications channel with the Nazi leadership which did not involve using third parties. It did not matter at what level that communication took place as long as it was reliable. Eden believed that there were already good communications between Russia and Britain and Churchill had said that he was happy for these to be strengthened still further.

So what Cadogan and Maisky did was develop a plan for a special diplomatic enclave in neutral Sweden. Negotiations for it were delicate and slow. It first of all required the support and approval of the Swedish government. Then the German government would have to be approached through neutrals. Sweden did agree and after appropriate assurances had been given was happy to facilitate any moves to bring about a reduction in hostilities. Britain approached Germany through the Swiss government. Russia approached Germany through the Turkish government. All parties agreed to proceed on an experimental basis. The most difficult part of it all had been about creating safe communications of all sorts between Stockholm and the three capital cities. Those communications had to include at least a weekly air service which was guaranteed freedom from attack as it crossed enemy territory. Even that was agreed. The British government arranged for BOAC, a civilian airline, to operate its weekly flight.

That diplomatic link proved to be a very important one for all three countries.

The flight schedules from London, Berlin and Moscow were all co-ordinated so that all three aircraft were on the ground at Bromma Airport, Stockholm at the same time. That meant that anyone needing to go from Britain to Berlin or Moscow could do so easily.

* * *

June 23, 1941. Things have really changed over the last 24 hours. We have been up throughout that period listening to the intelligence reports about the German invasion. German advances have been very rapid. We have also started getting military information directly from Russia. I do not know why this is but I guess that it because they want us to know the damage that is being inflicted on them.

* * *

The German invasion of Russia began on 22nd June 1941. It began six weeks later than planned because Hitler was determined to complete the conquest of Greece and Yugoslavia first. Why he should have been concerned about two small and militarily weak states has never really been explained. He may have just become obsessed about gaining territory. The plans for Barbarossa called for virtually all of Russia west of the Ural Mountains to be overrun by massive German forces before the Russian winter really set in, probably by mid-November. Moscow was to be captured, so was the whole of the Ukraine. Additionally Germany planned to capture the Don industrial basin and the Caucasus oil fields. It was the most ambitious military campaign ever planned for a single summer. It was so ambitious because Germany believed the Russian forces to be very weak and incapable of fighting over so much territory at the same time. Had the attack been launched at the beginning of May it might just have succeeded in its entirety. Whatever the date and whatever the effect that invasion was an immense relief to Churchill. It was everything he hoped would happen when he had first had that briefing from Eden and Samuel months earlier.

* * *

Within days of Barbarossa starting Stalin made a plea to both Britain and America for any sort of aid; military equipment, food and clothing were the most important items needed. Both Churchill and Roosevelt immediately agreed to provide support but both warned that the very lengthy supply chains and shortage of shipping capacity would mean that initially the aid that would in any practical sense be small. Roosevelt agreed to provide aid to Russia on exactly the same terms that applied to Britain. It had to be Lend/Lease. From what Ponsonby had already provided in terms of information Stalin already knew everything about Lean/Lease. He had every intention of taking as much equipment as he needed, but he had no intention of paying for any of it.

That aid was indeed almost invisible in 1941. It could only be provided then through Russia's southern frontiers via Britain's colonies by road or via shipping convoys into Murmansk. The southern routes were virtually impassable to heavy transport and any convoy route to Murmansk was exceptionally hazardous because of the existence of numerous German naval bases in Norway. In any event any convoy to Russia reduced the capacity to operate convoys across the North Atlantic and to other parts of the world. Also anything that went to Russia meant less for Britain. Roosevelt had also insisted that America treat Russia exactly like Britain. No military involvement and all the transactions had to be with civilian suppliers. It was to be a long while before there was anything like adequate shipping capacity to be available for both the North Atlantic and Russian convoys. It was also to be a long time, nearly two years, before there was anything like reasonably safe operating conditions for any of those convoys.

* * *

July 1, 1941. Winston told me today that the dates for his meeting with Roosevelt had been fixed. I will be going with him in to Canada in August.

* * *

Contact between Churchill and Roosevelt immediately after the German invasion of Russia resulted in agreement that they would meet as soon as possible. It would be their first meeting. Roosevelt had no wish to go far from Washington at that time so it was agreed that they would meet off the coast of Newfoundland. Winston would travel there in a battleship and they would meet on board her. After extensive prevarication Churchill eventually agreed to meet Roosevelt between 9th and 12th August, 1941 in *HMS Prince of Wales*.

Two days before Winston left London he met with Sally Monroe. It was very much a private meeting and it took place at Chartwell. It was her first visit there. They had lunch together and then walked through the brilliantly coloured grounds on a fine summer's afternoon. Winston did not enjoy Sally's company but he recognised that he had no alternative. Despite not liking her he was prepared to be civilised and he certainly wanted to show her what stylish country living meant in Britain. This was the first time that they had been able to talk together outside the hothouses of London politics. Despite initial misgivings, what Winston was expecting to hear from her was that America was making its own entry into the war after the German invasion of Russia and that it would provide whatever resources were available to help its beleaguered friends. He did not get that message. What he got instead was that America was prepared to make a further commitment to bring the war to an end but that it needed to agree that with Britain and that it would impose conditions in return for any commitment it made. Sally had no further detail on any such conditions.

That same day Winston got a message from Bradman in Washington. Basically it said that Roosevelt intended to put to him a deal that would require many changes in Britain. He knew that it would be tough but if Britain wanted American help it would have to make those changes.

* * *

The day before Winston left for Newfoundland he had another lunchtime meeting with Alice.

"Alice, the way that I see it is that I have an enormous opportunity to press Britain's case very hard with Roosevelt on a face-to-face basis. It is possibly a one shot chance to get the President not only firmly committed to backing Britain in the war, but to backing Britain's ideas as to what the status of the victors should be at the end of the war, particularly Britain's status as the only world power.

"Alice I am sure you will remember the evening when we both met von Ribbentrop for the first time. That evening he described the German aspirations as being to go back to the pre-1914 status of their country. He went on to say how important it was that Britain's status as the largest imperial power should be protected at the end of the war. I fully understand that view and I fully respect the German position, if that is what he described.

"But I am very disappointed with the messages that I have been getting from Washington for more than a year about that because America seems to be looking for some new world order with a very much diminished role for Britain. I really do not understand this. I cannot see what it is that Roosevelt wants.

"He has surely got to oppose German military aggression and that means that he must support Britain but he seems reluctant to do so. He seems to deny us the vital support that we need.

"I have to talk with him directly within a few short hours and I have to work out just how I can get him to commit him to support us in our hour of need."

They talked until nearly three.

Her advice to him was:

"Winston, you know as well as I do that you can only obtain everything you want in negotiations when you start from a position of very considerable strength. Realistically Britain does not have that strength at this time. What you have to consider as you steam across the North Atlantic is what your bottom line really is. Perhaps the minimum position might just be the survival of Britain. Perhaps it might be more than that. Another thing is that we just do not know what the American military capability is right now and we certainly do not know just what they are capable of achieving.

"It seems to me that you have to assess the man, assess his arguments, assess the true capabilities of America and then decide how far you can push him or how far you are going to allow him to push you. It sounds easy to say that you must take the maximum from him in return for the minimum price. But you know that. Only you will be able to work it out while you are there. But public opinion here very much wants a large American involvement quickly. You will lose respect quickly if you do not achieve it.

"It is going to be a tough few days for you. I will be thinking of you all the time."

Winston kissed her and thanked her as he left.

* * *

August 4, 1941. We have just left Liverpool on HMS Prince of Wales. There will be complete radio silence throughout our trip. We cannot draw attention to our position at any time because of the risk of attracting U-Boats. For the first couple of days it looks as if we will have good weather. It will be a very frustrating time for Winston because he always likes to be in contact with everything that is going on in the war. Only some of the war cabinet know that he is making this trip and the British people have certainly not been told.

Winston is in a buoyant, even aggressive mood and he is certain that he is on the verge of a great breakthrough with Roosevelt. There is no evidence for that because there has been an entirely consistent message from the President since the war began. I do not know why Winston believes that he can change the man's mind. I just hope it is not just wishful thinking.

One thing is certain is that we will have plenty of time to rest and gossip over the next five days.

When we are in Canada we will be able to get a war update and that will be of great interest to us all.

* * *

HMS Prince of Wales was a very unlucky ship. She was a 35,000 ton battleship completed only in March, 1941. In late May, before her sea trials and operational working-up had been completed, she was deployed to help in the search for and sinking of the *Bismarck*. During that battle *Prince of Wales* received damage from German gunfire which damaged the bridge and killed all those on the bridge except the captain. .

Her first assignment after repair was to take Churchill to Newfoundland. It was to be a thankless task. On those two transatlantic crossings she was escorted by six destroyers that had been removed from convoy duty for the purpose. 20 ships were lost in convoy while *Prince of Wales* was away from Britain.

After *Prince of Wales* returned from Canada she went to Malta and then the Far East where she was sunk in the Japanese raids on Singapore on December 10th 1941. She had a life of only nine months.

* * *

The conference between Roosevelt and Churchill took place in Placentia Bay off Argentia in Newfoundland. Roosevelt travelled there on *USS Augusta*, a 9,000 ton light cruiser that had been built in 1931. Augusta was a lucky ship and she was usually at the forefront of American naval activity. For most of the 1930's she had been the US Navy Flagship in the Far East. She was modernized in 1940 and then became the Flagship of the Atlantic fleet. She was to be involved in several major wartime events. Augusta only had one escort vessel and that was the destroyer *USS McDougal*.

The only advisers Churchill took with him to Newfoundland were senior military offices. He did that because he was certain, despite what he had been told, that the discussions would mainly be about preparations for America entering the war.

* * *

August 8, 1941. We arrived at Placentia Bay this afternoon. What a bleak desolate place it is. There is absolutely nothing here, it therefore makes a perfect secret location for this big meeting. An hour after we arrived a Canadian destroyer tied up alongside us. It brought our High Commissioner who had with him the latest war reports. It took him a couple of hours to brief Winston on everything that was going on in Canada and then we all settled down to read the war papers. Most of them were about continuing German advances in Russia and bombings in Britain. Winston has been in a very buoyant mood throughout the crossing.

* * *

It was at that first meeting between Roosevelt and Churchill that the shape of future American policy towards Britain became obvious. After all the ever more strident requests for American involvement in the war that had been coming from Churchill, a meeting between the two men was inevitable after Germany had attacked Russia. The whole war had suddenly seemed to get a great deal larger. But it was that German attack on Russia that gave Roosevelt the opportunity he needed to bring into effect his personal policy towards Britain and its Empire that he had thought through and decided upon in that month after Churchill's first request for those destroyers. The reason it did was that blatantly Britain had no capability at that time of being able to fight such a vast army as the German Wehrmacht in Europe. The sheer scale of the German attack had changed everything. Roosevelt knew that and intended to take advantage of it.

Long before he first met Churchill, Roosevelt had studied the Versailles Treaty that formalised the end of the First World War and set the terms for the subsequent "peace". He had become firmly of the view that Versailles had been far too hard on Germany in that it had set conditions for Germany that were incapable of achievement. At the same time it had been very soft because it had done nothing to discourage and prevent Germany from waging war again. Roosevelt had looked on in dismay as the fledgling German democracy had collapsed under hyperinflation, war debt, reparations and resentment over the treaty terms. Well before 1941 he had decided that if America did have to enter a war in Europe for any reason any peace settlement would have to be entirely different. But he also decided that before any peace negotiations could even begin with Germany that country would have to be completely beaten in any military sense. That would certainly be one of his lines of discussion with Churchill.

As Roosevelt had thought so many times, almost everything that could go wrong in Europe after The First World War did go wrong. Many of the things that went wrong were as a result of the Versailles Treaty. The 1920's and 1930's were, in historical terms, appalling times for the whole European continent. That catalogue of problems started with parliamentary impotence, and it included civil war, economic chaos, colonial wars, industrial strife, poverty, racial and religious discrimination on a huge scale, political purges, the rise of several dictatorships, government fraud, mass brutality and appeasement of evil. Almost all of that was caused by the failings of individual politicians and entire political systems. Roosevelt often thought that things were going to have to get far worse even than that before they could get better.

* * *

The foundations of what Roosevelt wanted were all written into his State of the Union address on January 6th, 1941. He knew from Sally that Churchill had read that speech many times and was seriously disturbed by it. Basically in writing that speech Roosevelt was thinking about the fundamental freedoms that did exist in America and how they contrasted with the "freedoms" available to the vast majority of the peoples in the British Empire.

On the way up to Placentia Bay in *USS Augusta* Roosevelt read that speech again several times as he rehearsed what he was going to say to Churchill. The speech read:

"As men do not live by bread alone, they do not fight by armaments alone. Those who man our defenses, and those behind them who build our defenses, must have the stamina and the courage which come from the unshakable belief in the manner of life which they are defending. The mighty action that we are calling for cannot be based on disregard of all things worth fighting for...

"For there is nothing mysterious about the foundations of a healthy and strong democracy. The basic things expected by our people of their political and economic systems are simple. They are:

"Equality of opportunity for youth and for others.

"Jobs for all those who can work.

``Security for all those who need it.

"The ending of special privileges for the few.

"The preservation of civil liberties for all.

"The enjoyment of the fruits of scientific progress in a wider and constantly rising standard of living.

"These are simple, basic things that must never be lost in the sight of the turmoil and unbelievable complexity of our modern world. The inner and abiding strength of our economic and political systems is dependent upon the degree to which they fulfil these expectations...."

Having stated these principles from a standpoint accessible to the average American citizen, Roosevelt then universalized them so as to apply them to the rest of the world, not from the standpoint of an existing world, but as principles of change, to move the world from its current wretched state to a new and better post-war world. He knew that it was a message that Churchill and the British government did not want to hear.

"In future days, which we seek to secure, we look forward to a world founded upon four essential human freedoms.

"The first is the freedom of speech and expression--**everywhere** in the world.

"The second is the freedom of every person to worship God in his own way--**everywhere** in the world.

"The third is the freedom from want--which, translated into world terms, means economic understandings which will secure to every nation a healthy peacetime life for its inhabitants--**everywhere** in the world.

"The fourth is freedom from fear--which, translated into world terms, means a worldwide reduction of armaments to such a point and in such a thorough fashion that no nation will be in a position to commit an act of physical aggression against any neighbour--**anywhere** in the world.

"That is no vision of a distant millennium. It is a definite basis for a kind of world attainable in our time and generation. That kind of world is the very antithesis of the so-called new order of tyranny which dictators seek to create with the crash of a bomb.

"To that new order, we oppose the greater conception--the moral order. A good society is able to face schemes of world domination and foreign revolutions alike without fear.

"Since the beginning of American history, we have been engaged in change--in a perpetual peaceful revolution--a revolution which goes on steadily, quietly, adjusting itself to changing conditions--without the concentration camp or the quicklime in the ditch. The world order which we seek is the cooperation of free countries, working together in a friendly, civilized society.

"This nation has placed its destiny in the hands and heads and hearts of millions of free men and women; and its faith in freedom under the guidance of God. Freedom means the supremacy of human rights everywhere. Our support goes to those who struggle to gain those rights or to keep them. Our strength is our unity of purpose.

"To that high concept there can be no end save victory."

In his State of the Union address Roosevelt had deliberately enunciated the word "everywhere," as he repeated it in cadence with each of the Four Freedoms, and in relation to the struggle for human rights and freedom. According to his aide, Sam Curtisman, Roosevelt had dictated the draft of this section of the speech himself. As he dictated, his trusted advisor Harry Hopkins questioned the use of the word "everywhere," saying that the American people didn't care about people in Africa or elsewhere. "They had better start caring, Harry," replied the President.

* * *

When visual contact was made between the two ships Roosevelt instructed the captain of *Augusta* to invite Churchill over for dinner that evening. He was to be told that it would be a getting to know you session and that the main business would start the following morning when they would meet on *Prince of Wales*. Roosevelt was determined to get a better measure of the man before their serious discussions started. Churchill readily accepted the invitation. In any event there was nothing else to do in or near Placentia Bay. They had only gone there because it was a good safe anchorage.

Churchill arrived on board *Augusta* at six that evening. He was taken on a tour of the ship and then to the Admiral's cabin where Roosevelt was waiting for him.

Roosevelt was not interested in negotiating anything serious with Churchill that evening. It was the first time he met the man and what he really wanted to do was understand more about the British Government and about how it was managing the war. He also wanted to learn more from Churchill himself what life was like in wartime Britain.

So Churchill explained about how he was head of the government and responsible for the war effort. He said that that included all the military effort and specific war time production requirements such as aircraft and ships. He told Roosevelt that his deputy, Clement Attlee, was responsible for everything else including all home matters and the Empire.

"Mr. President, you have to realise that things are very tough in Britain today. Right at the beginning of the war we had to introduce rationing of food and fuel. That is because Britain has to import more than half its food and we have to import all our oil. Supplies of both have been drastically cut by the convoy losses. We also have to import most of our iron ore and all of the aluminium we need to build aircraft. On top of all that some part of Britain is bombed every night when the weather is favourable.

"Our factories have had to be converted for wartime production and this has drastically reduced our once massive exports.

"It is a time of very great hardship, but the spirit of the British people is very strong. There is a very strong will to defeat Hitler and return to our way of life that prevailed before the war. Everyone would like to see a quick end to the war but Germany is a very powerful country militarily."

They talked until ten. Churchill was pleased that Roosevelt had some excellent drinks on board the ship and that a very good dinner had been provided.

* * *

August 9, 1941. Winston told me over breakfast that he had much enjoyed his evening with the President. Apparently they had not discussed any political or military matters but the President had seemed genuinely interested in conditions in Britain. He said the evening had provided a good foundation for the real business they were going to discuss that morning.

* * *

In that first meeting together on *Prince of Wales* that morning Roosevelt took control of the meeting immediately it started:

"Look Winston. I know that you have read my State of the Union speech many times. It is something that you are going to have to take very seriously, because it is a statement of American policies that has prevailed since independence and will prevail for many a long time to come. I hope that it will prevail for many centuries. The way I described it is just my own way of doing so but if you read Lincoln's great Gettysburg address you will get exactly the same flavour. It clearly reflects our constitution.

"The most important part of it all is that part about those four freedoms. Those freedoms apply to all Americans but few other people on the globe. They only apply in some respects to very few people in your colonies, mainly Canada, Australia and New Zealand, but those countries have very sparse populations. The only basis on which America will continue to help Britain in this war is if you adopt those freedoms implicitly and agree to apply them to all the people that you currently control as soon as possible. If you don't there will be no more help. I say this because if there is to be any larger American involvement in the war in Europe the American people will expect their government to use the opportunity to spread American values. Please remember that a very large part of our electorate comes from countries which did not have democratic values when they left and which do not have democratic values now. If at any stage America does enter this war as a participant a major objective of ours will be to spread those values. That will be a pre-condition of any agreements that we reach. Do you want me to go on?"

Churchill was already getting angry. He loathed that speech because it challenged every tenet of the British Empire. Now Roosevelt was making adoption of those principles a condition of any further American assistance. It was going to be a tough meeting but Winston desperately needed as much American assistance as he could possibly get. He did not want to go but he knew that he could never tell the British people that he had met the President and not reached an agreement. He had been warned about the importance Roosevelt attached to it all but he had taken little heed of those warnings. He wanted a much better deal for Britain than anything suggested by that speech.

"Mr President, I do understand the implications of your address and I believe that it was deliberately aimed at Britain. I do have an American mother and I am well aware of American values. We, too, have our values and are fighting this war as a democratic country and in seeking to save our country we are also seeking to save democracy. But just following the ideas in you speech is not in my view a good way to proceed. Equally I do not believe that it can be all that you have to say to me. We are not meeting here to discuss your speech. My requests for assistance are the main reason why I am here. So please tell me everything that you want me to hear and then we will discuss the details."

"OK, Winston. I am willing to ramp up American arms production and the production of support equipment such as trucks and food as far and as fast as is necessary to help both you and Russia. I personally think that Britain needs much more help than Russia. I have had several requests for aid from Russia but they have neither been as frequent or as strong as those for you and your people. They have asked me to bring America into a land war in the west of Europe and I have declined that request in exactly the same way that I have declined your requests for help.

"It is certainly my assessment that Britain is going to need a lot more aid from America than it currently gets now. In fact I do not think there is anywhere else that the aid can come from. The production facilities simply do not exist in your colonies or in Britain itself.

"But I have three problems. The first is that for domestic political reasons I cannot commit America to going to war at this time. The only conditions under which we will go to war are if some nation, logically Germany, Italy or Japan declares war on us. We currently do not see that as an imminent or likely possibility. If it does happen then a different situation will arise. I cannot discuss what we would do if that event did arise but I can assure you that the American people will want any such threat to them to be dealt with effectively and quickly. But as I say there are no current indications that any such situation is likely. If such a situation does arise I can assure you that you and I will need to meet as a matter of urgency.

"Perhaps the easiest issue that I have is who pays for any aid that we do provide. America does have the capacity to provide you with more military equipment, food, iron ore and aluminium or indeed anything else you need. We are starting to build a new type of cargo ship which is likely to be of considerable interest to you. We can provide as much as you want of anything. We can certainly take some of the pressure off your factories by building more equipment in the Unites States. That we can and will do but Britain is going to have to pay the full cost of everything that she acquires from us. We will simply take the role of supplier on wholly commercial terms. At the rate at which you are taking stuff at the moment it will take you a very long time to pay. That does not matter to me. We have plenty of capacity to be your banker, but pay in full you surely will, even if it takes a century, It will be the people of Britain who have to pay the bill, which they will do through high taxes for many years to come. That will probably be judged by future generations as a reasonable price to pay for the appalling failings and sterility of British policies for a very long time. Britain has been looking at the wrong ball on the wrong playing field for a very long time. It was looking at the Empire when it should have been looking at the rottenness it had helped to create in Europe. That is not just my personal view. It is view that is widely held by many in my government and in this country and is a major reason why there is such hostility about getting into a war in Europe at this time. You may not like that but it is the way it is seen this side of the Atlantic.

"My third problem is with that Empire. It will be a condition of any further aid that you adopt those four principles in my speech and that you apply them fully throughout that Empire. It is an all or nothing deal. Saving Britain will mean that the Empire has to go. You cannot apply those freedoms and still rule those territories from London. If you agree to that you will get all the aid that you want. Those freedoms cannot be real if your colonies are still ruled from London. They must be able to live their own freedoms. As and when I have to tell Congress what I have agreed with you the main concern that they will have is about how I have used the opportunity to extend democracy through the world.

"Now let us get down to the specifics. America will do nothing to help Britain in any country which forms part of your Empire, except Australia. We see them as an important long term partner in the Pacific and if they are attacked we will go to their defence. But we will not help anyone else.

"In return for the help we are giving you now we demand that you help us at any time in the future when we believe that such help might be valuable. But it will be our call. You will have no choice. I cannot predict when we might call your country, but you must do as we say. That agreement will last for a minimum period of 150 years.

"So as I see it, Winston, you have a clear choice. Either Britain survives with American help on our terms or it does not. You can now choose your future. But before we leave this ship we must have a written agreement. What parts of that are published we can decide but you will not have any agreement for us to provide any further aid unless you agree to get rid of your empire."

By now Winston was very angry and not prepared to respond in any detailed way to what he had been told so he asked for an adjournment. He had to think through the consequences of what Roosevelt was telling him. But there were three things that he needed to say immediately.

"Mr. President, You have said things that are critical of recent British governments. As you know I have been critical of many things that out governments had done or not done in recent years. But whether you agree with what has been done or not you have to accept that the British people, just like the American people have views about what they want to be achieved on their behalf. In the Great War every parish in Britain lost young men. There was not a single family in Britain that did not lose a relative or a friend. In many cases all the young members of families were killed. Some of their bodies have never been recovered. Every family learned just what the horrors of war were. You must accept that after that there was an overwhelming desire for peace across the entire nation. If that desire for peace contributed to the weaknesses of our position at the beginning of the war then that reason needs to be understood.

"Since the Great War British democratic institutions have been strengthened. We now have a universal franchise, for example. Trade unions have gained greater authority and respect and we have introduced regulation into some industries to achieve a better balance between owners of industries and their customers.

"One other thing I will say at this stage is that Britain is a shining light in Europe in that it is a democracy. The two nations that we are fighting are not democracies. But what seems the most important issue of all at this time is that we win the war against those countries. I am sure that it will be easy for us to agree that democracy should replace the totalitarian regimes that exist in Germany and Italy.

"I think we should adjourn now as I will need to think over everything that you have said so far. When we talk again in the morning I think I should be allow to state my case more fully."

He took all the rest of that day and all that night to think it through. He did have dinner on *Augusta* that evening with Roosevelt and some of the advisers that they had both brought with them. Roosevelt talked over dinner about the Tennessee Valley Authority and why it had worked so well. He could not think why similarly imaginative schemes had not been adopted in Europe. After dinner Roosevelt and Churchill talked about American history. An issue that Roosevelt stressed was the impact that the emancipation of slaves had had as a result of the American civil war. Churchill thought that was interesting but not relevant to their discussions that would have to resume in the morning.

* * *

August 10, 1941. I went with Winston for dinner of USS Augusta last evening. It was a splendid meal and completely different from the mean fare we are able to have in Britain at this time. Winston was in a sombre mood all the evening just as he had been after the main session with Roosevelt in the morning. He has said nothing about his talks. All afternoon he brooded in his cabin. If they had talked about military matters I am sure he would have told me. That means that they can only have discussed political issues. I know that Winston did not want that. He had hoped that they would start on military issues and get agreement on those before making further progress.

* * *

Later Roosevelt and Churchill met again on *Prince of Wales*. As they had discussed Winston was able to lead the discussions at the beginning. He started:

"Look, Mr. President, yesterday you presented me with a very stark choice. As I understood it you said that I had to accept your pre-conditions or not agree with you. That is not the way that I see things at all. I think we should start with trying to resolve the problem that we both share. My country is at war and the defence of democracy is at the heart of that war. It is going to be stunningly difficult for us to achieve victory in that fight without massive help of all kinds from America. If that help is not forthcoming then democracy will disappear completely from Europe. That is a position which is completely inconsistent with your stated aim of ensuring that there is democracy everywhere. We should therefore explore how we can help each other achieve that aim.

"Most of what you said yesterday would make impossible reading for me or any other British Prime Minister in the newspapers in our country. There is no way that any British government could be seen to agree to the conditions that you were proposing yesterday. There is no agreement that might be possible between us that could be be presented in that way. Politicians simply do not create their own suicides by publishing anything like you proposed yesterday. Equally I simply cannot tell Parliament at any time that I have agreed to dismember the Empire.

"If any one of the conditions that you proposed yesterday, let alone the whole lot as a package, was put to Parliament they would be rejected. Every member would be instructed by his constituents that Britain simply could not accept conditions like that. The government would certainly fall. There would be nothing that I could do or say that would prevent such an outcome. There would immediately be a call for me to resign as soon as I presented any such proposals. There is no way that I or any other British Prime Minister will ever be able to do anything like that.

"Probably the toughest condition of them all is about the Empire. In Britain it is seen as a huge national achievement and it is a huge source of pride for our nation. At the moment large numbers of people from those countries are serving in our armed forces and are seen to be a great strength for us at this terrible time. Whatever else we might agree it is simply not possible for us to have any sort of public agreement which links the supply of military materials to any commitment to re-organise or abandon the Empire.

"The overwhelming view of the British people is that we do need support in this war and that that support must come from America. It clearly cannot come from any other nation in the western part of Europe. Russia is only a theoretical possibility. But there is very little interest in Russia in Britain and the political system that they now have is so alien to our own that it is impossible to see what benefits could arise from any such relationship. In any event all the information we have from Russia is that they have been very focused on internal reforms and that those have been the overwhelming national priority. It is certainly true that the present

German invasion reduces the pressure on us in the west but there are still very large numbers of German forces along all the North Sea and Channel coasts and the threat to us very much remains.

"I cannot see Russia being of any great help, in any event. German forces have advanced very rapidly against weak defences and the most likely outcome at this time is that Germany will achieve its objectives. In those circumstances there will not be a Russia to help us.

"So, as it always was, it is back to America. Britain does not know that I have made this journey to meet you and neither does America know that we are meeting. They will both have to be told within a few days and they will have to be told what the outcome has been. As I have already said I can never tell my government, or Parliament, or the nation what you have said to me. But I do, I believe, have to tell them that a strengthened relationship between the two countries has been agreed and that it will help Britain's war effort.

"Most people will understand that America cannot go to war at this time but they will be very disappointed by that view. The reason they will be disappointed is that if no war is declared on America there will be no direct involvement in the war in Europe by America. When Germany has overwhelmed Russia, as I fully expect, then we will be back in the firing line. It could well be that Britain might be attacked next year. We currently have nothing that even vaguely approaches the 153 divisions that they are believed to have used against Russia, and we have no capability of producing or equipping anything on that scale.

"So the real issue with which we are dealing today is not what America provides but how it is done and how it is presented. After we spoke yesterday I was able to give much thought to what you said and how things between us can be reconciled. I have a proposal which I would like you to consider.

"So what I propose that we do is tell the world that we have created a powerful Atlantic Alliance under which America recognises a special relationship with Britain and that a new set of supply contracts have been agreed under that special relationship. I think we can easily agree on all of that. I personally believe that with America making those manufacturing facilities available to us you will have made major strides towards the extension of democracy across the world which should be sufficient for the achievement of your objectives. We can both treat it as a great success. I suggest that we defer discussion on any other matters of interest to you.

"I believe that we can now look at what you said yesterday about the commercial terms for example. There is logic to that. It is that manifestly obvious that Britain cannot pay until our factories are exporting on a large scale again. That can only happen at the end of the war. Therefore no action needs to be taken now to fulfil that part of any agreement.

"Equally it is obvious that no action can be taken to deal with the Empire issues again until after the war. As a minimum there would have to be consultations with those colonies on a wide range of issues before any action could be undertaken. A good example is that their currencies are linked to Sterling and all their international trade is undertaken in Sterling. Britain provides a central banking facility for them all. They are all dependent on Empire trading agreements. No thought has ever been given in Britain about how those sorts of issues can be resolved. So in a practical sense there is nothing that I can discuss about the Empire while I am here. We must make progress and towards that end I would appreciate your comments on what I have said."

Roosevelt thought about what he had said for perhaps twenty minutes. Winston arranged strong drinks for both of them. When Roosevelt had got his Beefeater Martini he responded to Churchill;

"Winston, please accept from me that I fully accept the plight of Britain and her people at this time. America has only two choices. It can either stay out of world chaos and continue to heal the wound caused by the great depression. Or it can enter that chaos. The people have chosen that former course. I will consider what you have said. And I certainly appreciate what you have said about democracy in Europe. You can be absolutely certain that if we were involved directly in your war an essential outcome for us would be the achievement of democracy throughout the continent.

"Like you I will give it all some more thought. What I suggest we do is meet again this afternoon and try and see what we can finalise then. I will come back here at about four."

* * *

August 10, 1941. Over lunch today Winston was much more forthcoming about his talks with Roosevelt. He told us he was certain that Roosevelt would agree to a large increase in American aid to Britain. There were commercial terms that had to be agreed but he thought he would get a deal that he could proudly present to Parliament and the people as a triumph for Britain. He was asked several questions by me and his other advisers but he declined to answer any of them. As I think I know Winston well I interpret that as meaning that there is something that he does not wish us to know. I do not think I can believe that things have been going as well as he has suggested.

* * *

When Roosevelt returned he was in a very determined mood and he offered a package solution to Winston:

"Winston, I have taken account of everything that you have said. We are ready to agree to a Lend/Lease package which goes far beyond anything for which you have asked. You can have whatever you want from us in terms of food, machines, equipment, materials, aircraft and ships. We can start to increase our production facilities immediately. We have plenty of spare capacity in many industries. We can regulate the producing companies to ensure that you get a fair price. We will finance it all for you. You will not have to pay anything until after the war. But you will have to pay all accrued interest on all sums owing. That deal can be as public or as private as you like. I am certain that you will want to describe it a huge triumph of your negotiating skills. That does not give me a problem. It cannot be an exclusive deal. We will deal with Russia on an identical basis as we will with any other country that wants us to help them.

"But the quid pro quo of all of that is that we must have another deal to be called the Atlantic Charter or the Atlantic Alliance. I am not hung up about the words. It can and should be a secret agreement. There must be three parts to that:

"The first is that there must be substantial technology transfer from America to Britain through the transfer of patent rights. Our industrial companies must be able to get benefits in return for all the work that they will be doing for you. Britain currently leads the field in several industrial fields and we will need the benefits of technology transfer without payment in order that they can invest heavily in the next generation of machines and equipment. Britain's work on jet engines is perhaps the best example.

"The second part is that there must be a commitment from Britain to help America in any military conflict of ours at any time over the next 150 years. The request for assistance will come from us and cannot be refused.

"The third is a commitment that democracy will be introduced to all your colonial countries as rapidly as possible after the war has finished. You can still call it an Empire if you wish but there will have to be full democratic rights in all those countries and that includes the right of self-determination. As long as they are free to make their own decisions they will be free to have whatever relations with Britain that they desire.

"If you can agree to those conditions I will authorise our industries to trade with you on an unlimited basis. If not I will only allow our industries to trade with you on current terms. That will be taken to mean no credit and no war materials other than those being supplied currently.

"I think we should try and wrap this all up in the morning so that a final agreement can be drafted before we both have to return to our countries. It really is up to you now. I have put my final proposal on the table. There is nothing more that I can give."

* * *

August 11, 1941. Winston wanted a private talk with me early this evening. He told me that he had to make a decision by the morning on a package put to him by Roosevelt. He could not discuss it with the service chiefs he had brought with him and he had to discuss it with someone. I assumed from that that he was having to grapple with political matters and not military ones. He explained to me that there were two elements to what Roosevelt had proposed. The first was about an unlimited extension of Lend/Lease. It would cover anything Britain wanted but it had some strings about technology transfer linked to it. He was certain that if that deal was not linked to anything else it would be easy to accept. But he went on;

"Samuel, he has linked that Lend/Lease deal to a new political understanding that will limit our freedom to deal with other countries around the world for a very long time to come. There are some aspects of those political arrangements which are neither a surprise nor difficult to accept. But there are others that I could never even tell my colleagues about let alone try to sell to Parliament or the British people. There are some that I do not believe that any Briton could ever accept.

"You and I know from the military intelligence we review almost every day that we have a very long and difficult fight on our hands if we are to beat Germany. They have mighty armies, more powerful than anything previously assembled and when they have defeated Russia they will probably attempt to invade Britain. At the moment it is highly unlikely that we will be able to resist them. They already have a numerical superiority against us of about 10 to 1. If they are able to absorb some of the Russian armies into their own that will get even worse. They are making great gains in Russia just now and they will probably conquer Moscow within the next couple of months. That will be the beginning of the end in the east.

"The only way that we can increase the capability of our armed forces is to take the expanded Lend/Lease. Amongst my colleagues whom I consulted before I came here there was an expectation not only that we would achieve that but that we would get a commitment from Roosevelt to deploy large numbers of America personnel to help us as well. He cannot send us any troops at this time and I do not now believe that I can persuade him otherwise. So we remain on our own but with potentially greater equipment resources.

"But there is no possibility of my getting cabinet approval for the political arrangements. I do not even believe that I can tell them about them. They would certainly require me to resign if I did. What is more I do not believe that even if I sign an agreement with Roosevelt I can ever personally implement it. I would be surprised if any British government would ever

voluntarily do so. It could only be implemented under duress. But I have to decide what to do by the morning. It is made worse by the fact that Roosevelt I insisting that it is all or nothing. If we do not sign the political deal we will sink militarily.

"I need some help in thinking my way through it all."

It was not a conversation that I had ever expected to have with him. But what I recognised was that making the decision he had to make was a true burden. Only the great can make the right decision in those circumstances. There was no way that I could help him politically. I simply did not have any useful experience in that area. The only thing I could do was assist him with some of my military experience but before I did so I asked him whether he could give me more detail about the content of the likely agreements. It was when he told me the detail that I realised the true burden of the decision that he had to make.

Before he did that he said; "Samuel, you may well be the only person to whom I recount the detail of what Roosevelt is demanding. You must agree that you will never disclose the detail to anyone.

I gave that undertaking and then said to him:

"Winston, the only real experience that I have which might be able to help you is my military experience. In the military you only win if you have very clear objectives. If you attain those objectives you will win the battle and then the war. If you are confused about the objectives you will usually fail. I am sure that the expectations of the British people about you are that your role is to win the war. You have certainly positioned yourself with them as the man to do it. So if that is your objective you must make the decision that best achieves that."

Winston did join us that evening for dinner but it was a rather serious occasion. The only thing he wanted to talk about was the huge damage caused by the Bismarck battles. He was particularly hurt by the loss of those ships in convoy and by the loss of the battleship Hood. He was, as always, taking all naval losses personally.

There was a new footnote to this diary entry dated June 6, 1970. It was written a few days before Samuel died. It reads:

"Since then I have not spoken to anyone about what Winston told me that evening. Nor have I seen any statement from any British or American source which describes any detail of the Atlantic Charter. But what I have seen are many events which are consistent with what was agreed at Placentia Bay. Those events include the dismemberment of the British Empire and British involvement in the Korean War."

* * *

August 12, 1941. This morning Roosevelt came back on board. Within a couple of hours they had finalised whatever it was they agreed. They signed documents and then Roosevelt left. As soon as he had gone we departed from that dreadful place to return to Britain.

* * *

When I was able to read Roosevelt's personal papers I found one document which set out his conclusions about the Placentia Bay talks. It was obvious from what he wrote that he was in excellent form as he steamed back to Virginia on board *USS Augusta*. He had done the deal of a lifetime. It would make America very powerful. It would crush the British Empire It was exactly as he wanted.

It was also obvious that he regarded America's entry into the war as inevitable. He was pleased that Britain would need vast amounts of military equipment. That meant that he could expand America's defence manufacturing capacity without making Congress suspicious as to the reasons for that. When the time came America would be well prepared.

* * *

What Churchill told the Commons was something quite different. Even in wartime Parliament had a summer recess. But it was recalled to hear a statement from the Prime Minister. He started to speak at two in the afternoon. *Prince of Wales* had arrived at Faslane in Western Scotland during the night and he had then flown to London.

"Mr. Speaker, I have just returned to Britain after having several days of talks with President Roosevelt. I could not announce the plan for these talks in advance because of overwhelming security considerations. These were most particularly concerned with the safety of my travel across the Atlantic.

"In our talks we reviewed the actual war situation that Britain currently faces as well as the developing situation on the Russian fronts. I do not have to remind this house of the difficulties that we face in these islands from German bombings, food and fuel rationing and the need to build up our armed forces so that we can beat the might of the German armies. It will be a long battle before we triumph.

"At this time Russia is facing the largest military assault that has ever been created. They have asked us to assist them by the opening of a land war with Germany in the west. But realistically we cannot do that at this time.

"This House will know that I have always believed that American support is essential if we are going to win this war quickly. Within days of the war starting I had negotiated the first Lend/Lease deal with America that provided us quickly with extra convoy escorts. Since then many other deals have been negotiated. They have been very valuable to our island nation.

"In our recent talks we have agreed a major extension of this programme. There is one particularly interesting and useful new addition to the programme. It is in relation to merchant shipping. We have all been concerned about the loss of merchant shipping on the North Atlantic convoys. America has been developing a new type of cargo vessel that can be mass produced. These are called Liberty ships and can carry 9,000 tons of cargo. They will be bigger than most of the ships that have sailed in convoys so far and they can be assembled within a few days. The first is due to be launched in a few weeks time. The President has agreed to make an unlimited number of these available for us to acquire and use on our convoys. I expect the first one to be in a convoy in October. They will be essential in our programmes to provide our nation with additional military equipment and civilian supplies.

"The President will also be providing Russia with much enhanced aid through similar programmes to those that he has set up for us.

"I wish to express my gratitude, through this house, to the President for all he has been able to do for us despite the fact that America has no state of war with any country at this time.

"The agreement that we signed is called "The Atlantic Charter" and it is designed to extend our co-operation as and when it may be required.

"Mr Speaker, with this additional American aid we will continue to prosecute the war in every way that we can as we move towards a successful conclusion."

Not a word about the duration of the agreement, nor any word about the principles within it. No word either about American refusal to help Britain with any colonial country. Not a word about Churchill's commitment to dismember the Empire.

In due course Roosevelt smiled when he read the text of what Winston had said. It was very much the smile on the face of the tiger.

* * *

It was a much chastened Churchill who went to see Alice the following day. She was the only person other than Samuel to whom he ever spoke about the Atlantic Charter. He told her exactly what had happened on board *Prince of Wales*. She was good at debating and she debated the whole issue with him at great length. He did not have any other appointment until dinner at eight with Anthony Eden. Then he would be going to the Cabinet War Rooms for another night of battle news.

Alice's analysis was good for Churchill. He needed to be very clear that he had really had had no alternative but to sign up to everything that Roosevelt wanted if he was going to continue to get aid from America. He also knew that Britain could not survive without that aid. There was no way he could have survived politically without bringing back that additional aid. But he did tell Alice just before he left that there was no way that he personally would do anything to change Britain's relationship in any way with any country in the Empire. How he would get out of that commitment he had made to Roosevelt he had no idea. But he had survived at least for the time being. Survival was something dear to every politician.

* * *

November 10, 1941. Today we have heard even worse news from Russia than we have heard for some weeks. Russian armies commanded by Guderian have now reached the outer suburbs of Moscow. Goodness knows how long that city can survive now. Winston believes that the Russian government will have to leave soon and find a safe place much further east.

* * *

In Russia the main German attack had been in what Germany called the Centre; that was from southern Poland, east and south towards Kiev and north east towards Smolensk. Beyond Smolensk the target was Moscow. Guderian led the attacks on Kiev and then on Moscow. All through that summer and autumn the German troops advanced relentlessly against inferior Russian armies.

Germany succeeded in getting into the outer suburbs of Moscow and in taking over Kiev and much of the Ukraine before the winter halted effective German military operations. They were also able to overrun much of the Don Basin and get to the very edge of the Caucasus. By any normal standards it would have been regarded as a military triumph.

* * *

November 12, 1941. Coming hard on the heels of the bad news about the German advances towards Moscow is the news that a German army corps has landed in North Africa. The only objective for this army can be to try and clear British troops from Egypt and the Middle East. Winston is very depressed about it all. Things seem to be getting even worse. The only good news is that convoy losses have dropped off in the last few weeks but that may just be because of bad weather in the North Atlantic. The shortage of ships has also meant that fewer convoys have been able to sail.

* * *

In November 1941 the German General Erwin Rommel arrived in North Africa with his Afrika Corps. Rommel had led tank armies in Poland. France and in Russia with great distinction. Now Hitler wanted him to drive Britain out of Egypt and the Middle East. His first encounters with British armour were at Tobruk in Libya on November 23rd. Over that winter British lines in Libya became seriously undersupplied with food and fuel because of the great distances to their supply depots in Egypt but the battlefield remained stable.

* * *

December 6, 1941. Today Winston held reviews with all the Services chiefs. For weeks he has been fretting about the lack of progress we have been making in the war. The only successes on the ground have been in North Africa and now those are threatened. We have not been able to attack the heartland of Germany in any real way although we have been flying regular bombing raids. The loss of ships in convoys has destroyed a large part of our merchant fleet. Hood was sunk in the battle for the Bismarck. Russia has been overrun. Rationing gets tougher each month and many of our cities have been bombed whenever the weather has been good enough. It is in Winston's view still a disaster with no clear victories in sight. He fears it is all going to get worse. He remains angry about America. I think he will go on being angry until such time as something happens to bring her into the war. But as yet there is no sign of anything like that happening.

We have been at war for more than two years already and Britain is in a tighter situation of siege than it was then. It is all very grim.

Another thing that is worrying Winston is the mood of the British public. When we came back from Canada there was euphoria about what he had achieved there. But now the newspapers regularly contain articles asking when all that extra aid will reach Britain. People are getting very tired with all the deprivations. It is certainly going to be another tough winter.

The Defeat of Germany

December 7, 1941. This afternoon we were told of a devastating air raid by Japanese forces on the American Pacific Fleet anchored at Pearl Harbour in Hawaii. Winston was ecstatic at the news and was certain that America would now enter the war. He said "Our long wait is now over."

* * *

The whole horrible shambles of the war was given a wholly new dimension on 7th December, 1941 when the Japanese Navy attacked the American naval base at Pearl Harbour in Hawaii. A large part of the American battle fleet was destroyed. Throughout America that attack was entirely unexpected. It turned the war from being a European conflict into a global one.

America immediately declared war on Japan, Germany and their allies. Roosevelt then sent a telegram to Churchill demanding that he visit Washington as soon as possible. So Churchill flew there in December 1941, within a few days of Pearl Harbour. The call from Roosevelt was an instruction, not an invitation.

* * *

December 10, 1941. Devastating news both for Churchill and the nation. A Japanese air raid on Singapore has sunk Prince of Wales. In view of our recent voyage on her this has come as a shocking blow to Winston. He has sent personal condolences to all the families of the crew who lost their lives.

* * *

Before he left for Washington Winston sent a message to Bradman asking Washington for an assessment of Roosevelt's current mood. It took a couple of days to get that and send it back to London by telegram a few hours before his plane was due to depart for Washington.

He met with Sally at Chartwell again for her assessment of his mood as well. All she was able to say was that the President attached the highest importance to the meeting and would be setting out what America now intended to do. That was not what Winston wanted because he intended to tell him what Britain wanted him to do.

As usual Roosevelt asked Angela to have lunch with him so that he could explain to her the position he was likely to take in his discussions with Churchill. Despite the new pressures on him she found him to be in a genial mood when she was shown into his private sitting room. It was Dry Martini time and they were already poured. They sat near the large window that looked out over Washington Mall. The winter sun was streaming in.

"Angela, when I met with Winston a few months back I did tell him that we would need to meet urgently as and when any situation arose in which America was seriously attacked. No one could have predicted then just how soon such an attack might be made and just how devastating it would be. I have never been on any of our ships which were sunk or damaged at Pearl but I did meet with Winston on *Prince of Wales* and I have been very distressed about her loss. I have asked Joseph Kennedy to pass on my condolences to all the families affected.

"Although we were not prepared for this attack I have given much thought in recent times about what would happen if America was forced to enter the war. We have been increasing the capabilities of our forces, increasing our training capacity and introducing more and better weapons. As a result we are far better prepared than we would otherwise have been. But war is not just about weapons systems it is about the complete commitment of a nation to win that war.

"I am going to tell Winston about that commitment and I am sure that he will be satisfied that it is very large and that it will be effective. But as with our last discussions there will be choices that have to be made. The reason that I need to meet with him is to go over those choices and see how we can get Americans involved in the war in Europe quickly. Those choices are not easy for us and they will not be easy for Winston either. But they have to be made at the outset and they will affect the entire way the war is conducted after that. They will also affect the way that the transition to peace can be managed and about the shape of that peace.

"One of those choices is about the convoy system. We can put some of our own destroyers and cutters on to North Atlantic convoys within a few days but we will need to set up a command structure under which they will be effective. It would be sensible for him to bring a suitable British officer with him who can get that work going immediately. We will be able to put some of our merchant ships on to convoys within the month.

"Something else you can tell him is that we have to reach agreement while he is here. You know that he has been pressing me continuously since the beginning of the war for American intervention. He has stressed Britain's desperate need. Well, now is the time to turn that all into action. Action he will see on a spectacular scale as long as the right conditions can be achieved.

That was exactly what she passed back to Winston. He ordered Admiral Max Horton to join the flight. But Winston did not like the overall tone of the message.

* * *

December 12, 1941. I am writing this as I travel with Winston to Washington. We are on a BOAC Skymaster plane. It is the first time any of Winston's party have flown across the Atlantic. Winston seems to like the experience and I suspect that from now on he will choose to fly wherever possible rather than use a battleship. We left Northolt this morning and had to stop at Prestwick, near Glasgow, for fuel. Admiral Max Horton joined the plane there .We will have to stop again at Gander. Winston wants to spend several hours with him going over the options for American involvement in the convoy escort programme.

As soon as we had taken off from Prestwick he asked me to sit with him. He showed me the message he had received from Washington during the night. It was from the agent we call Bradman. We really wanted to know what I thought of the phrases in the message about choices. It seemed to me that the choices about the convoys were obvious. There simply had to be efficient ways of getting ships across the Atlantic safely. Perhaps one of them was for American ships to operate in the western part of the ocean and British ships to operate in the eastern part. That was how we already operated with the Canadian Navy. It could be done the same way with long-range aircraft. But I could not see what other choices were implied in what Roosevelt had sent.

We arrived in Washington in the late evening. Winston went straight to the Ambassador's residence for the night. The rest of us went to a hotel.

* * *

Winston went off to the White House for a breakfast time meeting. This was going to be his first visit to the White House and he hoped that it would be a pleasant experience. But what

Roosevelt told him within a few minutes of his arriving went far beyond anything that was imaginable.

"Winston, I have already broadcast over the radio to our people saying that I have committed the entire resources of this nation to winning the war in the Pacific and in Europe. It is not a commitment into which I entered lightly. Over the last couple of years I have had plenty of time to consider what America might do if we were attacked. I have taken steps during that time to build up our military capability just in case. It was essential that we did not repeat the same problem that Britain, France and Russia have had which is inadequate preparation for war. We had not expected the threat to come from Japan. We had actually expected German air raids on New York. We know that Germany has been developing aircraft with exactly that capability. There have been several submarine attacks on our warships. We have not publicised these but we were anticipating that sooner or later they would lead to a sinking. If that had happened we would have gone to war with Germany. The real issue about that is that we are already at an advanced state of readiness.

"Now I said a few minutes ago that I have committed the entire resources of this nation to war. Not just to go to war but to winning that war. That is a completely open ended and unlimited commitment. We will win the war however long it takes. We will beat Germany and we will beat Japan. We will beat them both simultaneously. We will go on building up our armed forces until we have achieved all of that. We are the only country in the world with the manpower and industrial capacity to do it.

"It is going to be America's war now. But I said in my broadcast that we would be fighting with our allies, Britain and Russia in order to bring about those victories. The words I used to describe that victory were "we could accept no result save victory, final and complete." It is that final and complete victory which will distinguish this war from the last one. Both Germany and Japan will be completely crushed in the onslaught that we will create.

"When we have crushed both countries we will install democracies there. Neither country has ever had any sort of democracy. As you will know from our meetings on *Prince of Wales* democracy is the very heart of our political thinking and it is the very heart of our foreign policy. I am making it the very heart of our military objectives as well.

"America is already largely financing your war. We will soon be your largest supplier of tanks, guns, aircraft, and merchant ships. We have the manpower to put into the field vastly greater numbers than your country can provide. We have the capability to fight on several fronts at the same time. That is why America will be controlling this war from now on. We will control it wherever our forces are involved. Wherever there are British forces operating in the same theatre they will be subservient to America. It will be run by America and it will be America that brings about victory, in conjunction with our allies. We will co-operate with our allies to achieve our military and political objectives.

"As we see it now Britain has only been able to make one significant military advance and that was against weak Italian forces in Libya. Even that gain is now threatened. Britain has been developing expertise fast in the convoy wars and that expertise is one that we value. I have listened to you about those battles and about the importance to Britain of achieving a high level of safety for all those ships. We can learn from you there and it is, I believe, the first area where we can work together.

"But there is a price for you to pay for the victory that we will surely achieve. You must allow our troops, navy and air forces unlimited access to Britain, immediately. And you must agree that the overall military command structure will be under the control of American officers. You don't have any choice but to agree to that. I will nominate a senior officer to go to London to plan for a ground force landing to take place somewhere in Europe as soon as a sufficient troop build up has been achieved. We will send aircraft to Europe immediately and we will provide air patrols over the North Atlantic immediately in order to try and prevent U-Boats attacking the convoys. We will also provide all the convoy escorts needed in the western part of the Atlantic within a few weeks.

"I must stress that the price of an unlimited American commitment to achieve unconditional surrender both by Japan and Germany is that it will be America's war. You simply have to accept that in addition to the agreement that we made last summer on *Prince of Wales*.

"You cannot possibly have any idea of what an unlimited American commitment is until it happens but I can assure you that you ain't seen nothing yet."

Churchill felt as if one giant knife had just been stabbed into his back. He told Roosevelt he needed time to think it all through. They agreed to meet again the next morning.

All afternoon Churchill fretted and worried about the issue. It seemed to be like a horrible re-run of the *Prince of Wales* meetings. But it quickly became clear that he had only two options. The first was to accept it and recognise that Britain's role in managing the war would slip away. The other was to reject it and if he did he would have to resign as Prime Minister. But he really knew that that would be impossible for him personally. He could never resign and he had to go on fighting for the best possible American involvement. What he had read into what Roosevelt had said was that America was going to take on Germany whether Britain was involved or not.

One thing that Churchill did know, and it had been pressed on him by Alice and Clemmie, was that the British people expected him to get help from whatever source so that the increasingly tiresome war was brought to an end as soon as possible. On that basis he simply could not go back to Britain without a deal. He also remembered what he had been told by Samuel about the clarity of objectives. If the objective was to win the war then he probably had no alternative but to agree to Roosevelt's requirements.

But gone were any remaining dreams of his about his controlling the war and leading all the enemies of Germany to a triumphant victory. Late that afternoon he felt as if it might all slip away from him quite quickly. It was a very hard message for him. But he knew very well that Britain had no capacity to win the war on its own. And he knew that America would not let Britain do that anyway now.

But the biggest realisation of all that afternoon for Winston was that Roosevelt had been planning for months and years about how he was going to handle Britain. He had objectives of his own for Britain and he was now going to use the war to make sure that they were all achieved.

For that evening Roosevelt had arranged a dinner for Winston to meet several members of his cabinet. There was no talk about any new deal between the two countries that evening. Roosevelt, in any event, would not have consulted any member of his cabinet about any talks with Churchill. He rarely consulted anyone about anything. He was the master political architect, the master political chess player. All the plans he followed were his plans and his plans alone.

It was an enjoyable dinner, held in the White House, and the talk was largely about American history. It was a subject that seriously interested Churchill and he was pleased to talk about anything other than the way that Roosevelt had gained mastery of the war.

As he was driven back to the British Ambassador's residence, where he was staying, he reflected on the appalling barrenness of British politics after the First World War and then through the 1930's which had led to these terrible humiliations at the hands of a ruthless American President.

But what he did know and for which he would always be grateful was that it was now possible to see a route through to the completion of the war. He had no doubt that Roosevelt meant it when he said that he would commit the entire resources of the nation to the task. He had no doubt that as the men and equipment became available the results would start to show through very strongly. He personally hoped that the first results would be in the North Atlantic.

Before the dinner had started that evening Roosevelt had asked Churchill what his personal priority would be. He replied that everything depended on being able to get much larger convoys through safely. Getting more escorts and more planes flying over the Atlantic was essential to that. He pressed upon Roosevelt that that should happen very quickly. Roosevelt agreed to do what he could.

Churchill then said;

"I have brought an Admiral with me to Washington, as you suggested. His name is Max Horton and he commands our Western Approaches. He is an anti-submarine expert and he is making good progress in his work but there is always far more to be done. He is very expert on the state of the forces available to us and the ways in which they are working. I think he should get together your people in the morning and they can work out a plan. You will find him very appreciative of any useful and urgent contributions that you can make."

The next day Winston and Roosevelt met at the White House again. This time Winston was not in fighting mood. He realised that there was no alternative to America being in the commanding role in the war from now on. Their discussions that day were about how they were going to make it work.

* * *

December 14, 1941. Winston wanted to talk after our aircraft took off from Washington. He wanted an update on developments in the war. The biggest one I was able to report to him was that the German advance had stalled around the western suburbs of Moscow. The weather had deteriorated and that was making military operations impossible. All the reports I had received suggested that it was likely to remain like that until the spring. But the same reports indicated that Russian reserves had been more or less completely exhausted and that the front was therefore very fragile.

We went on to talk about his discussions with Roosevelt. He said to me that he thought it was a bit like Placentia Bay, only much worse. He never mentioned those talks in the White House again to me.

* * *

In December 1941, immediately after Pearl Harbour, Eden, as Foreign Secretary, visited Russia. He actually went to Russia when Churchill was going to Washington.

Since Russia had been attacked there had been frequent telegram exchanges between Churchill, Roosevelt and Stalin. These provided little basis for any agreed conduct of the war between Britain, America and Russia, let alone any agreement in which America might be involved in the war in Russia over and above the supply of equipment. In the post Pearl Harbour situation clarity was even more important than before.

So Eden went via that special air service through Stockholm to see Molotov to try and get some clarity on what might be possible. Russia adamantly insisted that the main thing it needed was for Britain to open a second front in France so as to draw German troops away from Russia and increase the overall pressure on Germany. Their second objective then was to protect for Russia, in any peace deal at the end of the war, the territorial gains it had made in Eastern Europe as a result of the Molotov-Ribbentrop agreements. Molotov went into considerable detail about what Russia expected from those territorial enhancements. It was to be a recurring theme throughout the remainder of the war.

Britain was clearly not in a position to agree to either of those demands. Eden was left in no doubt both by Stalin and Molotov that Russia could not agree to anything less than the achievement of those two objectives. Stalin made no mention, of course, of his designs on British territory in the Middle East. Those were to come later.

In addition to assuming that America would inevitably become drawn into a land war in Europe as soon as they were able to move the troops and equipment across the Atlantic, they were able to make progress about how Russia, Britain and America might be able to work together. Molotov did say that he expected America to step up its level of support for Russia as a priority. Eden agreed to help that along in any way possible. Eden committed Britain to running more convoys into Russia. The American Liberty ships would help that effort.

* * *

The day that Churchill arrived back in Britain after an exceptionally bumpy and noisy flight across the Atlantic he reported to the House of Commons on his latest meeting with Roosevelt:

"It gives me great pleasure to tell this House that I have just returned from America where I have had a further meeting with President Roosevelt following the tragic events at Pearl Harbour. He advised me that America had now made an unlimited commitment to bring about the defeat of Japan and Germany. They will be discharging this commitment in conjunction with Britain and Russia.

"I have no personal doubts that the much higher level of American support which will now be possible will result in the defeat of Germany.

"We can expect within the next few months to be welcoming American armed forces to our islands as they prepare for a joint invasion of the European mainland that we will now prepare."

He was given a long standing ovation.

* * *

Soon after Barbarossa was launched Stalin formed STAVKA, which became a very effective High Command Headquarters. General Zhukov became its Chief of Staff on 29th July, 1941. Zhukov's first field command in the war was the defence of Leningrad. He saved Leningrad from being overrun but the city was virtually surrounded and under siege for the next 900 days. On 10th October 1941, virtually at the eleventh hour, Zhukov was ordered by Stalin to go to Moscow and was made responsible for the defence of the city. There were two main parts of his approach to this task.

On October 7th there had been virtually no Red Army troops between the Germans and the centre of Moscow. Reserve troops were moved in from the Far East and from other areas in Northern Russia under Zhukov's direction. Bridges and roads were destroyed. Fortunately sleet and rain made it impossible for the Germans to advance for three weeks. But it was enough time for Zhukov to get his forces organised.

The Germans did advance to the outer suburbs in November but in early December the snow started to fall and the temperatures dropped to well below minus twenty degrees Celsius. The German armour could not operate effectively in those conditions and the German armies were driven back about 100 miles. But Moscow was saved. As result of that victory Zhukov remained the Chief of Staff of STAVKA for the remainder of the war and conceived and led all the main campaigns after that.

It was on December 13th, 1941 while Roosevelt and Churchill were meeting in Washington that a series of events started in Moscow that were to have a far more profound effect on the conduct of the war and the shape of the subsequent peace than anything that Roosevelt was then planning.

* * *

It was late on a December afternoon in 1996 that I started to find the information trail that would lead to the corroboration of the ideas that Samuel had about the battle of Kursk. I was in the National Archives Library in Moscow. Even by Russian standards it was an exceptionally hard winter that year. The streets were piled with snow and the temperature in the middle of the day was around -20 degrees C. It was already dark when I arrived at the library. There were only two other people studying there that afternoon. The warmth of the place was a welcome change from the agonies of being outside. The library closed at eight so I would be able to study there for about four hours. Over the previous months I had got to know the librarian well and she always had the papers I wanted ready for me. That afternoon I wanted to go through the private diaries of General Zhukov

Georgii Konstantinovich Zhukov was born on 1 December, 1896 in the village of Strelkovka, some two hundred kilometres south of Moscow. His father was a shoemaker with little income. His mother was physically very powerful and she supplemented the family income by carrying 180 pound bags of grain. When he was eleven Zhukov became an apprentice furrier in Moscow. He was conscripted into the Russian army at the age of nineteen and there he stayed. By 1929 he was a brigade commander. His real rise to fame and an important command came in 1939 when he defeated a Japanese incursion across the Mongolia-Manchuria border. He was promoted to General, decorated and given command of the Kiev district. Thereafter he went on to command the defence of St. Petersburg, the defence of Moscow, and then the long series of battles to destroy the German armies as they retreated from Stalingrad and then through Kursk, Minsk, through Poland and on to Berlin itself. He was undoubtedly one of the greatest military leaders of all time. It was easy to see why Samuel regarded him as one of the supreme influences over the war.

I had started reading those diaries a couple of days earlier. I had already read about his early years in the army and then about his victorious campaign in the Far East. That afternoon I wanted to read about his role when he was District Commander in Kiev. Commander in Kiev was one of the most important commands in the whole Russian army. If there was ever a threat to Russia from the west then Ukraine would inevitably be the front line. It had been in the Great War and would always be so. Geographically it had a long border with Western Europe and its territory was suitable for invasion by tank armies.

It was round five o'clock that I found these entries in Zhukov's diary:

March 3, 1940 Since I have been here in Kiev I have been familiarising myself with the command here. I have already made some changes in the senior ranks and have designed some new training programme. I am now going to tour the main areas in my command to get to know the terrain and identify opportunities for battles here should the need ever arise.

March 10, 1940

Over the last week I have been in the area of Kursk. Until I had been there I had no idea that we had such a military gem in our country. It is perfect military territory for defence and counter attack. I have driven over large parts of the area to the west and south west of the city and flown all around the area in excellent weather conditions.

* * *

Studying the Russian archives provided a deep insight into how STAVKA worked. Apart from the Communist Party itself it was at that time the most important institution of the Russian state.

STAVKA met every day, usually in the afternoon. Each morning Zhukov had to be at his own Headquarters directing the defence of Moscow or visiting hot spots in the battle in order to instruct and guide local commanders. Zhukov usually dreaded STAVKA meetings. They were almost always chaired by Stalin and he always seemed to be in a brutal and sadistic mood. There were always demands for instant action and instant results. At that time Stalin had little understanding of any detailed military requirements. They were things that other people had to sort out.

But no one who had any regular contact with him could possibly have underestimated his absolute determination to beat all the German armies and his absolute hatred of the German people and their leader for what they were doing to Russia. His endless demands, the critical battlefield situation around Moscow and the needed to defeat Germany often gave rise to conflicting demands which could never be easily resolved. Arguing with Stalin could easily lead to the offender disappearing for ever.

It is probably impossible for anyone who did not experience it directly to understand the sense of fear that Stalin instilled into almost everyone he met and into every level of Soviet Russian society. Stalin had had a brutal past with several of his younger years being spent as a terrorist and bank robber. He had had many years in jail as a result of those terrorist activities. The general opinion of him, especially those that knew him and had to work with him, was that he was vindictive, rude, cruel and oppressive. He was known to be very happy to use violence openly and widely. Most people who had to work with him would happily submit to his moods and oppression rather than challenge him or show any signs of independence. Stalin, in his turn only wanted people round him who would accept his instructions and get on with the tasks assigned to them. Even that was not a formula guaranteed to create any sort of security for them. If he changed his mind they could be sent off to a Gulag on his simple instruction. Stalin's was a brutal and despotic regime.

One of the few people who ever exercised any independence of command under Stalin was Georgii Zhukov. He had largely come to Stalin's notice because of that independence. It was in 1940 when he had had to deal with a persistent problem of Romanian insurgents stealing railway and factory equipment from the Odessa military district in the southern part of the Soviet Union. The problem had been going on for years without solution. But Zhukov found a solution which he did not bother to clear with Moscow before implementation. His successful clearance of the Romanian insurgents resulted in diplomatic protests at the highest levels. When Stalin heard about it all he laughed. What mattered to him was that Zhukov had solved a problem for his country. The incident was etched on Stalin's excellent memory and when he needed help the next year it was to Zhukov that he turned.

Zhukov's relationship with Stalin after that was largely determined by a combination of Stalin's moods and Zhukov's successes in battle. But all the time there was the underlying thread that Stalin trusted nobody. In particular he would never give any independence of command to anyone who might challenge him in any way.

It was largely because of that that STAVKA was formed. STAVKA was to control the war effort with Stalin as its chairman. Other members would be appointed from time to time as necessary but there would not be any other single person in the organisation that would be able to challenge Stalin. If they came close to challenging him they would be sent off to Siberia.

Even Zhukov who was the architect of so many military victories during the war was under constant threat of removal from office as the senior Soviet military commander. He could not act without the approval of STAVKA even though he was the Chief of Staff of that organisation.

But equally Stalin did not have anything like sufficient command of military practices and skills to be able to lead STAVKA without a massive input from Zhukov and other military commanders.

The whole situation led to an uneasy peace in the Soviet command all the way through to victory in the war and well beyond that. The only thing that provided any sort of personal safety for Zhukov was military victories. The relationship between Zhukov and Stalin was a very obscure form of symbiosis. Zhukov needed Stalin's patronage. Stalin needed Zhukov's command skills.

* * *

The first of the tasks with which STAVKA had to deal was quite simply trying to stabilise the whole war front with Germany. Initially that proved to be completely impossible as the western part of the country became completely overrun.

After the first couple of months of Barbarossa and as Stalin was emerging from his severe depression about how he had been outwitted it became obvious to him and to STAVKA that defending the whole front was going to be impossible. The Russian armies were simply being overwhelmed. As summer turned to autumn the defence of Moscow became the priority. Stalin made his view perfectly clear to STAVKA that if Moscow fell the entire Soviet Union was threatened. So Moscow had to be defended at all costs.

It was Stalin personally who decided that Zhukov should be moved from the defence of Leningrad to take over the command of the Moscow defences. That proved to be an excellent move. Zhukov was able to halt the German advances and start to force them to retreat.

Making Moscow safe was the greatest task for all of them, indeed for all Russians at that time and Zhukov was achieving it.

But that was not enough for Stalin. He was determined that they should develop plans to destroy all the German forces in Russia. He was determined that never again would Russia be under any threat like a German invasion again. He was angry and he was demanding that everything be done. Nothing would satisfy him other than the complete annihilation of all those German armies. A massive problem that STAVKA had not really addressed was that Germany occupied a large part of Russia. Making Moscow safe was actually quite a small but very visible part of the whole problem.

Their second priority was therefore what to do after Moscow had been made safe. STAVKA was trying to develop at least the first thoughts as to how they prepared for whatever spring and summer campaigns were likely to be needed to deal with German forces that were spread out over vast swathes of the country. It was proving to be tough and difficult work and Zhukov could do without it at this time. But he had to go to STAVKA as he was the only successful Soviet military commander in the war so far. He was the only commander in whom Stalin had confidence at that time. He had to plan for next year and defend Moscow at the same time. What he was increasingly thinking about was that Russia should find a suitable place of her choosing at which to make a stand against the enemy, force them to a halt and then launch a massive counter attack. It could not be Moscow. It had to be well to the south. It had to be a place well beyond the existing German lines. He knew he would win the argument eventually. But they had to go over it so many times.

* * *

It was late in 1996 that I read a stunning entry in Zhukov's diary. It read:

December 13, 1941 It has been a cold bright evening and I have been out to visit some troops serving in the northwest of the city. The STAVKA meeting was over early and I then went to my headquarters. They told me that it had been a good day on the battlefield. There have been no German advances today. In some areas they are starting to retreat. So I decided to go and celebrate with some of the troops that had done such good work.

It took nearly two hours to get there through the blackouts and across the broken up road system, but the driver was a very good one and clearly knew the way well. I sat down by a coal brazier with some of the troops, we shared some thick meat and potato stew then we sang Stenka Razin, the song about the legendary Cossack leader who had captured the city that later became known as Stalingrad in 1670 for the Russians. I played the accordion and the men cheered me as I left.

I then went to the HQ of Rokossovskii's 16th Army. He appraised me of the relative positions of both the Red Army units and the opposing German forces. I set their targets for the next day. It was to be a determined offensive across the whole of that sector to start at first light. The target was to force the Germans to retreat by at least ten kilometres. The planners would be up all night preparing for it.

On the drive back into Moscow I was able to think through very carefully what I must say to STAVKA at our next meeting about how we can set about achieving the destruction of the much larger German armies to the south. A plan is forming in my mind but it will take a lot of selling to Stalin. I must think it through very carefully.

* * *

The STAVKA official records for December 14, 1941 show that the plans that had been drawn up by Zhukov and Rokossovskii during the night resulted in the German forces in that sector being forced to retreat over a distance of 12 kilometres that day. It was recorded as the best day for any Russian army since the invasion had started in June.

They also give a full account of the STAVKA meeting that afternoon which includes what looks like a verbatim report of the presentation given by Zhukov to the meeting. The subsequent discussion and the decisions taken are fully recorded.

I had already read large volumes of German records dealing with the planning for the battle of Kursk. None of those started before April, 1943. German ideas for a major battle at Kursk, according to the records, simply did not exist before 11 April, 1943. They only existed because there was a large salient west of the city that had been formed during the army movements in Ukraine after the battle of Stalingrad and the subsequent taking of Kharkov by Germany. The German Chief of Staff, Zeitzler and the Commander in Chief of Army Group South, von Manstein, believed that the Russian salient was vulnerable to a major assault by Germany. It was on April 11, 1943 that Hitler instructed them to consider plans for a battle there.

Samuel had been baffled by why there should have been a battle at Kursk and also in awe of the consequences. He told me many times that Kursk changed the war and dramatically undermined the strategy being pursued by Roosevelt. It was therefore very important for me to find out what I could about why such a staggering battle took place.

I knew that Samuel had been right about it all when I read the STAVKA records of their meeting on 14 December, 1941.

The record of Zhukov's presentation shows that he said:

"I believe we have now stabilised the front line to the west of Moscow. Indeed if things go as well as they have today we should be able to push the German lines back over the next few weeks. I am now sure that we can do that but while it will make Moscow safe it will make little other contribution to Russia winning this war.

"The only way that we can win the war is by defeating the German armies. At all times that must be the overwhelming objective. At this stage territory is almost unimportant when compared with the task of defeating such vast armies as the Germans now have.

"The numbers of German troops round Moscow are relatively small compared with their deployments elsewhere in our country. Whilst Moscow might be of symbolic importance to them all the evidence of their troop deployments is that the agricultural areas of Ukraine, the industrial areas of the Don Basin and the oilfields of the Caucasus are their main objectives. That is why so many of their troops have been driving south east. Last summer their biggest armies went in that direction. They will continue that way when they start moving again in the spring or early summer.

"To attempt to destroy their armies now, or even in the coming summer would be foolish. We simply will not have enough men or equipment to make it possible.

"To win this war we must fight on ground of our own choosing. The German armies are so large that we will have to fight them several times. When we have found the right places we will have to prepare everything well in advance and then lure the enemy on to that battle ground. So far in this war we have only been able to fight on ground of the enemy's choosing. There is no way we will win if we allow the enemy to choose the ground for any future major battle. We have to fight on our terms if we are going to win. We have to stop thinking about defending things. We have to think at all times about attacking things. The purpose of war is to destroy the fighting capability of your enemy. We are going to do just that.

"The first battleground that we choose must be a strategic target for the Germans otherwise they will not be drawn onto it. There is no point in it being open countryside. That will be of little use to them and it is always less easy to defend open fields than it is to defend a really difficult target. The toughest targets are always in mountains or large cities. The Germans are unlikely to have a mountain as a major strategic target. The only large cities that would seem to have any strategic interest for them are in the south in Ukraine, the Don Basin and down in the Caucasus. We have to look down there for somewhere to fight.

"The place I prefer at the moment for our first large battle with them is Stalingrad. To use the factories in the Don basin effectively they will need access to the river docks at Stalingrad. It simply has to be the most important strategic target in the south for them. We will lure them there next summer and fight them in the streets there until the river freezes over next winter. Then we will surround them with reserves stationed well outside the city, push the Germans out in the middle of winter and then destroy whatever armies they have sent there. Stalingrad has one other advantage for us; it will further stretch the massively long German supply lines. We will use the time to build up our reserves of men and equipment and we will then be well placed to start the long march right the way through to Germany.

"I know Ukraine well from my time in command of the Kiev District. I deliberately went round as much of my patch as I could to assess the military opportunities that it presented. The best of those by far is Kursk. It has a combination or hills and flat plains that provide both for good defensive positions and manoeuvring space for large tank battles. To fight there, though, we will have to start protecting some of the site soon. It is a very large area covering thousands of square miles.

"To make it all possible at Stalingrad we will have to start the training of the urban guerrilla troops that we will need now. We must have people of the highest experience and skill if we are going to succeed. We will also have to build up our reserves at a very rapid rate. Stalingrad will probably not be the biggest battle that we will have to fight. That will almost certainly be at Kursk. At Kursk we will need a numerical superiority of at least two to one, preferably more to guarantee success. There is no point in exposing ourselves to any major confrontation until we have the strength to win it. To get those sorts of numbers ready for Kursk, which will have to be fought in the spring or summer of 1943, we will have to start creating several new armies now. The production of tanks, guns and aircraft must start immediately. All the training and manufacturing will have to be done well away from German eyes. That in turn will mean that we have to improve transport links in order to bring all that material up to the front line.

"We must also prepare Stalingrad itself. There must be defences against tanks and infantry. The attrition rate amongst the Germans must be high before they even get into the city. But it will probably be impossible to evacuate the civilian population before the Germans arrive. There must be mines and booby traps everywhere. Our snipers must have clear lines of fire so as to make German advances almost impossible. We must also have clear supply lines across the river for our troops fighting there.

"Kursk will require defences on a vast scale. We will probably have to start preparing that site well before we start fighting at Stalingrad. It will be a huge engineering task. Even to do that we will need air defences there which will prevent any German aircraft seeing what we are doing.

"All in all it will be an enormous task. None of it can be cobbled together at the last moment. If we intend to win those battles we have to start work on it now.

"I am happy to go into more and more detail as the days, weeks and months go by but I very firmly believe that whatever we do, we must take plan now for those big battles to take place.

"One final thing is that our objectives at all times must be to destroy all German fighting capability. That is much more important than protecting or gaining territory."

Stalin was silent for several minutes. He then launched into several hours of intense questioning about it all. Why Stalingrad? Why Kursk? How many armies? How many men? How many tanks? How everything?

At the end of it all Zhukov and STAVKA were authorised to turn it all into operational plans. They became the plans from which they never deviated in any substantial way.

There were two issues that concerned Stalin most of all. The first was that the objective of destroying the German armies had to be attained. He made it clear that there was no cost that Russia would not accept. The number of casualties, civilian or otherwise was not a constraint. Whatever factories had to be built to supply all the tanks, guns and aircraft would be built. Work would start on them somewhere beyond the Ural Mountains within days.

His other issue was even more important to him. It was security. He was not prepared to risk any possibility of Germany discovering anything about it all. Nor was he prepared to share any of it with America or Britain.

After he left the meeting we called Lavrenti Beria, his Secret Police chief into his office. He was given instructions about surveillance of all the key people involved and the appointment of extra political commissars to all the units that would be involved in the formation of those great armies. Beria was instructed to prepare a disinformation campaign for Russia's allies. Stalin undertook to provide a cover for that with an endless series of demands to both America and Britain that they open another front with Germany in the west. Finally he resolved to put intense pressure on Zhukov himself to try and bring forward the plans and get earlier results.

Other Soviet archives show that he wrote to Roosevelt and Churchill that evening to demand the opening of a second front in Western Europe in order to take the pressure off beleaguered Russian forces.

* * *

That night Zhukov went out again into the cold night to visit troops to the south west of the city. It was exactly the same as the night before. With the soldiers there he sang Stenka Razin again. When he left he was cheered by all the men there.

The following day the troops in that sector also advanced; this time by 17 kilometres. That forced all the German troops between those two areas to have to retreat. In a two week Russian offensive directed by Zhukov the Germans withdrew generally by 140 kilometres..

Moscow was safe. During the remainder of the winter and into spring the Russian defences around Moscow were strengthened to make it impossible for there to be any further German advance on the city. Zhukov started to plan in detail for Stalingrad.

* * *

January 10, 1942. The intelligence we are getting from German sources suggests that the lines round Moscow have stabilised. They have had to withdraw but they blame the appalling weather conditions for this. It does not seem possible for there to be any significant fighting in the diabolical weather conditions there. All the messages are saying that it is this that has caused them to move to safer positions. Our sources close to the German High Command are beginning to suggest that their plans for the summer campaigns in Russia will involve the final annexation of Ukraine and the Caucasus. Although Moscow remains a key it is less important than the Russian industrial targets in the south and the Caucasus oilfields, but they will come back to Moscow when they have won in the south. They expect Moscow to fall in the early autumn.

All the German reports indicate that they believe that the Russian armies are seriously depleted and that most of their reserves have been exhausted. They are therefore expecting to make massive gains in their summer campaigns.

We have started to get intelligence reports from within Russia. That is a huge benefit from becoming formal allies with them. It is early days to be able to test the reliability of the Russian information but it does support the information we are getting from Germany.

* * *

January 20, 1942. There has been a big meeting today with all the service chiefs to consider Britain's strategic position following Pearl Harbour and the loss of Singapore. Winston chaired the meeting which lasted all day. It started with Ronnie Harford giving an overview of the intelligence position on all the war fronts. All the information was grim. The update we were given on the military situation was worse.

Winston's own assessment was even worse than that. He said; "The start of 1942 sees us in an even more perilous position than we have faced before. In the Atlantic convoy losses have dramatically increased and the enemy has taken the battle to the shores of America. In two weeks we have lost 25 ships totalling 200,000 tons. In the Far East the advance of Japanese forces continues unchecked. In Libya we are facing a powerful new German army. We must expect that Russia will collapse under German aggression this year. At home the bombing of our cities continues. Rationing continues to seep the morale of our people. Whilst we have very strong American support it will be many months before that will have any impact on the battles and our plight at home. There is every indication that things will get very much worse before American aid and military support enable us to turn the tide.

The meeting debated the options all day. The only conclusions were about the position that should be taken as the command structures with America were established.

Winston and I talked afterwards. He feels very lonely at this time. He raised with me a new fear that he has. It is that the Japanese advances in South Asia will force us out of Malaya and Burma and that then the way will be clear for Japan to invade India. As there are no plans to defend India and no capability of doing so anyway he fears that country might be overrun. As he regards India as the jewel in the Imperial Crown he feels that that might be the ultimate disaster to befall us so far in this war.

* * *

From the moment I discovered that in December 1941 Zhukov had first suggested that a major battle be fought at Kursk I decided to look deeply into all the STAVKA records covering the whole planning period for the battle. I told my friendly librarian what I wanted and she told me that the files were immense. She said that I should look into some of the files from Stalin's office as well. As I had already read the German files I was getting into a position in which I could verify the assertions that had been made about the battle by Samuel. I already knew from German records all about Hitler's planning for it and I had been able to confirm that Hitler had indeed been at Kursk on June 9, 1943 as suggested in Samuel's diary for that date. Over the following months I was able to piece together an account of how it all happened and about the endless tensions within STAVKA as Stalin bullied them relentlessly about the conduct of the war.

At the same time I read about Zhukov's relationship with Nikita Khrushchev who had been appointed by Stalin as the political commissar to his headquarters. Khrushchev was very much a rising star in the Communist Party at that time. In order to protect his own position Stalin was going to ensure that no Russian army officer was going to have an opportunity to develop any power base which could threaten him in any way. That was one reason why Khrushchev was there. Khrushchev was also there to spy on everything that Zhukov was doing.

In the months following the successful defence of Moscow tensions arose within STAVKA. Moscow had certainly been saved. Stalin was grateful for that but was constantly demanding more victories. There seemed to be no way of satisfying his lust for more triumphs over the German armies that were occupying Western Russia. There seemed to be no way of satisfying him that everything possible was being done to neutralise and then eliminate the German threat. It did not really matter to him that Zhukov had succeeded in successfully defending both St. Petersburg and Moscow. He had to have more victories as soon as possible.

Had Stalin not directed the Second Revolution the manufacturing facilities for the war could never have been available. But even with those changes it was still a brutal process to set up the capability of making several thousand tanks and aircraft thousands of miles away behind the Urals. Even moving the necessary people to work in the new factories would have been impossible without the changes that Stalin had forced through in the Second Revolution. Everyone involved in those new factories and all their support facilities including the new rail lines that were needed had to endure a thoroughly brutal experience. Thousands were moved east against their will and under armed escort. They had to work staggeringly long hours and many perished. Their families never knew what happened to them. But to Stalin none of that mattered.

It was much the same in the military training camps that were springing up in numerous parts of Russia. Over the remainder of the war around 20 million people were press-ganged into military service. Few of them ever saw their families again.

Despite the diabolical winter around Moscow things had certainly improved. The German front lines had been pushed back so far that they no longer posed any sort of threat to the centre of the city, or indeed any part of the city. There was no German artillery that could threaten any part of Moscow. It was certainly the case that air raids were a threat but generally the weather throughout that winter was so bad that it was in any practical terms impossible to conduct any real air raids. Occasionally German aircraft were seen over Moscow but they did no damage. Most of them were shot down.

To make the city safe Zhukov organised a series of fixed defences to make any German land advance impossible. There were three concentric lines of defence that completely surrounded the city. Deep ditches, concrete traps, mines and artillery were installed despite the appalling weather. Any German armour that did advance would be cut to pieces before it could have moved more than 5 kilometres. If anything got through the first ring it would have faced an even more awesome second ring. By late January STAVKA was satisfied that under all circumstances Moscow was safe from any land attack.

But that did not satisfy Stalin's anxiety. Although he had accepted Zhukov's plan in principle in December he still wanted instant results. The Germans had to be removed from all Russian soil. Every STAVKA meeting started with demands along those lines from Stalin. The pressure to meet those demands fell entirely on Zhukov and Khrushchev in the first instance. They were the two people in the firing line and they were the two people who had the most contribution to make to ensuring Russian success at that time. They were not friends and there was constant tension between them but they did share a common objective. But they were driven by entirely different personal motives. Khrushchev was driven by his political ambitions. He was effectively Stalin's eyes and ears in Zhukov's headquarters. His expectation was that his influence on a victory over Germany would make him the natural successor to Stalin. He pursued that ambition by putting constant pressure on Zhukov for the organisation of a battle that would defeat the Germans. Every day he had to convince Stalin that he was doing just that and that he was making progress.

Neither Stalin nor Khrushchev had the slightest idea of the implications of military logistics and they both constantly hoped that instant results could be achieved. Zhukov was the only military expert in that triumvirate and it was a endless battle for him to convince them of the military realities, let alone the realities of beating the largest army ever assembled in the world. His ambitions were all about military leadership. He cared little about national politics but he did care about military success. His greatest concern was that he was being driven towards military success without regard to the costs, particularly in human terms.

It was in late January that Zhukov took Khrushchev on a flight down to Stalingrad. The day they left Moscow was cold and clear. It was an excellent day for viewing the ground from an aircraft. Zhukov's plan was to show the Stalingrad area to Khrushchev from the air and then to tour the city over the following two days. After that if the weather was clear they would fly west from the city towards the German lines so that Khrushchev could see the land that the Germans had to cross before they were drawn into the planned trap at Stalingrad. They would then spend two days looking at the key features of the intended battleground at Kursk.

They left Moscow in the early morning and flew non-stop to an airfield near Stalingrad. They re-fuelled there and spent the rest of the day flying round the city and the surrounding areas. As they flew round Zhukov explained why the city was the ideal site for containing and reversing any German advance. He pointed out important features that could be used in the defence of the city and in the subsequent encirclement of the German forces that he envisaged.

That evening they dined together in the officer's mess at the Headquarters of the Stalingrad military district. It was the first time that they could have unlimited time together. It was certainly a time that Zhukov was going to use to his advantage. In every officer's mess in Russia vodka was the fuel of conversation. It certainly was that evening. Zhukov started by explaining the most basic of military tactics after their second vodkas had been served:

"Comrade, as I said to that STAVKA meeting in December when I first proposed to fight the Germans at Stalingrad, it is the most basic military rule that if you want to win a battle you have to fight it on ground of your own choosing. There is no way that we will ever win a major fight against the Germans if we attack them on ground where they have defensive positions. I cannot think of any way that we could dislodge them from a powerfully defended position at this time. But if we bring them here we will have the double benefit of drawing them on to positions of our choice and we will bring them a very long way from their supply lines. The combination of good defences here and their logistics problems will halt their advance. What we will do, though, is only have the number of troops in the city just to halt them. When they are well and truly stalled we will counter attack. We will keep the main body of our forces well away from them until they are stalled. With any luck they will have no idea of just what power we will be able to unleash against them until they are completely trapped by a combination of our defences and the weather.

"Over the next couple of days we will drive through the whole of the Stalingrad area and I will make notes about the terrain and key features in the city. Then I will draw up some plans based on that which will form the basis of my defence of the city. After that we will fly over the land that Germany will have to cross to come here. That they will come here I have no doubt.

"We will then do it all over again at Kursk. I am sure that you will be convinced that the terrain is right and that if the necessary men and materials can be provided to give us numerical superiority we will be able to trap and destroy the German armies that we will face in those battles.

"When I get back to Moscow I am going to seek the approval of Stalin for the appointment of three Generals to help me with the planning. I want the best and they will be Rokossovskii, Vatutin and Chuikov. They will probably each need a couple of hundred people to work on the detailed plans. As soon as the thaw starts we will start building the defences and the defiles needed to trap the Nazis completely. Trust me and it will work. I want you to sell it hard to Stalin. If it does work you will be made and we will all have a command structure that will take us all the way to Berlin. But we have to start in Stalingrad."

Khrushchev was uneasy about giving so much trust and responsibility to a military officer. All his training and all his beliefs had taught him that politicians should be in charge of everything. But he certainly had no better ideas than those of Zhukov and however powerful he felt himself to be he had no detailed knowledge of military requirements that might possibly enable him to overrule Zhukov. As the vodkas kept coming he warmed to the man. He knew that in that brain there was a plan that might save Russia. It was that night that he decided that he would support Zhukov at least until the climax of Stalingrad and obviously thereafter if it all worked. He would sell the plan to Stalin and he would use Zhukov's success to develop his own powerbase in Moscow. He had little alternative at that time because Zhukov was the only Russian General who could claim any real success. He recognised that whatever it was that drove Stalin he was not going to get rid of his only successful general at this time.

They did tour the city and the surrounding areas for two days and Zhukov made copious notes. Whatever personal doubts he might have had before he went there were completely dispelled by what he saw. He regarded the ground as ideal for the sort of defence he had in mind. But several times he warned Khrushchev that the city could not be defended without a very large loss of life. He had come to the view that no attempt should be made to evacuate the city in advance of any German arrival. The Germans were bound to have spies in the city and if any general evacuation took place it was bound to be reported to them. The risks of that triggering off German suspicions were far too great. In any event Stalin had already ruled that the human cost of a victory was not a consideration.

When he had seen all that he wanted they flew out over the steppe to the west of the city. Because they were flying towards German lines there was a risk that they would be intercepted by German aircraft. To deal with any such eventuality they had an escort of ten fighter aircraft. Fortunately they were not intercepted at any time that day. It was a flat landscape with few features. There was nothing to impede German armies and there was nothing to defend either. But Zhukov was able to explain to Khrushchev just how he could place small numbers of soldiers so that they could draw the Germans inexorably towards Stalingrad.

It was easier for Khrushchev to understand the terrain around Kursk. Zhukov explained the concept of a military salient and just how dangerous it can be for the defendants. This time, though, he was going to trap the Germans between two salients and then cut them off.

It was a Sunday afternoon when Zhukov presented his plans to STAVKA. They were enthusiastically endorsed by Khrushchev. Zhukov's plan became the official STAVKA plan for halting the German advances into Russia but despite giving his approval Stalin said that he wanted earlier action. But Stalin refused to endorse Zhukov's choice of generals at that time. He had different ideas of how the campaigns were to be planned. All the planning work was to be done under STAVKA's direction. That meant that there would be direct political control of it at all times. There was no way he was going to allow any general to develop any independent plans for anything. He told Zhukov that the choice of generals for each of the commands needed for the battle of Stalingrad would only be made much nearer the time.

That was a directive that Zhukov did not need and it was to lead to continuous difficulties for him in his dealings with Stalin. The real practical problem that it gave him in the short term was that he personally had to supervise all the plans for the retreat to Stalingrad and the battles that would take place within the city. He had wanted to use the time to develop the training and the command structures in the army overall. Stalin's decision that day was to cost the Red Army hundreds of thousands of deaths.

Zhukov's personal diary describes his thoughts about Stalin's decision that day.

31 January, 1942. Today has been an intense frustration for me. At STAVKA we have made progress toward preparing for Stalingrad in the autumn. The outline plans were approved but Stalin did not accept my ideas for the command structure. It is something I will have to raise with him again and again. Unless I can have the right people I will have to do the work myself and it will probably have to be done in Moscow. It would much better de done by the commanders who will be leading the battles there and done in the Stalingrad area. What I had hoped to do over the next few months was improve officer training in the whole army. It was seriously weakened by the army reforms introduced by Stalin a few years ago and much needs to be done to get it up to the standard of the enemy. But Stalin cannot get away from his apparent need to keep the armed forces under tight political control. I do not understand this at this time because the army passionately shares his objective of getting rid of the Germans.

A major problem I have with his position is that I have to be able to have army commanders who I know will work with me and lead their commands successfully. I dread any prospect of his choosing his own people. Whatever he chooses to do I will speak to Rokossovoskii, Vatutin and Chuikov in the next couple of days. I want Chuikov to lead the defence of the city and all the fighting within it. The others, I hope, will lead the reserve armies which will encircle any German forces.

It is going to be tough fighting the politics as well as leading all our forces in these great battles.

* * *

February 1, 1942. Today Winston showed me a report from Bradman. It sets out what are claimed to be the steps that America has taken over the last two years to increase its military capability. Although America was not at war with any country until December, 1941 it seems that Roosevelt has taken steps to increase the size of the armed forces and increase their equipment levels just in case America did get dragged into a of war. When Winston was in Washington Roosevelt had not given him any clue that America might have done so much already and he is furious that Roosevelt was resisting providing us with help when he was obviously making his own advance war preparations.

Some of the information in Bradman's report corroborates what we have learned from Admiral Horton now that he has returned to Britain at least so far as America will contribute to the convoy escort problems.

An interesting part of the report covers the people that Roosevelt will be sending to London. He was going to do this within days of the meeting with Winston and it has now all been finalised.

* * *

One of the beneficiaries of the expansion of the US army in those times when Roosevelt had authorised additional recruitment and training had been Dwight D. Eisenhower. In 1940 he had been a Lieutenant-Colonel working in the Philippines with General Douglas MacArthur, the American Chief of Staff, to establish a local defence force there. Immediately after Pearl Harbour MacArthur promoted him to Brigadier-General and put him in charge of the War Plans Division. Very soon he was promoted again and put in charge of the US Forces European Theatre of Operations, based in London. Roosevelt intended that he should become the Supreme Allied Commander in Europe as soon as that was politically feasible.

Before he left for London he was briefed personally by President Roosevelt as to what was expected of him. That briefing took place in the Oval Office:

"Ike, I am very pleased that you will be in charge of our operations in Europe. The task you have to achieve is very clear. It is the complete and total destruction of all German military capability. I have every reason to believe that the Russians have exactly the same objective but they appear to have exhausted their capabilities at this time and I do not believe that we can rely on them to make an effective contribution. As it looks now they will probably be destroyed within a few months. There is no other objective that you can or should pursue. I have never been convinced that that objective is shared by Britain. They seem to have a lot of confused views about protecting their Empire. That seems odd to me when there is such an obvious enemy out there who simply must be beaten before anything else can be considered.

"You will have a key role to play in developing the plans to achieve that single objective. The military objective cannot be separated from the political one which is to restore peace and democracy to Europe. The military victory will be the first stage in achieving that. At some stage I envisage that we will be having high level talks with Britain and Russia about how we achieve that political objective. But in the meantime nothing must deter you from preparing the plans for a complete victory that will result in the unconditional surrender of Germany.

"I am very sceptical about what Britain has already done to prepare for that victory. There do not appear to be any dates in mind, for example, as to when there might be a ground invasion. I will need you to report back to me at the first possible moment about what you find there. Please contact me with a full assessment as soon as you can after you get there."

Eisenhower arrived in London a few days later. He took General George Patton with him. Patton was very pleased with that because he would be able to see Sally Monroe in London.

It was three weeks after he arrived that he sent a very bleak assessment of the position in Britain to Roosevelt. It read:

Mr. President, the most positive thing I have to report is that the spirit and determination of the British people is very good. They face frequent bombings but they seem disciplined and forthright in such adverse circumstances. They also face great hardship through all the shortages forced on them by the rationing system.

The bad news is that there are no plans for any land invasion of Northern Europe. To have any chance of success, even if Hitler is pinned down in the east, will require something between 35 and 50 divisions together with appropriate air force support if any such invasion is to be successful. I regard it as my first duty to plan an invasion of Europe on that scale. It will require a huge political commitment after that even if the necessary troops and arms can be made available. It will take a long time to organize and get the necessary troops and equipment in place.

The first problem about an invasion is the suitability of conditions for a major land offensive. Because of the climate this will have to take place between March and October. It is always possible that that window will open a little wider but it is not possible to plan on that basis. It is much more likely to narrow down. That means that the very earliest date at which we could plan for an invasion is sometime next spring. For reasons that I will explain I think that that is a completely unrealistic date. The following spring appears to be very feasible, though. That really means that we cannot help Russia by opening a second front before, say, May 1944. The issue of how that is handled with Russia is a political one.

The constraints are all logistical. Let us assume that the target is to have fifty divisions ready and trained for ground combat before an invasion of Europe starts. Britain currently has four divisions under training and can increase this to about ten within a year. Another year would generate another ten divisions. That means that America would have to generate thirty divisions within two years if an invasion is going to be successful in 1944.

The transport of that number of men across the Atlantic, together with all the equipment needed could not under any circumstances be completed safely inside a year. It could only be completed within two years with a huge increase in the number of ships available and with an increase in convoy safety. As I write convoy conditions are very bad.

There is a strong appetite here for bombing Germany. That is both in the public and in their politicians. I do not know what such a campaign will achieve in military terms. That will all depend on the targeting and the result, but it is something that will prove popular here. They are hoping to start large scale bombing in May.

Unfortunately Britain has very little capability for such bombing missions just now. They have designed a very capable bomber called the Lancaster which looks to be a very good tool for night bombing missions and the RAF seem to have some very good crews as well as the capacity to train many thousands more people to operate these impressive machines. The bad news is that this machine only came into service last Christmas. The attrition rate of bombers is already proving to be very high and in order to run viable bombing raids several nights a week there will have to be around five thousand bombers in service. There are just three hundred at the moment, but this number is expected to rise rapidly in the coming months. The real problem is that the production rate is going to have to rise to about fifty bombers a day in order to deal with the attrition rate. I have met the British Minister involved in managing war production, Max Beaverbrook, and he will be coming to Washington shortly to see whether these machines can be manufactured in America at much quicker rates than they can in Britain.

If we are to station large numbers of American bombers in Britain in order to help the British bombing efforts, our first priority must be to build large numbers of new airfields to accommodate them. This is a political issue that I must ask you to take up with them.

One remote area in which Britain has done well so far is in North Africa. The main objective there has been to protect the Middle Eastern oilfields from German attack. I am cautious about future prospects there because a substantial German army was landed in that area last November and it is commanded by Rommel who is known to have had an excellent record in commanding armour in Poland, France and Russia. Although it is peripheral to the main efforts I believe that we should support that British effort with a landing in North Africa of our own as soon as it is practicable.

There is one area of British warfare in which there are plans and affirmative action and that is in the convoy battles. Please do not underestimate the importance these convoys have on British life. Some very good new tactics have been invented by a British escort captain called Frederick Walker and these are now being applied across the whole escort service. Plenty of high quality escorts are being built and Britain is building some seaplanes called Sunderlands which are capable of providing long range air cover for convoys right out into the middle of the Atlantic. I think this is an area where we should accept that they are well ahead of us and work with them to provide higher levels of air and naval cover.

My best current guess is that an invasion of Europe in the spring of 1944 is the most likely option at the moment. The logistics of doing anything earlier than that look severe just now. With the current rate of losses in the convoys it would be very dangerous to bring large numbers of our men over here. We have little option but to wait for safer times.

Yours,

Ike

* * *

Soon after that message had been delivered Beaverbrook sent a telegram to the British Ambassador in Washington to say that he intended to visit in early March in order to set up a licensing agreement so that an American manufacturer could build large numbers of Lancaster bombers there.

The Ambassador read out that telegram at his routine prayers meeting the following morning. Angela was at that meeting. She wrote immediately to Max and said she had heard that he was coming to Washington. She would book somewhere for them to go over the weekend that he would be there.

He arrived in Washington on a Tuesday evening and was immediately taken away by Pentagon officials for the formal negotiations that had been scheduled. It was an early spring in Washington that year and the city looked superb. But before he could get to their car he was intercepted by Sid at the airport who told him that Louise would meet him in the bar of the Willard hotel at five on Friday evening. They would be going out of town immediately and would not be back until the Sunday evening. It was a very welcome message.

They did meet that Friday evening at five and Sid did drive them out to a small but very luxurious hotel out on the Skyline Drive a couple of hours west of the city. It was called the Nathan Bedford Forrest Lodge. It consisted entirely of very discrete suites. People only went there when they wanted to be alone. It was named after an American Civil War cavalry general who had had some spectacular successes in that area.

It was nearly three years since they had last been together. Louise had arranged a very special meal for them for the Friday evening. Definitely things that were not available in Britain at any price then. The starter was fresh lobster; they followed that with roast rib of beef au jus. They had Champagne as an aperitif and followed that with fine wines from California.

Max was very keen to understand what she was doing in Washington but she said not a word about that. All she did say was that it was very important work that seemed to be valued highly.

Over the weekend they went for long walks through the dogwood forests, which were coming into flower in the warm spring sunshine and sat out in a small park on the skyline looking out over the open plains of the Shenandoah Valley. Each day they took a picnic lunch with them and afterwards lay out on the grass in the warm sunshine.

They did not talk about what she was doing in Washington, although Max was very keen to find out. They did talk about the progress that he had been able to make in getting Lancasters built in America. He told her that an initial set of drawings had already been flown out and a complete set of jigs would be arriving within a few days. The engines would also be built in America under licence from Rolls-Royce.

It was on the Saturday evening while they were having dinner in a small restaurant a couple of miles from the hotel that he said to her:

"Louise, I do not know what you are doing in Washington but I would like you to consider doing something very different. My trip over here has been about finding ways in which we can increase substantially the production of military aircraft. We need many more if we are going to win the war. America can create the production facilities very quickly, so that is where we are going to build them. It will work. But I need someone over here that can provide a management overview of the whole programme. I need someone who I can trust implicitly and who can report to me immediately if there are any problems. I would like that person to be you. Is there any chance that you can do it?"

She looked at him as held his hand;

"Max, I think that most of the work that I can do over here in my present job has already been achieved. I would love to work for you again. But I cannot say this evening if I am free to work for you. I will need to talk with my present employer before I can say anything. That could take anything up to a month before I can get a decision from them. If you can wait that long I am sure it will be all right but I cannot give you a decision this evening.

"There is one thing that I have to tell you and it is that while I have been over here I have not been using my own name. I have had to use a name that was given me for security purposes. It is inevitable that if I do that new job for you that I will have to meet with people over here who have known me in this new name. I cannot tell you today what that name is but it will be necessary for me to get clearance to use it in any new role with you. That may or may not be a problem. It is something that I will have to resolve. But if there is a problem it will not in any way be possible for me to help you. Let us leave it like that for today."

Max then told her about life in Britain and about how people were coping with what seemed to be an endless war. He thought things were very difficult politically as well. Although the people seemed happy to trust the government to bring the war to an end they were becoming increasingly concerned about the effect on their lives and about the lack of any significant progress in stopping Hitler. There did not seem to be any real understanding of just how strong Germany was militarily and it was certainly not in the government's interests to tell them. The active involvement of America now was very welcome although there had not yet been any real impact from it.

That night they talked about the happy times they had spent together before the war. Max asked her several times what she had been doing while she was away on those two occasions and how she had been able to obtain such accurate information about the start of the war. She did not answer but held him very close to her. Each time he raised those issues she said; "My darling, let us not think about that. Let's just enjoy ourselves."

It was a superb and very relaxing weekend for both of them. Sid took them back to the Willard Hotel on the Sunday evening. As she was leaving him he told her that when the war was over he would guarantee her a job somewhere and if they could then spend more time together that would be great.

* * *

The following morning she rang James Westfield and asked for a meeting with Roosevelt. He told her that it would have to wait for a couple of days because he was busy in conference with General MacArthur about the detailed plans that were being prepared for increasing the war effort. But he told her that Roosevelt had already asked to see her for lunch on that Wednesday to tell her about those plans. So that was when she went to see him.

It was a dreadful morning. It had started snowing heavily at dawn and by the time she had to leave to go to the White House there was at least 20 inches of snow on the sidewalks. Snow ploughs were battling to keep the streets clear in the government area but they seemed to be fighting a losing battle. Fortunately the embassy had a couple of four wheel drive vehicles ready to be used in just such conditions and Sid was able to use one of them. Despite that the journey was slow and difficult even though it was less than a mile. Sid promised that he would stay at the White House and somehow he would get her back later.

Lunch was at the same table in the window but there was nothing to see but driving snow. After the hazards of the drive the first martini was especially welcome. She wondered whether it might even be her last with him. If so, it would mark the end of a very enjoyable period in her life.

"Angela, I know that you asked to see me but before I will let you say why you wanted to come here I need you to pass a very important message to Winston as soon as possible. This time I am sure it will be something he welcomes.

"Over the last couple of days we have been working through exactly what we can do over the next year to increase our war effort. I was not prepared to do that until I had had a report from General Eisenhower in London. I got that from him a few days ago and it makes bleak reading. What we have identified are the things that Britain needs to do to accommodate the men, ships and aircraft that we will be sending there. The requirements are immense. It will probably be necessary to build at least a hundred airfields for our bombers alone. There will have to be a dock expansion programme so that the ships taking all our equipment can be unloaded. Britain will have to build barracks for at least one million men. Then we will need harbour facilities for all the naval ships that will be going there. And so it goes on.

"Not everything needs to be done immediately but it will be essential that progress is made across all these items at a rapid rate. For example, the first bombers will be going there in May and they will need airfields to be ready when they arrive. I will go over some of the details with you shortly but the message that I want you to pass to Winston is that we are ready now to deliver the start of the unlimited commitment to ending the war in Germany about which I spoke to him. It will be up to him to ensure that the necessary facilities are available in Britain as and when they are required.

"Eisenhower has given me details of the people he needs over in Britain to plan the next steps in detail. Around 200 people will be flying over within the next week. They will need to be alongside him in London. A week after that we will be sending over people who will be working with your commanders–in–chief to pave the way for Eisenhower to take command of all the joint forces. There are a hundred other items in the document and it will be updated probably every week until the joint command structures are in place, hopefully by May.

"Yesterday we received a list of urgent supplies that are required by Britain. They will all be provided as soon as the necessary shipping space can be found.

"Angela, the pace of this war is going to get a lot quicker very soon. We have our own serious problems in the Pacific right now. The biggest one is trying to destroy the Japanese Navy. But we are very happy that we can do that at the same time as ramping up the war effort in Europe.

"You can tell Winston that we have been conducting a review of what we think the Russian capabilities are. Our present assessment is that they are in a very weak state and are unlikely to be able to survive any German onslaughts this summer. But our commitment is to liberate that country as well. We have no idea yet what level of resources will be needed to achieve it but we will work on that over the next few months.

"I would like you to ensure that Winston gets the whole of the document within the next few hours.

"Now what did you want to talk to me about? But before you start on that let me fix you another martini."

While he did so Angela looked out at the swirling blizzard. She just hoped that it would stop soon so that she could get back to the car and get Sid on to sending that huge document to London. She did not like snow and had had more than enough of it in Russia. She was then not surprised to see that the second martinis came in larger glasses. The President was obviously going to make a long afternoon of it.

"What I want to talk about is something quite different. I have been here since September, 1939. I came when there were problems about the communications between our governments. I have been in the frontline of difficult communications between my Prime Minister and yourself. We have now moved on from all of that to the point where thousands of people will soon have to communicate with each other every day. Much as I enjoy working with you I have to question seriously whether there is enough of a role left to keep me properly occupied. I need your views on that before I can consider what has been presented to me as a very important career opportunity. It is one that will be very important as part of the war effort but it will be outside the diplomatic service. It will be based here in America but it is still too early to say exactly where.

"I have to consult with several people before I can come to a definite decision and you are the first. Winston is another. I cannot take this new job if either of you have problems with my moving on. I am talking to you first because I deal with you here frequently. My British counterparts are at the end of a communications channel in London, it will therefore probably be easier for them. I think I am likely to have less difficulty with them than I am with you.

"It seems obvious to me that I have been in a very special and very privileged position since I have been here. I think that both you and Winston will agree that the work that I have done has made a valuable contribution to your communications and to the implementation of the numerous Lend/Lease deals. But things have moved on. Britain and America have a very public relationship as allies and as America moves more and more into the war there will be thousands of people involved in communicating between the two governments. Because the management of the war will be based in London, that is where most of the communications will take place. The role that I have fulfilled will quickly become a thing of the past now. It therefore seems to me to be the right time to move on. I would very much appreciate your support in that. That is what I wanted to say to you today. Maybe what you have asked me to convey to Winston will be the last message that I handle."

As she finished talking the snow stopped. Roosevelt looked out of the window as the skies started to clear and suggested that they start lunch. They did not talk about the war over lunch. Roosevelt wanted to tell her about the taming of the Wild West and the part his uncle Teddy Roosevelt, who had been President after his western exploits, had played in that. At the end he said to Angela;

"You know, Angela, he was very popular in America because Americans loved his confidence and self-reliance. They loved his determination to win. Americans love those qualities today. They will stand us in good stead in this war.

"I shall miss you. I have certainly enjoyed out many meetings together. Yes, you must move on. You will always have my full support in everything you do. I am sure that your new venture will be a success. When you are free to do so please come and tell me what it is."

She kissed him as she left.

It took Sid several hours to encode that message and send it to London. It was the last one he would send for her.

When he had finished he sent a private message from her to General Harford. He noted that in it she said wanted him to go to work for her when she moved on. He was very happy with that.

* * *

March 9, 1942. Winston got a long message from Roosevelt today. It took him quite some while to digest it because it was so detailed. When he had read it all he was delighted. He told us that at last America was taking real practical steps to help us. He called in the Cabinet Secretary to ask him numerous questions about what, if any, procedures were needed to enable more than a hundred airfields and barracks for a million men to be built. He was told that it would require a simple Act of Parliament. It could all be authorised within a single day under wartime emergency powers. Winston instructed him to go ahead and organise it all.

When he had gone Winston wanted to talk to me about the situation in Russia. He said to me:

"Roosevelt's assessment is that Russia is completely exhausted and is unlikely to survive any German onslaught during the summer. Every briefing you have given me has said the same thing. I have had several letters from Stalin all of which almost instruct us to open a second front in the west immediately so that the pressure is taken off Russian forces. In his most recent letter he accused me of deliberately making Russia take the strain so that Britain and America would have an easier war. Even if that is what we wanted to do it is impossible to organise at this time.

"It is very important that we do know what is going on in Russia. Until we do we cannot know just how big our enemy is. It is easy enough to see that just trying to conquer German territories as they were in 1939 will be a vast task. Roosevelt has now understood this; at least that is what I have understood from the message I have received from him today. If Germany really does control those vast territories to the east our task of conquering them will be vastly larger than anything we have imagined before.

"What that suggests to me is that somehow or other we must provide Russia with the support that can ensure that they are not destroyed by Germany. Given our own problems I have no idea how we do that. But the consequences of not doing it are potentially far worse. It is a nightmare scenario.

"We will never know whether that nightmare scenario exists without high grade information about what is going on in Russia. Are you satisfied with what you are getting?"

I explained to him that the intelligence we received was only as good as the sources we had. We were certain that what we were getting from Germany was good. We were far less certain about Russia. We did not have a spy network there nor did we have any Russian informers known to be close to real hard information. The Foreign Office appeared to have access to some high level information through the Embassy in Moscow although this was often vague. What was known for certain was that Russia had tightened all its security procedures in recent months. We had concluded that that was because they did not want the world to know just how weak they were, but we could not be certain.

Winston was not happy with that. He wanted me to do a thorough examination of it all and try and find a way of validating everything about Russia.

There is a footnote to this entry dated June 6, 1951. It reads: *"I had several meetings over the following few weeks with Ronnie Harford and others. We never found an effective way of getting what we would regard as high quality data from within Russia in 1942 or in the first half of 1943. None of the embassy staff had any freedom to leave their compound and look for information, still less travel to any military area. Every time they travelled anywhere they were always followed by the secret police. It was impossible for them to leave central Moscow. Some of our embassy staff were given weekly briefings on the war situation by the Russian Foreign Ministry but we regarded these as suspect. All these briefings were passed on to George Ponsonby at our Foreign Office. We did try and infiltrate agents into Russia across the borders with Afghanistan and Persia but the distances that they had to travel to get to any active area proved to be too great, so we really got nothing from them.*

After Kursk our military attachés in Moscow were allowed to visit the battle areas under escort and we were then able to see the huge scale of all the military activity in Ukraine, Belarus and Poland. But by then Russia had become totally dominant on the eastern front and they were proud to show what they had achieved.

* * *

Angela went to see the British Ambassador two days after she had had that lunch with Roosevelt. She said to him:

"Sir, this is a discussion I never expected to have. When I came here I anticipated that I would remain in my post as long as London wanted. I have always accepted that someone there determines the length of any assignment and that I move on as directed. But I have to tell you that I have been offered a very interesting post outside the diplomatic service. It is a frontline job supporting Britain's war effort. It will be based here in America and I will be able to use my contacts to good effect. It is a job that I would very much like to do. Before I can give any response about it I will need your approval and that of London as well. It will be working for Avro, the makers of the Lancaster bomber and I will head up their organisation in America as they start building those machines over here. I hope it will be possible for you to support me in this and that it will be possible for me to be released very soon.

"I have come to the view that the role that I have been performing has been overtaken by events. Now that the joint war effort is rapidly gathering pace it no longer seems to be necessary to have the role that I have been performing."

The Ambassador agreed to support her and promised that he would contact London about it.

* * *

In 1997 I found some files in the Russian archives that contained reports written by Yuri Butkov. They described how he managed Guy Burgess during the early years of the war. There were no entries after June, 1943 because Butkov died from a heart attack then. But the diaries do describe the information he was able to obtain from George Ponsonby in the early war years. They show that Stalin was privy to any policy information that was available to the Foreign Office.

I went through a very detailed analysis of the information that Bradman, in Washington, had passed to Churchill and I found that only those messages that had been copied to the Foreign Office had eventually gone through to Guy Burgess. None of the messages that had been passed only to Ronnie Harford or direct to Churchill had found their way to Russia. It was a damning indictment of the failures of the British security services.

* * *

Zhukov's diaries for 1942 for the period from January to September reveal an intense frustration about the way he was required to manage the war. He was subject to constant political interference. There was an entry almost every day. It must have been a very difficult period for him. What I have tried to do is consolidate his thoughts into a coherent description of what was going on in the Russian high command at that time.

His most difficult task was the planning for the counter attacks against Germany which would be made in deepest winter and after the German armies had been thoroughly weakened. The daring part of the plan for Stalingrad was that the extra troops needed for those attacks could only come from the defence of Moscow. There were none available from anywhere else in any real quantities although training for millions of extra forces had been commenced east of the Urals. Stalin would not agree to the release of any troops or aircraft from Moscow until the main stages of the Stalingrad plan were underway, probably in the early autumn.

Zhukov disagreed with that view and had numerous fierce arguments with Stalin about it but the man was simply not prepared to change his view in any way. The arguments were sometimes so fierce that Zhukov was certain that if he had not had those achievements in Leningrad and Moscow he would have been sacked by Stalin. He was certain that he would be sacked if Stalingrad failed but that was a possibility he refused to contemplate then or ever.

The plan was based on winning and he and the whole of the military staff in STAVKA knew that western Russia was doomed unless they won the battle to come in Stalingrad. Stalin's views made the balancing of the defence of Moscow with the counter attacks that were going to happen in Stalingrad a planning nightmare.

It was all made rather worse by the fact that Stalin would not even release to Zhukov the commanders he would need in Stalingrad to complete the planning and then run the battle on a day to day basis. Stalin told Zhukov several times that he would only release them when he could see that things were going to plan. This really meant that Zhukov had to spend a lot of time in Stalingrad directing the preparation of the defences. But every time he went there he was called back to Moscow for another STAVKA or some late night meeting with Stalin at which he was usually drunk and always ate copiously. He had his own aircraft with crews ready to fly at all times but it was a long flight between Moscow and Stalingrad and sometimes the weather made any sort of flying impossible. It led to a very stressful life.

If Zhukov could have had any choice about what he could do it would have been to return to a field command. That was what he liked most about army life and he was good at it. But that was not to be. Instead he was in the frontline of Stalin's arguments several times a week. As the spring of 1942 gave way to summer he longed for the Germans to start their advance and for battle to be joined in Stalingrad itself. He knew that he would be proved right and that Stalin's caution was unnecessary.

Something Zhukov found very hard to get used to in STAVKA was the endless politicking. There were senseless discussions about whether it was good communism to do this, that or the other. Zhukov could not understand what communism had to do with it but he was not in any way free to criticise that doctrine. So instead he adopted a line from which he never wavered that the issues were all about the defence of Mother Russia herself. That was the overwhelming objective, that was what he was going to do and Stalingrad was merely the next stage in achieving that. Despite the endless arguments he never lost his confidence. But he never became a friend of any civilian member of STAVKA nor would he ever describe himself as a friend of Stalin. He doubted whether Stalin even had any notion of friendship. Friendship or not Zhukov knew that the most important thing of all was retaining Stalin's confidence. That could only be done by winning battles.

* * *

March 16, 1942. Ronnie Harford told me today that the agent we call Bradman is leaving the White House shortly and therefore the sort of communication Winston has had through him will no longer be possible. I was concerned that it might lead to weakening communications with Roosevelt but he assured me that nothing of that kind would happen.

When I told Winston he seemed delighted. .He said; "I hope that means that I will never have to meet that bloody Sally woman ever again." I had no idea what he was talking about and he did not answer any questions about it.

* * *

April 2, 1942. All this year we have been getting grim news from the North Atlantic. Today we got the final tally of shipping losses for the first quarter. We have lost 225 ships since the New Year. In that time we know that Germany has commissioned 49 more U-Boats and we have only sunk 11. It looks as if things can only get even worse. Last year 25,000 people lost their lives in the convoys. To make it all far worse those machines are now patrolling deep into American waters. They have even sunk ships in the Gulf of Mexico. Winston is appalled by it all. He had really thought that things would start to improve immediately America entered the war but they have only got worse. Each day for about three weeks now he has been telling us that he wonders just how much longer Britain can take all this punishment. Outwardly, of course he puts a brave face on it all. Yesterday he told the Commons that American forces were already arriving in Britain and that joint planning to bring an end to the Nazi menace was already well advanced. It is nothing of the kind. There are huge tensions about the level of control that America will have. Eisenhower comes to see Winston every other day and each time he comes he has a new list of demands. Winston feels humiliated by what he is expected to do at Roosevelt's behest.

Perhaps the only bit of good news around at the moment is that the building programme to accommodate the American forces is going well and we should be welcoming their first bomber squadrons within a couple of weeks now. Their first bomber base to be completed will be at Ridgewell in Essex. Winston will be there to welcome them when they arrive.

* * *

May 9, 1942. Winston was apoplectic all day today. Two things have angered him. There has been a large loss of shipping to U-Boat attacks in the Caribbean. This seems to have been caused by American reluctance to introduce a full convoy system there. That area has become so dangerous that some of our Escort Groups have had to be withdrawn from the Atlantic to counter the threat. He is especially angry about this because Max Horton had recommended a total convoy system for all shipping in and out of American ports immediately. The American failure to do this has already resulted in the loss of a million tons of shipping. Now the protection we have been building up in the North Atlantic has had to be diverted to help them. The result was immediate. In one convoy last night 9 ships were lost.

The other reason for Winston's anger was that we heard this morning that America had won a large sea battle with the Japanese in the Coral Sea. He thinks that America is putting more effort into the war in the Pacific than into Europe. He fired off an ill-tempered message to Roosevelt about it all.

What really irks him, though, is that America has already achieved a major victory in that battle and Britain still has precious little to show for its war effort. He has decided that there will be no reports of the Coral Sea battle in any British media. He told me that there will be no reports of any American victories until such time as Britain has a great triumph to report. As things look today, that might be some long while away.

* * *

May 25, 1942. Winston has become so angry about American success in the Pacific without there appearing to be a comparable effort in Europe that he has decided to talk directly with Roosevelt once more. We left London this morning to fly to Washington. Over the next few days Winston hopes to be able to persuade FDR that America should make a large scale landing in Morocco later this year. He has already talked it over with Eisenhower several times. He believes that such a landing will make it impossible for the German forces in Libya to attempt any major attack on our forces there. He hopes to impress Roosevelt that such an American landing will make the Middle East safe from any German attacks.

It was a noisy and bumpy flight across the Atlantic. We flew in cloud most of the way. This was my second trip to America with him by air. I feel that I am already getting used to the refuelling stop in Gander. What a desolate cold place that is.

* * *

May 27, 1942. Things have suddenly got a lot worse. This morning the Germans launched a massive attack against our forces in Libya. All day long we have received reports of our forces retreating under overwhelming German firepower. Winston has been very angry about it and has ordered a news blackout. It could not have happened at a worse time. W. was confident that our Eighth Army in Libya would be able to contain the German armies there indefinitely and then move forward towards Tunisia as the American landings in Morocco he wants took place. Now he feels very exposed to anything that FDR can throw at him. Just spending a few moments with Winston is enough to realise that he thinks that we probably cannot get to any worse position than we now have. But he never gives up fighting. He intends to use the occasion to force Roosevelt into more urgent action in Europe.

* * *

On May 27th, 1942 Rommel started a major offensive against the British Eighth Army. Within a few days the symbolic British fortress of Tobruk had fallen and Eighth Army had started a long retreat which was to take them all the way back to within 60 miles of Cairo. Initially the retreat was a complete shambles but command of Eighth Army was taken over by General Auchinleck, the British Commander in the Middle East, at the beginning of June. Auchinleck managed the British withdrawal back to the natural defensive lines at El Alamein within 60 miles of Cairo.

* * *

May 29, 1942. Despite the dreadful setbacks in North Africa Winston seems to have won his verbal battle with Roosevelt. The President had agreed to there being an American landing in Morocco later in the year. It will be directed by Eisenhower and the field commander will be George Patton. The date has yet to be fixed, but it will be sometime in the autumn. Roosevelt has said that the date will be determined solely by himself in consultation with Eisenhower. He is not prepared to go ahead until America can commit what he calls overwhelming force to the campaign.

Tonight we go back to London. Winston regards it as a successful trip despite the dire news from North Africa but he is confident that we will be able to resist that German army there.

Winston pressed FDR about American progress in the Pacific but he got no useful information from him.

* * *

June 6, 1942. We got news today of another American naval victory in the Pacific, this time at Midway. Winston is appalled that America should be having these victories while we are suffering the grief of the retreat in North Africa and another escalation in the convoy losses. April and May have been diabolical months on the convoy routes. We have lost more ships in the last 2 months than in any comparable period in the war. To make it worse another 58 U-Boats have been commissioned since the end of March. There are now 61 of them at sea in the North Atlantic.

* * *

June 9, 1942. Winston called an intelligence meeting for today. At it he got some of the best news that he has had in a long while. The intelligence service he set up in 1939 has become well established at Bletchley Park. It has been staffed by some very brilliant people, mostly taken from top teaching positions in our universities. That investment is now paying off. They told us today that they have broken most of the German military codes. Some of the Luftwaffe codes remain to be cracked. When they are able to decode a message they are getting very good information. The problem they now have is sorting the messages so that they can find the ones with the key messages in them. There are many thousands of messages sent every day by German commanders and it is only possible to decode and translate less than a hundred of them. But each day they are getting excellent information about German troop deployments. Winston is happy with what we are receiving.

The most important information they are getting now is about Rommel's intentions in Libya. There is no doubt that he is going to increase the intensity of his offensive. That is not a surprise but the information we have received has been passed to General Auchinleck in Egypt. Winston is satisfied that it will enable him to react much more positively to events as they unfold there.

We have also received information from the Russian front that General Paulus will start to advance with his 6th army within a month. They have been held up by a lack of supplies. One of the messages that has been intercepted was from Paulus to Hitler and it was an assessment of the current strength of the Russian forces in Ukraine. He is very confident that he will face little resistance as he advances into the Don Basin and then on to the Caucasus. It looks like the end for Russia.

* * *

June 25, 1942. Winston addressed the Commons today. He has been preparing for it for days. There is absolutely no good news that can be made public but he has judged it essential to give the British people an optimistic account of things more as a morale boost than anything else.

The final draft that I saw just before he left for the Commons started:

"Last month the first American bomber squadrons arrived in our country. I was at their new base to welcome them here. Their arrival marks a turning point is this war. Throughout this year the Royal Air Force has been increasing the intensity of the bombing raids that it operates over Germany. The arrival of the Americans will enable the bombing efforts to double over the next few months. That represents a real advance in our capability to defeat Germany.

"So far this year we have been destroying enemy U-Boats at twice the rate that we have achieved in ay previous period. Although the rate of shipping losses remains high we have been able to increase the rate of new construction ......"

Little of it bore any resemblance to reality but it did go down well in the Commons. He was cheered when he had finished speaking.

* * *

July 3, 1942. The news from the North Atlantic seems to get even worse. In the first six months of this year 465 merchant ships have been sunk on Atlantic convoys. This is a much larger total than for the whole of 1941. In this dreadful carnage 18, 000 lives have been lost.

On top of that we are getting daily news about the retreat of Eighth Army in North Africa. We seem to have lost all the gains we made there in 1941. The North African campaign then was seen as a beacon of hope and did a great deal to boost public morale in Britain. Now everything there seems to have been lost. Winston, of course, is angry about it all.

* * *

July 13, 1942. After the Eighth Army in North Africa has been retreating for weeks we finally got some comforting news today. General Auchinleck seems to have done a magnificent job against overwhelming odds of getting Eighth Army to safety. The army is now dug in at El Alamein. We have been looking at the maps of the area. The El Alamein line seems to be a natural defensive position between the Mediterranean and the Qattara Depression, a huge very low area surrounded by high cliffs. The army line stretches for 38 miles between the sea and Qattara. Auchinleck is happy that the army is now in a position that it can hold indefinitely but they have lost vast quantities of stores in the retreat.

Winston is furious about the whole business and has decided that Eighth Army must have a new commander who will not retreat. He is determined to beat the Germans in the Western Desert, and he needs a commander who can deliver just such a victory. He is not concerned with the cost. All he wants is a victory so that he can prove to Roosevelt that Britain has got what it takes to win the war.

He seems to be obsessed with the fact that America has had two very successful sea battles and Britain has achieved nothing. He has become determined that Britain must achieve a major success in a land battle soon and El Alamein offers the only opportunity. He wants to smash Rommel's army there.

He has decided to go to Egypt in August to agree the strategy for that battle with the new army commander whom he will appoint soon. There can be no doubt that politically he is in desperate need for a major victory.

All day he was in turmoil but he calmed down this evening and over a very large brandy he asked me what I thought of it all. Although I knew it would not be popular with him I did say that I thought that Auchinleck had done a brilliant job of rescuing the army against overwhelming odds. He would not accept that. He said to me that the only thing that mattered now was a British victory. Parliament would demand it and he would be removed from office unless he achieved it. He made it very clear to me that he was not in a position of quitting for any reason and therefore the largest possible priority for him in the coming weeks was to get that army in the desert advancing again.

He was truly depressed about the British Army's performance today. I am sure that, as always, he just wanted to prove to everyone that he was doing a good job. I will probably remember forever the final words he use that evening; "Look, Samuel, we heard about the retreat in Libya when we were in Washington trying to persuade Roosevelt that an American landing in Morocco was essential. They are going to go ahead with that landing. Even while it is still being planned we have retreated more than a thousand miles. It places us at a huge disadvantage. We cannot afford disadvantages of that sort. I am therefore going to find a commander for Eighth Army who will get us out from such a shambles for ever."

* * *

July 15, 1942. Winston told me this morning that he has decided to go to Moscow to talk with Stalin. He has had several phone calls with Roosevelt about some demands that Stalin had made about retaining Russian control over territories in Eastern Europe after the war. Stalin attaches much importance to the pact between Molotov and Ribbentrop and the territorial gains that it gave Russia. Although that pact is well and truly dead Stalin has wanted to keep the territories that it promised to Russia. However, yesterday he sent a telegram to Roosevelt suggesting that he would drop those demands if Britain and America opened a second front in the west immediately. Winston told me that he had agreed with FDR that he would go to Moscow to explain why such a front was impossible but also to explain what the campaigns in Africa were so important.

After he has met with Stalin he will then fly on to Egypt to finalise plans for an advance from El Alamein.

Just as I was about to leave he told me that he had selected General Bernard Montgomery to be the commander of Eighth Army. I have never met him and have no knowledge of his record so I could not comment but I did decide to find out more about the man.

* * *

July 18, 1942. A fascinating lunch today with Ronnie Harford and several of his cronies. The consensus view was that Montgomery was a very curious choice for Eighth Army commander. He is not popular in the army and is widely regarded as a loner and self-opinionated. He is not recognised to be a military strategist but an expert on logistics. Time will tell as to whether Winston has made the right choice. I shall doubtless meet the man when I go with Winston to Egypt in August.

* * *

July 20, 1942. For days now we have been following the movement of convoy PQ17. Every day the news has been getting worse. This convoy was one of the largest ever formed and it was carrying military equipment to Russia. There was enough equipment on it for several armies and it would have been of immense help to Russia. It now appears that almost the entire convoy has been destroyed in the Barents Sea. It is by far our worst convoy disaster and it will wreck Anglo/American efforts to help Russia. Winston is in by far his worst mood yet.

* * *

August 12, 1942. Arrived in Moscow today. On the flight Winston was just as optimistic as he had been before all those meetings with Roosevelt. He always seems to think that he can conquer the world with a robust argument with any other leader anywhere. He is sure that he will achieve something with Stalin. But I am very unclear what the real objective of this meeting with Stalin really is.

We had a big meeting in London a couple of days ago in order to come to a consensus as to what the real strengths and weaknesses of Russia are at the present time. Everything available to us suggests that they are very weak and that the German assessment that Russia is about to collapse is correct. If that is the case there is no possible point in Winston meeting Stalin because Russia will not then be able to make any contribution to ending the war. Another view point is that Russia is weak but could be saved by a large scale invasion in the west during the next few weeks. That seems to be what Stalin wants. But there is nothing that Britain or America can do to achieve that. Again there is no point in talking to Stalin. The trigger for these talks anyway is that Stalin wants to depart from the demands that he gave Eden earlier that after the war he wants to control those territories that Russia gained in the deal with von Ribbentrop. This again looks to be academic unless somehow Russia has physical control of those territories at the end of the war. If Russia is weak that will be impossible. All in all there does not seem to be any point in meeting with Stalin at this time. But according to Winston Stalin was very insistent that the meeting take place.

The brief that Winston agreed with Roosevelt and Eisenhower was for him to explain the planned landings in North Africa to Stalin.

* * *

August 14, 1942. Winston called a breakfast meeting today to explain to us what had happened at his meetings with Stalin yesterday. They apparently achieved nothing. Stalin was actually very insulting about British military performance and he was furious about the disaster to PQ17. He was very unconvinced that any military activity in North Africa would make any contribution to the war in Europe. He refused to accept that it would help Russia in any way at all. Stalin had apparently ranted for a couple of hours about the desperate situation that Russia faced. He had taken Winston into a map room and had showed him the positions of the large German armies and the positions of the very much weaker Russian forces. There were apparently hardly any Russian forces in Ukraine and two German armies were advancing rapidly there. Winston told us that if everything from Stalin could be taken at face value it was highly likely that all of western Russia would be lost within three months and that was likely to include Moscow. There were no decisions of any sort made at the meetings.

But Stalin did invite W. to a late night drinking session at the Kremlin. Stalin had drunk a huge amount of vodka and had got very drunk. At two in the morning he had ordered a whole suckling pig and this was brought within a few minutes, so it was obviously something he did regularly. He ate it all and then went to bed.

* * *

I was able to find a reference in Stalin's papers to this meeting. Stalin's account of it was very much more optimistic than Winston's. He noted that he had enjoyed talking with Churchill particularly in the drinking session and that it had been a good opportunity to get to know him.

* * *

August 14, 1942. It is early morning and we are still on the BOAC Skymaster to Cairo. After we left Moscow we had to fly well east of any Russian military activity and that meant stopping in Tehran for fuel. The only passengers on the plane are Winston, myself and Lord Moran, Winston's doctor. Moran is a good friend of mine and he is very much trusted by Winston. I know that W. confides in him even more than he does in me. We have often talked together about Winston but Moran has never disclosed to me anything that he has said to him which could possibly be classified as a confidence. The weather for the flight has been mostly good so it was much better than the bumpy flight we had had from London to Moscow. After take off and a few brandies Winston slept all the way to Tehran.

After we left there he wanted me to help him with something that Stalin said to him while he was eating that suckling pig. He had been trying to work it out for himself but had not come to any conclusion. Although Stalin had painted a grim picture of Russia's weaknesses during the day he nevertheless told Winston that Russia was planning a major battle that would start soon. He had not said where it would be nor did he give any indication of how they could possibly do it given their weakened state. Winston wanted my view as to what it could possibly mean.

We knew from German sources that Germany was advancing rapidly across the steppe at that time. There was no significant Russian resistance to their advance. The general direction of the German forces was south east towards the Volga River. It looked to be a certainty that they would reach that river within a month and within a couple of months after that they would mop up the whole of the Caucasus and the Donets Basin. We knew from our sources that that was their intention. Winston confirmed that that was exactly what Stalin had told him as well. What mystified him was that there were no significant Russian forces marked on the maps that Stalin had showed him of that area. So Winston wanted to talk at great length about what that phrase "We are planning a great battle" really meant. We were not able to reach any conclusion. What we were certain about was that within a few weeks we would know exactly what was going on in Russia. If they were beaten by Germany it would be soon.

* * *

For the rest of the flight Winston thought about the progress of the war on all fronts. He was going to North Africa to review the plans for the forthcoming battle that was being planned to take place at El Alamein. The only active war fronts in which the British were involved at that time were the North Atlantic, North Africa and some operations on a much smaller scale in the Far East.

There was not a lot for him to be happy about. The initial victories over the Italians in North Africa had turned to despair after Rommel had brought his army there. The convoys were still being bashed to pieces in the North Atlantic and although British capability there had improved markedly there were still large numbers of U-Boats out there and still more were being built.

Britain's interests in the Far East had been shattered by the Japanese. But in the Pacific at least America was beginning to see progress in its naval war with Japan. It had won the battles of Coral Sea in May and Midway in June. Even as he was in that aircraft they were fighting the Battle of Guadalcanal. That went way beyond a naval battle because it also involved an initial landing of 15, 000 marines as the advance party of hundreds of thousands of American soldiers. It looked as if America would soon drive the Japanese off that island. If they did they could start the long haul task of driving the Japanese off every island all the way back to Japan. Roosevelt had kept him informed of what they were doing but Churchill had ordered that those American victories be kept out of the newspapers and off the radio in Britain until he had a victory of his own to celebrate. He desperately hoped that that victory would come at El Alamein.

As soon as Churchill arrived at Cairo he was driven out to Montgomery's headquarters. He had arrived in Cairo in the early morning and it was about a three hour drive from the airport to Monty's HQ just to the east of the El Alamein lines.

Churchill had decided on the plane exactly what he would say. It was to be an ultimatum. A classic stick and carrot approach:

"Monty, Let me fill you in on the strategic situation. Britain has had no victories for a long while now. Sure we did beat the Italians in this desert at the beginning of the war and sure we did sink the *Bismarck*. But that is about it. We have not got anywhere near winning the U-Boat battle. Meanwhile America is getting some successes in the Pacific. They have won two big naval battles at Coral Sea and Midway and they are now starting the task of clearing Guadalcanal of all Japanese. Those battles have not been the subject of any publicity in Britain so far because we have not had any victories to announce so far.

"At the moment Russia is planning a major battle. I cannot see how they can win it because of their depleted forces but if they do it will be a disaster for us. It would really put us in the shade and sharply reduce our credibility with Roosevelt. We cannot allow that and we must therefore have a victory here at El Alamein before we can know anything about that Russian battle. You must therefore win here. If you fail you will be sacked and there will almost certainly be a no-confidence vote in the House against me. I dread the consequences of that.

"If you win you will become the senior British field commander but I have to tell you that you will report on all military matters to General Eisenhower who is going to be in charge of all military operations in Europe. That is the price we have had to pay for American aid.

"What I will also do to provide you with assistance is send you one last convoy with whatever people, equipment and supplies I can assemble. It will be sent as soon as I can get back to England.

"So that is the deal. You just have to get on and do it. Britain's credibility depends on your success in the desert here. You are ordered to win that battle as soon as you can."

Churchill then told him that there was a planned American landing in Morocco in November to be called Operation Torch. Eisenhower would be in overall command of it and Patton would be the army commander. But Churchill wanted El Alamein to have been a success before then. Montgomery knew nothing about either of them until then, but they would both plague him for the rest of the war.

They talked all day, but in the end Monty realised that he had no option. It was all or nothing. It was a gamble on a single throw of the dice.

* * *

When Churchill got back to London two days later his first meeting was with Beaverbrook:

"Max, I require you to round up all the fast merchant ships and passenger liners that are in Britain or America at the moment. They must be filled with soldiers, tanks, guns, ammunition and food and they must sail for Egypt as soon as possible. Montgomery needs as much of all of those as he can get. You must form convoys escorted by the fastest escorts and whatever capital ships are available to take them all safely into the South Atlantic. Please just get on and do it."

Beaverbrook loved logistics and transport problems. He worked day and night to organise convoy OG 219 which sailed at dusk from Liverpool five days later. It steamed at 19 knots all the way from Southern Ireland to the Equator. It was the fastest convoy of the war, operating at well over twice normal convoy speeds. It contained twenty five ships including three liners and fifteen escorts. It reached the Equator in a week. There the escorts turned back and returned to England. All the merchant ships reached Egypt well before the end of September. A further convoy left Charleston, South Carolina, at the same time laden with tanks, guns, ammunition and vehicles.

Montgomery would have had far less hope of winning El Alamein without that extra help.

* * *

14 September, 1942. There is still no sign of the large battle about which Stalin spoke to Winston. We are getting masses of information from German sources about the fact that their 6th Army has been prevented from advancing beyond Stalingrad. Apparently there were large and effective defences there which initially stalled the German army but since then they have advanced into the city which is being progressively destroyed. It is apparently continuous house to house fighting. If Russia has planned for a battle there it is odd that there are no signs of large numbers of troops in the area. That means that Stalin must have had somewhere else in mind. That is odd, too, because winter will come soon and then any normal fighting will be impossible.

* * *

October 14, 1942. Winston is getting more anxious with every passing day about El Alamein. When he was there in August he was hoping that battle would start early in October and that Rommel's armies would be completely destroyed by the end of October. In his heart of hearts he would dearly love Eighth Army to finish off the task so that the Torch landings in Morocco were rendered redundant. That would certainly strengthen his position with Roosevelt.

Those extra convoys arrived in mid-September and a division of troops was moved from India to Egypt. Despite all this Montgomery has asked for a postponement of the operation twice already and it is now scheduled for the fourth week of the month. Nothing irritates Winston more than any delay in a military operation. He always thinks the commanders are being too cautious in those circumstances. What he really wants Montgomery to achieve is a knock-out blow on the first morning of the battle. Only that will satisfy him.

It is all made rather worse because Roosevelt phones him a couple of times every week to press him into getting the operation started quickly. He fears that if Montgomery does not get going soon the Torch landings will be prejudiced.

* * *

El Alamein started on the 23rd of October. Far from being the knock-out blow that Churchill wanted it rapidly turned into a bloody grind. It took 12 days to dislodge Rommel's armies from their El Alamein lines despite Britain having a solid firepower advantage At the end of those 12 days the German armies slipped away and were never seriously engaged in battle again in Africa. The German retreat was followed by a slow and methodical advance by the British. Montgomery was never able to catch up with Rommel let alone destroy his army as he had been instructed to do by Churchill. It did eventually succeed but it was a hard bloody grind.

* * *

November 5, 1942. Winston has been to the House today to announce a major victory at El Alamein. He was cheered wildly because he portrayed it as the big breakthrough and the beginning of the end for the German armies throughout Europe. I have no doubt that all the newspapers tomorrow will be full of it all. The news of the battle even taking place had been held back so that Winston could announce it as a great triumph to a surprised but inevitably delighted nation. All day he has been getting messages of congratulation from all around the country. Interestingly, he has heard nothing from Roosevelt.

* * *

In my researches I have looked into numerous accounts of every aspect of El Alamein. At the end of the war Churchill said;

"Before Alamein we never had a victory, after Alamein we never had a defeat."

That statement was not true on either count. There had been the earlier victories in North Africa. The *Bismarck* had been sunk and so had the *Graf Spee*. There were still several months of defeats in the convoy battles after October, 1942. The advance through Italy was to be a long bloody grind. Then there were Caen and Arnhem, which both severely damaged the British war effort. The British commander in both those encounters was Montgomery.

His reputation in Britain in late November, 1942 was close to that of a deity. He retained his job as the senior British land commander because Churchill had promised it to him if he succeeded at El Alamein. Despite the failures at Caen and Arnhem he retained his reputation and it was still intact when he died.

Much later historians revised their judgments about him. By the 1990's it was widely recognised by them that El Alamein was entirely unnecessary. The British lines were virtually impregnable. They were certainly impregnable to Rommel's army which could not be reinforced and was at the extreme end of a very long supply chain. Montgomery could easily have waited there until the Torch landings had taken place in Morocco in November. As soon as those landings had taken place Rommel would have been forced to withdraw whether Hitler liked it or not.

El Alamein took place because Churchill had to have a victory in the west before either America or Russia. He knew that it would be an easy victory for America in Morocco. There was only the possibility of light resistance there. He knew that Roosevelt would make the most of it as America's first successful intervention in the war in Europe.

He had no way of knowing whether Stalin really was planning a major battle or not and if he was he had no idea how it could be successful. But politically he could not take the risk. He was certain that Russia would use any victory of theirs to full propaganda advantage.

That all meant that Britain had to achieve a major victory before either Russia or America. That was why El Alamein was so important.

That phrase "Before Alamein we never had a victory, after Alamein we never had a defeat." has become a central part of the British public's view of the war. It was widely believed that Britain alone brought about the final phases of the war by staging that battle at El Alamein.

There is an interesting corroboration of this view in Samuel's diary. An entry dated November 12, 1942 he records a conversation he had with Churchill that day. It reads:

"Winston was in a very talkative mood today. He told me that he knew that El Alamein was a gamble. He knew that it was risky despite the British superiority in both men and equipment. The problem about El Alamein, in his view, was that it was a superb defensive position for both sides. He acknowledged that Auchinleck had selected an excellent position in which to save and protect Eighth Army. But it was also a position from which it would be hard to dislodge any German army of the strength available to Rommel. But, and these are the words he used:

"'I had to have that victory. I had to beat America or Russia to a large land victory. It did not matter what it cost and it did not matter what the downside consequences were. It simply had to happen. As Wellington had said after Waterloo - It was a close run thing. But I am now relieved that it is all over. I know that for many a long year all Britain will see it as the turning point of the whole war and I will be credited with achieving it"

That was how it all happened and that was why El Alamein became central to the entire British view of how the war was won.

* * *

November 23, 1942. The Torch landings led by USS Augusta took place this morning. There was little resistance. The army is safely camped ashore and will start to advance tomorrow morning.

* * *

Zhukov's diary for June 27, 1942 read:

We have now received confirmation that the German Sixth and Fourth Panzer armies are on the move. Stalin has agreed today that Chuikov can command the defence of Stalingrad. Tomorrow I will be going to Stalingrad with him and Khrushchev to plan the final defences.

* * *

The German supply lines in southern Russia had become so long and the ravages of the winter so great that it was impossible for them to renew any large scale offensive actions until late June, 1942.

The German armies had over-wintered on a front line that ran roughly from Kharkov in the north to just west of Rostov in the south. The line was approximately four hundred miles west of Stalingrad. Between the Don basin, where they had spent the winter, and Stalingrad there was a completely flat grassy plain, called steppe, that ran for six hundred miles all the way to the Ural River. In summertime it was always dusty and hot.

It was easy country for tank warfare but there were few military targets anywhere short of Stalingrad. As Zhukov had indicated in his conversations with STAVKA the previous December it was all about getting the Germans right into Stalingrad itself. That was where the fight would take place.

The principal German forces to be used in the campaign were the Fourth Panzer army and the Sixth army.

General Paulus led his Sixth army eastwards on June 28th. The campaign to capture that steppe and Stalingrad itself was called Operation Blue. It was under the overall command of von Manstein. On the way the German Fourth Panzer Army quickly captured the town of Voronezh. By August 5th they had captured the railway centre at Kotelnikovo just seventy miles southwest of Stalingrad. That evening Hitler told his friends that he believed that the Soviet Union was about to collapse and that its reserves were now non–existent.

By August 23rd the German forces had crossed the Don River about 40 miles west of Stalingrad. All the while Russian troops were harassing them lightly in accordance with Zhukov's plans and withdrawing steadily towards Stalingrad.

Zhukov left Moscow on August 27th to take charge of all Russian armies in the general area of Stalingrad. He made his headquarters at Malaya Ivanovka, 50 miles north of Stalingrad. By September 2nd all Russian troops had withdrawn into the city. Paulus had no further opportunity to fight them on the open plain. Blitzkrieg was at an end.

* * *

September 11th, 1942 was a crunch day for Zhukov. His diary records that he spent most of that day with STAVKA. The purpose of the meeting was to review the defence of Stalingrad and to put in place the next steps to trap and destroy the German armies. His diary entry that day was obviously written after hours of intense frustration. It had been a very difficult day at STAVKA.

Stalin had been happy that an entire German army had become embroiled in the elaborate defences around the city. He was happy that it would be impossible for them to advance further until the city had been taken. But he was not happy that it was likely to take so long.

Zhukov wrote:

"For most of the day I was trying to tell him that our original plan required that we trap the Germans in the city and that we destroy them when the winter makes it impossible for them to fight. I told him that we must stick to that plan because it is the only one which will maximise our chances of success. He kept going on about how Britain and America had plans for land attacks on German armies over the next few weeks and how it was impossible politically to allow them any advantage, however small.

"I told him that it was impossible for us to do what he wanted in Stalingrad until we had the advantage of winter weather. That was the original plan and that was the way it had to be. It is rarely a good idea to get aggressive with him but I needed decisions and I was fed up with all that politics. So I told him that I needed his immediate approval to appoint Rokossovskii and Vatutin to command the armies that would encircle the Germans. I promised him that if he approved those appointments today then I would guarantee victory in Stalingrad by January, but not before.

"It took another two hours of hard discussion before he agreed. Tomorrow I must have a meeting with them both so that they know exactly what is expected of them. They will only have a couple of weeks in which to plan the detailed deployment of troops away from the defences of St. Petersburg and Moscow and organise their movements down south. It will be a hectic time."

* * *

From September 11th until November 19th in Stalingrad it was continuous urban guerrilla warfare. In the process the city was entirely wrecked. Legends were made there, though. The street fighting encouraged new forms of military skills. The greatest legends were Lieutenant Vassili Zaitsev, a sniper who is known to have killed 242 Germans each with a single bullet fired at long range and his lover Sergeant Tania Chernova who also had a distinguished record as a sniper. Tania was even selected for an assassination attempt on General Paulus. It only failed because one of her escort team was blown up by a land mine and Tania was concussed and had to be taken away from danger.

In early November the weather had become extremely cold and the Volga and Don rivers froze over. It was becoming exactly right for Russia to launch counter attacks just as Zhukov had planned. In the German HQ's there was a widespread belief that all the Russian forces in the area had been destroyed and General Paulus was confident that the fighting would cease completely within two or three days. It was now becoming almost safe for Germans to move around the wrecked streets of Stalingrad.

On November 16th Zhukov and Rokossovskii started to move the Russian 5th and 21st Tank armies across the Volga River. They moved out from their bridgeheads on November 19th to approach Stalingrad from the northwest. The following day three Russian armies under Vatutin encircled the city from the south. Paulus's Sixth army was completely cut off within the perimeter of the city. It was a complete and sudden shock to Paulus and the entire German High Command. As Hitler had thought, they had all believed that the Russian armies were at an end.

At the time von Manstein was garrisoned near Rostov well away to the southwest. He was ordered by Hitler to undertake an operation to relieve Stalingrad. All the German troops within Stalingrad were to be rescued and von Manstein was to destroy those Soviet armies. All the German troops within the Stalingrad area were at that time sure that they would be relieved. Von Manstein was revered throughout the German armies because of his victories in France and at Sevastopol. They were all certain that he would lead them to safety.

Von Manstein's relief operation began on December 12th with a dash from Kotelnikovo directly towards Stalingrad. The combination of appalling weather and endless attacks on his forces by Russians meant that he could not get anywhere near Stalingrad. Within four days his advance had effectively been halted.

The German High Command had had no idea that Russia had any reserves left before Stalingrad. They were astonished that such large armies could have been formed without their having any knowledge of it. It was only after Soviet papers had been released after the end of the cold war that it was possible to work out where those troops had come from. Zhukov knew that the troops that he had withdrawn from the cities in the north were the only ones available then.

* * *

December 1, 1942. We are getting very strong indications from German sources that they are facing a major catastrophe at Stalingrad. The Sixth army has been encircled in the appalling weather conditions there. They seem to be mystified as to how it can have happened.

* * *

December 26, 1942. Well, it has been a better Christmas than last year. Not much normal Christmas cheer, though. Shortages of everything have meant that there is very little to eat but there has been plenty of drink available. Our wine cellar still has good stocks left. There was virtually nothing in the shops for giving as Christmas presents. But it was much better than last year because most of the war news has been encouraging.

Winston gave a small party in the bunker on Christmas Eve. All his immediate staff were there. He gave a gracious speech thanking us for our efforts during the year. He also set out what he thought were the advances we had made in the year. Obviously El Alamein was the most important for him. Then he cited the U-Boat killings. There had been nearly a hundred and it was by far the best figure so far. He said that he hoped that it meant that we were starting to win the convoy war. Finally he mentioned the large scale bombings of Germany that had started in May.

He said he was very pleased with the American successes in the Pacific. He mentioned Stalingrad using the words "Our Russian allies are at this moment still fighting a desperate battle in the snows of Southern Russia where they are trying to drive a large German army from the city of Stalingrad. Our thoughts go out to them at this hour of peril for them."

* * *

December 31, 1942. We have heard today that the Japanese Emperor has authorised the withdrawal of all Japanese forces from Guadalcanal. Winston has spoken to Roosevelt on the phone today and he has congratulated him on a fine American effort there.

* * *

When I was able to study Roosevelt's private papers I found a draft of his State of the Union speech that he was due to give in January, 1943. The speech he actually gave was very different but that draft provides a very interesting insight to his thinking over that Christmas period.

It read:

"Fellow Countrymen, America has now been at war for a little over a year. It has been a year in which America has been able to exert its authority over the war in Europe which had been threatening to spiral out of control. We have had some notable victories over Japan in the Pacific.

"Let me tell you in detail about our achievements. On the battlefront we have stopped the Japanese advances in the Pacific. They reached the Solomon Islands and had they continued unchecked they would have been in a position to invade Australia. That country is a much treasured friend of America and any Japanese invasion of her would have been treated by us as an invasion of our own homeland. We have been able to prevent it by successfully beating large Japanese forces at Guadalcanal in the Solomons. We have beaten them at sea off Guadalcanal and we have landed a large army there which has defeated the Japanese land forces on that island. The way is now clear for us to move northwards and clear them from all the territories that have invaded throughout the Pacific.

"We have engaged them in two other naval battles in the Coral Sea and off Midway and on both occasions we have won decisively. In winning these battles we have clear proof of the quality and commitment of our armed forces.

"A notable advance has been made on the other side of the Atlantic. In November we landed a large force in Morocco. This is now moving east and within a few weeks will meet up with British forces that are driving German armies out of Africa. This is a joint Anglo-American operation and in under the overall command of American General Dwight D. Eisenhower. He will command all joint Anglo-American operations for the remainder of the war.

"We have continued to provide aid to Britain throughout the war. It was only the provision of American tanks and guns which enable them to take on the German Afrika Corps in Egypt.

"American bombers are now based in Britain and are conducting regular sorties over Germany.

"With the plans in place I expect that we will make major advances in the Pacific over the coming year. In Europe we will be leading a land invasion that will intensify the pressure that we are already placing on Germany.

"I will be meeting Prime Minister Churchill shortly to plan further stages in the implementation of the Atlantic Charter that we signed in August 1941."

That speech was never made but it does clearly indicate that Roosevelt's priorities at that time were American domination of the war effort and the implementation of the Atlantic Charter.

* * *

January 6, 1943. Today we got the final listings for convoy losses for 1942. Over 1,000 ships have been lost; that is well over 8 million tons of shipping. Not even the massive Liberty ships programme in America has been able to compensate for that. As always Winston is depressed about the rate of losses. But he is far more anxious about the numbers of new U-Boats that have been commissioned in the year. At 248 it is far higher than ever before. We have only been able to destroy 87 of then in 1942. A truly awful situation. Nevertheless Winston is confident that with our large building programme of new escorts and with increasing American support and much better air cover over the Atlantic we should be able to control this problem now.

* * *

January 8, 1943. We are due to go to Casablanca within a few days for a conference which will shape the next stages of the war. All the planning for it has assumed that Stalin and Roosevelt will be there with Winston. It was to be the first time they have all met together. But Stalin cannot now come as the battle at Stalingrad is reaching its climax. The whole plan has got worse today because Lord Moran has diagnosed that Winston has caught pneumonia. His view is that Winston cannot possibly fly to the conference. Winston is having none of that and has demanded that Moran cure him. He has adamantly refused to accept that he cannot go to such an important meeting.

So what Moran is going to do is give him an experimental drug called penicillin. It has done well in trials but has never been used in any normal treatments and may well have side-effects. He has told Winston of the risks and he is not prepared to accept that any of them apply to him. So he is going ahead and will use the stuff. When I was with him a few minutes ago he was very ill and running a high temperature. Let us just hope that it works.

* * *

The Soviet records show that Stalin was first invited to the conference in Casablanca the previous November. It was certainly his intention to go but he did say that he could only reach a definite decision shortly before the appointed date and that it would depend on the military situation in Russia at the time. His own notes record that he was deeply suspicious of every aspect of the conference. He sent telegrams to both Roosevelt and Churchill demanding that if for any reason he could not attend the conference should be postponed until such time as he could attend.

The same records show that when he had to withdraw he was appalled that Roosevelt and Churchill still planned to meet and he sent furious telegrams to them about their failure to open a second front against Germany. That he claimed was inflicting appalling punishment on Russia as the main nation opposing Germany on the ground at that time. He went on to allege that this was a deliberate Anglo-American plot to allow the Germans to bleed the Soviet Union dry before reaching their own separate peace. At the beginning of 1943 things were not easy between the allies.

* * *

January 11,1943. Winston is much better and that potion being fed to him by Moran certainly seems to be working. So, we will be travelling to Casablanca tomorrow.

* * *

In order to get to the Casablanca meeting Roosevelt commandeered a Pan American Clipper flying boat. It took forty-eight hours to get there. That was largely because it had a fairly short range and had to go via the Caribbean and South America and then up the West African coast. Its last stop was in Gambia, a British colony, at the town then called Bathurst, so named after one British governor of the colony. Roosevelt took a tour ashore and was appalled by the conditions in which the people lived. He was certain that those miserable conditions were as a direct result of poor colonial rule by Britain. That visit increased his resolve to ensure that all vestiges of colonial power by Britain were disbanded. It was actually the first time that Roosevelt had visited any colonial country.

When he arrived in Casablanca FDR told his son who was in his delegation;

"I simply have to tell Winston about the deplorable conditions I found in Gambia this morning. There are none of the basic facilities of life like education, sanitation, decent standards of living, and minimum health requirements. The average life expectancy there is 26. These people are worse than livestock. Winston may have thought that I wasn't serious when we spoke about it in Newfoundland. He will sure get to know what I think about it all this time."

The only documented outcome of that conference was a statement jointly made by Roosevelt and Churchill that they would go on fighting until they got the "unconditional surrender" of Japan and Germany. There was no discussion about the conduct of the war. There was no discussion as to what might happen when "unconditional surrender" was achieved. Churchill essentially accepted the Roosevelt doctrine of "unconditional surrender". He did so in a way that was consistent with his negotiating brief from the Cabinet but largely because he was so grateful for the American aid received so far and because he was so pleased that he had such a powerful ally, even if the terms of that alliance had not yet been made public.

One decision that they did reach there was that when operations were complete in North Africa all troops there would move across to Sicily and when they had eliminated German resistance there they would invade Italy itself and drive the German armies progressively northwards. There was little discussion about a landing much further north in Europe. Sicily was Churchill's plan but the Supreme Commander there would initially be Eisenhower.

A little known American demand made at Casablanca that was accepted by Churchill and which was consistent with the agreement negotiated at the conference on board *Prince of Wales* was that, if Japan was still in the war after Germany was defeated, Britain would redeploy whatever forces were necessary to the Far East in order to help America finish the war there.

Privately the two leaders also talked again about Britain's colonial interests. Roosevelt made it very clear to Churchill what he thought of the Gambia and what he thought about Britain's neglect of its colonies.

* * *

January 15, 1943. Winston was at a private meeting with Roosevelt for hours today. When he returned from it he was very angry. Apparently he had been given a dressing down for what Roosevelt described as appalling conditions in Gambia. Roosevelt seems to have told him that after the war he would establish some kind of international commission that would be tasked with ending such abuses. He also promised that any abuses such as he had seen in Gambia would be well publicised.

* * *

January 31, 1943. We have heard today that General Paulus has surrendered at Stalingrad. Initial reports indicate that the army he surrendered totalled 94,000 men. Winston sent a telegram to Stalin congratulating him on a great win. All Stalin said in acknowledgement was that Russia had been very much helped by the winter and that their equipment had been more suitable in the dreadful conditions. Our German sources are indicating that there is deep shock in von Manstein's HQ about what has happened.

Many years later it was estimated that as many as two million people had died at Stalingrad. It was thought that all but a few hundred of the 500,000 people who had lived in Stalingrad in the early summer of 1942 had died. Of the 94,000 Germans who surrendered only about 5,000 were to survive the war.

* * *

Zhukov's diary for February 1, 1943 reads:

"Stalin is content now that we have destroyed the German Sixth Army. But we now have to get on with the next phase which is far more important. We are currently moving the bulk of our forces away from Stalingrad so that the Germans cannot get any accurate estimates of numbers or equipment levels. One of Rokossovskii's armies will be retreating through Kharkov to Kursk. I am certain that the enemy will follow. They cannot risk attempting further advances in the south until they have destroyed this army.

The risks we took in taking defenders from Moscow and St.Petersburg have worked There was, however, nowhere else from where they could be taken at that time. But by the spring of 1943 the recruitment and training programmes under way in the Soviet Union together with the weapons production that have been developed east of the Urals will mean that Russia is about to have a vast superiority in numbers. We should achieve that well before we have to fight at Kursk.

* * *

After Stalingrad there were extensive exchanges between Churchill and Roosevelt about the implications of the Russian victory and what it meant for the future war effort. What Roosevelt had done after Pearl Harbour was make an unlimited commitment to achieving American victory over both Japan and Germany. He had not anticipated any challenge to that and he had taken numerous steps to make Britain subservient to that objective. In his view America had to be the clear victor on all fronts. He had never anticipated that Russia might be a competitor to America in any way at that time, nor had he anticipated in any way that Russia would be able to make any substantial contribution to the overall war effort. All of his thinking had been on the basis that only America would conquer Germany. To the extent that he had even considered any future role for Russia in the war he had assumed that they would be an ally of America and largely supplied by America. They would therefore be subject to whatever it was America wanted to do. Over the coming months he was to change his views about Russia.

* * *

It was on a cold early spring evening in Moscow in 1997 that my friendly librarian, Oxana, in Moscow told me about some interesting files she had discovered. We had spent many hours talking over my work and she was very interested in it. Our talks in the library office had migrated to talks over dinner and then one night in February that year she had suggested that she come back to the hotel with me. She claimed that she just wanted to talk with me about some new files she had found.

She spent that night with me and many other nights as well. But it was not until we had been sleeping together for perhaps a month that she talked about the new files she had seen. She had been re-organising the papers from Molotov's office when she found some that had not been indexed before. They covered the period from July, 1942 until February, 1943 and dealt with a deliberate misinformation campaign that the Foreign Ministry had to follow about Stalingrad in all of its dealings with other countries.

The first document in the files was a copy of the minutes of a meeting held on July 21, 1942. The delegates were Stalin, Molotov, Beria, Khrushchev and Zhukov. It was about the request that Stalin had had for a meeting with Churchill and what they were going to tell him while he was in Moscow. But perhaps even more significantly it set out a plan for telling both Britain and America a completely fabricated story about the true Russian intentions so that until after Kursk they would have no idea what was going on within the Russian defences.

It was recorded in those minutes that Stalin would invite Winston to that late night session in the Kremlin, would attempt to get him drunk and would give him a deliberately vague hint of a big battle to come.

After that they defined the sort of messages that Molotov would feed to Guy Burgess with the certain knowledge that they would be passed on to George Ponsonby in London.

There were other accounts of actual meetings with Burgess including full details of the messages he had been asked to pass on. I was able to corroborate these with files in the

British Foreign Office and I found that every message that had been given to Burgess and was described in those files had indeed been passed on.

But Molotov's files also contained the details of the British viewpoint at that time. All the information is attributed to George Ponsonby. Molotov was certain that that was where it was coming from and he was sure that it was not coming from anyone else. The person who organised the relaying of the information was that same officer who had originally taken Ponsonby to the gay sex club in Moscow and who was then based in London. Ponsonby must have been seeing him regularly.

In the light of what we now know the information getting to Molotov was an accurate reflection of policy making in London. I was not able to deduce who was Ponsonby's source but I did establish that many of Ponsonby's messages included exact phrases taken from War Cabinet Minutes. As those were on an extremely limited circulation list and were classified at the highest possible security marking I had to conclude I could only conclude that Ponsonby must have had access to a copy of those minutes. He was certainly not on the circulation list. I have made the assumption that he was somehow able to access Anthony Eden's copies of the minutes but it not something that I have been able to prove.

There were several strands to what Ponsonby was passing to Moscow:
1. That Britain and America together believed that Russia was very weak and that in 1942 it had little, if any, capability of fighting Germany on its own.
2. America and Britain were planning to destroy Germany without Russian help even if they had to go into Russian territory to fight German armies
3. That Britain and America were going to determine the date for any land invasion of Europe and would not be influenced by Russian thinking on the subject
4. Britain was basing all its planning for the ending of the war on the basis that it would still be the most powerful nation on the earth then and that its empire would still be intact.
5. Britain could not have survived without Lend/Lease but recognised that it would be very costly over the long term.
6. The only basis on which Britain and America would bring the war to an end in Europe was when Germany agreed to unconditional surrender.
7. That Britain deeply resented the fact that all of its forces operating as part of Anglo-American operations would be under American command but recognised that that was the price that had to be paid for all the Lend/Leased deals.

Oxana found some papers from Stalin's office which showed that as early as September, 1942 he was planning to do a deal with Roosevelt about dismembering the British Empire. Stalin had plenty of information about Roosevelt's attitude to empire and democracy and it was obvious to him that sooner or later America would put pressure on Britain for major changes. I have no doubt that Churchill would have been appalled that British thinking at the highest levels should have been conveyed at all to Stalin. He would have been even more appalled at just how Stalin was planning to deceive him on that first trip of his to Moscow.

One thing we know for certain is that before and during Stalingrad and indeed right up to the middle of the battle of Kursk Winston and the British Government believed that Russia was perilously weak.

* * *

When George Ponsonby retired he went to live in North Essex. His house was by co-incidence just a few miles from where Samuel had lived in his retirement. He shared it with Michael Curtis.

The only place I ever found any record of Ponsonby's deceit was in Moscow. There was no record in any British government archives of any deceit by either Ponsonby or Curtis.

After the war both of them continued in the diplomatic service. Ponsonby became British Ambassador to the Soviet Union and Curtis became Ambassador to West Germany. They held those posts at the same time in the 1950's.

There were numerous documents in the Foreign Office archives written by both of them but there was nothing approaching any private papers that I was able to find out about either of them in Britain. I had, of course, found some Ponsonby papers in Russian archives and I was keen to find out whether Michael Curtis had been involved in any similar activities.

He had died in 1982 and had no family. I could not find out whether he had written a diary and still less to whom he might have left such a document. But I wanted to find out more about him.

The only clue that I was able to find was in one of Ponsonby's documents in Moscow. It described the Royalist International organisation and how Igor Molotov and Otto von Papen had been members. I asked Oxana to look into any Russian records that might have linked the young Molotov and Michael Curtis but she was unable to find anything then. She thought she might be able to do so one day but the records were in such a jumble that it might take ages. So I started to look in German records again to see whether Otto von Papen was recorded at all and if so what it was all about. What I found was truly enthralling.

* * *

It was widely believed in British political circles in 1940 that the end of Hitler, through death or assassination, would lead to a swift end to the war. There was no basis in fact for such a view and its proponents could not describe what a post-Hitler situation might be like then. Germany was very strong at that time and the Nazi party was very much in command. It was certainly unclear who might have replaced Hitler but there were certainly several contenders. The concept of overthrowing Hitler was certainly very attractive to Anthony Eden.

So when he returned to the Foreign Office in 1940 he had set up a new secret unit in addition to the one run by George Ponsonby. This new unit was to be run by Michael Curtis. Its purpose was to liaise with any serious dissident groups in Germany and in particular with anyone who was both interested in and capable of managing a coup d'etat in which Hitler could be overthrown. At best it was going to be risky and dangerous work, but Michael Curtis was qualified to run it and he knew exactly who to recruit to help him

Ever since Hitler had first become Chancellor of Germany there had been reports of possible assassination attempts and of potential coups. The only way to know whether they were credible was to get good intelligence on the participants and their plans. That was what Michael Curtis had to achieve in the first instance.

When Eden briefed him he said to him:

"Michael, in this role you will report to me and you will not communicate any details about your work to anyone else in the British Government. If there are any serious plotters against Hitler out there they will always be in great danger so we cannot afford any leaks. We know already that Hitler is very suspicious about possible plots. It may just be paranoia, we do not know. But what we do know is that he has had several people assassinated who have been alleged to be in plots of various sorts and soon after he came to office he purged his party and other parties to get rid of any potential rivals. That is exactly what happened to von Hammerstein and his co-conspirators back in 1933 and to a similar group led by von Schleicher in 1934. After that things quietened down on the coup front but the purges went on.

"I do not care how you track down anybody who might be a credible plotter but I am sure you will find a way of doing so.

"What you do not know is that the British government was approached several times before the war about participation in a coup against Hitler and about a new understanding between Britain and Germany should such a coup have been effective. The most important of those approaches came in September 1938 when we were approached by Brigadier General Boehm-Tettlebach. He came to London bringing some very important state secrets with him. He claimed, and we had no reason to doubt him, that he was an intermediary for a group called the Beck-Goerdeler group. It was named after General Beck, who was then the army Chief of Staff, and Dr. Carl Goerdeler, who had been Mayor of Leipzig. What we were told was very interesting and we agreed to keep in touch. Britain said that it could not participate in any direct coup but it would certainly want to talk constructively should a coup be successful.

"We do know that Winston Churchill was aware in 1938 of plans for a coup against Hitler. We believe that he was told about the plans by Fabian von Schlabrendorff who had written a book called *Offizere gegen Hitler.*

"Boehm-Tettlebach came back again in 1939. Since then we have not heard from him, but we do believe that he is still alive. Also in 1939, September in fact, Lord Halifax, as Foreign Secretary, had a visit from a man called Adam von Trott zu Solz. He had many contacts in England. He seemed to be determined to try and prevent the war spreading. After he had seen Halifax he went on to America to talk to Roosevelt as well. At the time we were never clear exactly what he wanted and for whom because when he was in America he was found to be a master spy for Hitler. He was arrested and his activities ceased.

"You might find that tracking down any one of those names might be a useful start."

Michael Curtis knew that Otto von Papen had been posted back to Germany well before the war had begun and that as soon as the new diplomatic facility had been opened in Stockholm he had been moved there. Curtis had not been in contact with him since he had left London but he decided that he would go on the next plane to Stockholm to do just that.

It was five days before the plane was due to leave. Curtis used that time to look into whatever files he could on the matter. There was not much and none of those state secrets that Boehm-Tettlebach had brought over were included in any of them. But what was in those files were accounts of several meetings with German officials and officers, all of them on the same theme. There were notes in the files indicating that the writer was suspicious of a visit made by von Manstein and Guderian to Churchill's country house back in 1937. There were several German names mentioned in the files and Curtis took note of all of them.

Eden never told Churchill of what he had arranged.

* * *

The evening he arrived in Stockholm Eden had dinner with Otto von Papen. It was a fine warm Thursday in late May. It never gets dark in Stockholm at that time of the year and when the weather is fine it is a perfect place for late night dining in the open air. They went to a large restaurant on the waterfront opposite the Royal Palace. They had a table right by the water's edge. It was quiet and they were able to make useful progress in their discussions. But the subject was too big for them to complete then. So von Papen suggested that the following afternoon they went out to a log cabin on an island that he had rented for the summer. They would go out by boat and would stay there until the Sunday evening. They could take plenty of food and drink with them in the boat. He explained that whenever he went there he took two security guards, who were a husband and wife team, from the diplomatic mission with him. Their role was to look after him and any friends he took with him. They also drove the boat, prepared the food and kept the place clean.

The island was about two hours on the motor boat from Stockholm. It was a fast and very comfortable boat. The island was about a kilometre square and there was only one log cabin on it. The nearest island was about half a kilometre away. Otto explained that in the summer going out to places like that for weekends was one of the very attractive features of the Swedish lifestyle.

They did not talk business on the boat. However much trusted the staff were, what they had to discuss had to be done in as much secrecy as possible.

Over the weekend Otto told Curtis that when he had been in London he had been well aware of the first visit of Boehm-Tettlebach and who was behind him. Indeed he had personally arranged the entire visit. He had also been aware of the visit by von Manstein and Guderian to see Churchill. He had de-briefed both generals after that visit and he had only passed on some of what they said to von Ribbentrop. He had passed on nothing about the possibility of a coup against Hitler, although they both mentioned that it had been discussed.

They talked about the Beck-Goerdeler team. Otto was currently not in touch with any of them although that would be easy enough to arrange.

What they did agree was that Otto would talk to them and to his uncle, Franz von Papen, who was now German Ambassador to Turkey. When he had been able to make some progress he would contact Michael again and they could meet up again in Stockholm. He thought it might take up to a month, particularly with all the security arrangements he would have to put in place to ensure that there were no leaks.

* * *

It was a little under a month later that he invited Curtis back to Stockholm. It was now late June and even warmer. School holidays would start in Sweden within a few days. They went down to a different restaurant for dinner. This one was also right down by the water but it was a few minutes walk away in the old part of the city.

Talk at dinner that evening was mostly about old times. Otto asked about the mission that they had arranged some years before for someone to go to Germany. He wondered how successful it had been. Michael Curtis told him that it had struck a very rich seam of information. It had been excellent intelligence for the British Government but the political situation had meant that there was not much that could be done with it.

They went out to the island again on Friday afternoon. It was while they were there that Otto was able to tell him matters of the highest interest. First it was all about the Beck-Goerdeler plans. What they were doing was preparing to launch a new government to be effective as soon as there had been a successful coup. There was no point in speculating on when and where a coup might take place until plans had been completed for a successor regime.

He went on to list the members of the Beck-Goerdeler team. The team included:
- Ernest von Weisacker, Secretary of State
- Erich Kordt, a very senior official in the Foreign Office
- His brother, Theo, who had been in the German Embassy in London
- Admiral Canaris, the Head of State Security
- General Halder, the Chief of Defence
- Fabian von Schlabrendorff, who had been to London before the war to see Lord Halifax
- There were also several diplomats and ministry officials
- The person doing the planning for the assassination itself was Colonel Count von Stauffenberg
- Generals von Manstein. Guderian and Rommel

What was even more important was that Beck and Goerdeler wanted to open an on-going dialogue with Britain at a very high level, initially just to inform them as to what was going on, but later to negotiate a provisional agreement that could be put in place as soon as the assassination of Hitler had been successful. They would want peace to follow on just as quickly as possible after that.

When Eden was told about it he decided to go to Stockholm as soon as he could to meet with Goerdeler and try and reach a provisional agreement with him along those lines. They met two weeks later. It took three more meetings over a six month period to hammer out all the detail but at the end of it Eden had an agreement that he was prepared to recommend to Churchill as soon as there was a firm plan for a coup.

He never did tell Churchill about any of it; that was largely because he knew that Churchill had met von Manstein and Guderian at Chartwell long before the war. He wondered whether Churchill knew of that plot, perhaps even whether he had maintained contact with them through the war.

* * *

In late February 1943, about three weeks after the German defeat at Stalingrad Michael Curtis was asked to go back to Stockholm; Otto von Papen needed to see him urgently. Stockholm then was very bright and cold. It was not possible to go by boat to the island but it was certainly possible to drive there across the thick ice. The same couple as had been with them on those summer visits drove them out and would look after them over the weekend. The log cabin was superbly equipped for the winter. It had thick well insulated walls and was very warm, with seemingly minimal amounts of fuel needed to make it very comfortable. But it did get dark early and it was hardly light before ten in the morning.

They decided to have their secret talk by walking round the island as soon as it got light on the Saturday morning. What Otto had to report was that Russia had captured a senior German intelligence officer in the surrender at Stalingrad. He described exactly what had happened:

"He had worked in Sixth Army headquarters and had reported directly to General Paulus. One of his roles had been to manage the communications between Paulus and von Manstein as the latter had tried to force the relief of the city. The Russian interrogators had concluded that he was seriously disaffected by everything that had gone on in the final weeks of the Stalingrad cauldron. In particular he blamed Hitler for issuing a series of insane orders that were completely incapable of any useful implementation. The officer's name was Rudi Zweigle.

"He had been taken to Zhukov's headquarters for further interrogation and Zhukov had become convinced that he could be a useful informant for Russia. No one in the remaining German forces would have had any idea whether he had been captured or not but what they did know was that some personnel at all levels had been able to escape from Stalingrad and had managed to hole up in remote places for a few days. Zhukov did a deal with Zweigle. He would be put in a place from which he could reach German lines in return for becoming an informant to Zhukov personally on German military intentions. They agreed on communications procedures.

"Zweigle was found hiding in a remote barn by von Manstein's forces as they crept northwards a few days after Stalingrad. Von Manstein met him in order to get a briefing from the most senior officer who had escaped from Stalingrad. In any event he knew him because they had worked together before. Von Manstein was very keen to get him into his own team and Zweigle had no problem with that but he did ask for a few days home leave before starting another assignment.

"von Manstein arranged for him to go to Berlin, which was his home city, but he had to be back within a week. While he was in Berlin he contacted General Beck. He had known for a long while that Beck represented people who were strongly anti-Hitler and he wanted him to know just how bad things had been in Stalingrad as a result of Hitler's crass orders.

"Beck had known Zweigle for many years and they had worked together on many occasions. Zweigle liked working in any team led by Beck. While he was in Berlin they met many times. Beck told him of possible assassination plans, but those were proving really difficult to implement. Hitler was guarded very closely and security around him was increasing all the time. In addition to that his movements were very unpredictable. It all made for very difficult detailed planning of what they might do with at least a reasonable chance of success.

"But what Beck had thought was that more defeats along the lines of Stalingrad were more likely to bring an end to Hitler than, possibly, any other course. He had been thinking that passing some secrets to the Russians might help very well in that. He wanted to know what might be feasible from the front line. Zweigle was as likely as anyone to have a good view on that.

"Zweigle did not tell Beck what he had already arranged to do, but they did agree that good intelligence passed to the enemy might be as good a way as any to bring an end to the war sooner than might otherwise be the case.

"When Zweigle returned to the front to von Manstein's headquarters he was very clear exactly what he was going to do.

"So that is how things stand on that issue. Weakening Germany's military power is currently more important than any assassination attempt. It is a very ruthless policy and many lives will be lost but at the moment it seems the best way to proceed. If Britain can help in that it will be invaluable.

"In the meantime there is another issue that has arisen that seems to involve Britain and I wondered what you knew about it.

"There is a secret agent who goes by the code name of Lucy who has been passing certain German secrets directly to Stalin. That is known. The quality of the information getting to Stalin is very patchy and always very incomplete. We have no idea who Lucy is but whoever he or she is seems to have exactly the same motives as the Beck-Goerdeler group. What we were rather hoping is that it might be possible to combine the efforts of Lucy and Zweigle and produce more of better quality information to Stalin. Do you think that might be feasible?"

Michael Curtis had never heard of Lucy but agreed to look into it all and meet with Otto again as soon as he had anything to report.

* * *

Oxana proved invaluable in helping me with my research. Once we had become lovers it was much easier to talk about the information that I needed and she was then prepared to spend more time finding it.

I had studied Zhukov's diaries for the period immediately post-Stalingrad and they said very little. He did describe a process under which the Red Army would move generally northwest, would appear to look very weak and would leave some plum sites for the Germans to capture, the city of Kharkov being the most important. But they did very little to explain how the battlefield of Kursk came together.

Oxana looked into the STAVKA records for me and they did not help much either. It all looked rather like an information vacuum. Indeed it started to look as if someone had purged the files of all useful information about what history showed to be the biggest single event of the whole war.

As she explained to me, as many of the Russian files were randomly stored and without a proper indexing system it was difficult to locate many of them. There were millions of documents in the archives and it seemed to be like looking for a needle in a haystack.

Then we had a lucky break. Because we could not find what we wanted in any of Zhukov's papers or in any STAVKA files we started to look into the files of the individual army commanders. It proved to be a frustrating experience because most of them had written nothing. But in the early morning one day in early summer she had an inspiration. She decided to leave my bed and go to the library to look for the records of General Pavel Rotmistrov. She knew enough about the Russian archives filing system to know that it would be difficult to locate anything he might have written; that was because he always seemed to be changing units which he commanded. Any records of his could be stored with the records of many different army units. So she mapped his career and then looked into the records of all the units with which he had served. Had Oxana and I not been lovers I am certain that I could never have found the crucial documents about Kursk.

All the crucial records were stored within the records of the Fifth Guards Tank Army which he had commanded at Stalingrad. There cannot have been any doubt that someone within the Soviet administration had deliberately concealed all the crucial files in the records of that army. It was impossible to tell who did it or when but all the principal documents about the planning and preparations for Kursk were stored in that single place. There were STAVKA records, memoranda from Stalin, papers from Zhukov, Khrushchev, Rokossovskii and Chuikov and a set of maps detailing the build-up of Soviet forces in the Kursk area. In researcher's terms it was a veritable goldmine.

What all those documents showed was exactly how Zhukov moved his armies to Kursk and prepared the battlefield there. They showed just how the Germans were deceived and how eventually the trap was sprung which led to the destruction of so much German fighting power.

The plan was to create two vast salients to the northwest and southwest of the city of Kursk. These were to be heavily fortified defences on lines of hills. Between these hill was a broad valley leading from the west to the town of Prokhorovka which was south of Kursk. As it would be impossible for the enemy to take those hills initially the first area of battle was to be in that valley. It was superbly suited for tank warfare. It was obvious from the maps that Germany could not hope to control Ukraine unless it eliminated the Kursk salients. It was thus the perfect trap. But for success it depended on Germany believing that Russia was impossibly weak.

It was not the geography which proved to be so important; it was how a massive Soviet build-up at Kursk was completely hidden from any German observation. The documents show that Zhukov knew in January the likely scale of the forces that he would be able to command at Kursk. His problem was that if Germany had any inkling that he had forces on that scale they would have avoided battle at all costs. He therefore had to prepare Kursk with a very small force and only bring up the larger numbers available to him at the very last opportunity. It was an enormously complex logistics exercise.

Work started on the outer concentric rings of defence on both lines of hills in early February. That consisted of anti-tank obstacles and gun emplacements. At the time there were no significant numbers of German troops in the area it was thus possible for the work to be largely unobserved. At the same time most of the forces that had been deployed at Stalingrad withdrew to the east across the Volga River.

By April all the defences had been completed on the hills and some troops were moving into their final positions. By May almost all the available Soviet forces, army and air force, were within two day's travelling time of the planned battlefield. All the mine laying had been completed by the end of May.

Rotmistrov's files show that the spy called Lucy had informed Stalin on April 12th that Hitler had agreed the previous day to the preparation of a plan for a large battle at Kursk. It is obvious that Lucy's source was someone who had been at the meeting between Hitler and Zeitzler, the Wehrmacht Chief of Staff, that day. The words in the file say "Hitler spent the best part of an hour studying the maps of Ukraine that were on the conference room wall. At the end of that he said that it was obvious that there would have to be a battle at Kursk. The weak Russian position had forced them into a dangerous salient. By attacking through the centre Germany would be able to encircle any Russian forces there and destroy them."

Stalin had added a note to the document in his own hand which read: "That will pay back the bastard for what he has done to Russia."

From that moment on Russia was ready for whatever battle Hitler wanted.

* * *

March 1, 1943. Winston is intensely frustrated by the slow speed with which Montgomery is advancing towards Tunisia. When he was with Roosevelt in Casablanca they were assuming that the North African campaign would be finished by the end of February and that the invasion of Sicily would start in April. Now there is no such likelihood. W. has had to fend off endless complaints from FDR about the delays.

* * *

March 5, 1943. We are about to enter one of the tensest times of the war so far. It will be at least as tense as El Alamein, possibly worse. What is likely to be the worst convoy battle is certain to take place over the next few days. Winston and I have been in endless meetings with the Royal Navy about it for some days now and there really does not seem to be any alternative. There are three large convoys, SC122, HX 229 and HX 229A waiting to leave North America for Britain. Between them there are 164 merchant ships and 27 escorts. It is essential that these convoys get to Britain because their cargoes are critical for both survival and for the continuation of military operations. The largest single cargo is oil. If they do not get here we will have no oil of any sort in Britain by the middle of April. It is also certain that ration allowances will have to be reduced sharply. Winston has decided that either of those situations cannot be contemplated and that those convoys must sail.

But there numerous problems. Because of the expected weather conditions and the amount of ice at this time there is only one route that all three convoys can take. Across those routes we know already that there are 46 U-Boats. All three convoys are made up largely of slow ships and the maximum speed may have to be as low as 6 knots when the weather is poor. It is all very high risk but essential for survival. Because of the weather it is very unclear that adequate air cover will be possible. Worst of all, the escort force is very weak and there are no supports groups that can be in that area for any part of the voyage.

W. keeps telling us that it is a nightmare scenario. But one thing is absolutely certain and that is that Winston will be up every night while those ships are at sea. It is he who has ordered them to sail and he will take every loss personally.

* * *

March 10, 1943. Those convoys lost 4 ships last night. The atmosphere in the war rooms is very gloomy

* * *

March 15, 1943. Another 12 ships were lost during the night. Horrendous. Winston is in a vile mood.

* * *

March 24, 1943. The last of the ships from those three convoys arrived in Britain today. 23 ships were sunk but all the escorts survived. 2 U-Boats were sunk.

* * *

March 25, 1943. Air Marshal Arthur Harris came to brief Winston on the rapidly increasing capability of Bomber Command. He claimed that as a result of the plans that Max Beaverbrook had put in place to build more Lancasters and because of the successful training programmes for more air crew the RAF now had the capability to bomb Germany every night when the weather was suitable. He was hoping that it would be possible to bomb on 10 nights a month as we moved into summer.

He explained that the key to success was not running missions with just a few aircraft but running vast missions in which continuous streams of bombers attacked single cities in waves. The optimum size for a bomber stream seemed to be about a thousand aircraft. With that density of flying it was possible to provide an adequate level of defensive fire when the stream was attacked by German fighters, as it always was. The survival rate was always higher when the operation was conducted with large bomber streams.

He said that the new factory for Lancasters in America was producing 30 aircraft per day and these were being flown across the Atlantic largely by female crew. It was proving to be popular and low risk work for them.

Winston told me afterwards that he was amused by the fact that we seemed to be dependent on female crews to deliver our best bombers to Britain. Although he fully supported the efforts of women to contribute to the war effort I do not think he had ever envisage that flying aircraft would be one way that they could do so. He reckoned that farming and office work were more suitable.

* * *

On April 2^{nd,} 1943 Max Beaverbrook travelled to Washington. It was just a year since Louise had been appointed to supervise the Lancaster bomber building programme in America. During that time he had received regular business reports from her about the building of the factory and then its performance as the production rate increased. All those reports were signed with the name of Angela Smith.

The initial production rate had been only one aircraft per day but this had progressively increased and was now running at 30 per day. Together with the production in Britain that was sufficient to cover any losses during battle. Bombing Germany had proved to be an exceptionally dangerous business and few aircraft accomplished more than 3 missions. To support the bombing plans of the RAF the production rate of Lancasters might even have to be increased. That was the official reason why he was going to Washington.

But his real reason was personal. Throughout the year he had received regular letters from her and they were all signed Louise. He longed for the time when it would be possible to get rid of the subterfuge of her official name, but he knew that that could only happen after she had left America. But far more important than that was his need to be with her again.

They spent a day at the factory, meeting staff and reviewing production plans. Then they went to Myrtle Beach in South Carolina for a weekend together. It was easy enough for her to arrange for an aircraft to take them there.

On the Saturday morning they lay on the beach in what was an unseasonal heat wave. Max talked about the war at home, Churchill, his newspapers, the disasters that Britain had suffered and what he detected as extreme war weariness amongst the British people. He said;

"My dear Louise, every day we get perhaps 200 hundred letters at the newspaper office about the war. Almost all of them are about hardship and they all ask questions about why the most powerful nation on earth cannot get its act together and defeat Hitler. My readers simply do not understand why it is taking so long to get back to peace. They simply do not understand why they have to endure the hardships of rationing. They still have faith in Winston but it is wearing thin. He has promised them that Britain is leading the fight but they do not see anything happening.

"None of my readers has the slightest idea of what the truth is anymore. I am in the Cabinet and I know what the official reports show. I am a friend of Winston's and I know what he asks me to do and what he tells me. It is all very different from what he tells the public. I fully understand why he makes the broadcasts he does and I am sure that there is no alternative. But what it does say is that we are all being corrupted by this war. I am just thankful that I have been able to make a real contribution to getting a solution.

"But it all looks very grim just now. Last year was completely disastrous as far as supplying Britain was concerned. We lost more than 1,000 ships in convoys to German U-Boats. Winston has hailed as a triumph the battle in Egypt last October at El Alamein. But in reality it was a hopeless bloody grind. It has achieved nothing and has not changed German behaviour in any way.

"Right now we believe that Germany is preparing the final knock out blows for Russia. If they succeed, which our military chiefs believe to be most likely, then Britain will be in the firing line again with a probable invasion next year.

"It is all rather grim and there is no obvious solution to it all.

"Right here on a deserted Myrtle Beach all those problems seem to be very far away. Tell me something good instead."

"I love you Max and as we are alone here I intend to prove it. Just relax and we will enjoy ourselves for the rest of the day."

* * *

May 9, 1943. Winston was in an excellent mood today. Since those ferocious convoy battles back in March things have gone much quieter in the North Atlantic. Not only that but the U-Boat sinkings have increased dramatically. So far this year we have destroyed more than 70 of the things. That is nearly as much as the total kills last year. Since those battles in March our shipping losses seem to have halved. On top of all that the mammoth construction programme in America is now bearing fruit. Already this year new construction has vastly exceeded losses. It is the first time that that has happened since the war began. American construction now exceeds our own by a factor of more than ten to one. It is the greatest example yet that America is really making that unlimited commitment to bringing the war to an end. No wonder Winston is in such a buoyant mood.

* * *

When Michael Curtis got back to London after his meeting with Otto von Papen he went to see Anthony Eden. He could not think of any other way in which he could find out about the informer called Lucy but he also needed to update him on what he had learned in Stockholm.

Eden told him that an agent by the name of Lucy was known to the British security services. He was known to have communicated information about Germany to Russia but the original source of the information was not known. His or her identity was not known. Eden promised that he would tell Curtis if and when he found out more. He never did. Eden knew all about the information being handled by Lucy. It all came from British sources, mainly from coded messages that had been broken at Bletchley Park. There was no way that he was going to divulge that source to anyone.

* * *

"June 9, 1943. Today has been dominated by a long conference about the forthcoming battle that will in all probability be fought at Kursk quite soon now. We have been getting information both from spies and through radio intercepts about a big German build up around the city of Kursk. From all that we have heard the German build up there is greater than anything they have assembled for a single battle before. Their only intention can be to destroy the Russian fighting capabilities completely. Winston stressed the vital importance of knowing what is going on there and planning for the outcome."

* * *

It was in 1994 that I found the German records that validated the information that Samuel had received that day. There was a very close correlation between the information that Samuel had received and the information in those German records. Hitler had been to visit von Manstein at that time and the discussion had been about finalising the battle plans for Kursk. The only thing that was not in the accounts that Samuel had received was that Hitler wanted one additional Panzer army to be brought in and that would have to come from France.

What I had not expected to find in those German records was a report that after Hitler's aircraft had landed at Rastenburg it had been inspected by mechanics and they had found a bomb in the luggage hold. The bomb was connected to a timing mechanism which was powered by a battery. When they tested the battery it was found to be defective. If the mechanism had worked it would have caused the bomb to explode. That explosion would have taken place an hour after the aircraft had left the airfield near Kharkov. A massive investigation had been launched into who was responsible but no perpetrator was found. Nevertheless Hitler ordered that all the ground crew who had handled the aircraft in Russia should be shot. Their names and the date of execution are recorded in the file.

* * *

By the middle of June Russian preparations for Kursk were complete. The full details of the Russian defences were not revealed at the time but when the Russian war records were made available for inspection they showed that preparations had been made on a scale that could not possibly even have been imagined by any other nation.

* * *

July 1, 1943. Yet another meeting today about Kursk. Winston is convinced that Germany will win it.

We still know virtually nothing about the military capabilities of Russia despite their success at Stalingrad. Of course that had been a great victory, but had it been a freak? It had certainly been a surprise to Britain and America.

Winston's own view is that Russia had been lucky there and gained supremacy just because that battle was fought in the middle of winter. It was inevitable in those circumstances that Russia would have the advantage. They had a similar advantage at Moscow the previous winter. Sure, their victory at Stalingrad had been a huge triumph under any circumstances but Kursk was different. Kursk was going to be fought in the summer and Germany had had many months to prepare for it. If Germany won, the rest of the summer would be spent mopping up remaining Russian forces and the war in Russia would end quickly.

He argued that the propaganda messages coming from Germany were all about a supreme and victorious German army facing the final obstacle before it overcame and destroyed Russia. The German troops would be commanded by the victors in France, Poland and throughout the Barbarossa campaign itself. Germany had huge resources and more experience than any other armed forces in the world. The German army clearly understood the concept of blitzkrieg and were surely going to apply it again at Kursk. In his view they certainly had the capability to beat any Russian armies at Kursk.

In Winston's estimation the Russian armies would not only be beaten at Kursk. They would be routed. Everything he had heard from Stalin was about Russia being on its knees and desperately needing relief from the war by the opening of another front in the West. He explained yet again that Britain could not deliver that front at that time whatever level of support America might have been able to provide. He said he had sent another message to that effect to Stalin that morning. Russia would therefore be confronting Germany on its own at Kursk. He was certain that there was no way that Russia could be properly prepared for such a confrontation.

What he had thought through was what the consequences would be of a Russian defeat at Kursk. He had no doubt that any such defeat would be regarded by Germany as something approaching the final victory over Russia. It was the most likely option. The Germans would in all probability resume the offensive against Moscow and St. Petersburg almost immediately. They could probably do that as well as mopping up in the Don Basin and the Caucasus. Russia would be doomed within a few months. If that happened Winston knew that it was only a matter of time before Germany turned its interest again to the west. He anticipated that in those circumstances there would be a German invasion of Britain by the summer of 1944. The only way to deal with that would be to ensure that there would be sufficient American troops in Britain by then to guarantee that any such invasion would be a complete failure. He had discussed that possibility with Roosevelt. If Germany won at Kursk the build-up of Britain's defences would become the overwhelming priority. Fortunately the improved situation in the North Atlantic was likely to make it possible for there to be a big American build-up in Britain. But what always concerned Winston was the sheer power of the German forces.

What he had not thought through was the possibility of a Russian success at Kursk. Not just any success but one which was so great that it overwhelmed the German forces. Indeed it was almost impossible for him to think in those terms. Britain had had a long, bloody slog to defeat 12 enemy divisions at El Alamein. Britain had committed 10 divisions to that battle and many of them had been equipped with the latest American equipment. Eventually Britain had prevailed. It had been very tough and they were fighting out from superb defensive positions against an army which had exceptionally difficult supply lines. His conclusion was that with fewer advantages than El Alamein offered overwhelming numerical supremacy was needed to destroy the German armies at Kursk. He was certain from what Stalin had communicated to him that that advantage was not available to Russia.

None of us at the meeting had any way of knowing exactly how many German or Russian troops were likely to be deployed at Kursk but we assumed that it could be as many as 30 German divisions. But what we were all certain about was that there would be German superiority of numbers, both in men and equipment. There was no information to us to suggest otherwise.

After the meeting had finished Winston wanted a private talk with me. I was unclear just what I could do to help his thought processes but that was what he wanted. He said to me; *"My position all along is that I want Britain to lead the winning side in this war. I have had a drubbing from Roosevelt about that many times but that remains my ambition. If Russia, by any miracle, wins this battle then that ambition is impossible. If Russia wins it will be in a position to dominate the land war from now on."*

I think he is genuinely troubled that Russia might win this battle. If she does it will mean that Germany no longer has the military initiative in the east. That in turn will mean that Russia will be able to take a far larger part in the remainder of the war than anything we have *previously envisaged. Because he thinks that to be so unlikely he has given it very little consideration.*

One thing troubles me and it is that he has not thought through what a Russian victory will mean for our alliance with America. Only the outcome of the battle will be able to answer that question.

* * *

It was in June 1943 that Michael Curtis contacted Otto von Papen again. He had looked into the existence and identity of Lucy. Otto was correct about there being such a person. Curtis agreed that Lucy would provide even more information for Stalin which could be used to help destroy German forces. He wished Otto luck in using Zweigle.

* * *

The first real details of the Battle of Kursk became available to Western researchers in 1992. That was when I first saw any Russian archives on the subject. At that stage the only information available was about the battle itself. It was much later that I was able to examine Zhukov's papers and those of some of his commanders. The original archives to be released were very much an edited version of the headlines. But what they did show was that by mid-June Zhukov had created numerous concentric rings of defences along the salients around Kursk. These consisted of mines, deep sheer ditches that would stop any German tanks and miles of concrete spikes that would prevent movement by any vehicle. The land forces consisted of 120 divisions including 70 rifle divisions, 42 tank brigades, 4,500 tanks and the placement of 3.000 self-propelled guns. They were supported by 2,500 aircraft. Those that were not yet at Kursk were already moving forward by then.

Ranged against them were German forces which included 33 army divisions of which 12 were armoured divisions. All of those divisions together deployed 2,700 tanks and 1,000 assault guns. They were supported by 1,800 aircraft.

German estimates at the time put the maximum Soviet forces at 10 divisions.

* * *

On July 4[th,] 1943 it was a horrible, sticky, hot, thundery morning in Kursk. The battle started with German attacks at 0245 local time with heavy air raids. In the first few days there were strong German advances towards the town of Prokhorovka south of Kursk but by July 10th these had been contained.

The official Russian archives reveal that intelligence information from Lucy and Zweigle were of great importance to the efficient deployment of Russian troops. Stalin is quoted as telling STAVKA that he had specific information about German intentions including the time and place of the initial attacks. Zhukov told STAVKA about specific troop deployments as they were being planned throughout the battle. Neither of them disclosed their sources of information but both sources proved to be very accurate and helped the Red Army to victory.

* * *

July 4, 1943. All day we have been receiving intelligence information from German sources. It does not appear to be an all out German attack today but they have advanced strongly and now hold some strategic high ground. We will have to see what tomorrow brings. Unusually Winston has been in the bunker all day waiting for news.

* * *

July 5, 1943. There appears to have been fierce fighting at Kursk today. There have been strong German advances along a wide front.

* * *

July 11, 1943. The messages from Kursk seem to have changed today. For the last five days we have been hearing of German advances but today it has been different. It might even be that the German armies have ground to a halt.

* * *

Zhukov's diary reveals that on the evening of July 11th he decided that he needed another evening with some of his frontline troops. He went out to the headquarters of General Rotmistrov who was then the commander of 29th Tank Corps at Prokhorovka with the intention of going together to spend the evening with some of his tank soldiers. It was another hot thundery night. The place to which they then went was in the middle of a deep pine forest to the south of Kursk. When he got there Zhukov was presented with an accordion and asked to play. The legend of what he had done at Moscow had spread through all the Soviet armies. He played Stenka Razin. The soldiers sang it several times. They all regarded it as a good omen.

His diary also shows that after he had finished entertaining his troops he spent the rest of the night with his senior commanders. They were putting the final details to the plans for a massive counter attack.

* * *

July 12, 1943. We have been getting messages all day about ferocious Russian counter attacks in the northern part of the battle field at Kursk. But today has been the day that our first joint army with America has landed in Sicily. Winston is ecstatic about that but increasingly concerned about what is happening in Russia. It is absolutely clear that Germany has not achieved any sort of major breakthrough at Kursk. Everything seems to be changing fast.

We are getting news that Russia has mounted strong and widespread counter-attacks around Prokhorovka today.

* * *

July 19, 1943. It is obvious now that the German forces are in full retreat from Kursk. Winston is in despair. On the one hand he is getting excellent reports about the progress of our forces in Sicily. But he also now knows that Russia has the power to defeat Germany on its own. For him it creates awesome problems He believes that it could easily mean that Russia will dominate military operations in Europe and may well be in a position to dominate any arrangements for peace .To prevent any public speculation about the implications of Kursk he has ordered a complete news blackout on the subject.

He has been in contact with Roosevelt today. As usual FDR told him to calm down. But he did apparently assure him that it did not make any difference to America's unlimited commitment to end the war with the unconditional surrender of Germany.

* * *

It was at Prokhorovka, exactly as Zhukov had intended, that the battle reached its climax. Between 13th and 19th of July the Russian counter attacks destroyed the German armour. The air attacks destroyed more than half of the German aircraft and tanks in the area. Kursk was where the world's largest tank battle took place. It was where Germany lost more than 1,000 tanks in just 3 days. That was where Germany started to lose the war. It was on those wheat fields of Ukraine that the German military might was wrecked. The sheer ferocity of Kursk will never be repeated. It was the fiercest tank battle ever. It was the fiercest air battle ever. It caused the highest daily loss of life in any battle ever. In those two weeks nearly a million Germans had been killed or taken into captivity. After that it was steady retreat by the German forces. Virtually none of the captives survived the war.

There is no Russian record of just how many of their people lost their lives at Kursk. It was probably well over a million. That did not matter to Stalin. All that mattered to him was destroying any military capability that Germany had. Kursk went a very long way to achieving that.

The battle had been fought on the basis of Zhukov's plans that had first been formulated during the defence of Moscow.

* * *

July 20, 1943. In the middle of last night Winston was in a complete panic about what was going on in Russia. He is absolutely certain that any sort of Russian victory at Kursk will destroy British hopes of leading the efforts to destroy German forces and win the war. He has been phoning Roosevelt about it endlessly since it became clear that Russia was winning at Kursk. FDR was been trying to calm him down but Winston is still in a panic about it all.

It was just before dawn that Winston told me that he was going to have it out with Roosevelt. He is determined to have a ferocious face-to-face row with the man. So we will be leaving very soon now to fly to Washington to meet him.

* * *

July 20, 1943. We are now flying across the western Atlantic. In about an hour we will land at Gander to refuel. All the way Winston has been rehearsing the arguments he will use with Roosevelt. I find it very difficult to understand what W. thinks he will achieve. FDR's views have not changed in any way throughout the war and I do not know what has happened that might cause them to change now. But Winston is convinced that Kursk will do that.

* * *

July 21, 1943. We are now flying back from Washington. W. got an absolute drubbing from FDR. As a result Winston is very angry. He simply cannot understand why FDR does not see the threat that Russia is now. He simply cannot understand why FDR does not see the importance of being first into Berlin.

The only thing the two leaders agreed on at this futile meeting was that there would be no official record of it. FDR had told W. that there was no point in meeting like and that no good could possibly come from it.

It all has to have been a sad and angry episode. All in all it has achieved nothing. If anything Winston was seen by Roosevelt to be very petulant. It was a very long way to go just for Winston to vent his temper.

The BOAC crew has been magnificent in the way that they have dealt with W. He is now nursing a very large brandy and will probably be asleep soon. The crew must be very tired as we only were in Washington for a couple of hours. They cannot possibly have had any sleep.

* * *

Although Samuel had talked to me about Kursk the first time that I had any idea about the scale of the battle had been that first day that I had met Celina. It was that RAF Canberra pilot that I had met at the evening barbecue who had told me about the sheer size of the battlefield.

In 1997 I went with Oxana to Kursk to study the battlefield there. I was staggered to find that it had still not been completely cleared of wreckage from the battle. There were still the remains of burnt out tanks in the fields and orchards. There were still human bones beside those tank remains. I saw numerous crashed and wrecked aircraft everywhere. It was almost as if the place had been preserved as a monument to Russia's greatest military triumph. But it was a truly awe inspiring and humbling place. It is impossible to imagine the scale of it without going there. The battlefield is the size of Wales. Just to think that two million people died just because they were there in those two tumultuous weeks is something that is very difficult to understand. But what is certain is that the sheer violence of the place destroyed the ability of Germany to win the war. It changed everything. I was already convinced by the documents that Samuel had been right about Kursk. Going there proved it beyond any doubt.

It was also easy to see Zhukov's brilliance in selecting it to be the place to destroy the German armies.

* * *

July 23, 1943. Winston is still trying to get to grips with the stunning Russian victory at Kursk. Since our trip to Washington he has spoken on the phone with Roosevelt several times about it. The only thing on which they have been able to agree is that it creates an entirely new dimension to the war.

I spent a long time alone with him today and it is obvious that he is deeply disturbed by what has happened at Kursk. He has done some simple calculations and has concluded that if Russia follows though at the sort of pace demonstrated at Kursk she will be able to over-run Germany long before any Anglo-American alliance can do so. In his mind that means that Britain will not be in control of the peace process that will follow the war. To him that is a complete disaster.

I have had a couple of chats with Moran during the day and he tells me that Winston seems to be obsessed about Russia. According to him he feels that he has been deceived by Stalin and that any peace in Europe may well be dominated by Russian thinking rather than British thinking.

It must be a very difficult time for him. All those of us who have worked closely with him have known for years that his big dream has been that he would lead the world to victory and would go down in history as having achieved that. Ever since they first made contact Roosevelt has been trying to diminish any British war effort and now Stalin has proved that he has the capacity to defeat Germany on his own. It is all going to make for tense times in the next few months.

But Winston never gives up. If he was a quitter he would have given up long ago. This war is proving as horrendous for him as it is for the British people. He is currently in a state of despair but he is still thinking about the future of himself, Britain and the empire. What he has started talking about today is the need for a big conference where he can set his own agenda for the completion of the war and the subsequent peace. He will be talking with Roosevelt about it and he hopes that they can agree on a joint approach to Stalin about it.

* * *

July 24, 1943. Winston obviously had a bad night last night. There was no reason for him not to go to bed and sleep easily. There was not expected to be any convoy battle and the front in Sicily is proving to be quiet every night. But he came into the bunker this morning looking awful. He told me that he had instructed Moran to give him something to sleep but the wretched pills had not worked.

What he did want to do was talk. He certainly wanted to talk to me. What he said was: "Samuel, the Russian victory at Kursk is going to change everything. It is going to affect the whole way the war is conducted from now on. It is going to affect any peace negotiations at the end of it all.

"What we know from Kursk, which we did not know before, is that Russia has massive military capabilities. The details of German casualties there are sketchy but by any standards they must be very large. We know they had huge armies ready to destroy what we thought remained of any Russian military capability. Instead they have been forced to retreat and all the indications are that they are being chased hard.

"I am sure that you have worked it out for yourself. What sort of military superiority is needed for such a victory? Probably at least two to one. That means Russia must have had at least two million soldiers alone at Kursk. It is totally incredible but the facts are beginning to speak for themselves. You cannot achieve a victory like that without massive superiority.

"So what are they going to do next? There can only be one answer to that. They are going to drive all Germans out of Russia. They will then drive them out of Poland and invade Germany itself. The distances they have to travel are vast and the German forces must still be formidable. So it will take time. Significant military activity after November might be difficult because of weather problems. So it will not be this year that they get to Poland but it might well be next year. On that basis they could be in Berlin next year.

"We cannot launch an attack on France, Belgium or Holland before next spring at the earliest. The weapons we will use and most of the people will be coming from America. There is absolutely no way that we can get them all here before next year in sufficient numbers. That means that there is a real risk that Russia will overwhelm Germany before we and America have any chance to do so.

"At the minimum that means that Russia will be able to dominate the peace process. I have no doubt that they will demand unconditional surrender.

"I have been in touch with Roosevelt several times in the last few days to tell him of my fears about potential Russian domination both of the peace process and about their potential physical domination of Europe. To me it is a nightmare scenario which will both destroy our empire and make real peace in Europe impossible. Roosevelt has made it clear to me that his view is that the objective is the unconditional surrender of Germany. He says it does not matter how that is achieved so long as it is achieved. He rejects my arguments about the Empire as he always has. I fear that he is now looking to a stronger relationship with Russia.

"Whichever way I look at it it seems impossible for Britain to end the war in the way that we began it. Then we had a clear objective that we would beat Germany on our own but with help from America. Now it seems that America is taking little notice of our interests and Russia has the capability to end the war in Europe on its own.

"There seem to be numerous lessons in this for us all. The first is that it is not possible to trust Russia. Last summer, when we went to Moscow, Stalin told me that he was preparing for a large battle. We had no idea at the time what he meant. After Stalingrad we assumed that that was it. But we can now deduce that what was really in his mind was Kursk. If that was indeed the case he has duped us all along. All that talk about being desperately short of military capability when they were in reality building up the largest armies the world has ever seen was intended to blind us to the truth.

"One of the reasons we fought El Alamein was because we thought that Russia had minimum military capability and we simply had to start defeating German armies. The other was that we needed a victory for propaganda purposes. Although I have said great things about El Alamein and will continue to do so, I doubt very much that future generations will judge it to have been of any importance. If we had been able to wait, every German soldier in North Africa would have been withdrawn in order to shore up the armies in the east. We would not have had to fight there.

"One thing Roosevelt and I have been able to agree on is that we should both meet Stalin face–to–face as soon as possible. I hope it will be as early as September. Roosevelt thinks it will be longer than that. He wants to know the results of the summer and autumn campaigns in the east before the meeting. Stalin has agreed in principle but is noncommittal about any date.

"Whichever way it goes I feel more and more that our control of the war is slipping away. That leaves me in a state of despair. It is bad news for Britain."

There was always brandy where we worked. Winston normally only drank it at night but that day he was more depressed that at any time I had seen before. It was almost as if his entire world had fallen away. So I poured him a large one. We talked for perhaps an hour after that and he then had to go off for a lunch appointment.

* * *

August 12, 1957. Alice came to stay for a couple of days. I really wanted to talk to her about the effect of Kursk on Winston as she saw it. I knew that he must have talked to her about it. What she had to say was very important.

"Look, Samuel, I never kept a diary or anything like that. But I always remembered things that happened on dates with which I had a particular association. July 24th was my late husband's birthday. I always remembered things that happened on that day. In 1943 Winston came to see me for lunch that day.

"As you know I had known Winston for many years. I had met with him in good times and bad. I was always satisfied that he was prepared to share his greatest anxieties with me and I always talked them through with him in order to try and find a way forward for him.

"Before the war when he was in the political wilderness I had been able to help him crystallise his position and I was able to help him find a new direction which ultimately led to his becoming Prime Minister.

"But that July lunchtime it was far worse. The person who came to see me that day had all the signs of being in despair. I had never seen him in such a state before. My first job was to calm him down and stop his ranting on about bloody Russians. It was almost as if he saw their victory at Kursk as a personal attack on himself.

"So I sat him down and gave him a large glass of red wine. It was only after the second glass that things started to improve.

"I used my usual technique with him which was always to find out the real problem and then try to look for a solution to that problem. When Winston was confused and angry, as he certainly was that day, he usually had difficulty in separating out the various components of a problem. It was obvious that he was having a problem with Russia. But that was a very large problem and unlikely to respond to a simple solution.

"So we had to look much deeper into the problem. After a couple of hour's discussion and a good lunch we had worked out that there were two main parts to his problem. The first was what was proving to be the awesome power of the Red Army. When we talked about that in detail we found that Britain actually knew very little about just how big and effective that army was. It was clearly very big and very powerful and after Kursk it was likely to be very confident. It was impossible for us to speculate on just why Kursk had forced the Germans to retreat after what seemed to be a spectacular win. What we did conclude was that an enormous task remained for them to defeat the still very large German forces in the east. That would take time and the distances they had to cover were vast. There clearly was no immediate likelihood of their overrunning Poland let alone Germany. At the very earliest that was next year's problem. The only mitigating strategies seemed to be to speed up the deployment of American forces in Europe so that Germany could be conquered from the west before the Russians had any chance of getting there or reaching some kind of agreement with Russia about where their advance would stop.

"That led quickly to what turned out to be Winston's much larger problem. He had previously told me about the discussion he had had with Stalin the previous August. The discussion with Stalin had all been about Russia dropping demands to control territory ceded to it under the Molotov-Ribbentrop agreement. That afternoon he explained to me that at the time he had not even understood why Stalin regarded the matter as so important. Winston had no expectation then that there would ever be any likelihood of Russia ever being able to control the ceded territories in Eastern Europe. At that time Russia was being mauled by Germany and any expectation that she would be able to advance west would be ridiculous. But it now looked as if that might be a real possibility. He had realised that as a result of Kursk that all along Russia had a plan not only to beat Germany but to control several states in the east of Europe as well. That was what was really hurting him that day. He had been duped by Stalin.

"After a long discussion we agreed that the only strategy he could pursue in the circumstances was to seek, with Roosevelt, a new approach with Stalin that kept Russia out of Eastern Europe. The prospects did not look good, though.

"I think the impact of his discussion with Stalin the previous August haunted him for the rest of his life.

"He left in a better mood than when he had arrived. But it was obvious to both of us that he faced many months of gruelling difficulties as the impact of Kursk changed the war and as the *implications of Russia's plans to control territories in Easter Europe came to be worked through."*

* * *

February 4, 1958. Louise came to lunch today. I wanted to know whether she had any knowledge of what was going on in America in the days after Kursk. I knew that by then she no longer had regular contacts in the White House but she had told me that FDR was in occasional contact with her. She had quite a story to tell:

"FDR rang me on July 21st, 1943. He said he needed to talk with me urgently and that we should meet the following day for lunch. He would make the whole afternoon available if necessary.

"When I got there he had arranged everything as if I was still doing my old job with the White House. The martinis were already mixed and he poured them as soon as I arrived. He always went quickly into business. What he said was:

"You will have no way of knowing that over the last few months Russia and Germany have been preparing for a huge battle. All the intelligence available to us indicated that it would be won overwhelmingly by Germany. We were getting very little information from Russia but what we were getting indicated that their forces were very weak.

"Well that battle has now been fought. There will probably be nothing about it in the newspapers for many years because both we and Britain have decided to put a news embargo on it. But the result was an overwhelming Russian win. What it means is that Russia has armed forces on a scale and with a capability far beyond anything we have previously thought. The implications of that are immense.

"It was just eight days ago that the tide turned in Russia's favour. It happened at a tank battle near the city of Kursk We have no idea exactly what happened; that will probably have to wait for the historians but it caused the Germans to start fleeing the battlefield

"Since I got first got that news I have spent most of my time thinking through the consequences.

"I have been contacted several times by Winston on the subject. He even flew here to talk to me about it yesterday. He seems to be more concerned about the effects of this one battle than by any other war issue. He believes that the Russian victory heralds a disaster for the west as Russia overruns first Poland and then Germany. He continues to remind me of the impact on the British Empire if Russia does control the peace process if she gets to Berlin first.

"I have also had several communications from Stalin. He maintains that Kursk has bled the Red Army completely dry and that the price of the victory at Kursk has been immense. He is arguing that if Britain and America had done what he wanted earlier and opened another front the price all round would have been much lower.

"I have asked you here today because I want to rehearse an argument with you before it is conveyed to Winston. You well know from all the discussions that we have had that America's objectives in this war are to achieve the unconditional surrender of Germany and Japan. You also know that I regard it as highly unlikely that the British Empire will survive for long after the war.

"What I have had to do is consider whether a Russian victory at Kursk affects the implementation of those objectives in any way.

"I have come to several conclusions. The first is that this Russian victory does indeed destroy Winston's hopes of leading any peace process in Europe. I know both from him and what you have told me over the time we have worked together that his main ambition was to lead the war effort, win the war and then lead the peace process. Once he approached me back in 1939 that was never going to be possible if at any stage America entered the war. He continues to behave as if the agreement we reached at Placentia Bay is not binding on Britain. It is. What is more, after America entered the war I set out the terms on which America would lead the war effort in Europe. Those terms are binding although he continues to believe that he can pick and choose from them. He can't.

"I have agreed with Winston and Stalin that the three of us will meet during the next few months to plan for the remainder of the war. The main agenda at that meeting will be about how Russia and America are going to bring about the unconditional surrender of Germany. Later I hope we will be able to deal with peace issues when that is achieved. You will have noted that I spoke about how Russia and America are going to achieve German surrender. I did not mention Britain.

"The second conclusion I have reached is about whether Russia really can contribute to the swift elimination of German military activity. I have concluded that she can. I did not think so a few months ago but what they seem to be achieving at Kursk requires a complete re-think. It may be cynical but every Russian life lost is potentially an American life saved. Stalin has pressed me hard in the last few days about more American aid for Russia. In particular he wants trucks that will enable him to speed up the advance of their armies. I have today ordered a massive increase in military truck production. I have set the target of doubling production within three weeks with a further doubling in production within two weeks after that. All those extra supplies will go to Russia. I have also ordered a massive increase in the production of Liberty ships. If Russia wants those trucks it can have them on whatever scale they need. If that helps them to get to Germany quicker then so be it. Our support for them on this will be unlimited. I believe that their current capability substantially reduces American risks in this war. We have to recognise that.

"If Winston thinks that increasing the transport capabilities of Russia is threatening to Britain then so be it.

"The third conclusion is that America must deploy many more personnel in Europe both in our Air Force and in the Army. I have signed an order this morning drafting in another two million men into our armed forces.

"The fourth is that those men are going to need much more equipment. I have therefore ordered a doubling in equipment production of all sorts. That is ships, aircraft, guns, vehicles, tanks, whatever. That will include the production of those excellent bombers that you are managing over here. There is going to be a huge increase in bombing activity over Germany as a result. We simply have to destroy all their production capabilities.

"Finally, and this has been the most difficult of all I have concluded that manpower and equipment alone will not solve the problem. I have therefore ordered an increase in research and development to make our weaponry far more effective. Under the terms of the agreements I reached with Winston America has the right to technology transfer from Britain without the payment of royalties. I shall therefore be instructing him later today that certain distinguished physicists currently working in Britain must move to America immediately. They are needed here on our research projects. They will be leaving tomorrow on Air Force flights. Our military police over there have already been given instructions to protect them.

"We will also be demanding the transfer of jet aircraft technology. The development of jet engines is going all too slowly in Britain just now. The development rate must be speeded up

"None of it will be welcome to Winston but it is all a natural next stage of our unlimited commitment to bringing this war to an end".

"Over lunch he was keen to hear what I thought the impact on Winston might be. The only thing I could really tell him about that was that it seemed to have the usual mix of good and difficult messages that had characterised their exchanges ever since the war began. I told him that anything which would shorten the war would be widely welcomed in Britain. But I also told him that Winston would be shattered both by the decision to provide Russia with much enhanced transport capabilities and the decision to invoke the technology transfer provisions of the Atlantic Charter. I thanked him for the additional investment in Lancaster bombers and I assured him that it would prove to be a good investment.

"He listened intently to what I was saying and when I had finished he went on to talk about American progress in the Pacific. That gave me time to think more deeply about what he had told me. In America, just as in Britain, there was total government control of all military news. Until he told me that day I had no idea of the advances that America had been able to make in the Pacific. They were still thousands of miles from Japan but they were winning battles.

"I think I really knew that day just how awesome American military power had become. They were fighting a massive war in the Pacific dominated by naval battles and they were preparing to fight an equally large war in Europe. And he had just told me that he had authorised another huge increase in the American war effort. It became truly obvious to me that day that Britain was going to get swamped by the American effort. No wonder Winston was troubled by the impact of what was happening in Russia as well.

"So I said to him: 'Mr. President, you have made it very clear to me over these last four years exactly what ambitions you have had for America in this war. At the beginning I do not believe that you had any clear idea how you were going to be able to implement them. It was certainly not obvious then that America would even go to war. But America is now at war and is putting a staggering effort into winning that war. I am sure that she has the capability to succeed.

"All along I have conveyed your messages accurately to Winston. He has always been reluctant to accept them and I am sure that it will be the same with what you have told me today.

"But what I sense about what you have told me today is that it is different from most of those earlier messages. This one is about using the opportunity of the unexpected Russian win at Kursk to turn the screw on Britain. This is a very large step on the way to American global supremacy. As the plan unfolds so do the steps by which you are going to achieve it. I am sure that Winston will see it exactly that way too. So a faraway battle at Kursk in which America did not participate is the opening chapter for the final stages of the war. In Washington you are known as the master politician. This sure proves it. But it does nothing to improve relations with Winston. While you share the common objective of defeating Germany things will go on but what happens after that? There can be no doubt that that is what will be concerning Winston now and possibly forever.

"I do not think you have asked me to do anything as a result of what you have told me today but if there is any message you want me to pass on I will try to do it."

"No, my dear, there is nothing I want you to do. I just wanted you to listen to me and tell me what you thought. I will be speaking to Winston later today. The transatlantic line is always poor but it is important to try and use it. It will not be an easy conversation. As always you have assessed my position correctly. It has been very good to talk with you again."

* * *

It was in 1996 that I was able to see both the STAVKA minutes for the days surrounding Kursk and Zhukov's diary for the same period. It was just a few months after I had been able to inspect the detailed German archives on Kursk for the first time.

Some German records had been made public around 1990 but these only covered the main battlefield events. From them it was possible to piece together what had actually happened each day. But the records published then were incomplete. They did not fully account for the actions of each of the deployed armies and they did not deal with any of the consequences of the battle. In particular they were silent about casualties and on the long term impact on both the Wehrmacht and Luftwaffe.

One key section of the records which dealt with the main tank battle at Prokhorovka was also missing at that time. When I was able to read it the extraordinary nature of the battle there, particularly on July12th became apparent. The phrase 'armoured brawl' neatly described what it was like. The battle involved more than a thousand tanks and took place at short range. A thousand tanks compressed into about three square kilometres of wheat fields provided little room for manoeuvre and did not favour the German machines which were only really effective at much longer ranges. Tanks were ramming each other and many were involved in multiple collisions. There were constant air attacks by both sides. It was truly a military maelstrom.

Numerous personal accounts of the battle by German soldiers talk of overwhelming Russian strength and apparently inexhaustible supplies of Russian armour and men. Almost universally those personal accounts concluded that Germany had no chance. Many of those personal accounts state that they felt as if they had been drawn into an inescapable trap. It was exactly as Zhukov had intended.

When I was able to read the complete German version of these events it was possible to see the true impact on the German forces. In the six week period starting at the beginning of July and ending when the retreat was fully underway Germany lost 976,000 men either in death or as captives. Only a handful of the captives survived the war and returned to Germany.

* * *

In the last two weeks before the battle commenced STAVKA met twice a day. Stalin chaired all the meetings before and during the battle. On July 2nd it was recorded that Zhukov was given permission by Stalin to leave Moscow and take command of the battle preparations from a command headquarters in a train parked in a siding in a forest south of Kursk. It was very close to the likely fighting. The minutes record that Zhukov insisted on that. He said he had to be near both his commanders and frontline troops. But he had to be on a secure phone line for all the STAVKA meetings.

Before the battle commenced the minutes record both rising expectations and rising tensions. Zhukov reminded every meeting that this was the battle to which they had agreed back in December, 1941. Everything they had done since then was part of the deliberate plan agreed then. The battle plan had been resourced with huge sacrifices by the nation, the commanders appointed, the men trained, the defences around the Kursk salients had all been built and heavily mined. They were now ready to destroy the German armour and aircraft. He urged patience and always said that he was sure that the Red Army would deliver. He sought and obtained permission to chase the Germans as far as they could go after victory at Kursk was secured.

The same minutes record that Stalin gave instructions that both during the battle and afterwards there was to be a strengthening of the political supervision of the army and its commanders. It was clear from those minutes that Stalin was terrified that successful commanders at Kursk might be tempted to gain control of the government. He desperately wanted the victory that Zhukov had promised him but he was going to do everything he could to prevent him from taking any personal or professional advantage of it. As a consequence Khrushchev was given increased powers and instructed to visit the headquarters of all the senior commanders in the army around Kursk and in doing so build up the powers of the political commissars attached to each of them.

Zhukov's diary contains no entries in the last days leading up to the start of the German attacks on July 4th. There is little of any interest until July 12th. But that evening there is an entry which reads:

"The whole battle plan came together brilliantly today. There has been a ferocious battle at Prokhorovka involving thousands of tanks fighting at short range. Last night I was out with some of Rotmistrov's men and the confidence they all had gave me great hopes for today. The last few days have been very hectic as I have visited all the armies in this area and have co-ordinated their battle plans. It was very tense when the Germans started their attacks on July 4th. Although he had agreed to the battle plans many times Stalin was nervous. He feels a great sense of shock at the loss of any Soviet territory even though the losses here have been part of a plan to decoy the German armies into a place where we can fight on ground of our own choosing. The arguments over this in STAVKA meetings have been time consuming and have not added anything to our military capability. Every day I have had to remind them over the phone that the plan is a good one and that we will win.

Stalin is worried that I and my generals will use a victory here for political gain. On every visit to my commander's headquarters I have been accompanied by Khrushchev. He has clearly been given instructions by Stalin to ensure that we are all politically correct.

To me that is all a waste of time. I am here to deliver a massive military victory over Germany. That is exactly the view of all my army commanders. That is our only objective. If we fail we are all clear that Stalin will eliminate us but we are not going to fail. It is all going to plan.

I saw today's battle from a hill south-west of Prokhorovka which was where Rotmistrov was based. The view of the battlefield was excellent despite all the smoke and fire. Over the whole fighting area every living thing was destroyed.

I spoke to Stalin several times during the day and he seemed pleased with what we have been achieving.

Tomorrow we start the task of forcing the Germans back and well away from this area. There are so many of them that it will take a few weeks to ensure that they are really in full retreat. But we have the power to make that happen now.

The rate at which trained personnel are being released for frontline service means that whatever our losses here we will vastly outnumber German forces on our soil. The rate at which new equipment is being made available is brilliant. Our tank production rate is now well in excess of 1500 machines a month and is still rising. There is no doubt in my mind that we can now win this war. But it is going to take time because the distances over which we will have to chase the Germans are vast. Our supply chain will be the most important determinant of our speed.

While I would like to be able to get to Germany in 1944, I do not believe that it will be possible. We have a major discussion about this tomorrow within STAVKA and I will be advising them that the spring of 1945 is the most likely date for the destruction of Germany."

* * *

July 23, 1943. Winston has been raging all day about the message he has received from Roosevelt. He has complained to me many times today about Roosevelt making unilateral decisions without any consultation. He is incensed that some of our top scientists are to be taken to America without regard to the impact on Britain. He is furious about FDR's criticism of our jet engine development programme when the government has given unlimited funds to Rolls-Royce to ensure the device is developed with maximum speed. Goodness knows what will have to happen to calm him down.

* * *

July 25, 1943. Winston was up all night. One of his favoured war projects is large scale bombing raids on Germany. The RAF Chief of Bomber Command is Arthur Harris. He is very much in the Winston mould. He passionately believes that bombing will destroy much of the German industrial capability. But successful bombing requires huge bomber fleets. A thousand or more for each raid seems to be the optimum. There was an attempt to bomb Cologne in this way last summer, but we simply did not have the resources then to operate any other raids in this way. The huge build-up of bomber production that has been organised by Max Beaverbrook, especially in America, has now made it possible for us to conduct such raids every night when the weather is favourable.

Yesterday Harris came to see Winston. He wanted to share his plans for the most aggressive bomber raid yet. What he told Winston was that weather conditions were perfect for a raid on Hamburg. What was planned was for sixty RAF squadrons to bomb the city last night and for fifteen American Bomb Groups to bomb the city today. In total that means that around 3500 bombers will have been deployed against a single city within about twelve hours. Winston gave him full support. But he had to wait up all night to hear what was happening.

We got the first reports around midnight. Large numbers of bombers had been able to hit their targets in the centre of the city. It was a hot night with a slight wind. That made conditions excellent for incendiary bombs. All the crews at the end of the bomber stream reported that there were huge fires right across the city.

After the American bombers had gone in this morning the photo reconnaissance flights followed. It was evident that the entire centre of Hamburg has been destroyed. Large areas of the docks have been devastated and the industrial areas are still burning. It was everything that Harris had promised. He rang Winston early in the afternoon to tell him all about it. Winston was ecstatic. He told Harris to get on with it and bomb everywhere else in Germany.

The bad news part of it was that the RAF lost 118 aircraft in the raid; that is around a thousand aircrew. With an average of ten raids a month that means we could lose a thousand or more aircraft a month and more than ten thousand air crew each month. It is a staggering price.

Last night there was yet another convoy battle. There were sixteen U-Boats in the path of a convoy bringing military equipment and oil from New York. Five U-Boats were sunk during the night without the loss of a single allied ship. Winston was delighted about that.

Because of all that good news he has not mentioned Russia all day.

* * *

August 6, 1943. Winston has been getting news all day about sustained Soviet attacks designed to force the Germans out of the cities of Belgorod and Kharkov. He is amazed that Russia has been able to pursue the German armies so quickly. He feels thoroughly deceived by Stalin. He remains very fearful about the consequences of it all.

* * *

August 8, 1943. Winston told me today about a strange meeting that is due to take place in Santander, Spain today. Apparently he has been in discussion with Roosevelt for some months about an approach made to FDR by Franz von Papen about possible peace overtures by Germany. He said he was very doubtful about it all in case it impeded any process leading to unconditional surrender. FDR has the same view. But they did agree to exploratory talks.

It all sounds very odd to me. Just the sort of thing that devious diplomats would involve themselves in. With things improving on all our war fronts it would seem to be madness to make any concessions to Germany at this time.

Winston did express the view, though, that if it opened an intelligence channel right through to the highest levels in the German government it might be worthwhile. I cannot see how.

* * *

After America joined the war Franz von Papen, Otto's uncle, undertook on behalf of Beck and Goerdeler to approach Roosevelt and get him to agree to a deal similar to the one they had agreed with Eden. Roosevelt was at that time prepared to talk and he appointed Colonel Earle as his intermediary. Useful progress was made and a possible deal was hammered out. It was not a process in which Roosevelt had any confidence, as his diary makes clear, but at that time he thought it desirable to follow any avenue which might lead to peace. Even he at that time had not worked out what unconditional surrender meant. Until he had, as he records in his diary, every possible avenue had to be pursued.

Initially Churchill was not told of these discussions. But Roosevelt did eventually raise the matter with him in order to have a tri-partite meeting set up between Britain, America and

Germany. Churchill readily agreed, but he had never been told of the various approaches Eden had made on the same subject and he never told Eden of the meetings to which he had agreed. The meeting eventually took place in Santander, Spain in the summer of 1943, after the battle of Kursk. Roosevelt was always nervous about such a meeting but he did think that after Kursk the weakness of Germany might make the overthrow of Hitler a practical proposition.

Germany was represented by Admiral Canaris, the Head of State Security. He was a key member of the Beck-Goerdeler conspiracy to eliminate Hitler. Franz von Papen had made that clear to Roosevelt. America was represented by William J Donovan, the Head of the Office of Strategic Studies in Washington. Britain was represented by General Menzies, Chief of British Intelligence, who had recently taken over that role from General Harford. Eventually it all came to nothing because Roosevelt in the end decided that he was not prepared to negotiate with Germany about anything. As he thought through the doctrine of unconditional surrender more carefully he realised that even dialogue with Germany was impossible.

Eden went on negotiating with Goerdeler until after D-Day but he found it increasingly difficult to reconcile what he was doing with Roosevelt and Churchill's demands for unconditional surrender. If unconditional surrender was the requirement there could be no basis for any deal prior to that happening.

* * *

In August 1943 the German armies were retreating steadily to the northwest, across the Dnieper River and towards Poland. Their losses at Kursk had been so severe that they would never again be any serious challenge for the Red Army.

Over the following three months the German armies were forced westwards by around 300 kilometres but it was still another 2,000 kilometres to Berlin.

No one will ever know exactly how many people died in battle during that war or how many died as a result of their subsequent imprisonment or deprivation and disease or how many civilian casualties there were; but the latest estimates (made in 1996) are that for Soviet Union citizens alone the figure was higher than forty million people. This means that the war between Germany and the Soviet Union between 1941 and 1945 killed more people than all the other wars ever fought on the globe put together. It was the first war in which civilian casualties even exceeded let alone overwhelmed those in the military. At the end of the war there were estimated to be fifty million refugees.

From November 1942 until May 1945 the German forces were in almost constant retreat all the way from Stalingrad to Berlin itself. That was a distance of about 2500 kilometres. But it was not a single military front. Fighting took place on several fronts simultaneously. Even in logistics alone it overwhelmed anything that had ever been contemplated previously in any field of human endeavour. Most of the ground over which the two armies fought had been decimated in their struggle during The First World War about a quarter of a century earlier.

* * *

September 3, 1943. It has been a day of drama. Eighth Army has left Sicily today after its successful conquest of that island. They have landed at Reggio di Calabria in the toe of Italy. It is a good sign of steady progress against the German forces.

Our spies in the German armies have been telling us that von Manstein has been to Rastenburg today to urge Hitler to agree to a withdrawal of all German troops to new lines west of the Dnieper River. That will mean a retreat of more than a hundred miles for most of them. That means that Kiev is likely to be the next big Russian target. If Kiev falls then Germany will be out of Ukraine. Winston believes that that will be the starting signal for a race to Berlin. It certainly looks like that.

* * *

September 8, 1943. All of today has been spent in preparations for the forthcoming meeting of the Big Three. Stalin and Roosevelt agreed yesterday that they would meet in Tehran in November. Winston is furious that he was not consulted about the date or the location.

Winston has fired off messages to both of them about British expectations for the meeting. He has also spoken to Roosevelt today. What he told him was that America and Britain must contain Russian ambitions to enter Germany. What he proposed was that the planned invasion of France should be brought forward to give the western allies a chance to get into Germany well before Russia had any chance to do so and that they should get as far east as possible before they met Russian troops. Whatever happened Russia had to be kept out of Germany.

Roosevelt's response apparently was that it was a matter to discuss in Tehran. He would not reach any decision on the matter until then.

* * *

After the great victory at Kursk Stalin resolved to keep up his pressure on Britain and America for them to open a second front. By then he had long since stopped thinking about the defence of Mother Russia, he had started thinking of the supremacy of Russia. After that battle he had enough confidence in his armed forces and in his military commanders to believe that complete and outright victory over Germany was possible. On many occasions he thought that that victory might be possible without any British or American assistance. At the time of Russia's direst need after the Barbarossa invasion they had not been able to make any contribution to Russia at all. To him friends were people to whom you turned in the hour of need. By that judgment in 1941 Russia had no friends.

He doubted whether they could make any useful contribution but he decided that he would put pressure on them to do so. In doing that he would seek long-term advantages for his beloved Soviet Union. He was certain that he would enjoy putting pressure on the other Allied leaders, Churchill in particular. He regarded Churchill as representing aristocratic arrogance, and that was something that he could not endure.

* * *

I had gone into the Russian archives office early one morning in September, 1996. Oxana and I had spent the night together. It was immensely enjoyable as ever. She told me at some unknown hour that the previous day she had found some of Stalin's diaries that had been filed in the wrong place. They seemed to her to be very important as they covered some of his thoughts after Kursk. We got there as the office opened.

She was absolutely right. There were numerous entries but perhaps the most important was dated 28th, August, 1943. It was at the time that the Red Army was moving rapidly west from Kursk and attempting to retake the cities of Belgorod and Kharkov. The record shows that within a few days after that they would start chasing the Wehrmacht to Kiev. It was at a time that Russian supremacy was obvious but not yet total.

The relevant section of the diary reads:

"It has been more than two years since we were invaded by Germany. It is impossible to calculate in detail at this time the effects on our country. What I do know about those effects is that everything has had to be reorganised to make it possible for us to defeat the invaders. Our entire industrial production capability has had to be moved east of the Urals to make it safe from any German attacks. We have had to acquire vast amounts of machine tools from America under Lend/Lease in order to build up our production capabilities. We are grateful for their support and will pay for it but it does not create any basis for friendship.

It has been necessary to order changes in the lives of millions of our people so that they can fight in the army, support the army or produce war materials. That is a small price to pay for the protection of Mother Russia.

What is now clear to me is that we will now beat Germany. Kursk proved that to me. So far as we possibly can we are going to do it on our own. I will continue to press America for their maximum effort but even if they do nothing we will defeat Germany.

My political strategy will be to put maximum pressure on the generals to move more quickly towards Germany. Roosevelt has agreed to provide large amounts of transport for this. It will help immensely.

But the real issue is clearing all Germans from Russia as quickly as possible. There is no doubt in my mind that this has to be done without regard to the cost in human or material terms. So that is the way it is going to be.

After the sacrifices Russia has already made it seems only obvious that we should be seen as the conquerors of Berlin. I do not know whether we can get to Berlin before the Americans. We have such vast distances to cover. Despite all our resources an advance of 2,000 kilometres in one year seems impossible despite any pressure that I can exert through Zhukov. If the Americans land in Holland in the spring they will only have to travel around 400 kilometres.

It is therefore inevitable that I must do a deal with Roosevelt, so that at the worst from the Russian point of view, we both enter Berlin simultaneously. All the information I have been getting from Washington for the last two years is that Roosevelt is against the British Empire. I therefore plan to do a deal under which we agree to the final plan for Berlin in return for an understanding that we will jointly bring that pathetic institution to an end.

That is why I am going to meet him in Tehran."

It was no surprise to me that that should have been the case, but too see it in writing but a discovery of great importance. It certainly explained the plans that were then being developed for Tehran.

* * *

Roosevelt's exchanges with Stalin after Kursk were altogether different from the ones he had with Churchill. He recognised that Kursk had changed everything. If armed forces could inflict the damage they had on the German armies at Kursk they had to be enormously powerful. As soon as it was clear to him what might be happening at Kursk he called a conference of his most senior Generals. Between them they worked out that to inflict damage on that scale on the German forces would have required a Russian numerical supremacy of at least two to one across all items; men, tanks, guns and aircraft. They worked out the likely level of German forces that had been engaged and then extrapolated the likely size of the Russian forces. They were staggered by the answers. They had no idea that Russia had resources on that scale let alone the capacity to equip them.

What those answers showed to them was that the availability of men and equipment to Zhukov at Kursk was far beyond the total size of the American armed forces at that time. It also showed that Russia had an army which was far bigger than any army even in the First

World War; that made it far larger than any army before in the world. It was not only awesome in size; it had proved itself to be awesome in capability as well. At Kursk it inflicted the greatest damage on any army that had ever been inflicted.

Roosevelt knew at that meeting that whatever his intentions had been it was unlikely that America would bring about the end of Germany. It was likely to be at least nine months before American troops could land on mainland European soil and by then at their present speed the Russian armies would be very close to Germany itself. That meant, at the very least, that America would have to share any victory over Germany with Russia. If Russia was able to speed up its advances it was likely that she would become the sole victor over Germany. That was not something that he could contemplate. As the arch political manipulator he recognised that he would have to do a deal with Russia at some point to prevent that happening.

Roosevelt made some decisions at that meeting. The first was that he would seek a much closer alliance with Stalin. It Russia had that much military power America then was not going to confront it but try and cooperate with it. The second was that he was going to try and encourage Russia to be his ally in his quest to end the British Empire. The third and perhaps the most important was that if Russian troops could take the brunt of the casualties in Europe he would encourage that. If Russian lives could ensure an American victory that was a worthwhile objective in itself. It might be cynical but Roosevelt knew that the American public would want the lowest possible level of American casualties. Make Russia do the dirty work was his view. But at the same time he decided that he would make available whatever supplies that he could. Stalin had asked him for large numbers of large cross-country vehicles to make his armies more mobile. Roosevelt would certainly supply them and whatever else Russia needed.

Roosevelt's diary for that day includes this entry:

"At a meeting with George Marshall and his senior aides today we cast the die that will deliver us victory over Germany."

* * *

In the autumn of 1943 Stalin was getting ever more angry about the Anglo-American failure to start a second front. He sent an endless stream of telegrams both to Churchill and Roosevelt complaining about their inaction.

To try and calm things down Roosevelt sent his Secretary of State, Cordell Hunt, to Moscow to meet with Molotov. Anthony Eden was there at the same time. Hunt was scarcely fit to go to anywhere, let alone Moscow. He suffered from diabetes and tuberculosis and was physically exhausted before the trip had even begun. He kept his illnesses secret. In addition to all that he had never been on an aeroplane before.

The trip over to Moscow was sheer hell for him. He coughed up blood several times and was very uncomfortable almost all the way.

The conference in Moscow was essentially about the dismembering of Germany after the war and about punishment for war criminals. It actually made real progress on both issues and there was increasing agreement between America and Russia on just what should be done. At the end of it the parties issued what was known as the Moscow Declaration. It included the phrase drafted beforehand by Churchill that war criminals be "sent back to the countries in which their abominable deeds were done."

Whatever else may have been achieved at Moscow it was a prelude to the Tehran conference held in November, 1943. It was in Tehran that Churchill, Roosevelt and Stalin met together for the first time.

* * *

October 20, 1943. We were de-briefed today by Eden Stalin had been in a very belligerent mood. All he wanted to talk about was reparations. He wanted to remove every possible asset from Germany at the end of the war. But he left Eden in no doubt that if Britain and America did not open a front with Germany then Russia would finish the war on their own.

* * *

As Roosevelt prepared for his forthcoming meetings in Tehran his thoughts were dominated by what Russia had been able to achieve so far. At the time of Pearl Harbor he had made his decision that America and America alone was going to win the war. Yes, they would take whatever support was available but the victor had to be seen to be America. Now he had to balance that objective with the objective of eliminating the British Empire. Russia was doing far better in the war than he could ever have imagined and seemed to have the capacity to eliminate Germany on its own. He had made those decisions after Kursk about which he spoke to Angela; the time had now come to implement them.

To him that meant that he would have to find some way of forging an alliance with Russia, however temporary, which met American objectives. He was certain that he could not go to Tehran with confused objectives. Every day he received intelligence reports about Stalin. They all said the same thing: the man was ruthless, cruel, vindictive and had no trust in any other person, but at Tehran Roosevelt had to leverage whatever he could from the man.

Based on the success of the system that the British had set up to involve Angela in the highest level of communications he had set up a similar system that would be used by him and Stalin. That communications channel told him something similar but it also told him that to Stalin Mother Russia was as important to him as his own power. In other words he had ceased to be just Stalin; he had become the saviour of his country. All sources told Roosevelt that nothing would distract Stalin from that course.

So what Roosevelt had to work out was what the common ground between them was. Was it just beating Germany or was it something else? Might it just be possible to convince Stalin that there was a common interest in eliminating the British Empire?

If that were possible then a very interesting deal might emerge. Roosevelt went to Tehran absolutely determined to do two things. The first was to achieve the maximum cooperation with Stalin about bringing the war to an end. The second was seeking his support and cooperation in eliminating the British Empire. He was sure that he would never be able to trust Stalin but he was equally sure that a deal based on material gain would work.

* * *

Any review of the Tehran conference shows that it occurred when the war experiences of the participants were entirely different. Russia had just had a truly wonderful year on the ground and it had thrown back the German armies. It had actually done far more than that. It had gone a very long way to destroying the entire German capacity to fight. True, there was a long way to go but the Russian star was very much in the ascendancy. That meant that Stalin would have a very powerful bargaining position at Tehran.

Britain had had a mixed year. She had been able to move out of North Africa and had been able to take Sicily without any real fight of any sort. But she had then got bogged down in some long and bloody encounters in Italy as she had tried, with American assistance, to move the German armies from some very secure positions. It was proving to be a long and very grisly haul there. In the North Atlantic it had been a good year. That big convoy battle in

March had indeed turned the tide. As the end of the year approached it looked as if they could have destroyed 200 U-Boats in the year. Shipping losses were well down as well. All the new tactics were paying off well, particularly the use of long range aircraft.

Britain and America were increasing their bombing raids over Germany but as yet no significant military targets had been destroyed in any of those raids although large amounts of urban development and numerous strategic factories had been destroyed.

America was not yet by any means fully engaged in Europe. But it was shipping over large numbers of men and equipment ready for D-Day planned for May 1st, 1944. In the Pacific it was making progress and was about to complete the removal of all Japanese forces from the Solomon Islands. But it was proving to be a very hard slog. What America was doing very well was producing large amounts of equipment, aircraft, tanks, guns and lorries.

But it was Russia that was wearing the victor's trophies at the first summit meeting between Stalin, Roosevelt and Churchill. As the conference neared Churchill was very aware of that.

* * *

November 20, 1943. Winston is in a very nervous mood today. In a few days we will have to leave for Tehran. Every day for weeks now we have been getting more and more information about the advances that the Red Army has been able to make. The weather in Ukraine this autumn has been exceptionally mild. There have been huge advances along a massive front a thousand miles long. There are now no German forces in the Caucasus nor anywhere east of the Dnieper River. Kiev will surely be retaken by the Red Army soon.

Winston is concerned that every mile of Soviet advance increases Stalin's bargaining power at Tehran. In the meantime our forces are trapped in another bloody slog in Italy.

The vile weather in Western Europe these last few weeks has completely halted all bombing raids over Germany.

The only area where things are going well is in the North Atlantic. Winston is delighted that all the efforts made there are now really working. He is satisfied that crossing the Atlantic is very much a low risk operation. For all daylight hours there are long-range aircraft over all known U-Boat positions. At night we have sufficient escorts to keep all U-Boats away from the convoys. Almost every day now more men and equipment arrive from America.

That all helps both Winston and FDR with the one thing that they can offer at Tehran. That is a firm date for an allied landing in Europe.

* * *

November 27, 1943. We arrived in Tehran today. We had to fly a very long way round to avoid all war zones and that made for a long and difficult journey. We stopped at Cairo for a conference with Roosevelt and the Chinese leader Chiang Kai-shek. Winston had hoped to be in on all the meetings but Roosevelt excluded him as he negotiated a dismemberment of the British Empire in the Far East with the Chinese leader.

Winston was furious about all that. On the plane from Cairo he was in a foul mood and spent several hours ranting about Roosevelt's obsession with the British Empire. It did not bode well for the big meetings in Tehran.

Things got worse when we arrived. It quickly became evident that Roosevelt, who arrives tomorrow, will be staying at the Soviet Embassy and in the same building as Stalin. We are staying at the British Embassy which is a couple of miles away. Winston is sure that it is a stitch-up between the two of them. He is certain that he is to be the victim. But as always he will fight. He always does and he will fight for his strongest belief, which is the British Empire.

* * *

One of the more curious aspects of the Tehran conference was that Roosevelt stayed in the Soviet Embassy compound. The outside world was told that that was on security grounds. The Soviet Embassy there was housed in a large walled compound with its own surveillance towers. But private telegrams between Stalin and Roosevelt, released only after the cold war had come to an end, showed that Roosevelt was asked to stay there by Stalin who wanted to have plenty of time for private conversations with him without there being any possibility of Churchill being around. It was an invitation that was easy for Roosevelt to accept. It proved to be very good for developing communications between them. It was ominous that the first occasion when they met face-to-face was the occasion when it was easiest for them to agree on downgrading Churchill's and Britain's roles.

I saw the relevant entries in Soviet files in 1998. Stalin clearly regarded it as a major advance in Soviet foreign policy.

Roosevelt's diary records a similar view.

* * *

On their first evening there Stalin and Roosevelt talked for several hours about their main shared interest which was the future of the British Empire. That evening that was more important to them even than the ending of the war.

It was late into the night when they got down to the nub of the argument. Stalin loved the late night. He rarely slept for more than two hours at a time and often woke in the night with his brain raging with ideas. It did not matter what those ideas were, they were all important. He had to write them down immediately he thought of them in case they were forgotten. It happened almost every night that he had new ideas and first thing in the morning he got some lackey or other to implement them.

But that night an idea began to emerge which Roosevelt found to be attractive. Stalin explained to him that the Russian people had had to endure so much pain at the hands of Hitler that it would be immensely popular in Russia if it could be seen all across the world that Russia had been the country to conquer Germany. It would enhance the prestige of his country and it would strengthen his personal authority. Although Russia had been victorious in the defence of its capital, had routed the Germans at Stalingrad and had absolutely thrashed them at Kursk the Russian sacrifices had been immense. There were doubtless many more sacrifices to come. But in return for those sacrifices he knew that the Russian people wanted to know that they had won the war. They wanted to know that Russia had fought off and beaten the aggressor. They wanted to know that Mother Russia had won. To Stalin that night it was all very simple: Russia had to be seen to be the conquerors of Berlin. If they could agree on that then all sorts of other things might be possible.

Roosevelt was equally clear that the only thing the American people would want was victory and then a return to their own domestic ways. They would not care about the details as long as the boys came home as soon as possible after the war. That meant that he had a very free mandate to negotiate anything that fell within that very wide target area. So what he negotiated that night was the freedom for Russia to be seen to be the conquerors of Berlin in return for support in eliminating the British Empire.

Neither of them could see any role for the British Empire after the war and they both agreed that they would work together to ensure that it was no longer the dominant world trade and political grouping. The agreement they reached together that first evening was to govern the negotiations between Russia and America for the remainder of the war and into the start of the post-war period. They shared common objectives that they were both very happy to pursue.

At the end of their discussion Stalin ordered a suckling pig and a bottle of vodka. He always ate a whole suckling pig when he had something to celebrate and he always slept better when he had drunk a large amount of vodka. Roosevelt did not want any share of that little pig at that time of the night but he did take a couple of large glasses of vodka.

* * *

The Tehran conference was the first opportunity for the Big Three, as they had become called, together to talk face-to-face about the future conduct of the war and about how to manage its aftermath. They made very little progress on the management of the war but they did agree that Germany should be dismembered and its industrial capacity should be destroyed. On every key issue Roosevelt sided with Stalin rather than Churchill.

On one item there was very strong agreement between Roosevelt and Stalin. It was that on the cessation of hostilities the 50,000 most senior German officers should be shot without trial.

At Tehran the three leaders decided that a newly created body called then European Advisory Commission should advise them exactly how Germany should be divided.

The only effective progress was made on the management of the war was that Stalin pinned down America and Britain to opening a second front through France on May 1, 1944. However in private talks Roosevelt agreed with Stalin that Russia would have the lead role in the final assault on Berlin. It was a promise that he was to keep, despite compelling advice to the contrary.

Stalin was the overall winner at Tehran. He had every reason to be satisfied with what he had gained. He had effectively won approval for his plan for Eastern Europe that had been discussed between Molotov and Eden in December 1941. He had also developed plans for Soviet expansion into the Balkans and at Tehran he had neutered Anglo-American objections to those.

Churchill left as probably the only loser. He realised at Tehran that Britain was losing its power to influence world events. What Roosevelt had said to him on the *Prince of Wales* was turning into reality. It was a sad and weary Churchill that left Tehran to go home.

* * *

December 2, 1943. As I write this we are flying home from Tehran. Again we have to go the long way round. Our first stop will be in Cairo. We will also have to stop in Casablanca and Lisbon to re-fuel. I cannot think how many hours we will be on this noisy machine.

What is absolutely certain is that Winston is in the worst state yet. He is furious at being stitched-up over the accommodation arrangements. Those in turn meant that he was excluded from all the main discussions between Roosevelt and Stalin. None of his ideas were accepted at all. Instead the other two agreed to some new borders for Poland. This was done without any consultation with Polish interests and it strongly favoured Russia. Winston did point out to them that Britain had gone to war in the first place in order to protect Polish interests and now those were being thrown away without regard to the consequences.

He was also angry that FDR and Stalin did a deal to provide Iran with substantial aid. Britain governs Iran and W. saw this as a direct assault on the Empire.

But above all he was angry because Roosevelt had been talking with Stalin about a deal on Berlin. Although they did not reach final agreement FDR accepted that Russia would be able to take most of that city. Next time they meet it seems certain that they will reach final agreement under which the Russian and American armies will meet in the south-western suburbs of Berlin. If necessary, American troops will slow their advances to make that possible.

Winston and FDR did agree that there would be major allied landings in the west in May of 1944. Winston is confident that as a result the war will finish in the spring of 1945. All three of them agreed that this was the most likely timescale. Stalin had told them he would dearly wish that it could be done more quickly than that but he still had to destroy more than a hundred divisions of German troops in the east and he still had to fight over 2,000 kilometres of land. He thought they might be into Poland by the summer of 1944 but the most difficult part was always going to be the assault on Berlin itself. It was a heavily defended city and there was some very difficult terrain on the way.

Winston did not like at all the fact that Stalin was in complete charge of the meetings. He was cocky and full of self-assurance after the Russian gains over the summer.

We are obviously in for a very different phase of the war now.

* * *

The British public may have detected Churchill's sadness. By 1944 he was certainly not the popular national hero he had been at the time of the Battle of Britain. Nor was he the popular hero that he became after the victory at El Alamein. More than three years on from the Battle of Britain and more than a year on from El Alamein nothing seemed to have happened on the domestic front. There was still rationing of all essentials, and this had been tightened. There was still no end to the bombings of Britain.

What did seem to have happened was that large parts of the countryside had been ripped up to provide airfields and barracks for both British and American forces. Within a year more than a hundred airfields had been created in East Anglia alone. The railways were choked with troops moving every whichway, to the point that any sort of normal public transport was becoming impossible.

What made it all a lot worse was that all the two million Americans who were stationed in Britain by the end of the year had no shortages of anything. They had generous supplies of food, they had no clothing shortages, they had all the fuel they needed and they had, in some cases cars without any petrol rationing. It all started to cause resentment for a war weary population. There was no one else to blame for it other than Churchill himself.

They started to make it felt. It was early in 1944 when he was visiting the site of yet another bombing raid in the East End of London that he was booed in the streets for the first time. It was not a comfortable experience. But it was to happen many times before D-Day.

* * *

February 3, 1944. When Winston came back to the war rooms today after visiting an area of East London which had been bombed during the night he was not so much angry as distressed. He has visited many parts of the country during the war and so far has always been welcomed. But today he was booed in the streets but what seemed to be an entirely spontaneous demonstration.

* * *

When Churchill was first booed in the streets of East London it was widely reported in the newspapers. The facts were on the front pages, the opinions were in the editorials. They almost universally described it as a natural reaction by a population that was completely fed up with war, that was hearing of distant Russian victories, hearing of American gains in its Pacific campaigns but yet there seemed to be no British gains and no end to the deprivations at home. And still the bombs went on falling and they were still losing families, relatives and friends in combat all over the world. They all advised Churchill that what the British people wanted was victory and then a swift end to the deprivations

Two days after that ugly street scene he was due to spend some time with Alice. The war situation was such that that he would be able to spend the whole evening with her. It would be the first time he could do that in what seemed to be many years since those seemingly care free days before he had become Prime Minister. He, too, was becoming war weary, although he would never admit that to anyone except Alice and his wife, Clemmie.

Another thing that concerned him was that the nearer Britain came to victory the nearer it came to having to pay that very high and demanding price that America had forced him to pay and which was still unknown to the British people. He sincerely hoped that it would never be known in his lifetime.

As he was being driven to Eaton Mews that February afternoon he thought of Tehran. He thought of a triumphant Stalin and an economically overwhelmingly powerful Roosevelt. He thought of how much they both enjoyed using that power. And then he thought of a bankrupt Britain that had only been able to get where it had in the war with vast amounts of American aid. Why even at El Alamein, which he had heralded to the country as a great and noble victory, most of the guns and tanks used had been American.

But one thing he was absolutely sure about as the car turned into Eaton Mews was that the war would end in Europe in the spring of 1945. He was sure that he would be given the benefit of the doubt as all that planning work that was going on just now resulted in a military campaign that resulted in unconditional surrender.

Alice had a large whisky waiting for him. She made him sit on the sofa close to the roaring log fire and take off his shoes and jacket. She wanted him to relax and enjoy himself that evening. This was above all a time for soothing and reflection. She also needed to boost his morale and find a way to help him over the next few gruelling months.

After he had sat down she said to him:

"Winston, there would seem to be lots of things going through your mind. I will listen to them all if you want to tell me about them. What I suggest you do is relax, enjoy your drink and the warmth of the fire and just talk to me about anything as soon as you are ready."

Winston took two large sips of whisky; he lay back with his head on the back of the sofa and gave her back the glass with a request for more whisky. When she returned it with rather more whisky in it than the first time round he started to talk.

"My dear Alice, today when I was booed in the streets I was very shocked. It was something that I had not expected. I have been round many bombed areas of the country and every time up until then I have been welcomed wherever I have gone. Bad as it was, a few people booing in the streets is by no means the biggest of the problems that I have to face.

"You know, Alice, all wars are unpredictable. They usually start with some clear objectives or ideals on the opposing sides and they very quickly get overtaken by events. That is something which must be very obvious to anyone who has ever read about any of them. It is certainly obvious from the books that I have written about them.

"The reason that they are unpredictable is that it is impossible to see in advance exactly what the setbacks will be and when they will occur and what the effect of them will be.

"The occasion of us going to war was the invasion of Poland. We had guaranteed to protect Poland only a few months before that at a time when we manifestly had no capability of doing any such thing.

"What happens follows what goes before, always. There is nothing you can do to prevent it. What went before our decision to go to war over Poland was two decades of trying to avoid any sort of conflict. Britain had in essence become a sort of pacifist country. We deliberately stood back from conflict; we deliberately disarmed. We got to the point in 1939 that we effectively had no useful fighting capability at all. We got to that dreadful position despite the certain fact that in most of the larger European countries chaos was developing at an astonishing rate or there was re-armament and aggression taking place on an unprecedented scale.

"I well understand why the British public wanted peace. What I do not understand is how the leadership of the country allowed it to reach such a desperate situation on almost every score.

"The legacy of those appalling years was that Britain had no money, no viable military, few ways of defending itself, and a much reduced industrial capability. The one real strength we had been able to retain was our Empire. It could be argued that another of our strengths then was the Royal Navy. But this was designed for large scale naval battles at which large capital ships tried to out-gun each other. In this war not a single battle like that has taken place. Our 1939 style of navy turned out to be nearly useless and their only real success was the sinking of the *Bismarck*, but that cost us dearly.

"The type of thinking that was going on in the 1930's turned out to be a real weakness for our country. What we actually needed turned out to be something completely different. The learning curve was very steep and the time taken to find the right solutions was long. A good example of that was in the convoys. If the entire capacity of the navy in 1939 was directed to convoy escorts the course of the war for Britain would have been very different and it would have been far less damaging for us in every way.

"We could not keep secret the losses we were experiencing on the convoys. The newspapers were able to get the names of every ship that was sunk. It was easy enough then to add up the tonnages of those ships. In 1942 we lost over six million tons of merchant ships. It was beyond the capacity of all the shipyards available to us to replace anything like that total tonnage in a single year. As a result the country was bleeding to death. When I went to the Admiralty in 1939 there had only been minimal planning for convoys and there were virtually no ships available to use as escorts. It took until 1943 to sort that out.

"There were dreams back in those days that sending two army divisions to France would stop any German invasion there. It was an absurd proposition when Germany already had at least 133 divisions available to it, possibly rather more.

"It has taken us until now to get to a size of army that will be able to defeat Germany in the west when we invade France in the spring. Even then we will have massive American support. In fact we have only been able to get this far with a vast amount of American help for which they have extracted an enormous price. That price will cripple our country for generations to come.

"In the meantime we have to contemplate the biggest surprise of all. Russia has been able to defeat and destroy very large parts of the German military machine with very little outside help. I have been astounded by their capabilities and the very fast speed at which they have been able to move westwards after Stalingrad. They would seem to have the capability to overwhelm the whole of Germany without any support from Britain or America. That is something we cannot and must not let them do. But what they have achieved is certainly the biggest single surprise of the war.

"Something else I could not have predicted was that America and Russia would have become, I won't say friends; perhaps co-conspirators would be a better term. When I was at Tehran it was very clear that they now have a shared agenda to reduce Britain's power in the world. I have no doubt now that that is something that they are going to achieve.

"Britain is bankrupt and we will have no capability of resisting that if they carry through with their intentions.

"At the beginning of the war Britain, together with its empire, was the most powerful state on earth. It was the only one with a global span. Long after my lifetime, when it is possible to take a long and dispassionate view of the events of the last few years it might just appear that Britain will have been the biggest losers of this war. That was certainly not intended at the outset and is not yet certain. A lot will depend on what it is possible to achieve in government after the war. The only certainties at the moment are that both America and Russia will be far more powerful than they were before the war began. Whatever happens there will be a whole new world order and we will have to take account of that.

"So, this February evening you can see that my whole mind is in a state of turmoil. At the beginning we could not predict the unpredictables. But it is now entirely those unpredicted events that are going to shape our world. I am certain that the British people do not know that. They are tired of war, I fully accept that. They are tired of the deprivations of war. They really want to go back to the pre-1939 situation, but that will not be possible under any circumstances."

He too another long sip of whisky and reached out and held her hand:

"Alice, see what you can do to help me with that lot."

Throughout the war years Alice had been able to get supplies of good food that went far beyond her rationed allowances. She had a cousin who was a farmer in North Essex and he was able to supply her with almost anything she needed. It was definitely what was called black market supplies. At the beginning of the war things had been difficult but they improved somewhat for him after the Americans arrived. His farm bordered the land occupied by the American airbase at Ridgewell that had been built in 1942. A small part of his land had been commandeered for it. As soon as they moved in he was given a contract to supply them with meat and vegetables. It was a very lucrative contract and it also enabled him to swap some of those items for things that they imported to Britain but which were not otherwise available in the country. Fresh citrus fruit was just one example.

For that evening he had been able to get her some trout from his own lake that she could use as a starter and a fine pork joint for the main course. There were suitable wines to match. Whatever else they were going to speak about that evening and night they were certainly going to have a good relaxing meal together.

She had filleted the trout and served them with a fresh lemon mayonnaise. After she had served them she said to him:

"Look, Winston, I have said to you many times before that you cannot solve problems by looking at the big picture alone. Solving problems is all about taking action. To decide what action is needed you have to break that big picture down into all of its constituent parts and then decide what action is needed to cure, correct or improve each single part. When you assemble them together again you should have a solution to the whole problem.

"Now some of the things you have told me this evening clearly have no solution at this time. For example, you probably can do nothing about the huge military power in Russia. That has obviously been developed in the short term to deal with an horrendous threat to their country. Back in 1939 no one could have predicted either the threat or the response.

"So what I am suggesting is that we try and break down your big picture into some much smaller units and then see what is possible. Are you happy with that?"

Over the hours that followed Alice was able to debate with him the priority issues, the things he could and could not do anything about, what Britain might want to achieve by the end of the war, what had to be done to achieve military victory in Europe.

It was a little after midnight that he completely accepted that he could not control the big picture. He could do nothing about Russia. Russia already had by far the most powerful and successful army in the world. That had to be accepted as a fact.

He accepted that he could do nothing at that time about the agreements he had entered into with America. They may or may not be re-negotiable some time in to the future. That would depend on relative positions at the time and whether Britain was then stronger than it was now.

The most important outcome was that he accepted that the most important thing for him to do was finish the job that he had been appointed to do; that was to win the war. Nothing really mattered until that was achieved. During that part of their debate Winston had argued that the implementation of the peace was a vital part of winning the war. But Alice pointed out to him that Roosevelt was due to face a general election that autumn. His war record would be judged by the American people then. She also pointed out that he would have to face a general election as soon as practicable after the war had ended. It was possible to be optimistic about the outcome and it was possible to plan for it but at the moment there were too many uncertainties for there to be any useful point in trying to plan for all the details. Win the war first and then try and win the peace was her advice.

Winston wanted far more than that. He wanted to be the architect of a lasting peace in Europe as well but he accepted that night that he had much more important priorities to pursue before he could get to that.

It was a quiet night in warfare terms. There had been no convoy battles and there had been no air raids on Britain; nor had there been any air raids on Germany. The weather had been far too bad for any of that. There was no need for him to be in the War Rooms under Whitehall.

He left around two in the morning. It had been snowing in London during the night. When his driver collected him the streets had only been partly cleared of snow and there was very little traffic about. It was a slow drive back to Downing Street. But on the way there he was quite clear in his mind that the only priority he could pursue was that the war had to be won. Everything else would have to wait.

* * *

March 15, 1944. For several months now Winston has been meeting General Eisenhower at least twice a week for a briefing on the build-up of allied forces for the landings in the spring. The date for the landings has been set as May 1st and this is now being called D-Day.

The landings will, take place in Normandy. All the intelligence we are getting from Germany suggests that they expect them to take place much farther east. This has caused us to create numerous army camps in the south-east, although some of them are dummies. We have been doing this to confuse the enemy's aerial reconnaissance.

Yesterday I went with Winston to inspect several camps in Dorset. We visited both British and American bases and we went to the naval base at Portland. It was obvious that morale was excellent and that they are all yearning to go.

We had lunch with the American General George Patton at a camp near Bridport. It was the first time Winston had met him. He had commanded the Torch landings in North Africa and was with Montgomery in Sicily. Winston was very impressed by his positive attitude.

* * *

It was not possible for the allied landings to take place in France on May 1st. There had been last minute hitches in the supply of key equipment and the weather was also too bad at that time. D-Day, as it was being called was initially postponed until June 1st but the weather then would have made safe landings on the Normandy beaches impossible. The weather started to clear by the evening of June 4th so the landings were ordered for June 6th.

The initial landings went far better than allied planners had dared hope. Objectives for the first day were all attained and armoured forces started to move inland. German resistance was persistent but not strong. Germany had not expected the landings to be in Normandy. Such defences as they had prepared were in the Pas de Calais area, far to the east.

* * *

June 6, 1944. The vast convoys carrying troops and equipment left ports all across the south of England during last evening for their destinations in Normandy. We went down to Portsmouth yesterday to see some of them off.

We started off there by going out into the Solent on HMS Nottingham. She is a destroyer which has been in many convoy battles. Winston enjoyed talking to her captain about his experiences.

The Solent seemed to be absolutely full of ships. There seemed to be every type there from tank landing craft up to battleships. In the early evening they all started leaving for France. It was a stunning sight. All day long the skies over all of southern England and the Channel were being patrolled continuously by both British and American aircraft. It was very noisy.

Eisenhower was there and he gave us a final briefing before the movements started. While we were with him he gave the final orders for movements to start at 1800 hours. Within minutes we saw the first ships leave.

As Winston saw them go he said: "Herr Hitler, we are now unleashing on you an armoured might which will surely crush you. May this soon lead to the end of this terrible war."

After that he stood still and silent for several minutes. After a final wave to those brave ships we returned to London to listen to the progress of the battle.

The landings were timed for dawn today, although thousands of parachute troops were landed during the night. All morning we have had a barrage of messages about the progress in Normandy. Eisenhower telephones Winston each hour to report on progress. All the indications are that the objectives are being met. Initial German resistance has been low, but this will obviously change. Winston is delighted with the way things are going.

* * *

June 7, 1944. Things seem to be going very well in Normandy. Eisenhower is happy that the initial objectives are being achieved. But there ware still massive German forces in the west and there are increasing indications that they are being moved to counter the threat that we have created for them.

There is equally good news coming from Russia. Over last winter and this spring they have made massive advances and are now developing a front round the city of Minsk. Stalin has told Winston that they will soon take that city and then drive for the Polish border.

I looked at the Russian maps with Winston today. The Russian advances have been massive. It can only be a matter of weeks now before the last of the German armies are ejected from Russian soil.

Winston is hoping that we will make such rapid progress in the west that it will be possible to get within range of Berlin long before the Russians have any chance of being there. But that will depend on us maintaining very fast progress. As Winston keeps saying the delays to D-Day have cost us dearly. If we had been able to launch it five weeks earlier we would now be five weeks nearer to Berlin.

* * *

July 3, 1944. German reinforcements have arrived in a big way in Normandy. Our forces have ground to a halt around the city of Caen. Eisenhower came to see Winston this morning about it. It is Eisenhower's view that the problem might not be with the German forces there which include large numbers of Hitler Youth Movement troops but with Montgomery who is the commander of all allied land forces. Eisenhower accused Montgomery of being stuck in trench warfare tactics and not able to think round the problem.

The result was another angry Churchill. He had appointed Montgomery to lead Eighth Army at El Alamein. He promised him then that a victory at El Alamein would mean that he was the senior British land commander. Montgomery delivered at El Alamein although it was a dreadful battle. So Winston feels loyal to him.

But Eisenhower made it clear that only days remained for Monty to win at Caen. If he had not solved the problem within three weeks he would be moved to another job and America would take over completely at Caen.

Winston phoned Roosevelt today to get some mitigation from Eisenhower's decision but FDR was not sympathetic. He reminded Winston that America had made an unlimited commitment to winning the war. If that included ditching failing British generals then so be it. FDR apparently told him that he would always uphold Eisenhower's judgments. W. was not happy.

He also spoke to Monty today. Monty was in his HQ near Caen. He was certain that he could grind down the Germans and that the constant American interference was not helping. W. was OK about that. But Winston did warn him that the pressure from the Americans was intense.

*　*　*

July 20, 1944. This has been an extraordinary day dominated by news that there has been an assassination attempt on Hitler. It was carried out by the same group of people who were involved in the meeting in Santander. Several hours after the attempt it is obvious that Hitler is still alive.

Winston is all for getting rid of Hitler but he is not tolerant of people who cannot achieve their objectives. He has told me he is relieved that the Santander meeting achieved nothing. Botched conspiracies are no part of his world. He hopes that that will be the end of the Beck-Goerdeler group. He is completely certain that unconditional surrender is the only option. Whatever his differences with Roosevelt he agrees absolutely about that.

Winston had never told me about this group before. I have no idea how long he has known about them. But it all sounds extremely odd. Winston categorically told me that they were a group plotting against Hitler. But for the German delegation to that meeting to be led by Admiral Canaris who is Head of State Security makes it very curious indeed. I wonder how he was able to leave Germany at this time. I am very suspicious of the whole thing. I cannot help thinking that diplomats must be behind it all. I must try and find out more about it.

*　*　*

July 23, 1944. Eisenhower came to see Winston today. I was present at the meeting. Ike said that he had just spoken to FDR and had told him that Monty had to be removed as Allied Land Commander. It was Ike's view that the man was completely incompetent and was seriously prejudicing the allied war effort. His campaign at Caen was causing massive allied casualties and delaying the advance of the armies. Accordingly he was going to tell him that day that he would be replaced by Patton as Land Commander. Britain could do whatever it wanted with the man but America was going to take over Land Command.

Eisenhower went on to say something which was far more important.

He said: "Tomorrow we are going to crush the Germans at Caen and we are going to move forward to Paris. We will crush them within a single day. You can say whatever you like about it but FDR has approved it. We cannot tolerate any more delays."

Winston was staggered that any American campaign could achieve within a single day what had already taken Montgomery several weeks to achieve. He tried to argue with Eisenhower but he was having none of it. So far as Ike was concerned the German forces around Caen were going to be destroyed tomorrow.

*　*　*

July 24, 1994. The Americans attacked the Caen sector this morning with 3,000 bombers. They called it carpet bombing. Within an hour they had destroyed all the fighting capabilities of the German defenders of that city. It was a truly awesome demonstration of what America can achieve. As a result the armies are now on the move towards Paris.

Winston is satisfied that we should not have tolerated the standstill at Caen even for a day. Although he does not like it he does accept that America has all the power to deal with a crisis like that.

But yet again the balance of power has changed. Eisenhower was proved to be right and his personal authority has increased considerably as a result. Winston is sure that Roosevelt will listen to him even more. Patton led the first American troops on from Caen. He will be in Paris now within a few days. Winston has been poring over maps all day. He is fearful that those wasted weeks at Caen will prevent us from getting into Germany this year.

* * *

Although the D-Day landings did secure a bridgehead for the allies in Normandy, the rapid advance into France that had been planned by General Montgomery as Commander of all allied land forces ground to a halt round the French city of Caen. Almost all of July was taken up with trying to destroy German forces that had ringed that city. The failure to make rapid advances caused severe tensions in the allied headquarters and the military campaign was ultimately successful only by the application of massive air power, mainly American, in destroying all German armour and communications prior to a big push by the allied tank armies towards the end of the month.

Caen has been called the "Stalingrad of the Hitler Youth", largely because a unit called the Hitler Youth Division lost 4,000 dead and another 8,000 wounded. The division was wiped out.

All in all the German losses at Caen were 210,000 prisoners and 240, 000 casualties. It was a small battle compared with most of those that had or were taking place in the east but it was by far the most important battle between the allies and Germany in the west. It was the biggest single battle in which Britain was involved in the entire war.

General Eisenhower was not happy with the command of the battle and relieved Montgomery of his post as Ground Forces Commander. After that his highest command in wartime was as commander of the 21st Army Group.

The allies made swift advances eastwards after that and by the late autumn they had reached the Rhine River and were poised to enter Germany itself. That they did not do so was the effect of the agreement between Roosevelt and Stalin at Tehran. They had agreed then that Russia would take most of Berlin. Eisenhower's armies had to wait on the Rhine River until Russia was much nearer Berlin. But in December the Anglo-American forces were far nearer Berlin than were the Russian forces. Eisenhower was in a position then to have taken Berlin well before any Red Army troops could have had any prospect of being there.

* * *

July 28, 1944. I had lunch with Ronnie Harford today. He moved to his present job of Commander of the Household Division about six months ago. I was certain that he must have known something about the Beck-Goerdeler plot in Germany. I was sure that if he did he would tell me about it.

I was stunned by what he had to tell me:

"Yes, we have been keeping an eye on that one for several years. It is a complete mystery to me that it has not done more to get rid of Hitler. von Manstein, Guderian and Rommel are active members of the group and they have unlimited resources to get rid of him if they wish. There must also have been plenty of opportunities. The first attempt on Hitler's life was made on a flight taking him back to Germany after a battle planning meeting for Kursk on 10th June, 1943. Everyone involved in managing that flight was shot. So perhaps fear of failure kept them back from making other attempts. The latest attempt was planned in great detail but botched at the last minute by von Stauffenburg. I would be surprised if anyone else tries now given Hitler's response and the summary justice involved.

"Something that has intrigued us is that the Foreign Office have maintained regular contacts with the group. The official involved is called Michael Curtis. There is circumstantial evidence that Eden has met them once but we cannot prove it.

"The group first met with the British Government long before the war. Our files include a reference to a meeting Churchill had with von Manstein and Guderian early in 1937 at Chartwell. We have no idea what was discussed. I have reviewed that file regularly and it is entirely possible that even then they were seeking Winston's support for a plot against Hitler. There is no evidence for that and we will probably never know the truth.

"As we now know the meeting in Santander came to nothing. It probably never had any prospect of success, so why did it take place? Did Winston know something very important about it? We will probably never know the answer to that either.

"All along I have been intrigued by the Foreign Office interest in this. Michael Curtis does not have anything to do with the German desk there nor is he in any policy role. As far as we can tell he reports directly to Eden, which makes his an unusual posting. We have recently come across evidence that he was a member of an organisation called Royalist International. That organisation does not seem to exist any more but when it did it seemed to be a talking shop for some very shadowy people in diplomatic circles in London. Maybe that is why he had been the link with Beck and his cronies. It is all very intriguing."

* * *

Throughout 1944 the Red Army continued to move steadily westwards. By the autumn it had reached Warsaw and was well to the west of Budapest. Its most successful operation that summer had been at Minsk, which started two weeks after the D-Day landings, where they had encircled several German armies and had taken half a million prisoners in the cauldron there. Few of those prisoners taken there were ever to return to Germany. Most died in captivity.

* * *

Another summit between the three leaders had been planned to take place in September 1944 at Quebec. Again it was impossible for Stalin to attend. He regarded the management of the war in Russia to be of far greater importance. The Red Army was already in Poland and he wanted to be able to take the maximum advantage of any German troop withdrawals.

But nevertheless Roosevelt and Churchill did meet. But they went out of their way to make progress in such a way that Russia did not feel shut out of the discussions. In particular the conference record was to show no possible trace of any conspiracy against Stalin.

* * *

September 9, 1944. We flew to Quebec today. It is such a long way across the Atlantic. It is always noisy on those damned aeroplanes and today's flight was bumpy as well. BOAC do their best to look after us and they provide good amenities on board but the Skymaster is still noisy and cannot cross the Atlantic without refuelling. As always we stopped twice today at Prestwick and Gander. BOAC always seem to provide the same captain for us. His name is Vivian Slight. He is a very genial man and I am sure that Winston will want him to receive a gong at some stage. When we eventually arrived we were greeted by Mackenzie King, the Canadian Prime Minister. Winston thanked him for the Canadian war contributions.

All the way across the Atlantic Winston was obsessed about the problem of Berlin. I cannot count the number of times he asked me the questions; "How can I persuade Roosevelt that we must gain control of Berlin before the Russians have any chance of getting there? We saw what American fire power could do at Caen. Why cannot they do that all the way to Berlin and ensure that the Russians never get there?"

They were questions that I could not answer. Only Roosevelt could and I was sure that he was going to reject any argument that Winston made on this. I tried to tell Winston that it had all been agreed at Tehran. But he was not listening.

* * *

September 10, 1944. We all met Roosevelt for breakfast this morning. He looked shockingly ill. It was also obvious that his concentration span was close to zero. He had to leave after about half an hour to have a rest. We could not meet him again for three hours. When he did talk he did not seem to be as sharp and incisive as he had been before. Winston is deeply shocked by it all. Whatever their differences W. has regarded FDR as a constant rock throughout this war. FDR has seemed to have a constant vision of the future. He has never deviated in any way from his commitment to bring about the unconditional surrender of Germany. He has ruthlessly followed that vision. In doing that he has probably saved

Britain. Winston deeply wishes that we could have done it on our own but after the American ruthlessness at Caen he knows that that was impossible.

He is now frightened that Roosevelt might not live to see the end of his work. He is seriously worried about what that will mean for Britain.

Roosevelt is facing re-election in two months time and no one knows who his vice-president will be. It all creates huge uncertainties in the allied position.

* * *

Churchill had been thoroughly stung by the rapid advance of the Red Armies through the Ukraine and Belarus towards Poland and Germany throughout the summer of 1944. The power and resources that they were displaying were truly awesome and far greater than anything Britain or America had ever imagined to be possible. Churchill had come to believe that armed forces on that scale and with that power would make Russia the dominant power in Europe for many a long year to come. After Kursk anything was possible but the sheer scale of it all still shocked Winston.

Lord Moran, Winston's doctor wrote in his diary at the time that "Winston never talks of Hitler these days. He is always harping on about the dangers of Communism. The advance of the Red Army has taken possession of his mind."

As a consequence Winston had started to re-examine his views about a post-war Germany. Just one of those ideas was that Britain might need German support in the future in order to counter any possible threat from Russia. It was then an extraordinary idea given the extreme hostility between the two countries. But Churchill was always looking to the achievement of his own ambition which was the protection and development of the Empire.

* * *

September 15, 1944. Before we left for the conference centre today Winston wanted to talk about the latest missive he had received from our Ambassador in Moscow. He was called into see Molotov yesterday. He had been warned by Molotov that Russia would not tolerate any future alliance between its war partners and Germany. Apparently Roosevelt had received a similar message at about the same time. None of us have any way of knowing why Russia might be so sensitive to that now when we are approaching the final stages of defeating Germany. The only justification that Molotov had offered was that both America and Britain had been extremely dilatory in responding to Russia's requests for the opening of a second front.

It is impossible to do a full analysis of such a message within a few minutes of receiving it but in naval parlance it certainly seems to be a shot across the bows. Winston is so fearful of Russian ambitions that he feels that we may have to bring Germany into some new alliance in order to counter those threats. It is all looking very confusing. I have no idea how he could possibly even begin to explain such a change of position to the British people. No doubt he will find a way.

* * *

September 15, 1944. Winston is pleased with the way that this conference is going. Lend/Lease has been so important for Britain that he wants it to continue after the war. Roosevelt readily agreed to that on the same financial terms as before. Later Winston was baffled as to why FDR agreed so easily. Eventually he put it down to his health.

Another thing Winston wanted was a statement about re-affirming the allied intentions to crush German industrial capability at the end of the war. This was baffling to me because he had publicly said something quite different before we left Britain. It was also something that had been discussed and agreed at Tehran. It was almost as if Winston could not remember what he had done then. That caused a huge row with Anthony Eden. It might have been a sop to Russia.

* * *

September 19, 1944. In phone links with Stalin today it has been agreed that Germany will be divided into three occupation zones as soon as the war is over. Britain will be responsible for all German territory north of the Ruhr and west of the final frontline with Russia. Winston wanted this to be based on the pre-war German borders but neither Stalin nor Roosevelt was even prepared to consider that. They reminded him that their agreement to for the armies to meet in Berlin was paramount and would affect everything.

This evening Winston expressed the view that despite the agreements reached Quebec seem to have been dominated by growing divisions between the allies.

* * *

October 6, 1944. We arrived in Moscow today. Winston has requested a private meeting with Stalin. Winston wants to do a deal with him about the carving up of territories in eastern Europe. In requesting the meeting W. had explained to Stalin that the purpose of it was to do a deal under which the two most powerful countries in Europe were to conspire together to find some mutual benefit by imposing some territorial solutions on smaller states. Churchill knew that he was going there in defiance of advice from Alice and FDR, but he simply could not resist getting involved in the design of post-war Europe. To him it was like a completely irresistible drug. He had to be involved in it all.

The circumstances of the meeting are not encouraging. Stalin has described Churchill in particular, but the British generally, as enjoying nothing more than tricking their allies. That hardly makes for a trustful or enduring agreement.

Winston has a more pragmatic view. He knows that, given the power of the Red Army, no one will be able to eject Russia from any conquered territory. There, therefore, has to be an agreement of some sort. He wants his name to be on that agreement. Whatever else he does he wants to save some part of Europe from communism. But he has a further ambition that has never been raised with Roosevelt or Stalin before and it goes far beyond Stalin's own demands for control over Eastern Europe.

Winston is prepared to concede far more territory to Stalin than has ever been discussed before but in return for Britain gaining control over Greece and Turkey.

* * *

October 7, 1944. Winston told me this evening that he presented Stalin with a hand written document, in his own hand, which proposed a new division of Eastern Europe after the war. It was neither approved nor disapproved by Stalin but it did go beyond Stalin's greatest expectations. It also set out exactly what Winston wanted and was prepared to concede.

Essentially W. proposed that in addition to the territories that Stalin had gained under the Molotov-Ribbentrop agreement the Soviet Union should also control Romania, Bulgaria, Hungary, Czechoslovakia, several Baltic States and what is to become Yugoslavia. By getting Greece and Turkey in return Winston is planning to incorporate both those countries into the British Empire. W. told me because the plan involved expansion of the British Empire he could never have discussed it with Roosevelt in advance.

It seems to me that what he has gained is insignificantly different, at least in principle, from what Chamberlain had wanted back in those years before the war had started. Chamberlain had been quite happy to give away the freedom of entire nations without consultation or negotiation involving those nations. Winston seems to be happy to do the same. He wants to control Greece and Turkey as part of his imperial dream. The price for that is to give away the freedom of several states. Bulgaria, Romania, Hungary, Poland, Estonia, Latvia and Lithuania are all sacrificial lambs on the altar of the last of British imperial dreams. I am staggered by it.

* * *

October 6, 1959. Alice told me today about her talks with Winston after that trip he made to Moscow in October, 1944. She said to me:

"He came to see me a couple of days after he had got back from Moscow. He always came to see me when he was hit by crisis. That was certainly the case that day. His main problem was that he was being castigated by Roosevelt for even having gone to Moscow. On top of that Roosevelt was furious that he had given Russian control to numerous states when it had been the American ambition to ensure that those same states were democratically controlled.

"I do not know why he went to Moscow then; there was absolutely no need to do that or any other deal. I have thought about it many times and the only conclusion I can reach is that it was a last attempt by him to impose his stamp on the future of Europe. It was probably the only time when he came to me with a problem that I was unable to help him. The whole episode was surreal. One of the things he told me was that Stalin had taken him to his dacha outside Moscow. He claimed that he was taken into Stalin's family and that they were friends.

"The whole incident has troubled me ever since because Russia did take control over all the territories suggested by Winston but Britain got nothing in return. It was such a shabby deal that President Truman, Roosevelt's successor, was later to deny that it had even happened.

"Winston told me several years later that that he regretted going to Moscow for that meeting. In his later reflections he had come to the view that it had seriously undermined his relationship with Roosevelt and it also undermined his own credentials to be anti-communist. It also gave Stalin the idea of a heavily defended frontier between Russia and Western Europe. It created in his mind the first notion of an Iron Curtain across Europe. But he was in no doubt then that it strengthened Stalin's hand in the negotiations they had at Yalta with a few months later.

"It was to turn out to be a short-term deal for Britain with no merit. I have never been able to work out why it was necessary. You were there, could you work it out?"

I had to answer that I could not.

* * *

As his dairy makes clear, in January 1945 Stalin regarded a Russian capture of Berlin as anything but certain. He knew all about his agreement with Roosevelt that Russia would be allowed to take most of the city and would meet with Anglo-American troops in the western suburbs. He also knew that the Anglo-American troops were far closer to Berlin than any Russian armies. For him it was a very tense situation, it was so tense that he simply did not believe that he could trust either Roosevelt or Churchill to keep to the agreement. Equally he did not trust the Germans to abandon their frontline on the Rhine in order to move forces east to weaken the final advances of the Red Army.

In talks with colleagues he was particularly doubtful of Churchill's position. He was sure that he would do anything to reach a separate peace with Germany in order simply to prevent Russian access to the city. Stalin's spies had been tracking Eden since he first met Goerdeler. They were certain that he was trying to negotiate some kind of anti-Russian deal. All the information to him indicated that Russia would have to look after its own interests and make its own decisions.

All the way through the autumn of 1944 Stalin agonised over the final solution for Berlin. The record shows that he had an endless string of meetings with STAVKA and Zhukov. All those meetings showed that Russia had the resources to overwhelm Germany. In the atmosphere of distrust which existed between Russia and her allies Stalin decided on December 10th, 1944 that he would not consult any further with them but that he would honour his agreement with

Roosevelt about the armies meeting up in the western suburbs of Berlin. He did that solely because he believed it to be the lowest risk option for Russia.

* * *

Stalin unleashed the Battle for Berlin on 11th January, 1945 but he was so worried about Anglo-American intentions that he hit on a uniquely Stalinesque solution to prevent them getting anywhere near Berlin before it could be captured by some part of the Red Army. In order to speed up the advance of the Red Army he ordered his three senior generals to compete for the honour to take Berlin. It was to be a race and they were all charged with getting to Berlin as soon as possible.

He gave the right flank to Rokossovskii, the left flank to General Konev and the most difficult centre to Zhukov. All of them had fought as a team all the way from Stalingrad through to the centre of Poland. They formed the greatest command team ever in all military history. Now they were forced to be rivals. They had to fight it out between them who would win. It was not something that Zhukov had expected and it proved to him just how devious Stalin was. But he was determined to be the general who captured the government area of Berlin.

* * *

Roosevelt left America to go to the final war-time meeting of the Big Three at Yalta in the Crimea on the cruiser *Quincy*. It was only a couple of days after he had been inaugurated as President for the fourth time. His health had been declining for a long time now and he could only move around in a wheel chair. He expected to be away for six weeks. Quincy took him as far as Malta where he and his party joined the first ever presidential aircraft, called *Sacred Cow,* for the flight to the Crimean town of Saki. It seemed an odd name for a Presidential aircraft. From there it was a six hour drive to Yalta. There was a Russian military guard throughout the entire length of the route. He arrived there on Saturday February 5, 1945. The American delegation to Yalta was so large that it actually needed 35 aircraft to transport it to Saki. Churchill said that in selecting Yalta Stalin *'could not have chosen a worse place in the world.'*

Roosevelt's first meeting with Stalin was the following afternoon. At that meeting Roosevelt said that he had been having problems with the British, the first was over the proposed division of Germany. Stalin asked Roosevelt what impact he saw on the British Empire as a result of the war. Roosevelt made no specific reply but he did tell Stalin that he thought that Britain would have to review its involvement in it all. There were obviously many big problems at home with which Britain would have to deal first. The second problem was the reduction in British power in the world.

The three leaders started out with very different objectives. Roosevelt wanted to pin Stalin down to help with the war in Asia as soon as European hostilities had ceased. He had come to the view that most of the European problems were impossible to solve.

* * *

February 5, 1945. We have arrived in this ghastly hell hole today. It might have been a nice city a few years ago. But it is now a wreck. The Germans reached this far and there is evidence of the fighting everywhere. There are still dead tanks and guns in the streets. I can only assume that Stalin has a vindictive sense of humour otherwise he could not possibly have selected Yalta for this vital meeting.

I cannot imagine that this will be a successful conference. All the preparatory papers indicate that there are huge differences between the allies.

Winston wants the so-called special relationship with America to continue after the war. In seeking that he wants continuing American involvement in Europe for a lengthy but indefinite period of time. His other objective is to create a new balance of power in Europe.

Stalin's objectives are all about the future security of the Soviet Union. His messages indicate that never again can his country expose itself to such an appalling invasion as it has suffered under Germany.

The American position is that they want to see the development of democracies. They want every country in Europe to be a full fledged democracy very quickly and they will do whatever is necessary to achieve that. They also want democratic standards to apply throughout the world. Winston is furious about that.

The other American issue on which Roosevelt is very keen is support for America in bringing the war in the Pacific to an end.

I have never been to a large international meeting before where the objectives of the participants have been so diverse.

* * *

February 10, 1945. This impossible conference is drawing to a close. I cannot imagine why we agreed to hold it and I cannot really understand why anyone thought there would be any useful outcomes.

Roosevelt has been seriously ill throughout. He has been brilliantly nursed by his daughter throughout but he has hardly been able to participate in any of the meetings.

Stalin has been in a victorious and complacent mood throughout. For most of each day he has been in military conferences as his generals lead what can only be called a massive Red Army storm devouring everything in its path as it advances towards Berlin. That is more important to him than anything that takes place here.

None of these key agenda items were progressed in any significant way. The first plenary session between the three leaders took place on the Monday. The meetings have lasted a week and they were difficult and fractious. Eventually the talks narrowed down to three main issues: the division of Germany, reparations and the treatment of war criminals.

They did reach agreement on German division which formed the basis of the last orders given by Roosevelt to Eisenhower a couple of days ago. They reaffirmed the Tehran agreement on Berlin. Winston is furious about that.

The meetings also fully met Stalin's expectations and the hopes that he had harboured after his meeting with Churchill in October. It is quite clear in hindsight that Roosevelt did not know to what he was agreeing on this point, but he did feel that he had been sold short by Churchill. He made that clear.

They did agree to set up a war crimes tribunal. That seems to be a more sensible solution than just shooting 50,000 German officers that was agreed to by FDR and Stalin at Tehran.

But they did not reach agreement on reparations. Soviet demands on this were for the equivalent of twenty billion dollars of reparations to be extracted from Germany. Winston's view on this was that twenty billion dollars, of which half would go to the Soviet Union, was entirely unrealistic. He doubted that any reparations would be possible. In his argument he added that "no victorious country will come out as financially burdened as Britain." In doing so he realised that Britain could get nothing from Germany other than a military victory.

The Big Three did discuss how long the military occupation of Germany might be but there was nothing in the communiqué or in the agreement about it. Roosevelt had told Stalin that America expected to be there for two years, at most.

The agreed communiqué at the end of the talks was typical of all government meetings at whatever level. It was very unspecific. It talked of "the unconditional surrender we shall together impose on Nazi Germany."

The three leaders did agree to meet again as soon as practicable after the war. They also agreed that such a meeting should be in or near Berlin. It would be up to Stalin to determine exactly where.

* * *

As they left to go home both Churchill and Stalin were well aware that their alliance was at best precarious and it probably would not last long after the war ended. Roosevelt was already moving on to other matters in the Far East where he was anxious to end the war as soon as possible. He knew that there would be intense pressure on him to achieve that as soon as there was a ceasefire in Germany. He had plans about that that he could not share with anyone.

Stalin also knew that he had won all of his demands about gaining control of European territories. His personal agreement with Roosevelt made on that Sunday afternoon in Yalta guaranteed that it would be the Red Army who would take control of central Berlin in the last battle there. They would also control numerous Balkan and Baltic states as well. Churchill had made that agreement inevitable.

Throughout the conference Roosevelt had been unwell. He had been looked after by his daughter, Anna, and two doctors but when he arrived back in Washington after five weeks away he was completely exhausted.

* * *

Towards the end of the war and as the Red Army began to close in on Berlin Hitler told his senior people that he had really had no choice about attacking Russia. He explained that his objective had been to force the British into a peace deal. He could then only envisage that happening if Germany was to destroy any British hopes of Russian intervention. Furthermore, he went on to say that for Germany to dominate Europe, Russia had to disappear. But what he really wanted was to force Britain to a deal under which Germany could gain control of British Middle Eastern interests. In other words Germany wanted exactly what Russia wanted from Britain. It did not seem to be a convincing reason for the most disastrous war in history.

* * *

On March 29th, 1945 Roosevelt went away from Washington for some rest in his own house in Warm Springs, Georgia. It was one of his favourite places and he had designed the house himself.

Just before he left he appointed General Lucius Clay as the German military governor of Germany. In the final interview Roosevelt told Clay that what was required for the whole of Germany was something like a giant Tennessee Valley Authority. That had done very well for America and was very popular, so the same model could surely easily be used in Germany. What he wanted to see was huge American investment in the re-building of Germany.

Roosevelt was certainly not looking well when he left Washington. He told friends that he needed lots of sleep. He had also lost a lot of weight in just a few weeks.

In his last few days Roosevelt had no idea that his illness was so severe. He talked with friends and colleagues about his expectations for the future and of starting all the post war efforts in Germany and Europe that would be needed for economic re-habilitation. He talked of leading America until the next presidential election in 1948. Although he was very tired and spent a lot of time asleep he was in an optimistic frame of mind.

When he woke on the morning of April 12th, his illness had taken a turn for the worse. By that evening he was dead.

* * *

Harry S.Truman had been American Vice-President since inauguration day in January. Although he had been a senator for many years he had never held any government office. Since inauguration day Roosevelt had never discussed any aspect of the war or any peace plans with him. Indeed they had hardly spoken about anything.

When he first had to take control of all government affairs on the morning of April 13th Truman was in a considerable state of confusion. Not only had Roosevelt just not told him anything, he had never confided his innermost thoughts in anyone else either.

But what he was told that first morning in the Oval Office was that Roosevelt kept all his wartime papers in a room called the Map Room. Truman had had no idea even that such a room existed. So he went there and started to read. What he read first of all were the agreements into which Roosevelt had entered: The Atlantic Alliance, Casablanca, Tehran, Quebec, Yalta, and the various Lend/Lease deals with Britain. He noted on Roosevelt's personal copy of the Yalta agreement that he had written in the margin at the appropriate place; *Let us hope that it will be possible for us to stay in Germany only for less than two years*. He read also some notes that Roosevelt had written about the Atlantic Alliance. He decided immediately that he would stick to the letter of all of those agreements. From the notes he knew exactly what Roosevelt had intended in relation to Britain. It seemed not only to be right for America, it would be enjoyable to carry it through.

He was staggered by the scale of Lend/Lease to Britain. During the war America had supplied 22,000 aircraft, 13,000 tanks and self-propelled guns, more than two hundred convoy escorts and nearly a thousand Liberty ships. The overall value of the British deals was $31 billion. The contribution to Russia had been almost entirely in transport equipment including a hundred thousand six wheel drive trucks and 2,000 railway locomotives.

He was called by Churchill later that day. The first part of the conversation was sorrow about the death of Roosevelt as a truly great leader. Then there were the congratulations and best wishes from "a true friend of the United States." Then there was a new assessment of the military situation in Germany. British and American troops had finally forced the surrender of 150,000 German troops in the Ruhr and the way was clear now to drive straight for Berlin. He proposed that new instructions be given to Eisenhower to achieve that before the Russians could get there. Truman had read the Tehran and Yalta discussions about that and knew that it was clearly agreed between Roosevelt and Stalin that Russia should have the key pickings there. Britain and America would only be allowed to get to the western suburbs. So he made his first executive decision as President and said to Churchill;

"Look, I know exactly what we have agreed with Stalin. I have no intention of changing anything in those agreements other than by negotiation. If we unilaterally deviate from those agreements how can we expect Russia to conform to them?"

Churchill knew that he had lost that argument for the final time. The sense of depression that had gripped him after Tehran returned with a vengeance. He was not looking forward to meeting Truman.

Next Truman met with Lucius Clay. He told Truman of Roosevelt's vision for Germany and about the industrial re-building that would be needed if Germany was going to become a peaceful and prosperous state again. They talked about the Tennessee Valley Authority idea. Truman was happy with all that and he told Clay that he would fully support him to achieve those ideas.

Soon after that Truman tackled the problem of Henry Morgenthau who had been Treasury Secretary throughout Roosevelt's presidential terms. Morgenthau was the only Jew in Roosevelt's cabinet and it was he who had handled the detail of the Lend/Lease deals. He had also been the author of the Morgenthau Plan which called for Germany to be dismembered of all its industrial capability forever after the war and returned to being purely an agricultural economy. The plan had been extensively published and promoted by Morgenthau but never adopted by Roosevelt. Truman had other ideas about it in his first few days in office.

So he called Morgenthau into the Oval Office one morning and told him that the Morgenthau Plan was not going to be adopted and was to be scrapped. He did not want to hear anything about it ever again. He went on to say that he could not possibly see how a plan to turn one of the greatest industrial nations in the world into a subsistence state could do anything other than provide a focus for revolution. He finished by saying "If you kick a man while he is down he will never forget it." He then sacked Morgenthau. The fact that he was a Jew was a particular source of satisfaction to Truman.

The thing that most astounded Truman was nothing to do with Europe or about being badgered by Churchill or Stalin or anyone else. It was the briefing by General Marshall the American Chief of Staff about a mysterious military establishment at Oak Ridge in Tennessee. Truman had been chairman of a senate committee investigating it but the truth about it was never disclosed to that committee. A few days after he had become President, General Marshall had rung him personally and asked whether he could come and brief him about it. Truman readily agreed because he was sure that something unusual was going on there.

Marshall began;

"Mr. President, the project that I am going to describe to you has gone under the name of The Manhattan Project. We deliberately chose to give it such a title so that if knowledge of such a project ever got into the public domain it would not be suspected as being one of the most secret military projects ever.

"It was many years ago now that your predecessor authorised work to take place on it on whatever scale was necessary. The only caveat he put on it was that secrecy had to be total. The only other member of his cabinet who knew about it was Stimson, the Defense Secretary.

"What we have been developing at Oak Ridge and at a site in New Mexico called Los Alamos is a weapon of immense destructive power. It is a least a ten thousand times as destructive as anything that we have used so far. The technology has been proved and it is based on splitting the atom. That releases huge amounts of energy. We have already had one live firing of a small version. That was done at Los Alamos a few weeks ago. I will shortly show you some pictures of that.

"We are now in the final stages of testing a definitive version of the weapon. If all goes well on that it had been our original plan to use at least one of these bombs to bring the Japanese war to an end. The schedule calls for two bombs to be ready to use live by the end of July. We could produce another fifty within two months after that. What I would like is for you to affirm that that plan can go-ahead. It has always been assumed that such a bomb can only be used against an enemy with the specific approval of the President."

They talked about it for more than two hours. At the end of it Marshall had Truman's authority to proceed. But each attack would have to have precise Presidential approval and that would have to include the name of the target city. In any event Tokyo could not appear on the initial target list.

Truman knew at the end of the meeting that he would have a very powerful negotiating hand when he met with Churchill and Stalin, whenever that was to be.

* * *

Berlin fell on 8th May, 1945 when Germany unconditionally surrendered. In the race to Berlin it was Zhukov's armies that got to the government quarter first and it was one of his troops who planted the Russian flag on the top of the Reichstag building. Konev's armies had reached the south western suburbs a couple of days earlier but had been held down by urban guerrilla warfare. American and British troops reached the western suburbs again a couple of days earlier and were held by street fighting.

That evening in London there was a vast celebrating throng marching down The Mall towards Buckingham Palace. That evening they cheered Churchill as he stood on the balcony with King George VI and the rest of the Royal Family.

The Post War Years

Louise left Washington when Roosevelt left to go to Yalta. There was no possible need for her to be there any longer. She had long finished her diplomatic work and the aircraft production programme would come to an end as soon as there was peace in Europe. It was Max Beaverbrook who persuaded her to return. He had a job for her which was likely to keep her extremely busy for a long time to come, but it was a job that would be based in Britain and it was also likely to involve considerable amounts of travel as soon as the war was over.

She had last seen Roosevelt about a week before he left for Yalta. It was the first time that she had seen him in about a month. She was very shocked by his appearance and by the fact they he obviously looked very unwell. His physical deterioration compared with their previous meeting was very marked. But he was in an excellent frame of mind, very optimistic about the forthcoming victory over Germany and absolutely certain in his own mind that it would be achieved before the middle of May. He was very pleased with everything America had done to bring it all about.

They had a long, leisurely lunch together. She knew that it would be the last time that she would see him; before she left that snowy, cold afternoon she would tell him that she would be leaving for London within a few days. She would also tell him what she would be doing there. She was sure that he would strongly support it. He might even make a financial contribution to it.

When she did tell him he agreed to arrange for ten million dollars to be sent to the appropriate account in London. It would be money from his family. It would essentially be a personal gift to her for all the good work they had done together.

He was completely unable to get out of his wheelchair that day and as she came to leave she lent down to kiss him. After that last kiss he said to her:

"Thanks, very much for all that you have done here. I know from Winston that you have always passed on my views and opinions to him very accurately. He did not like them and he never will. It is certainly going to be very interesting to see what happens as both governments go about the process of implementing the agreements that he and I made together.

"I was glad to help you with those aircraft programmes and I am very pleased that they have gone so well.

"Back in 1942 it was my view that America was going to find that dealing with Britain after the war was likely to be more difficult than disposing of Nazi Germany. That remains my view. Please do one last thing for me and tell him that."

* * *

The first serious problem with the so-called peace in Berlin in the aftermath of the surrender occurred on June 5th, less than month after the guns had fallen silent. It was at what was intended to be a routine meeting to sign documents which would have brought into being something to be called the Allied Control Council which was to be the supreme governing authority in Germany. Present at the meeting were Zhukov, Eisenhower, Montgomery and Lattre de Tasigny, the French general. France had joined the other allies for the process of governing Germany at the request of the British and she had been allocated a control zone along the French border.

Before the meeting could even get underway Zhukov had insisted that the signing of that document should wait until all the powers had withdrawn their troops to their designated control zones. He went on to say that until such time as those troops had been re-located all non-Soviet troops would be denied access to the Soviet zone of Berlin.

It was a threat that made the signing of the document impossible. America and Britain were astounded but did agree to start troop withdrawals by July 1st.

In the attempts to clarify the issues that followed and to get some resolution Stalin issued the invitation that had been promised at Yalta to Churchill and Truman to meet him at Potsdam in July. In Potsdam, just to the south west of Berlin there was an old German royal palace, called the Cecilienhof Palace that had survived all the fighting completely intact. It had all the facilities necessary for a large and secure conference.

Stalin saw that meeting as the opportunity to seal all the agreements that he had negotiated with Roosevelt and Churchill. He wanted to consolidate his power over Eastern Europe without any encumbrances. He also wanted all American and British forces to leave him alone while he got on with that. The final step in the process was to make sure that Truman was in line. Both Truman and Churchill readily accepted the invitation because they urgently wanted clarification and agreement on the control of allocated zones in Germany. Truman also wanted to consolidate America's position as the most powerful nation on earth.

What they could not have known at the time was that what Zhukov had done was create a state of tension in Berlin that was to last throughout the Cold War. He had indelibly marked the Soviet intentions on the entire governance of Germany.

* * *

June 7, 1945. Winston is very concerned about what has been happening in Berlin these last few days. He is sure that Russia is now going to close all the borders with the east. He is also sure that there will be no free access to the eastern part of Europe.

It is very difficult to talk with him about it all. After all he went to Moscow last October to do a deal with the Soviets that gave them control over the territories in the east. Now he regards that as wrong. It is impossible to work out his real position.

What he has welcomed, though, is that Stalin will be holding a conference at Potsdam in July. W. is hopeful that all these issues can be resolved then.

* * *

In the last years of the war Beaverbrook's title as a Cabinet Minister had been Lord Privy Seal. It was really the role of personal adviser to Churchill. He did not run any large government department but he was privy to many of the key issues that were coming to the fore as the war approached its end.

One that attracted his personal attention very strongly was the plight of refugees. Britain had only had to start dealing with them on a relatively small scale in France, Belgium and Holland as it had advanced from the Normandy beaches towards Germany. Even so hundreds of thousands of people were affected.

On December 7th, 1944 there was one short Cabinet discussion on the matter. Nothing was concluded but the general consensus was that the country of nationality would have to deal with the problem. As there were unlikely to be any significant numbers of British nationals as refugees it was easy for the British government to come to such a preposterous conclusion. Churchill had no serious interest in the matter then and he argued that Britain was in no position to contribute financially to any problem that there might be.

Beaverbrook was in his office at The Daily Express late that evening when he had a brain wave. He had been much disappointed by the Cabinet discussion which did not seem to offer any solution to any problem

His brain wave was that he would launch The Daily Express Refugee Charities Board. He would provide it with extensive free publicity through his newspaper and he would organise fund raising events. But above all he would seek volunteers who would be prepared to provide practical help including housing for any refugees that the charities could bring to Britain. He hoped that there would be large numbers of them.

Over the next couple of days he drew up a plan with the intention of launching the whole scheme in the New Year. He wrote to Louise and invited her to become Chief Executive of the Charities Board. He was delighted when she accepted and told him she would be flying back to Britain at the end of January.

Max Beaverbrook was under no illusions that the refugee issue was likely to be anything other than an overwhelming one for any government in Europe. He had no idea of the likely scale but it was certain to be huge. There was a vast task to perform all over Europe. Governments would have to have a role but getting the right people quickly into the refugee camps and everywhere else there were refugees was vital.

Max and Louise met yet again at the Savoy at the beginning of February. Louise was sad to see that it had become rather worn and tired since she had last been there with him before she went to Washington. They had obviously not had the money during the war to maintain their finest standards. It was a far cry from Washington where daily life seemed unaffected by the war. But they did still have plenty of Champagne. They did not go out that evening. All their time before bed was devoted to getting his charities scheme off to a very good start.

Max told her of the cabinet discussion on the issue and what had been concluded. He quoted Churchill's words exactly. She looked at him very quizzically as he was describing that discussion and why he had decided to do his own thing as a result. Basically his reasoning was that if the government was not going to do anything he would certainly have to draw the entire nation into doing something about it. It would be a great crusade for his newspaper. He was not worried that Churchill had been so negative in Cabinet. He was sure that as a personal friend he would support the cause.

The one clear decision that they reached that night was that Max would organise a launching event to take place as soon as possible after Churchill returned from Yalta. Louise wanted the Prime Minister to be the principal guest at the inaugural event and she was sure that Max would be able to persuade him to be there. Winston's support was essential for national credibility.

That event took place towards the end of February at the Strand Palace Hotel in London. Churchill was happy to be there and give the event the support of his prestige. He was also happy to speak in support of the cause at such an event. But beyond that he could not give any greater commitment at that time. It was certainly the most glittering event to have been held in London for many years. The pledges to contribute funds were announced at regular intervals. About half way through Beaverbrook announced what Roosevelt had volunteered to pay during his last meeting with Louise and after that the pledges increased rapidly.

It was after about the first hour that Louise found herself standing next to the Prime Minister. It was exactly the occasion she had wanted to happen. Anyway she had deliberately moved so that she would be next to him. She looked at him and said;

"Prime Minister, the only time we have met before was at that dinner party given by Max Beaverbrook back in 1936 when you met von Ribbentrop for the first time. You may remember me from then, but it is a long while ago now.

"When Max introduced the proceedings this evening you will have seen me on the podium and you will know that I am going to run this excellent charity for him. It is something that I look forward to very much.

"But there is something much more important about me that you cannot possibly know. It is certainly something that we need to talk about. You may be very surprised about it. I need to tell you about it and I am sure that as a result we will need to meet again very soon for a conversation that we cannot possibly have here this evening.

"You see, Prime Minister, I was your person in the White House. I was the person codenamed Bradman. You were probably very surprised when you heard that the Foreign Office had effectively managed to get someone into the White House who had access to at least some of Roosevelt's personal secrets and thoughts. But they did and that person was me. It was a wonderful job. I had an assumed name then, which I used while I was attached to the British Embassy; it was Angela Smith. I tried to pass on to you everything that was going on in Rossevelt's office but I always thought that what I was saying was not being fully understood in London. Roosevelt was really very anti-British, you know.

"Just before the war began you had lunch with Max and you agreed to write something for his paper about the war being imminent. It was me who gave him that information. You see, until a couple of days before that I had been a plant in the Russian Defence Ministry. I had access to many of their secrets and they were all passed back to London. I was very sad to hear later that very few of them had been acted on by London."

Winston interrupted:

"Well, well, it is a real pleasure to meet you. I often wondered who they had got do to do all that work. Yes I got lots of good information from you. I knew from the first stormy meeting that I had with him what his main agenda was. It will take a long while for it all to come out in public and I will be dead long before that. But you have to look at the choices available to me at that time and throughout the war. Britain could not have completed the war without American help. They were tense and difficult times and the British position may well be judged harshly by historians. I do not know. But what I do know was that I was always fighting to protect Britain's position as the leading world power.

"I would love to talk more to you about all this but as you have said we cannot possibly do so here tonight. Please come to Chartwell for the weekend, and we will talk more then. I will be looking forward to it."

* * *

Louise arrived at Chartwell in time for lunch on the following Saturday. It was a bright warm early spring morning. When she arrived by taxi from the local station of Oxted Winston was walking across the recently mown lawns admiring the spring flowers. There seemed to be masses of daffodil and crocus everywhere. They walked around the grounds for fifteen minutes and Winston showed her all the walls he had created in those wilderness years.

As it was warm enough to sit out for a while they had their pre-lunch drinks on a sheltered south facing terrace. Winston had whisky, Louise had gin and tonic. As soon as the drinks had been served he said to her:

"Louise, I was amazed when you told me the other day about the work you had been doing in Washington. I was even more amazed when you told me about your work in Russia. I never had any idea that we had ever had anyone so close to that government. I knew we had someone close to Roosevelt but it proved impossible for me to find out who that was. Anyway it did not seem important. The information we were getting seemed to line up with what we were eventually told by the man himself. Please start by telling me about Russia and what you found out there. I am also very intrigued as to how it was possible to get someone into any Russian government office. Perhaps you should start with that."

So she did:

"My first involvement in any government department was with the Foreign Office. I got in on the recommendation of a friend of mine. It was very soon after I joined that I developed a taste for clandestine operations. I was given an early opportunity to do some very secret work and for that I was trained by British military intelligence. The training was excellent and it stood me in good stead for the rest of my time in the diplomatic service. The Foreign Office also went to great lengths to protect my personal security. They did that very well and it was very rarely that I felt threatened in any way wherever I was working.

"My early assignments were all in Empire countries but then I went to America to infiltrate the activities of the Irish Republican Army there. They were seeking to de-stabilise the entire political process in Northern Ireland and had strong support from within the Democratic Party and Roosevelt was clearly aware of what was going on and supported it. It was that work which gave me my big breakthrough into the big time.

"After I met you at that dinner party I went on to an assignment to Germany. There I was able to penetrate deeply into the armaments build–up and provide Britain with masses of highly detailed information on it all. It was a fascinating assignment and one which I mostly enjoyed. I was able to do it because I speak excellent German. I cannot say now exactly what I found and I certainly cannot remember the detail of it all, but I did pass on a large amount of valuable information back to London.

"I went to Moscow in the late summer of 1937. I was able to go there because I also speak excellent Russian. I have no idea how the arrangements were made to get me there. Whoever did it must have been very resourceful. But I replaced a girl who looked very much like me. She worked as an administrator in Voroshilov's private office in the Ministry of Defence. I have no idea what happened to her but I lived in her apartment. I was told she had gone to somewhere safe.

"One of my main jobs in Moscow was organising and then taking the minutes of very high level meetings. After I had been there a few months most of those meetings were chaired by either Voroshilov or Stalin himself. Most people who worked in those offices were terrified of Stalin. He was rude all the time as well as being cruel and vindictive. Several people were taken from the offices and never seen again. They were undoubtedly shot because they might have revealed some useless secret or another. The information I got was excellent but every other aspect of the work was dull and the people who worked there were generally very dull. Being in Moscow was a very lonely time for me. I left the day of the final meeting between Molotov and Ribbentrop which sealed the fate of Poland and set the invasion dates for that country. I had taken the minutes of that meeting. I was spirited out of the country immediately after that meeting before I even could write up those minutes.

"The Foreign Office flew me in a Finnish aircraft to Helsinki. It was while I was going through my first de-briefing there that I was told that I would be going to Washington. I will tell you about that over lunch as it is quite a long story."

Churchill took her round the ground floor before lunch and showed her where he had done all that work on his great books.

When they got to the dining room the table had been laid just for the two of them. He showed her to a seat which had a splendid view out over the lawns. She was delighted to see that two bottles of claret had been opened. He obviously intended it to be a long and relaxing lunch.

"Now tell me about Roosevelt. I do not want to know anything more about what has been agreed with him although I might have to explain that to you later. To me he has been the man at the other end of endless phone calls and telegrams. I have not met him many times and when I have it has always been very formal. There has always been too much work to do for us to have any real opportunity to get to know each other."

She thought before starting to talk:

"To me he was always a very gracious and charming man. I found him very easy to talk to and he was always interested in talking to me. Several times he told me that it was always easier to deal with me than to have to go through all those formal diplomatic channels where people seemed to speak nothing other than mumbo-jumbo.

"He was a very powerful man. There was never any evidence that he consulted with his advisers or cabinet colleagues over any significant issue. He made decisions on new issues that I put to him without even talking to anyone else over the phone, still less asking them to come into our meetings. One of the reasons it worked so well with me was that he had been appalled at the way the British Foreign Office had penetrated, infiltrated and indoctrinated the State Department. He felt that as a result he could not trust the normal diplomatic processes. State used to send him lots of unsolicited advice on Britain and the war. He took very little notice of any of it and told me several times that he distrusted it deeply. But he did trust Joseph Kennedy in London.

"One thing that you must always remember about Roosevelt is that he is very opposed to any sort of imperialism. He absolutely loathes it and long before the war started he was determined to get rid of it completely. Because Britain was by far the largest imperial power he was very anti-Britain. He disliked our political institutions, he disliked the way we ran the Empire and he was determined to use every possible means to ensure that Britain was weakened and the British Empire dismembered. He never lost sight of this objective and he spoke with me about it frequently.

"Kennedy had been chosen as Ambassador to London because he was anti-British. He used to write to Roosevelt regularly about what he had been able to achieve in that direction.

"Kennedy had been able to give him very accurate information on the exact sate of Britain's finances. I do not know where he got it all from. It was certainly not published material and was not information that was available to our embassy in Washington. There was a very strong suspicion that he must have had a source of information at high levels inside the Treasury. I took this up with our Ambassador and he passed it on to Anthony Eden but he never got a report back as to what had been done about it. Before every meeting with you he got an update on the same information. I did tell you several times that he had very detailed financial information about Britain so I assumed that the need for more and more support for Britain was being made by you irrespective of the consequences and because there was no alternative. I had to assume that you always knew that you were negotiating from a position of weakness and that you had heeded the warnings that I was putting in what I sent to you."

Churchill interrupted her;

"Yes, I did read your warnings. I knew that he had been getting information about Britain which was not even available to my own cabinet. Eden did tell me that he had received that communication from Washington and we did start an investigation into it all. It took a long time to get anywhere but our suspicions eventually fell on one man. We were not able to prove anything but he was prematurely retired. Unfortunately we were not able to narrow it down until just a few weeks ago. He was at a very senior level in the Treasury. Anyway, carry on."

She drank some more of the excellent claret and continued:

"It was as he was preparing for the meetings on *Prince of Wales* that his thoughts took him in an entirely new direction. What he had begun to realise then was that if Britain was genuinely weak the Empire might collapse anyway. If it did there would be a power vacuum which, in his own view, only America could fill. From then on it did not matter whether he forced Britain to give up the Empire or whether it just happened as a result of Britain's weakness the result would be the same. America would win. His direction of the war effort after that was entirely dedicated to that aim. That was what you were up against all along."

Churchill then asked her:

"How did you get right into his mind as you obviously did?"

She answered truthfully, smiling:

"We used to get on very well together."

She then asked him who Roosevelt had sent to London to be effectively a counterpart for her.

He replied:

"Her name is Sally Monroe. She is black and the daughter of a black civil rights activist who was given a long jail sentence. Roosevelt pardoned him. She is also the girl friend of General George Patton who has been so effective in leading American armies through Europe. I will arrange for you to meet her."

During the afternoon and evening they went over more and more details of what she had learned and how each issue had been tackled by Roosevelt. Winston was able to explain each decision he had made about his negotiations with Roosevelt based on the facts and issues that were current at each stage of the process.

They were joined for dinner by Winston's wife, Clemmie, and their son Randolph and daughter Mary and Mary's husband, Christopher Soames. There was no political conversation at dinner. But there was a lot about wartime life in Washington. They also talked about the refugee crisis. It was that evening that Churchill agreed to make a strong government commitment to helping deal with that issue.

The last thing that he said to Louise that evening was;

"In making a government commitment to help you with your refugee work I will ensure that whatever happens in a general election that must take place after the war you will continue to receive that help."

Just before she left after lunch on the Sunday Louise said to Winston;

"I must tell you what the President said to me the last time I saw him. I will always remember it and I will quote it word for word. He said: *"Back in 1942 it was my view that America was going to find that dealing with Britain after the war was likely to be more difficult than disposing of Nazi Germany. That remains my view. Please do one last thing for me and tell him that."*

* * *

March 6, 1945. I met Louise again today. I had not met her since that dinner party in 1936. Winston told me that she had an interesting story to tell me. It took all the afternoon and evening. I am sure that I will meet her many times again.

* * *

Three weeks later Churchill hosted a cocktail party at 10, Downing Street for Louise's charity. At it he announced a government support programme for refugee charities that would be in place for as long as necessary. At that party he introduced Louise to Sally Monroe. Sally agreed to represent The Daily Express charity in Washington. If Roosevelt was prepared to give that money to it she would be very happy to do whatever was necessary. After all Roosevelt had been the saviour of her family. In return for that she would do whatever she could to save other families.

After the cocktail party was over Sally took Louise to her apartment in South Audley Street, just a couple of blocks away from the American Embassy. Sally, being an American diplomat, was not subject to any rationing and she was therefore able to produce an excellent supper for them. It was just like dining in Washington again.

Over their meal they discussed their respective experiences of dealing with the leaders of the two countries. Sally had found Churchill to be a very difficult person to talk with. He always seemed to be demanding things and never seemed keen to listen. She said that he seemed to be driven by personal objectives the whole time. Other people's views did not seem important to him. It was certainly not the easiest job that she had ever done but she did say that it was very enjoyable. She did say that Churchill had entertained her in Downing Street on a couple of occasions and she had found his talk about the history of his country to be fascinating.

* * *

With the formation of the National Government in the 1930's to try and deal with the endless crises at that time without party political wrangling and confrontation the whole electoral process in Britain had been suspended. National elections were also suspended for the duration of the war. But the legislation that suspended elections also called for them to take place again as soon as practicable after the war had finished. The election took place on July 5th, 1944. However the counting of the votes was delayed until Thursday July 26th to enable postal votes by the millions of British armed forces personnel based outside the United Kingdom itself to be included in the results. The counting was due to take place while the Potsdam conference was still in session. At the time the election was called the implications of that conference were unknown.

* * *

July 24, 1944. We are at Potsdam for the conference to finalise the whole shape of the peace process. For us British people the whole meeting has the air of unreality. Winston is here as leader of the British delegation. But Clement Attlee is also here. We have had a general election but the result will not be known for few days yet while they count the postal votes of all our armed forces around the world. If Winston wins the election he will be here for the final stages of the conference. If Attlee wins then Winston will play no further part in it all.

It all feels rather odd. Stalin is highly amused by it all. He cannot understand why a government has to call a general election and is not certain of the outcome. The results of the election will be counted tomorrow and all the politicians will be going back to Britain to hear of their fate.

I will be staying here just in case there are any military intelligence issues that have to be addressed while they are away.

* * *

That Potsdam was intended to be one of the most important conferences in all time can probably never be disputed. It was intended to shape the world after the largest and most devastating war ever fought, so its importance can never be overstated. That the opportunities presented to that conference probably exceeded the opportunities presented to any other conference can probably never be disputed. That the outcome bore no resemblance to the initial intentions of Britain can probably never be disputed either. That the outcome resulted in the creation of a very changed world cannot be disputed. But it was not so much what was said at Potsdam and what was apparently agreed at Potsdam that mattered. It was what it led to that was far more important.

Before Truman went to Potsdam he read Lincoln's speech at the ceremony honouring the war dead at the site of the civil war battle of Gettysburg in 1863. It included the phrase "the world will little note nor long remember what we say here." Truman wondered whether he would be judged by what he said at Potsdam or whether he would be judged by what he did for America there. So far as he was concerned the words he might use were almost irrelevant. It was the actions that followed that he hoped would lead to a far greater future for his country that really mattered.

One of the official photographs released at the time of the conference showed the three leaders sitting out in the sunshine on wicker chairs in front of a microphone. They were all smiling. Churchill was wearing something that resembled military uniform, complete with epaulettes. Stalin was wearing something that made him look like a waiter. Only Truman was wearing a suit and that looked to be very shiny.

The reality of it all was far less benign than that. This was not a conference where the photo opportunities meant anything at all. This was a power struggle. The principal protagonists were Stalin, who clearly controlled by far the largest and most successful army that had ever been assembled, and Truman, who was the head of government of the richest country ever known. Both Stalin and Truman were very confident that they would gain precisely what they each wanted. And then there was Churchill who was irrelevant as he waited for the outcome of a general election.

One reason, perhaps, for that benign appearance was that the conference was not dominated by issues about the war. There were no tensions about how the war might be won. The war was over in Europe. It was all about positioning for power in the post-war world. All three participants, at least at the beginning of the conference, were interested in that and in getting for themselves the best possible position in that new world. Only two would survive.

Truman went to Potsdam knowing that America was the only country in the world that not only had the atomic bomb but was prepared to use it. It was a negotiating card that he was determined to play. He told Stalin about the new weapon at the conference and he said that he intended to use it to destroy a city in Japan within a few days. Stalin urged him not to use it on any non-military target. But Stalin then instructed that the Russian nuclear programme be speeded up. He did not tell Truman that he had a similar weapon under development nor did Truman suspect any such development.

Back in 1941, when Roosevelt had imposed the Atlantic Alliance on Churchill he had insisted that it contain the clause *"to further the enjoyment of all States, great or small, victor or vanquished, of access on equal terms, to the trade and to the raw materials of the world which are needed for economic prosperity."*

The Russian Foreign Minister, Molotov, tried to address that issue both at the Potsdam conference itself and several times afterwards. He regarded those words in the Atlantic Alliance as seeming to suggest that there were 'equal opportunities' throughout the world. He knew that the reality was very different.

He pointed out at Potsdam and frequently thereafter that the gross domestic product of America in 1938 was 64 billion dollars. By 1943 it had risen to 149 billion dollars. In other words America had gained enormous economic growth, prosperity and profits from the war. No other country had ever gained so much from war. All other participants in the Second World War had been enfeebled by the whole process. In those circumstances there was no equality of opportunity. But it was an advantage that Truman did ruthlessly use at Potsdam and subsequently. It made for very unequal negotiations. Although Russia had been the principal military victor in Europe, in reality America had most of the negotiating cards because of its economic strength.

Stalin knew all of that and knew full well that he could expect Truman to take advantage of that incredibly powerful position that could have never been foreseen at the beginning of the war. He equally knew that Russia had had to pay a terrible price for its huge and largely unsupported effort to destroy the Nazi armed forces. With untold millions dead, and large parts of its entire country destroyed, Russia could have been nothing but a net loser in economic terms. But at least it did not accrue the huge debts that Britain had accumulated as Churchill had bought from America rather than produce at home.

Truman's intention all along was to ignore the other participants, agree to as little as possible and achieve a position in which America had as much freedom to do whatever it liked at Britain's expense. He gained all of that freedom. He turned out to be the greatest victor at the conference.

Potsdam turned out to be a mixture of pure fantasy, hopes that were realised, hopes that were dashed, illusions, deceit, lying and bullying.

There was never any realistic prospect of any worthwhile consensus between the parties. Their initial objectives were far too different for that to be possible.

Stalin was certainly a victor. He gained all the territories in Europe that he had discussed with Churchill and he also got significant new territories in the Far East in return for minimal intervention to help America win its war in the Pacific. The gains Stalin made enabled him to introduce communism to China and to gain control of North Korea. He also got control of the Sakhalin Peninsula and the Kurile Islands.

Britain only gained the right to govern Greece and Turkey.

Germany was divided and each governing power was free to take whatever reparations it chose from whatever part of that country that they governed. In practice Russia took everything from the Eastern Zone and America and Britain found that there was nothing useful to take. The industries in the west of the country had been far too damaged by bombing for anything useful to remain. In any case America was more concerned then about reconstructing Germany than taking reparations. Lucius Clay was going to apply all of Roosevelt's economic management practices to restoring Germany to prosperity.

The British team was not just Churchill anymore. The British general election had already taken place, but the results were not yet counted, at the start of the conference so Churchill took with him Anthony Eden, Clement Attlee and Ernest Bevin. Attlee and Bevin would be Prime Minister and Foreign Secretary if Labour won the election. If Churchill won the election Attlee and Bevin would not stay at the conference after the results had been counted. If Attlee won then Churchill and Eden would leave the conference. It was a situation that caused Stalin considerable amusement. He told Churchill several times that he could not understand why he was not able to control the results of an election that he had called.

All the British politicians left Potsdam on July 25th in order to be in Britain for the count of the votes and to hear of their fate. That morning Churchill was in a very depressed mood. Last photographs were taken of Churchill, Stalin and Truman together on the steps of the Cecilienhof Palace where the conference was being held. Many years later Churchill, in his memoirs, wrote of his thoughts on the plane as he was flown home that day. Most of it was about his dreams of what he would have liked to have negotiated. In those memoirs he also bemoaned the fact that his successors in government could not have been prepared for negotiations on the great plans that he intended to put to the conference. So what. They had other ideas anyway. Churchill's dreams, whatever they might have been, were never put to Stalin and Truman and if they had they would certainly have been rejected. Churchill may have understood that but was never prepared to admit that in world terms he had become irrelevant as two new super powers were starting to grapple with the implications of what they had achieved and what they wanted to achieve in the future.

Churchill and the Conservative Party did lose that general election and it was Attlee who returned to Potsdam as Prime Minister on Saturday July, 28th. It had not only been a defeat for Churchill it had been a resounding one. The Labour party had 48% of the vote and 200 more seats in the House of Commons than the Conservatives. The British electorate had wanted a change. They had been fed up with Conservative social policies before the war and were thoroughly war weary. They hoped that by changing the government all that could be put behind them.

Attlee went back to Berlin with Ernest Bevin, who had become Foreign Secretary. The civil service head of the Foreign Office was still Cadogan. He had been at Potsdam for the whole conference. He was there to welcome Attlee back that Saturday evening. He tried to sound as welcoming and friendly as possible. But in his memoirs that he published several years later he wrote; *"Bevin has a tendency to take the lead over Attlee, who recedes into the background by his very insignificance…"*

While Attlee had been away Stalin and Truman had negotiated the shape of the final deal between them. They had got so far, in fact, that Attlee was excluded from all the negotiating sessions after his return. His role there was completely pointless.

The Potsdam conference finished in the very late evening of August 1st. The communiqué turned out to be based on a ramshackle set of agreements; some of which were at best vague in their meaning.

America dropped the first atomic bomb on Hiroshima on August 6th.

* * *

Just before he left on the Presidential aircraft which was going to take him as far as Britain where he would join *USS Augusta,* Truman asked Attlee to visit him in his sitting room in the Cecilienhof Palace. It was a short and not very civil meeting. Truman said to him:

"Churchill met with my predecessor in August 1941. They negotiated the Atlantic Alliance. Churchill reported to Parliament on that as soon as he had returned to Britain. His account of that agreement was substantially inaccurate and he failed to mention some of the key provisions as they would affect Britain. I do not imagine for one minute that he will have given you or any other members of the British government a full account of what was agreed. But it has now fallen to you to implement that agreement so I suggest that you read it in full as soon as possible. You may be surprised about it, but what I can tell you is that America is going to insist on it being implemented in full. So I suggest that you read it as a matter of urgency. Have a good trip back to Britain."

All the way back to London Attlee fretted about what Truman could possibly have meant. As soon as he got to Downing Street he asked the Cabinet Secretary to give him the original agreement. It was produced within half an hour.

Attlee sat down to read it immediately. It did not take him very long to realise why Churchill could never have disclosed the true terms of the agreement to Parliament. He knew as soon as he read it that Britain had entered into virtually unlimited commitments to pay America vast sums of money over whatever period of time was necessary. He also knew why he had been humiliated at Potsdam. It was going to be a rough time. But he also knew that he could never tell his cabinet about what Churchill had agreed, nor could he tell Parliament or the British people. His premiership was already off to a heavily compromised start.

He asked the Cabinet Secretary to lock the agreement away in a very secure place. He certainly did not want to see it ever again, but he knew that it would haunt him.

* * *

On the Monday when Attlee was back in Berlin Winston was able to spend many hours with Alice. He felt as if he had been thrown against a brick wall, bashed all over, and mutilated. His whole life seemed to be in ruins. He had always understood that there was a risk that he would not be returned to government as Prime Minister. That can always happen in a democracy. But in trying to ensure the survival of Britain and in trying to win the war he had forgotten just how unpopular the Conservative's social policies had been. In the euphoria of victory he had also forgotten just how war-weary the British people had become.

There was no way that Alice could get him out of that mood in a single afternoon. It would probably take months. But what she was able to do that day was talk to him about the reality of it all. The reality of a national leader who is completely rejected and becomes nothing in an instant. The reality of a man who had big dreams for his country and is robbed of any chance to fulfil them. The reality of a man who has no faith or trust in his successors. The reality of a man who sees huge dangers in the way the Europe is going to be managed and is powerless to do anything about it. All those things were true of Churchill at that time.

They had started just before lunch. They went on talking all the afternoon.

Their conversations that day would be repeated many times over the months and years to come as Winston gradually learned the reality of a world without power. Alice would do whatever she could to steer him through all that mental turmoil.

* * *

On August 3rd, the day after he got back from Potsdam Clement Attlee went for a walk in St James's Park. He had been thoroughly humiliated by the treatment he had received over the last few days in Berlin. It was bad enough when Churchill was there leading the British delegation. It was becoming quite obvious then that Britain was regarded by both America and Russia as an unimportant participant in the talks. It was even worse after he had had returned triumphant after the election. Britain, by then, was not in the talks at all. Everything of substance had been agreed by the Big Two.

He had enjoyed the quick tour of war-ruined Berlin just before his plane had left Gatow airport to take him back to London. He was amazed at the amount of destruction that he had seen. A particularly poignant part of the visit was seeing the ruined Reichstag building.

Later that morning he had to preside over the first Cabinet meeting of the new Labour government. There was a huge and potentially forbidding agenda. That agenda was a mixture between practical realities and the need to implement the policies which his government had been elected to implement. The meeting could well last many hours and before it started he decided that he would like a walk in the fresh summer air in order to clear his thoughts. He liked walking in the London parks at any time of the year, but that was a very bright mild day with clear sunshine. It was likely to be very warm later.

What Attlee really wanted to think through on that walk was how he was going to handle the Cabinet meeting that day. He had chaired many cabinet meetings before, principally when Churchill was off on any one of his numerous war time trips around the country, the battlefronts or to his numerous meetings with Roosevelt and later Stalin as well.

The two conclusions he reached during that walk were that the agenda was effectively unmanageably vast. Although all the items were important they would simply take too long if there were all handled together or at the same meeting. The other decision he made was that the only way to handle it all was if the list was prioritised. He would get each member of the cabinet to select his own priorities and then score them. The one with the highest score would be regarded as the government's top priority. The second choice would be the second highest priority and so on. It was a risky way to proceed because there would be no way of ensuring that the selected priorities were in accordance with national needs. But any other way forward would have needed a lengthy debate as to what the national needs really were. Attlee dreaded that because it would inevitably result in a seriously divided cabinet.

But before the meeting could even start on the definitive agenda he would have to give the Cabinet a report on Potsdam. He had thought about that most of the way back on the plane. After he had seen the *Prince of Wales* agreement that had set up the so-called Atlantic Alliance he had decided that he could never tell his colleagues the complete truth about what had been going on. It would have to trickle out over many years. If the government was lucky it might never come out at all, although Attlee doubted that. Perhaps the minimum that he hoped for was that it would not come out during Winston's lifetime. But as he strolled round the edge of the lake in the park he decided that he would tell them the minimum about Potsdam. They would need to know something about it in order to proceed at all. In due course he would get Ernest Bevin to give them a more detailed account of it all.

Little did he know as he was walking back to Downing Street that he was setting in train a process that would complete the work of destroying Britain's place in the world that had been started by Roosevelt, continued by Stalin and then speeded up by Truman.

The one comforting thing to Attlee on that walk that morning was that several members of the team had been cabinet ministers for several years in the National Government. That meant that at least they knew the process. His Chancellor, Hugh Dalton had been one of those.

* * *

For many years the Labour Party in Britain had been trying to come to terms with its first disastrous period of office in Britain in the 1920's under its first Labour Prime Minister, Ramsay MacDonald. The loss of office at the end of that period had been a shock and ever since then the whole party had been searching for a formula that would appeal to the voters in such a way that Labour might enjoy a long period in office. That eventually turned out to be what they called *A New Jerusalem*. In truth it was not much more than a theory based on a popular hymn written by a controversial poet called William Blake around a century and a half earlier.

The Vision of A New Jerusalem in the hymn was at very best completely unspecific. The last three lines of the hymn read:

*"Nor shall my sword sleep in my hand
Till we have built Jerusalem
In England's green and pleasant land."*

It was then and still is a very popular hymn in Britain but it contains no detail of anything that could be remotely construed as a vision of any specific set of political programmes that could possibly be of any use to anyone.

The Labour Party was then completely undaunted by such realities and went ahead and developed its own vision of that New Jerusalem. Their thinkers had plenty of time to dream through a range of options both before and during the war. What emerged was a series of ideas based on the concept of state management of all of its people from the cradle to the grave throughout every phase of their lives. To make it even vaguely achievable they invented the concept of nationalising all basic industries; they argued that that was bringing them under the control of the people. In reality it was much closer to Marxism than it was to any other political doctrine.

In 1944 the annual Labour Party Conference specifically adopted the concept of A New Jerusalem as the way for the future and agreed that they would put New Jerusalem policies before the public whenever the next general election was called.

Those policies were put before the electorate in the 1945 election and they proved to be very popular. The central thread to all of them was state control of all key industries and public services. What was in the manifesto was that key heavy industries such as coal, steel, mining, ship building, railways, water, electricity, gas, long distance road haulage, most bus services and airlines would be nationalised. The current owners would be given the minimum possible levels of compensation. The lie was told that under state ownership every voter would have a stake in those industries. They would effectively be shareholders in industries that were only going to work for the national good.

The manifesto also proposed that all medical services should be absorbed into what was going to be called the National Health Service. There was only a vague concept of how that was going to be achieved but there was the promise that all health care would be provided free of charge to the patient, irrespective of his or her personal circumstances. How that was going to be achieved was left silent in the manifesto.

The public was also promised access to cheap housing that would be built by local councils. How that housing was going to be funded was also left silent by the manifesto.

In a sense it did not matter what was in the manifesto, the public were fed up with the National Government dominated by the Tories and wanted a change. But Attlee was left with the consequences of all that they had promised. When he had seen the full text of the Atlantic Alliance agreement he was fearful of what it might mean as they tried to implement their policies of social change intended to affect every single person in the country. It was completely clear in that treaty that Britain's priority had to be the honouring and servicing of that agreement. That was effectively the price for all of that help in the war. But Attlee equally knew that he could never divulge the detail of that agreement to his cabinet. It was clearly going to be a horrendously difficult time ahead.

* * *

It was an odd sort of Cabinet that Attlee had selected. By the time the election had taken place he knew that he could be required at Potsdam immediately after the results were declared. That meant that he had to select the whole team before he went there. It also meant that he had to select people who were likely to have large majorities in their constituencies so that they would be safe choices under all circumstances.

It was actually a very left wing cabinet. There had never been a British cabinet before that was anything like so radical. There had never been a British government before that was more likely to mount a challenge to everything that formed the basis of British life. In ideological terms the cabinet was closer to Marxism than anything else. If there were choices to be made it would side with Russia rather than America. But it was strong on Empire; it did then like the idea of retaining British power and influence in the world.

Two members of the government were open pacifists. They would resist war under all circumstances and they had said throughout the election campaign that they were in favour of disarming Britain completely.

Three of the appointments that Attlee made were in relation to the management of the Empire. They were Viscount Addison at the Dominion Office. Lord Lawrence at the India Office and Mr. G. Hall at the Colonial Office. That meant that they would be indicating to the world that they would be taking the Empire very seriously. It was likely to be a source of comfort amongst the electorate.

Organised labour and the academic world had more representation than any other groups. That was a source of potential conflict if ever there was one. Attlee dreaded the future when he had to debate every policy issue with teachers and trade union leaders. Every night when he went to bed he thought about how he was going to get through the next day. It was always a daunting prospect and it was only the tumbler of whisky, one of the few perks of the job, that enabled him eventually to have some deep sleep.

* * *

The agenda presented to that first Cabinet Meeting of the new Labour government was horrendous. It read:

1. Report on Potsdam
2. Getting the troops home
3. The economy
4. Health reforms and the introduction of the National Health Service
5. Reparations
6. The government of Germany
7. The future of the armed services
8. Nationalisation of key industries
9. The Empire
10. Trade Unions
11. House Building
12. Rebuilding industry
13. The consequences of Lend/Lease
14. Agriculture and rationing
15. Refugees and refugee immigration into Britain
16. Employment
17. Transport
18. Prisoners of war release programme
19. The Budget
20. Education

In setting out the agenda Attlee explained that he wanted Cabinet members to vote on the priorities. But even before they did that he needed to give them a summary of the conclusions from Potsdam. So that was how he started:

"The final agreement from the meeting in Potsdam dealt with the territorial division of the lands occupied by Germany and the division of Germany itself. It is actually quite a simple agreement but what matters in it is the division of responsibility between ourselves, America, France and Russia. We will deal with any wider issues at a future meeting but today I just want to set out the main obligations of the parties. They may well have an influence on the way that we deal with other items on the agenda.

"Broadly there will be a line drawn on a map that runs from the Baltic to the Adriatic. Most of the territory east of that will be in the Russian sphere of influence. That will include Poland, the eastern part of Germany, Czechoslovakia, Hungary and almost all of the Balkan countries. The only exceptions to that are that Britain will be responsible for the security of Greece and Turkey. We will have to deploy armed forces to both of those countries immediately.

"The western part of Germany will be divided into three zones. America will be responsible for most of the territory south of the Ruhr Valley. Britain will be responsible for all the territory north of the Ruhr. France will be responsible for a small amount of German territory that runs along its borders. We will have to start moving troops back into our part of Germany almost immediately.

"Berlin will be in the Russian sector but there is provision for the four powers to govern that city. Rights of access to Berlin remain vague.

"There is no time limit for the agreement. America expressed hopes that its role could be completed within two years but it was very unclear how that hope might be realised. I think that we must assume that our task there will go on until it is completed, however long that might take. If Berlin is representative of the rest of Germany there is a huge amount of war damage throughout the country and there will be a very large number of refugees. That means that there is likely to be considerable chaos for a long while to come. In those circumstances we will have to plan to govern our part of the country in such a way that optimises the chances for an enduring peace.

"But the point I do want to emphasise is that we do have on-going obligations there. It is all going to be managed rather differently from the aftermath of the Great War, and we will always have to remember our obligations to get it right this time.

"I also have to remind you all that we are still at war in the Far East. Even if that war is ended quickly, as I fully anticipate, it is by no means clear what the shape of any peace agreements will be. Equally it is very uncertain what our commitments there will be. But in the Far East there are some very important parts of the British Empire."

There were no questions or comments about that. They all agreed that if any discussion were needed it would be after they had been able to discuss the whole agreement, which they would do in due course.

After that he set out his proposed procedure for dealing with the main agenda. What he intended to do was ask an advocate in favour of each agenda item to argue why it should be selected as the highest priority. Each such argument would be limited to five minutes. That together with the inevitable overruns and the necessary comfort breaks would probably take anything up to two hours. Once that vote had been taken they would issue a new agenda in priority order. The Cabinet would then follow that new agenda very strictly. That was easily agreed and an hour was allowed after the supporting arguments for individual ministers to make up their minds, either individually or in consultation with others.

At the end of that hour a new agenda was produced. It read;

1. Health reforms and the introduction of the National Health Service
2. Nationalisation of key industries
3. Getting the troops home
4. The Budget
5. House Building
6. Employment
7. Trade Unions
8. Education
9. Transport
10. Agriculture and rationing
11. The Empire
12. Reparations
13. Report on Potsdam
14. The future of the armed services
15. The government of Germany
16. The consequences of Lend/Lease
17. Rebuilding industry
18. Refugees and refugee immigration into Britain
19. Prisoners of war release programme
20. The economy

Attlee was dismayed. He had a cabinet of twenty one members. Nineteen had voted for health as their highest priority. The number of cabinet ministers who had voted for issues relating to the aftermath of the war was trivial. What the voting had meant was that before any attention could be given to current issues a way forward had to be found on all those social reform issues. It was going to make for very difficult government. But at least he could start the process with a united government.

What Attlee did was agree that that would be the list of the government's priorities. In each of the following cabinet meetings they would address three items from the priority list. In each of those meetings he wanted the relevant minister to present his proposals for dealing with the issue in accordance with their manifesto commitments. At the next meeting, therefore, Aneurin Bevan, as Health Secretary, would explain how he intended to tackle health issues. Mannie Shinwell, as Fuel and Power Minister and Stafford Cripps as President of the Board of Trade would explain how they intended to deal with the nationalisation of key industries. Finally Attlee, who had overall responsibility for defence, would himself put forward proposals about how they were going to get the troops home.

But before they could leave the meeting and start their work Attlee wanted the Chancellor of the Exchequer, Hugh Dalton, to give the meeting a description of the British economy.

***

As was obvious from the selection of the priorities Attlee's first cabinet was high on idealism and low on realities, but that also reflected the views of the British people at that time.

Dalton's first presentation to the Cabinet as Chancellor of the Exchequer was a very sombre one. Dalton had first joined the Cabinet in 1940 as Minister of Economic Warfare. He had later gone on to become Minister of the Board of Trade. He was fully aware of the dreadful deterioration in Britain's financial position before and during the war. He was an odd choice for such a senior ministerial position and probably only got it because he had written a book in 1935 called *Practical Socialism* which had had a propound impact on Attlee. Decades later it is impossible to fathom out what that book was all about.

Dalton was a curious mix of the radical and the conservative. It was that curious mixture that infected that first presentation to the cabinet on the state of the Nation's finances. His presentation was actually very short because there was not a lot to say. He began;

"Prime Minister, what I have to say today is all about a gloomy view of the British economy. Before the war everything that Britain wanted to do was sustainable in economic terms because of the strength of our exports. We achieved a balance of payments surplus in every year over the last century and more. Britain was the largest exporter of capital goods in the world. At the beginning of the war that export surplus started to dry up as our factories were directed to make war equipment for our own use at home. We also needed to import large amounts of essential war materials particularly from the United States. In every year since 1940 we have run a trade deficit. Last year alone this amounted to 100 million pounds. It has only been possible to pay for this by reducing our gold reserves. These have now been depleted to the point that they represent only three months of trading deficit at the current rate. It is a grim position.

"In order to fund the war we entered into very large Lend/Lease deals with America. We have to start repaying them for those deals now but the repayment schedule is flexible. The less we pay in the short term the more we will have to pay in the long term. The only good news about those payments is that interest rates are currently low and are expected to remain that way. If they do remain low we may be able to defer some of those repayments.

"An additional source of revenue for the government during the war was the issue of War Bonds. At some stage these will have to be redeemed or replaced by new loan stock of some kind. The outstanding bonds currently equate to half our annual Gross Domestic Production. It is a level of borrowing that my advisers tell me is completely unsustainable.

"Those are the negatives with which we must deal. The only ways to deal with them are to increase taxes or increase borrowings. We must do one or both of those things as soon as we can.

"On the optimistic side we should be able to look forward to a period of sustained growth in the economy because the war has now ended. My advisers tell me that the resumption of exports that is now possible should produce immediate improvements in our balance of payments situation and should result in early improvements in our gold reserves. I certainly share those views and I do not believe that it is prudent to introduce crash economic measures until the effect of such an export boom is proven.

"Our legislative programme will take time to implement. That really means that in this current financial year we do not have to make any provision for payment to current owners of any businesses that will be nationalised nor will we have to make any provision for health facilities that will come under public ownership until that event actually happens. In any event the effect of taking all those industries into public ownership should be broadly neutral so far as public finances are concerned. But there will probably be a need to make some increase in taxation when we takeover all the health facilities just to replace the payments that people currently make to health savings clubs.

"I am optimistic that we can sustain taxation and all other forms of government revenue at the current rates for at least the next year. If that proves to be wrong then I would advocate an increased borrowing level as the solution to any problems that might arise.

"I propose to present a new budget to Parliament in October and what I have just said will be the basis of it. I would like the assent of this meeting to that today."

It was the most optimistic load of rubbish that could possibly have been conceived by anyone at that time and, as time proved, it was in no way an accurate assessment of the true needs of Britain. All it did was add to the economic gloom.

They debated that for a couple of hours. There were strong views held by almost all cabinet members on the subject. The widest consensus was among those who felt that taxes should be increased for the rich and reduced payments should be made for the industries that the government intended to nationalise. Some cabinet members suggested that there should be no compensation to the current owners of business that would come under state control.

Where it all fell down was that there had been no assessment done even of the government's current financial commitments, let alone any commitments that might arise from any nationalisation programmes. There was no recognition of the completely clapped out state of much of British industry. In other words it had been a speech about nothing and it was going to lead to a budget that was essentially about nothing.

There was no reference to why America had done so well during the war when Britain had done so badly financially.

* * *

The commitment Churchill had made to refugees had been incorporated in some emergency legislation. It was always possible to put forward such legislation in time of war, even if that war was coming to an end. In the years that followed Louise was very pleased that such legislation had been possible. Its nature was such that it was impossible to repeal. Whether people liked refugees or they didn't, there was a legal framework within which the government would support the whole effort to reunite families and provide them with homes.

What Churchill did was provide for 3,000 volunteers to leave the armed forces in order to join one or another of the charities formed to help refugees. They would each be able to take a military jeep with them to use as transport and the government would provide all the costs of operating those vehicles for five years. The idea that Churchill had worked out with Louise on the Sunday morning that she was at Chartwell, was that each driver would be able to travel around and between all the refugee centres trying to match names with relatives. They would use photographs, lists and government and local records. When they found a match they would arrange for a reunion. The next stage would be to take all such refugees to a place of their choosing or back to their native city, town or village. The Parliamentary bill included provision for 3,000 small buses together with volunteer drivers for that work.

* * *

August 5, 1945. There was a big party this evening so that Winston could thank all those who worked directly with him during the war. It was organised by Max Beaverbrook and took place at the Savoy Hotel. Winston made an excellent speech which was much appreciated by all but he is obviously still in deep shock about the way that he was booted out by the electorate.

Louise Harford was there and I realised for the first time what the real relationship is between her and Max. He is very lucky to have such an attractive lover. It is three years since I found my own lover and I can well understand just what it means to them.

Today has been a sad day for me. I was told this morning that I will no longer be needed in government. That was really inevitable from the time that Winston left office. I have no regrets about anything I have done with Winston these past few years. Rather I am very grateful for being given the opportunity to be so close to the centre of all the action that has taken place in that time.

Winston told me just before he left tonight that he wants to have lunch with me soon.

* * *

It was on August 9th, 1945 that President Truman spoke to the American people by radio about the outcome of the Potsdam conference. It was also the day that the second atom bomb fell on Japan at Nagasaki. He told them about that bomb and that the war had come to an end as a result. He claimed that it was a stunning victory for America, its enterprise and its technology. He did not mention the work of the British scientists led by Professor Rutherford of Cambridge University who had made it possible.

In that statement he categorically stated that Bulgaria and Romania were separate and independent states and not under the influence and control of any other power. He knew that not to be the case. He went on to say that he expected democratic governments to be created in those countries based on free and fair elections. It was a complete lie. He had signed away something completely different. Potsdam was clearly disappearing into some distant and useless part of his memory. It was clearly not important to him anymore.

As the world entered the autumn of 1945 it began to look as if Potsdam had never happened, or that it had made no difference to anything that might be in the mind of President Truman. Over that autumn and the following winter Truman made a series of speeches which essentially set out what he intended the American sphere of interest to be in the world. None of them bore any resemblance to what he had agreed at Potsdam. But they all used the freedom he had secured there.

Within six months Truman had not only set out a vision of American supremacy around the world. He had also indicated that he would be very happy with confrontation with the Soviet Union. It was all shaping up nicely for a long and very cold war. The real outcome of Potsdam was that it created the Cold War.

* * *

August 15, 1945. I had lunch with Winston today. He is finding it very difficult to adapt to his changed circumstances. He is still, of course, leader of the Conservative Party but to him that is nothing compared with the role of head of government during the war. He told me that his isolation from what is really going on is almost as bad as it was in the wilderness years.

He has plenty of friends in politics on both sides of the House now and as a result he is able to get the details of what is being discussed in Cabinet. That was really what he wanted to talk to me about.

"Samuel, it is extraordinary just how fast things have changed. When I was leading the government our agenda was a world agenda. Now all the cabinet talks about is a domestic agenda. It is almost as if the war never happened. There are huge threats out there and they are not even being discussed. America is trying to dismantle our Empire and this government is not even interested. Russia every day exerts more and more power in Europe. A few weeks ago they were our ally and we were fighting together to destroy Germany. Now they do not even want to talk to us. Everything I tried to do is being swept away.

"In these last weeks I have had plenty of time to think. To think about the war and how it changed over the years. There is no doubt in my mind that the biggest change of all was Kursk. Up and until then we had expected that the war would be won by Britain and America working together. Kursk showed that that was no longer even a dream. We all believed that Russia was then pathetically weak. But it was actually much stronger militarily than America.

"Since then things have changed again. That ferocious bomb that Truman unleashed on Japan the other day will change the balance of power forever. The thing that galls me about that is that it was our people who invented the thing. Roosevelt stole them from us. Now Truman can bomb anyone he likes out of existence in a few minutes. It is inevitable that a new climate of fear will develop in the world. While all that is happening all our government can do is talk about doctor's surgeries."

We talked for several hours that afternoon. Winston had no regrets about anything he had done but he was much saddened by what the country had done to him.

* * *

It was a hot and humid August day when Aneurin Bevan made his presentation to the Cabinet about how he intended to handle the formation of the National Health Service. It was essentially a presentation that encapsulated everything that was sterile and hopeless in the British political thinking process. In very much later years it would have been described as full of sound bites. It was certainly a presentation more attuned to local electoral hustings than it was to any decision making body.

He started with loads of numbers. About how there were more than 2,500 hospitals of various sorts in the country; about the numbers of doctors and dentists and nurses. It was not very interesting stuff. But he did then get into something more meaty:

"It is going to be a long and complicated business to create the National Health Service. There will, of course, have to be primary legislation and even though a parliamentary majority is assured for that it will still take the best part of a year for it to pass through all the procedures. It will probably take three months to draft the legislation. So about fifteen months from now it will become law.

"Before even it is enshrined into law we will have to start the process of consultation with the staff involved. Almost all the staff who are employed in hospitals or by local doctors at the moment are self-employed or are employed by small organisations. There are no national pay structures of any sort. Those will have to be created and terms of service agreed for all groups of staff. This will not be easy but there is no reason to believe that there will be anything other than goodwill from the staff involved. But there are a large number of them and we will have to start putting proposals to them very soon now. It will be our intention to advise them that the initial terms of employment will mean that they will all be employed directly by the National Health Service, with payment levels at or very close to their current pay levels.

"That is when the complicated bit will start because as I have said large numbers of them are self-employed. It will be our intention to offer them a level of pay which equals what they earned in the last 12 months before the new service formally comes into being. After that we will equalise the pay scales so that we will truly have a service which is equal across the entire nation.

"We will have to buy their premises and we will do that at the average of three valuations. That should be a purely mechanistic process and it should be possible to do that quite quickly and then draw up the necessary contracts.

"It will all be paid for by a new system of National Insurance, together with a contribution from central taxation. We have got to get into the detailed costings but the general intention is to start with a system that broadly costs no more than health care and pensions cost now.

"One of the intentions behind providing a national service is to improve the quality of health care particularly for poorer people. The legislation will ensure that improvements come about quickly so that people will feel that the quality of service has been substantially improved before the next general election. It is generally those improvements that will be funded by central taxation.

"The legislation that we will put forward will make private medical treatment impossible in this country. Everyone will have to be treated by National Health Service practitioners. It will genuinely be a cradle to grave service for everyone.

"What I propose to do is get the legislation drafted as quickly as possible and start all those consultations. My first meeting with the Royal College of Surgeons is next week. All the consultations will be on a confidential basis until such a time as we are ready to roll out the detailed plans.

"I propose that I give the cabinet an update on progress in, say, a couple of month's time."

The Prime Minister asked whether there were any questions. As most of the Cabinet had voted for health as the top national priority he did not expect there to be any. But there was one. It was from Hugh Dalton, the Chancellor of the Exchequer. He asked whether there were any reliable figures available as to what health care and pensions were costing the country at the moment. The answer he got was that they were being collected; they would probably be available in about six month's time but their quality could not be guaranteed until new contracts were with all those involved, at least in draft form.

It had been a question that would form the basis of open hostility between the Treasury and other government departments for many decades to come. It was also the first question about costs that had been asked in Cabinet since Churchill had become Prime Minister in 1940.

It had been a flimsy bit of skating over a pond that might have been icy at that time and safe enough for that skating at that time. But the pond was going to get dangerous very quickly.

Although Hugh Dalton was a rabid socialist and very much an architect of the New Jerusalem he had asked the question that was going eventually to destroy the concept.

* * *

Aneurin Bevan's idealistic and flimsy presentation was nothing to what Mannie Shinwell and Strafford Cripps had to say. But there was a very strong common bond between them. It was that they had all toured Spain during its Civil War in support of the Popular Front. They had all been expelled from the British Labour Party in 1939 for proposing a similar movement in Britain. They had been allowed to get back into the party by agreeing to keep to the rules of the party. But it was a very strong bond between them which no rules could put asunder. Bevan, Shinwell and Cripps were the most powerful grouping in the government.

Mannie Shinwell started by explaining that they proposed to nationalise almost all sections of heavy industry in Britain. Before they could do that, though, they needed to establish some key principles about the management of those industries. The first of those was that the sole shareholder would be the government. All shareholder rights would reside with the government. It was already a far cry from the position portrayed at the election that voters would effectively control those businesses.

The second principle was that all revenue from those businesses should go to the government and that all investment should be controlled by the government. Each year Parliament would be asked to vote on the appropriations relevant to each industry. Any funding that each industry needed would be put before Parliament in the Budget each year and would be limited to the requirements of that year alone. Any surplus made by that industry would go automatically to the government.

They would put forward something that they intended to call The Nationalised Industries Act which would set out the business management rules for all of them. They would be common rules for all of the industries that came under state control. Those basic rules were:
- Each industry should employ as many people as possible
- All employees would be required to be members of a recognised trade union
- All pay and conditions would be agreed between employers and trades unions through structures called National Joint Councils
- All nationalised industries would have monopoly status
- All directors would be appointed by the government

- The objectives for each industry would be set by the relevant minister
- All investment plans would have to be approved by the minister in addition to the board of directors
- All assets would have to be written off in the year of acquisition, just as they would be in government
- They would all have the right to bring criminal pCurtiscutions against anyone who failed to pay their bills
- They would generally be exempt from planning laws when they wished to develop any existing sites
- They could only operate from freehold premises
- They could not lease in any assets, they would all have to be owned

The industries that would be nationalised in the first instance would be:

- The mining of coal
- Railways
- Municipal and long distance buses
- Steel making
- Electricity production and distribution
- Gas production and distribution
- Airlines, although this was then a very small industry but it was regarded as having strategic importance
- All road haulage over 50 miles
- Canals
- Water
- Major ports
- Airports
- The Bank of England

Mannie Shinwell said that they would seek to expand that list when they had gained control of all those industries and they had been reorganised to meet the government's objectives of providing a fully socialist state. It was his view that the priorities were to get the energy industries under state control. That way every single person and organisation in the country would be affected very quickly.

Stafford Cripps set his priority as being the nationalisation of the railways. At that time there were four railway companies and they were all seeking immediate and urgent government aid. They all claimed that the demands of the war, as imposed on them by the government, had been such that state aid was essential for the necessary repair works needed. Again, it was to be an issue that would haunt governments for decades to come.

After that the priorities were ports, buses and long distance road haulage. Although long distance road haulage sounded like an obscure business to be under state control it was essential that it was nationalised in order to protect the railways from competition.

Hugh Dalton warmly welcomed the nationalisation of the Bank of England. That would enable the government to control interest rates which, in his view, was a long overdue reform.

All those ministers were cleared to get on with all the work that they had outlined.

* * *

As every family in Britain wanted their relatives back from whatever former war front in which they were then based it was clearly a political priority to achieve that. In August, 1945 there were three million people in the armed forces. Two million of them were still overseas.

Attlee explained to his cabinet that he had asked the Chiefs of Staff to prepare a plan for the most rapid possible return to Britain of the maximum number of the armed forces as possible. That plan had to take into account the need to protect British interests and to counter any possible remaining threats. Few threats were expected in the short term but there was a large amount of work to be done in policing freed territories particularly in the Far East and in Germany. He went on:

"Please remember what I said earlier about the outcome of the meeting at Potsdam. We have a number of major obligations as a result of that. Those obligations need to be worked on by the military planners so that the effect on our manpower deployments can be assessed. I cannot predict what the outcome of that work will be.

"But they do include the policing of Greece and Turkey.

"What I sincerely hope is that it will be possible to release 1 million men from the armed forces within the next 12 months. I hope to be able to report back to you about that within the next month."

The only comments on that were that the sooner the men could be released the better.

* * *

The tenth presentation in the series was made by Tom Williams in early September. If there was ever a perfect model of complacency that presentation was surely it.

Tom Williams was not by any means a distinguished politician but he was popular in the party and he had a large majority in his constituency. Many years earlier he had been Attlee's eyes and ears in the Commons as his Parliamentary Private Secretary. That was a very grand name for what was effectively the first level of selection as a future minister. But all you had to do was meet with your minister once a day when the Commons was sitting and report gossip back to him and in return for that responsibility you were given briefings which you had to pass on to backbench MP's. You got no extra pay for it but if you did it well you were likely to be selected for a Whip's post when one became available. If you did that well you might get chosen to be a junior minister.

Tom Williams had been a good PPS. He was good at passing on gossip and Attlee had been pleased at the feed-back he had received about the man. What Attlee did know about Williams was that he was intensely loyal both to him and the party. That was perhaps why he had been given the job of Agriculture Secretary. Reward for loyalty and a safe pair of hands were the thoughts in Attlee's mind as he told the man of his appointment.

On the first day he had been office Tom Williams did what every predecessor of his had done and what every successor was going to do. He met with the President of the National Farmers Union. That was an ultra reactionary organisation and the most powerful trade union in the nation. It looked after the financial interests of its members like no other trade union. Every farmer was a member. They all did well out of the cosy relationship that their union had forged with successive governments. In 1946 the president was David Scott Jones. He owned a 500 acre farm near Thaxted in Essex. By the standards of the time it was a very large farm.

They met in the Stranger's Bar of the House of Commons. They planned to have lunch in the Stranger's Dining Room later, but that would be after several drinks.

David Scott Jones's thesis was very simple, and he explained it in simple terms:

"Look, Tom, my members have done very well in the last few years. Sure, we had that agricultural recession in the early 1930's, but the government's policy of providing subsidies in order to protect a vital national industry enabled us to recover from that. We did well in the war, providing as we did more than 40% of the national food requirements. I think that the best reward for that excellent performance is that there should be a continuation of the policies that enabled all that to happen.

"So what we would like you to do is push an act through Parliament which enshrines all that in peacetime laws. The essential features of it should be the protection of British farmers from all forms of effective competition. There should be an annual price review to ensure that farmers get a fair return on their investments and there should be a system of licensing all imports so that they are only permitted when British farmers cannot meet demand.

"We are very happy that the wartime provisions that allowed people to use allotments and to keep the produce from them should remain. They should also be allowed to keep small scale animal rearing such as pig clubs, provided that each club is limited to a maximum of three animals per year. People should be allowed to keep as many chickens as they like. People should also be allowed to keep the fruit from any trees that they own.

"What we are worried about is the impact that large American and Canadian farmers might have on our members if they have unlimited right to trade their crops over here. It would be devastating for my members.

"So, Tom why not just continue those excellent policies that have worked so well for the country and my members?"

By the end of the lunch that is exactly what Tom Williams had decided to do. It was an easy option. It was bound to be popular with the cabinet. They had too many things to do without worrying about farming.

It was to be one of the worst ideas ever to be put before the cabinet because Tom Williams had not thought through the consequences of what was being proposed. He had failed to realise that the NFU plan would result in the continuation of rationing for many years. It would continue one of the harshest deprivations of war. It would continue one of the aspects of war that the electorate most wanted to see ended.

But when it came to cabinet Williams was able to get unanimous approval for his ideas and they were eventually incorporated into the Agriculture Act of 1947. He had rightly guessed that there were bigger fish to fry at those meetings.

What he had failed to realise was that what British farming needed then was massive investment so that it could produce a far higher proportion of the nation's food needs. It was not to get that investment at any time in which that Labour government was in power. But the incomes of the farmers were to improve throughout that period. It was not what was intended and it was to prove to be a bitter election issue at the next general election. It is always hard to convince a starving people to vote again for the government that allowed that starvation to continue.

* * *

The following week Ernest Bevin reported on Potsdam. His report was all about the Council of Foreign Ministers which had been established at Potsdam. Its role was primarily to draw up the definitive treaties that would establish the post-war world in Europe and lead eventually to the reconstitution of a German state. He would be representing Britain at those meetings and he would be seeking to achieve a harmonious relationship with Russia and a status for Germany that enabled that country to become an effective economic force but one without any military power. That way Britain and other countries could reduce their financial contributions to German reconstruction as rapidly as possible.

He went on to say that he thought that Potsdam had been a shambles in that it had appeared to be a conspiracy between America and Russia to expand their own spheres of influence in the world. He did not think that Britain had got much out of it and although he did not have access to all the details, and probably never would, he had no hesitation in blaming Churchill for the situation. He thought he had been pursuing some grand agenda or other which went way beyond Britain's interests. He thought it would have been better if Britain had simply tried to look after itself. Anyway that was what he would be doing in the Council meetings.

* * *

It was at the next meeting that the agenda changed abruptly. A couple of days before the Cabinet meeting Aneurin Bevan had been to see Attlee privately. He needed to agree with him how they would handle a rapidly developing crisis in the process of creating the National Health Service.

Their meeting took place in the Cabinet Room at 10, Downing Street. Aneurin Bevan was not in a good mood that morning. He went straight to the point:

"Prime Minister, when I set out the programme of work needed to create the National Health Service to the Cabinet I said that a process of consultation was needed with those currently employed in health care in this country. I suggested that we should be optimistic about the outcome of those consultations as there were good reasons to believe that all those involved would benefit from working within the NHS.

"Well, I started those consultations with the Royal College of Surgeons. They listened to the proposals that we put to them. They made no comment at the time but said that they would like to consider them and then come back to give us at least their initial conclusions. They did come back a couple of days ago. I can only describe their reactions as exceptionally hostile. They have made it clear that they will not give up their status as self-employed people at any time. They categorically refuse to become employees of any National Health Service and they will not give up their freedom to continue to conduct private medical consultations and cases. They are happy to discuss rates that would apply if they did work for the National Health Service and they are willing to do that work but the price for doing that work is that they are free to do whatever work they choose to do as self-employed people. They have even insisted that it will be a pre-condition of any further talks that that freedom is guaranteed.

"I asked them what their position would be if that guarantee was not forthcoming and they replied that there would be no further talks and they would do no work for the NHS.

"Things got worse when we had consultations with General Practitioners. They are all self-employed people who work from their own premises. They have also made it very clear that they will not become employees of any state system, nor will they sell or lease their premises to the NHS. They will happily talk about fees to be paid to them for each NHS patient who is registered with them but they will not give up private practice under any circumstances. I asked them what would happen if we could not reach agreement and their response was that they would rather give up medical practice completely than work for the state.

"We have had a similar response from the dispensing chemists. They claim that their current work in this field is profoundly unprofitable and that in return for handling NHS prescriptions they will require a substantial increase in revenues.

"It is perfectly obvious what is happening. Every single staff group and business interest is taking the opportunity to try and improve their conditions. We have two choices. We can fight them and try and impose our will and run the risk that the whole scheme gets off to a poor start. Or we can try and achieve the best possible compromise against some tight deadlines. That way we will be able to deliver an NHS well before the next election and we will be able to take the credit for that but it will be at a higher cost than anything we have contemplated before. I would like your guidance as to how we should proceed."

Attlee looked at him for a couple of minutes and then said:

"Aneurin, you know what we said in the general election campaign about health care. You know just how important a part of our campaign it was. You also know just how the cabinet gave it the number one government priority. After all that there is no way that we can allow any delays to interrupt the process. We will certainly not allow doctors, surgeons and chemists any opportunity to tell the country that we are bullying them just to deliver a political promise.

"That means that you just have to do the best deals that you can. If it costs more than we had previously thought, so be it. To give yourself some negotiating time I suggest that you make the legislation permissive rather than mandatory. That means that you will not have to spell out the precise terms of it all. That should also make it possible to keep the critics at bay for as long as possible.

"I will happily delay any further cabinet discussion on this matter until you have got quite a lot of the right ducks in the right rows. That way you can report success to your colleagues. We will include the legislation in the King's speech in November and you must have something to put forward then. But I would like you to work towards an early December deadline for solving these problems. If you can do it in that timescale I am sure that we can find a way of giving an optimistic report to the Cabinet and to Parliament. The only problem we will have is with Dalton. But I am sure that in the interests of political expediency we can get round him as well. Just get on with it."

That was the way it turned out to be. In agreeing the private contracts Bevan gave away one of the first principles of the NHS. Things have not improved at any time since then.

* * *

On October 27, 1945 President Truman used the occasion of Navy Day to deliver a major statement on foreign policy in New York City. It was an important statement and included references to Soviet influence in Europe and the role of the British Empire. In relation to the Soviet Union his statement was a flat denial and rejection of the agreement he had reached at Potsdam only a few months earlier. He said:

"We shall refuse to recognize any government imposed upon any nation by the force of any foreign power." That was despite the fact that he had agreed with Stalin that Russia could control Eastern Europe.

In discussing the role of the British Empire he used words that were very similar to those that had been used by Roosevelt:

"We believe that all states which are accepted in the society of nations should have equal access on equal terms to the trade and raw materials of the world."

In saying that he was effectively denying Britain any role in controlling Empire trade; that was denying to Britain something that was a cardinal principle in the whole management of the Empire. It was a very strong message to the British government. Its meaning was not lost on Attlee. Churchill read the words with dismay.

* * *

At the Cabinet meeting early in November Attlee managed to get the Empire to the top of the agenda. He reminded the meeting that it had been Labour party policy during the 1930's that India should be granted independence. The time had now come to re-consider that idea and do something about it. Having read the Atlantic Alliance documents Attlee was certainly in no mood to delay any action on the matter and he hoped that if India was granted independence then America might keep quiet for a while about the rest of the agreement.

He had taken private soundings amongst his colleagues over a couple of weeks and he had been most impressed by what Stafford Cripps had proposed. His plan was as clever as it was devious. What he suggested was that they should make India independent within the shortest possible timescale, hopefully well under two years. But he suggested that they give the job of achieving it to Lord Mountbatten, who had been overall British Commander in South East Asia. As a member of the Royal Family he would certainly command the respect of the British people and he would also certainly have the respect of the people of India. It would also be seen as an appointment without political bias.

Cripps and Attlee chose the planned date for Indian independence on an entirely arbitrary basis. It had to be within two years as suggested by Cripps so they chose August 1947. Just for good measure they also chose the date. It was to be August 14th, 1947. It was to be the start of a very long and tortuous process covering almost all parts of the Empire.

* * *

Max Beaverbrook had been absolutely right about the refugee crisis. When the war ended in May there were calculations that perhaps 10 million people might be affected. By late June that figure had been doubled. No one knew how accurate that figure might be nor had anyone any real idea then just how high it might go. In almost every sense the figure did not matter. What mattered was getting help to dispossessed people who might be a long way from their original home and separated from their relatives.

Louise first went out to Germany to look at the issue at first hand in July. She was taken by an RAF transport to Hamburg which by then was becoming an important British centre in North Germany. When the plane landed she was met by an army corporal called Ron Rawe who had volunteered to go on to refugee work. Such was the workload he was the only person available that day but Louise immediately saw his commitment to the task and the importance he attached to it all. He had his jeep with him and took her immediately to the centre they were using there to try and co-ordinate all their work. It was not much of a place physically. It was just a vast tent on what used to be a park in the northern part of the city. The nearest refugee camp was about a mile away and Louise would be going there later in the day. But that large tent was the administration centre for refugees in that part of Germany.

The main job they were doing there was the collection of records. Every person who came into one or other of the refugee reception centres had to be documented and photographed. It was essential to know from where they had come, who they were and who their relatives were. Only then could the search begin for any relatives so that they could be reunited as soon as possible.

Ron explained the process to her and she could see how all the details were recorded. All around that tent were notice boards. They were arranged in alphabetical order by family name. There seemed to be hundreds of them. Ron explained that his work involved taking a batch of names, going off in his jeep to a different administration centre and then trying to find a match for relatives there. All the centres managed the names of people in their area in exactly the same way so all he had to do was go and look at the alphabetical boards there and try and find a match.

In their area there were refugees from almost any part of Northern Germany, Poland, Estonia, Lithuania, and Latvia. Most of them had been driven from their homes by the onslaught of the Red Army in the autumn of 1944 and spring of 1945. They had all attempted to get as far west as possible.

He explained that he had free movement throughout all those areas and was often away for weeks at a time as he visited numerous camps to try and find relatives. Every trip was successful and each time he left Hamburg he was able to find people so that they could be reunited. Thereafter the next stage was actually to get people together and after that it was to get them back home or to a new home. Most people wanted to go back to their original homes if that was possible. He told her that the process was working well but it was inevitably slow. The distances that he and his colleagues had to cover were vast and the number of people involved was immense. But he said it was a very rewarding job because every success resulted in such huge satisfaction for all the people who were reunited and able to go back home. Even so it would take years. More resources were always going to be needed and there would always be the tragic cases of people who had lost everything. In his view it was those people who deserved and needed new lives in Britain and elsewhere.

After that he took her to the nearest refugee camp. Nothing could have prepared her for what she saw there. She had never seen so many people in a single place before. Ron told her that the whole place had been created since the end of the war and now housed around half a million people. There were sanitary facilities but they were very primitive and still involved long queues. There were shower facilities and people could use them as often as they liked as long as they were prepared to put up with the queues. There were catering facilities and two meals a day were provided; one in the morning, the other in the late afternoon. Clean drinking water was always available.

He explained that once a refugee had arrived at any camp they were documented and immediately after that the search began for any relatives. If the family was already complete when they arrived at the camp they were offered a choice of what they could then do. The first choice was to go back to their original home. If that was what they chose they would be given transport. But after that they would be dependent on whatever facilities were available there. They usually provided transport for one member of the family to go back there to see what it was like before they made a final decision. Going back home was always the first choice if their home existed and there seemed to be a chance of making a go of things there.

The other option was of going to a new destination. America was the most popular, followed by Britain, Canada, Australia and Holland. These choices were only offered when the family was complete or they had positive proof that the missing members were dead. Transport to America was easy. At the moment one liner was leaving every four days and typically three thousand people were carried on each one. The demand was such that more ships were likely to be needed quite soon. If they were going to Canada or Australia they often had to wait for up to a month for a ship.

In the meantime more and more people were streaming into the camps. Wherever possible they employed refugees to do the work of the camps, and more and more of them were now getting involved in the search for relatives programmes.

The camps were setting up their own political processes and in all cases had elected leaders who could deal with the allied authorities and the charities.

Ron thought that the work was likely to be unending for several years because more and more refugees were being found all across the battle zones. It had all been made more complicated because Germans had been fighting for the Russians rather than being taken as prisoners of war. Russians had been fighting for Germany, and these moves had scattered people across vast distances. At the end of the war all these mercenaries had been disowned and had become refugees themselves. In all cases they were widely separated from their families.

Fortunately, he explained there were no movement restrictions on those engaged in trying to re-unite families. He, personally, had been as far as Latvia, Ukraine and Hungary. The travelling was lonely but everywhere he went he was able to find relatives and arrange for them to be reunited. The pleasure of that made the job immensely rewarding.

The following day he left to take her to another camp well to the east at Breslau. It took two days to get there because of the poor condition of the roads. Frequently they had to drive through fields because the roads were so badly damaged and through small rivers because there were no bridges. Everywhere they saw lost people foraging in the countryside for their survival. It was easy for Louise to understand why the only feasible transport for Ron and his colleagues was the jeep. On the way they spent the night at a British barracks near Gatow airport in Berlin.

At Breslau they went immediately to the notice boards. On that trip Ron had a thousand names of people for whom he was searching. Within the first hour he had satisfied himself that 20 of them were in the Breslau camp. The method of contacting them was to pin a notice on the boards in the camps. Everyone looked at the notice boards every day. The new notice merely said that they should report to the camp office at four in the afternoon. Everyone there knew that that was good news. By the middle of the night he had found the names of another 15. Louise had taken a batch of names and she found 30. She fell asleep just where she was at about three in the morning. She had agreed to meet Ron for breakfast at eight.

They met with the camp elders after that. Everyone agreed that the whole programme was going well but that it needed to be speeded up. The refugee count was already far higher than could have previously been imagined. 10 million people had already been documented and there were still large numbers of people scattered anywhere from Stalingrad to the North Sea. 50 Million was beginning to look like a realistic estimate.

After Breslau Ron was going up to Lithuania and he would be visiting several camps on the way, so Louise went back to Hamburg with a different driver. His name was David and he was an army lieutenant from an armoured regiment. He was another volunteer. This had been a two week trip for him and he had identified nearly five hundred people who could be reunited with their families within a week. His plea to her was that more and more resources were going to be needed to sort what was an horrendous problem. On the way back they went to the British Brigade headquarters in Berlin and were entertained in the mess there by the

Brigade commander. He was very interested to hear Louise's reports on the refugee situation and what she was planning to do to speed up all the processes.

When she got back to Hamburg Louise took the first available plane to London. She had to talk to Max, far more action was required. She also needed to talk to Sally; everybody including all Americans needed to do more.

* * *

The evening Louise got back to London she met with Max Beaverbrook. She needed to tell him everything that she had seen in Germany. Above all she needed his help in increasing the effort made by everybody in getting the refugee crisis solved.

They met early that evening; they both wanted plenty of time to talk before they started to enjoy themselves. This time they met on the Riverside Terrace at the Savoy. It was a fine summer's evening and they sat in the evening sunshine as they sipped the first of what were likely to be many glasses of Champagne that evening.

Within a few minutes of her starting to talk Max rang through to the offices of his paper and demanded that the Editor come to the Savoy immediately. He arrived within a quarter of an hour, his name was Adrian Parish. It took Louise only a few minutes to repeat to him what she had already told Max, Adrian wrote it all down. He immediately realised the potential of the story and rang through to his office to say that he would be writing a new editorial for the next morning's edition and that the front page would have to change.

They decided then and there that the front page headline would be *HUMAN CATASTROPHE* and that the story would be a plea for far more government effort in trying to stem an impending tragedy on a vast scale. The paper would promise that the story would run and run.

The following morning a team of twenty Daily Express journalists flew to Germany in a chartered plane. They would tour the camps with the volunteers and they would report human interest stories every day. The stories would be good and bad but they would all be heart rending. Beaverbrook wanted his readers to cry when they read the stories. He wanted them to pressurise every politician in sight until such time as there was an overwhelming effort put in to solve an overwhelming problem.

As those journalists were leaving to go to Germany Max went to see the Archbishop of Canterbury, still then a figure of immense influence in the nation. He was so moved by the story in the Daily Express that he agreed to go to Germany later that very day in a plane provided by the Express so that he could see for himself what conditions were like. He agreed that he would preach on the matter at Canterbury cathedral the following Sunday morning. The Express would print his sermon in full. The theme of the sermon would be *The Innocent Victims*. The idea behind it was to shame politicians into doing something effective for a group of people who were likely to be larger in number than the entire British nation.

Then Max went to see Churchill. He needed his oratorical skills to stir the nation into action. Churchill agreed to speak to a rally to take place in the Royal Albert Hall that Saturday evening. It would be paid for by Beaverbrook and all the famous in the nation would be invited through the annals of The Daily Express.

In the event the hall was full and everyone there gave generously but the climax of it all was Churchill's speech which began with the words:

"Any nation victorious in war knows that victory brings responsibility. The destruction of an evil dictator in Germany was the result of the largest military campaigns ever mounted in the entire history of this globe. Many innocent people were hurt by those campaigns and their lives were ruined. We are now beginning to realise just how many innocent lives were ruined and it is our responsibility now to help those people to return to normal living. We are now beginning to realise just how many families were split by the overwhelming nature of those military campaigns. It is now our responsibility to try to re-unite those families….."

The following day, Sunday, Louise went to Chartwell for lunch again. They agreed exactly what he would do to publicise the need for more and more support and for more government money. It did a great deal to heal his mind as he was trying to recover from the crushing electoral defeat that he had suffered.

Churchill invited her to go with him to Eaton Mews the following Tuesday evening to meet with Alice again. He explained the nature of his relationship with her and how important she was to him.

As Louise left that little house late that Tuesday night Alice thanked her profusely for giving Winston a real cause into which he could put his energies.

* * *

Louise telephoned Sally as soon as she had got back to London. She had had a great idea on the plane back from Hamburg. It was that George Patton should be appointed to handle the refugee crisis for both Britain and America. He was very popular in both countries and he had been a most effective wartime commander. Louise was certain that his skills could be used to good effect in improving every aspect of the refugee problem. His status as a national hero in America would help immeasurably in fund raising and in creating practical arrangements to assimilate millions of European refugees into American life. It would be a huge piece of work.

He did agree to do it and he obtained Truman's permission almost instantly. Truman saw it as an opportunity to extend further American influence in Europe. He demanded of Patton before he left for Europe that he do a superb job that would forever be a credit to America. Funding would no longer be a problem.

The problem of the refugees was the only one on which Truman and Churchill ever agreed.

Under Patton's command the refugee problem did come under control but it was such a huge problem that it took several years before clear solutions were available for the vast majority of those affected. It was actually as big a problem as the war itself had been.

* * *

Winston Churchill was awarded an Honorary Degree by Westminster College in Fulton, Missouri. He went there for the award ceremony which was held on 5th March, 1946. He was introduced to the audience by President Truman who had travelled there especially for the occasion. In thanking both the President and the college Winston gave a long and eloquent speech which became known immediately as his "Iron Curtain" speech. It was very controversial both in America and Britain at the time. Winston could say what he liked at that time. He was not in government and was not bound by any official line. But he did use the Fulton speech as an attempt to change the fundamental basis of the Atlantic Alliance, and he did so in front of President Truman.

What he seemed to be doing was trying to put the past behind him. He had discussed the whole speech with Alice before he travelled to America and she had pointed out to him that he had an opportunity to distance himself from all those painful agreements into which he had entered. If he could find the words to make it look as if new challenges should unite Britain and America in a common purpose he might just be able to do that.

It was a long speech, its style typical of all his most memorable speeches. In an early part of it he made a plea for unity of purpose using the phrase "It is necessary that constancy of mind, persistency of purpose, and the grand simplicity of decision shall guide and rule the conduct of the English-speaking peoples in peace as they did in war."

He went on to claim that full democratic freedoms existed throughout the British Empire, which manifestly at that time they did not. It was the issue about which Roosevelt had lectured him onboard *Prince of Wales* and at Casablanca. At Fulton Churchill used the phrase; "We cannot be blind to the fact that the liberties enjoyed by individual citizens throughout the British Empire are not valid in a considerable number of countries, some of which are very powerful. In these states control is enforced upon the common people by various kinds of all-embracing police governments."

He then used an extraordinary set of words which indicated that he fully accepted the principles that Roosevelt had explained to him and over which they had fought on *Prince of Wales* until Winston had finally had to accept Rossevelt's terms for more American assistance.: "All this means that the people of any country have the right, and should have the power by constitutional action, by free unfettered elections, with secret ballot, to choose or change the character or form of government under which they dwell; that freedom of speech and thought should reign; that courts of justice, independent of the executive; unbiased by any party, should administer laws which have received the broad assent of large majorities or are consecrated by time or custom. Here are the title deeds of freedom which should lie in every cottage home. Here is the message of the British and American peoples to mankind. Let us preach what we practice- let us practice what we preach."

He did not say that Mahatma Gandhi had been fighting for exactly those freedoms in India for more than twenty years, and that he, Churchill, had opposed giving India those freedoms and had led the British opposition to granting those freedoms.

By this time Truman was seething. In his view the whole speech was turning into a smokescreen. He was certainly going to regret that he had introduced him to the audience. But things were going to get worse.

Churchill then turned to the situation in Europe. He described the deal he had done with Stalin on that disastrous trip to Moscow, about which he had had subsequent regrets about the effect it had had on his dealings with Roosevelt. It was that deal about Russia being able to control vast areas of Eastern Europe. He said: "From Stettin in the Baltic to Trieste in the Adriatic, an iron curtain has descended across the Continent. Behind that line lie all the capitals of the ancient states of Central and Eastern Europe. Warsaw, Prague, Berlin, Vienna, Budapest, Belgrade, Bucharest and Sofia. All these famous cities lie in what I must call the Soviet sphere, and all are subject in one form or another, not only to Soviet influence but to a very high and, in many cases, increasing control from Moscow. Athens alone-Greece with its immortal glories- is free to decide its future at an election…"

As he said those words Truman muttered to himself "That is the deal you did, just because you wanted to control Greece."

A few minutes later Truman was choking as Churchill finished with a section that began "Let no man underrate the abiding power of the British Empire and Commonwealth."

It included the phrase "If the population of the English speaking Commonwealths be added to that of the United States with all that such cooperation implies in the air, on the sea, all over the globe and in science and in industry, and in moral force, there will be no quivering, precarious balance of power to offer its temptation to ambition or adventure."

That was the very last thing that Truman wanted to hear. Whatever may have been Truman's former intentions he decided that afternoon as that speech came to an end that he was going to turn the screws on Britain.

He had already taken over management of the refugee crisis and now he was looking for something much more overtly political.

When Attlee read the speech he went apoplectic with rage. Churchill had signed that wretched agreement and now he was talking as if it did not exist.

In the meantime Attlee was having to pick his way over the carcass of war and try to find some way forward for the British people in desperate times. His difficulties were not helped in any way by Churchill giving a wholly different account to the world of what he had agreed with America and Truman inventing completely new policies which went far beyond anything that had ever been said at the great conferences at Tehran, Yalta and Potsdam.

Each night as he nursed his deep, long drink Attlee felt very lonely. He felt that Britain was being cut off at the knees and it was its own wartime leader who had set that process in train.

* * *

Winston's aspirations to bring Greece and Turkey under British control and eventually to be part of the Empire had been explicitly agreed with Stalin and were an integral part of the deal to give Russia control over most of the territory in the eastern and south-eastern part of Europe.

But Stalin never had any intention that British control over those countries would be the eventual outcome. Immediately the war was over and even before Britain had any chance to gain any sort of control in either country Russia had started aggressive campaigns to impose its own will in both countries.

In Greece, Russia organised the formation of a communist based insurgency group called the National Liberation Front. Greece was in economic chaos after the war and amid the growing collapse of its institutions the National Liberation Front, sometimes known as EAM/ELAS, was able to gain strong support amongst the population.

In Turkey the weak government there faced unrelenting pressure from Russia to give up all Turkish territory north of the Dardanelles. This would put the crucial waterway that Russia needed from the Black Sea to the Mediterranean under joint control.

Neither of these situations had been envisaged by Churchill and they effectively made it impossible for Britain to impose its will in any useful way on either country.

* * *

Britain in 1946 was dominated by the debates in Parliament over nationalisation and the plan to give independence to India. The first actual nationalisation was of the Bank of England. It was the first because it was by far the simplest.

Aneurin Bevan continued to have difficulty with all key staff groups in health care and with freehold owners throughout the year. As a result the eventual parliamentary bill was a fudge; so was the initial organisation of the National Health Service. It proved impossible to eliminate private health care because the consultants and doctors refused to work for the state in any way if private care was outlawed. It constituted such a large share of their personal incomes that they simply had to ensure that it continued. It was a principle that Bevan had to concede if he was to have any chance of success.

He failed to get a national pay structure without significant pay rises for large groups of workers, particularly nurses and all those that lived and worked in the northern parts of the country where wages had traditionally been lower than in the south. The whole pay issue became a nightmare in cabinet. Each time Bevan reported on so-called progress the cost had gone up substantially. There never had been the slightest chance that the national service could be provided within the previous cost to the country.

Each time he produced a new estimate there was a ferocious row with Dalton. He argued that it was impossible for the state to pay for such massive cost over-runs through taxation receipts. The public had been promised a free National Health Service and it would therefore be politically impossible to impose extra taxes just to cover the cost of such a free service. In those circumstances the government had no alternative but to borrow the necessary money. It was effectively borrowing money just to pay salaries. It was a gross misuse of any normal borrowing criteria but it was a political necessity. Basically the cabinet took the view that the public would never know; so who cared? It was to prove an expensive mistake.

The four railway companies could not wait to sell. They knew only too well just what difficulties they faced if they were to continue trading as independent companies. Virtually the whole railway infrastructure was clapped out and extensive replacement was essential. Competition between the old LNER and LMS had drained both companies of cash. The LNER had never paid a dividend and investor confidence there was very low. The railways had depended on a type of coal called Welsh Brown as the fuel for all their powerful locomotives. It was very efficient and all the most modern locomotives had been designed around its calorific capabilities. Supplies of that were now running out and the costs of new locomotive designs to use other types of coal were proving prohibitive. It was all a hopeless mess. It the government wanted to take on that shambles, so be it. It was the beginning of well over half a century of indecision, under-investment and political dithering that was to ruin a once great industry. Most of the cash paid by the government to railway shareholders was subsequently invested in America.

Stafford Cripps was the minister responsible for the railways. Shortly before the date for the completion of the purchase of the railway companies, he warned the cabinet of the investment requirements if the railway infrastructure was to be repaired and if there was to be any modernisation of the system. The figures were so high that the cabinet decided that investment on that scale was impossible. They therefore cut the plans by 50% and decided to borrow whatever money was required within that limit. Thus the national debt increased again. Dalton warned them that the interest alone on all that debt would require an increase in taxation but that warning was ignored.

It was much the same in all the other industries that were to be nationalised.

* * *

If state ownership of whole industries was proving to be vexing the independence of India was proving to be a nightmare.

Trying to rule India from Whitehall had always been difficult and the only way it had been possible at all had been to delegate power to the Viceroy and any local government formed by him. Mountbatten had asked for even greater powers and they had been conceded to him by Attlee before he had accepted his appointment. But whatever Mountbatten had to agree locally in India to achieve independence in 1947 still had to be agreed by the government and Parliament.

Mountbatten negotiated principally with Mahatma Gandhi who represented people of the Hindu faith and Jinnah, who represented people of the Muslim faith. The Muslims were largely but not exclusively in the north; the Hindus in the south. Tolerance and respect between these groups and faiths was more or less non-existent. It did not take Mountbatten long to find that it was likely to be impossible to create an independent state in which those two groupings would respect each other sufficiently for that state to be workable. His solution was therefore to create two states. One based on the Hindu faith to be called India; the other to be based on the Muslim faith to be called Pakistan.

That certainly proved popular on the sub-continent but the implications of it were a government nightmare. In order that the overwhelming majority of the people could live in an area in which their faith predominated there would have to be a migration of around 6 million people. The costs of that would have to be paid for by Britain. It was another huge blow to Britain's budget.

Mountbatten travelled back to Britain to persuade Attlee that there was no other way. It was a difficult meeting between the two men. Attlee knew that it was another huge cost that Britain could not bear. Equally he knew what he was required to do under the Atlantic Alliance. He knew he would not get any relief from that agreement by Truman. It was not even worth asking the question. He eventually concluded that the only answer to the problem was more government borrowing. He reluctantly authorised Mountbatten to proceed.

As soon as Mountbatten had returned to India and had agreed the main lines of the partition of the country with Gandhi and Jinnah he was presented with demands for on-going British aid because India was incapable of being self-sufficient at least in the short term. He had no option but to concede that as well.

Tom Williams continued with his complacent agricultural policies. There was very strong public clamour for the end of all rationing and there were powerful demands that Britain import whatever food was necessary to ensure that there were adequate stocks available for Britain to be free of all rationing as soon as possible. But he did nothing about those demands. He argued instead that British farmers needed the continued support of food trade protection in order that they could invest heavily in the development of home grown products. The fact that farmers were growing rich and that they were investing less in their farms than ever before seemed to be irrelevant to him. He had done that deal with the NFU and that was it so far as he was concerned. Anyway, rationing meant that the government was in control of what people were eating and he thought that to be excellent.

One piece of good news for the government in 1946 was that it was possible for servicemen to be released and to return home. The navy was able to release large numbers of people provided they undertook regular reserve training. The RAF also agreed to release people who had been associated with Bomber Command. In future they would have access to nuclear capabilities. Roosevelt had agreed with Churchill that Britain could have access to American weaponry technology and Truman upheld that agreement provided that overall command and control remained with America. But access to that technology meant that conventional bomber forces could be reduced in size almost immediately.

Releasing people was not so easy for the army because the commitments in Germany were very large and there had been outbreaks of terrorism in various parts of the Empire, particularly in the Middle East and in Malaya. But by August 1946 it had been possible to release 600,000 men to go back home. It was not as many as Attlee had wanted but it was a good start.

Despite Dalton's hopes the resumption of British exports on anything like the pre-war scale had proved to be nigh on impossible. British manufacturing capability had been far too drained during the war and most of the factories were in a poor state. There was no money available for product development and re-investment in the factories. It would be a long while before any large scale exports could resume and during that period the British economy would continue to deteriorate.

General Patton's efforts brought a much higher level of management and control to the refugee crisis. During 1946 10 million of them were returned to their original homes, two million went to America and another million went to other parts of the world. But another 2 million died of disease or from injuries. It was a year of progress but there was a long way to go. Louise had regular reviews with George Patton about how she could best deploy the resources of her charity and new targets were always set at those meetings. They were all achieved.

* * *

The post war world proved very unstable, especially for Britain. Russia was continuously angling for greater involvement in the Balkans and the Middle East. Britain was facing greater and greater economic difficulties and was coming under intense pressure from Truman to dismember the Empire which Churchill had agreed to do on the *Prince of Wales*.

There were real fears, widely held around the world, that Britain would no longer have the economic or military strength to govern and control those large areas of the Middle East that it had controlled since the First World War. If Britain had to withdraw from there it was felt that Russia would use precisely that opportunity to spread its influence southwards. The consequences of that happening in such an unstable part of the world were widely feared

There were similar fears about the impact of a declining British influence in the Far East. If Britain had to withdraw from Singapore, and Burma, for example, it was by no means clear that America would have had any interest in either. What then would have happened?

These fears were widely obvious very soon after the war. Hugh Dalton's first austerity budget after the war made it obvious that Britain was going to look to its own short-term financial survival before anything else. The cost of the war had been avoided by Churchill and the National Government. It had all been washed under a carpet called "the special relationship with America." The public had believed during the war that America was not only making an increasing commitment in terms of equipment and manpower but that it was also paying for Britain as well. They thought that that was what all those demands by Churchill of Roosevelt were all about. In reality America made no financial contribution to Britain's own war effort. It did finance its own efforts but all the rest was to be paid for by Britain on purely commercial terms.

Through the second half of 1945 and through the whole of 1946 the financial crisis got worse and worse. The public had hoped that with the end of the war the wartime austerity measure would quickly and progressively disappear. But they did not. The rationing of food, fuel and clothing continued for many years. It all made a war-weary public depressed, anxious and seriously de-moralised. People simply could not see an end to the misery.

But it was not a political act of any kind that caused the crisis to deepen. It was not an international meeting, or a row with Stalin or some kind of crisis in Berlin. Nor was it a demand by Stalin for more influence in the Middle East. But it was something that caused President Truman immense satisfaction. It was the worst British winter in the 20th century.

That winter was so bad that for large parts of January and February the temperature was below freezing by day and night. There were frequent blizzards that severely disrupted transport. Whole factories were closed throughout those two months. The clapped-out railway system, devastated by over-use throughout the war and un-repaired afterwards, could not cope with the bad weather. Whenever there was high pressure over the country there were severe smogs largely caused by the widespread use of coal as practically the only fuel available. The national budget was wrecked by that weather.

In February 1947 the British government could not continue with any pretence about anything anymore. The truth had come home to it in a very severe way. If it wanted to carry out all its New Jerusalem policies the Empire had to be diminished. The truth was that Britain could no longer afford to maintain an Empire so large. So in that month Attlee and his cabinet made what was probably an inevitable decision. They confirmed the final date for withdrawal from India. Britain's circumstances were so dire that there was no alternative. Soon after that they announced that they would also be withdrawing from Ceylon and Burma as well.

At that time Britain was fighting something that threatened to become very ugly very quickly, and there was little sympathy for Britain's position from around the world. It was all about the future of Palestine. Attlee did discuss the Palestine question with Truman on one occasion, hoping to get American support for some cohesive action. The reply he got was that America was not in any way obliged to help Britain in any of its colonies no matter how serious any situation might become and it would not do so. He went on to say that the creation of a protected homeland for Jewish people was not on any American list of priorities at that time. Protection of democracies was. So far as he was aware there were no democracies in the Middle East.

One of the legacies of the large scale slaughter of Jewish people in Germany and German occupied territories under Nazi rule, often called the holocaust, was a strong cry from Jewish people for them to have their own homeland. They wanted part of what was then Palestine, which was then ruled by Britain. Britain had neither the will nor the financial resources to fight the Jewish terrorist activities and the world generally was determined to let them have some sort of homeland, although Palestine was not the only place being considered. The others were Uganda and Uruguay. But the Jews wanted part of Palestine and they were going to fight for it. So Britain turned the whole problem over to the United Nations, and in doing so created the first stage of a rapid withdrawal from the whole of the Middle East. Within nine years Britain had left the area altogether.

The final decision made by Attlees's government that February was to withdraw all British troops from Greece and Turkey by March 31st. That was effectively instant withdrawal from an unstable area which was very vulnerable to any threats that Stalin cared to throw at them.

Although Truman had never been involved in Roosevelt's planning before the *Prince of Wales* meeting and the negotiation of the Atlantic Alliance he fully understood the benefits to America that would flow from Britain's withdrawal from anywhere. On March 12th he therefore launched what commentators called the Truman Doctrine. This called for America "to help free people to maintain their free institutions and national integrity against aggressive movements that seek to impose upon them totalitarian regimes." At the same time he sought congressional approval to provide financial assistance and the assignment of personnel to Greece and Turkey. It was the first step in the long process of America taking over power and influence from Britain all around the world. From wherever he had gone Roosevelt would have been very pleased. It was everything that Churchill had fought against in his early verbal skirmishes with Roosevelt. It was everything that Roosevelt had attempted to achieve.

* * *

At the very time that Britain had been making those decisions about Greece and Turkey Ernest Bevin was attending a six week meeting of a group called The Council of Foreign Ministers. It was taking place in Moscow. The American side was led by George Marshall, who had recently been appointed to be Truman's Secretary of State. Since Potsdam, differences between America and Russia had widened. For example America wanted the whole of Germany to be regarded as a single economic unit. Russia wanted the eastern part that it controlled to be under Russian economic control. The long meeting, involving 43 sessions, achieved very little other than to confirm those widening differences. But both Russia and America were convinced at the end of it that the dreadfully slow pace of recovery that was being experienced all over Europe was going to cause political chaos unless something was done about it very quickly. Marshall's view was that no government could long survive unless it was able to solve such problems.

While he was in Europe he deliberately travelled around so that he could see the true state of the continent. He was appalled at the remaining state of devastation nearly two years after the end of the war. In some places it seemed that nothing had been done to improve matters. What particularly appalled him was that whole factories still lay in ruins. In many areas the industrial capacity of Europe was still almost non-existent.

Marshall was a man of action. It was not for nothing that he had been the American commander in the Pacific. His command ethos had been to find solutions to problems. He was determined to find a solution to those increasingly overwhelming economic problems in Europe. He was sure that if he did not then the whole continent would collapse into political chaos. If that happened, he reasoned, Russia would be a very active predator. In finding solutions to those economic problems he proved to be a real dose of fresh air in the entire European political process.

As he travelled back to America he thought through a policy that was deliberately designed to get the war-ravaged European economies back to work. He was particularly concerned to ensure that German industry could re-start. What Marshall had realised was that the re-building of Germany was essential for progress across the entire continent.

By June 5th sufficient progress had been made for Marshall to set out his ideas in a speech at Harvard University. What he said at Harvard included:

I need not tell you gentlemen that the world situation is very serious....

In considering the requirements for the rehabilitation of Europe the physical loss of life, the visible destruction of cities, factories, mines and railroads was correctly estimated, but it has become obvious during recent months that this visible destruction was probably less serious than the dislocation of the entire fabrics of the European economy.

The truth of the matter is that Europe's requirements for the next 3 or 4 years of foreign food and other essential products -principally from America- are so much greater then her present ability to pay that she must have substantial additional help, or face economic, social, and political deterioration of a very grave character.

Our policy is directed not against any country or doctrine but against hunger, poverty, desperation, and chaos. Its purpose should be the revival of working economy in the world so as to permit the emergence of political and social conditions in which free institutions can exist.

It is already evident that, before the United States Government can proceed much further in its efforts to alleviate the situation and help start the European world on its way to recovery, there must be some agreement among the countries of Europe as to the requirements of the situation.....

Political passion and prejudice have no part. With foresight, and a willingness on the part of our people to face up to the vast responsibilities which history has clearly placed on our country, the difficulties I have outlined can and will be overcome.

That day Marshall Aid was born. Marshall Aid was essentially the provision of credits to enable most European countries to buy food and industrial materials from America. Anything bought had to be carried in American ships. No cash was provided at any stage. Each country had to produce a plan for what it needed and it was against those plans that the aid was provided. It was certainly Marshall Aid that enabled new investment to begin throughout Europe but it was also Marshall Aid that caused the differences between Russia and America to widen. Russia was offered aid but chose not to take any. It was still concerned with what it could take out of Europe, Germany in particular. Russia would in due course retaliate against Western Europe about that aid. Altogether America provided 13 billion dollars worth of aid (probably equivalent to 260 billion dollars today).

* * *

Britain eventually drew down over 3 billion dollars of Marshall Aid. The Cabinet were happy enough to agree to it but they were not prepared to change national spending priorities in any way to accommodate it. They re-affirmed that the national priorities were health and the nationalisation of the major industries. They also decided that they would not use Marshall Aid in any way that detracted from the requirement of the nationalised industries to employ as many people as possible. A good example of that was in railway locomotives and railway equipment in general. A conscious decision was therefore made that railway equipment could not be part of the Marshall Aid package despite a desperate shortage of modern railway equipment in the country. There were, for example, no freight trains with powered braking systems at that time although such equipment was used throughout America. That made for diabolically slow freight trains in Britain which had the effect of making passenger trains slow as well.

The American owned Ford factory at Dagenham was re-built and re-equipped with Marshall Aid and was therefore quickly able to resume exports but that was the largest industrial scheme to benefit.

Tom Williams made a plea that as much of that aid as possible should be used for food, because British farmers did not have the capacity to grow enough. A much better plea would have been to use a large chunk of it to modernise British farms and start using the industrial farming methods so common in America. But his deal with the NFU would have prevented that.

One new idea did emerge in Cabinet and it was that the availability of Marshall Aid might make possible some re-jigging of the overall budget so that they could start the construction of large numbers of houses to be owned and managed by local councils. A plan to achieve that was eventually conceived by the Treasury and as a consequence some large scale importing of building products, particularly timber and asbestos, took place.

The net effect of all that aid was really in food and council houses. A great opportunity to re-build British industry was lost.

In Germany all the Marshall Aid was used to re-build factories and modernise the agricultural system. Food rationing was ended in Germany long before it was ended in Britain.

* * *

In 1947 Dalton had to resign as Chancellor of the Exchequer because he was found to have leaked his own budget speech to a newspaper. He was replaced by Stafford Cripps who took a far less complacent view of Britain's economic circumstances. He immediately introduced an austerity budget, the like of which had never been seen in Britain before. Interest rates were jacked up to the point that personal and commercial borrowing became almost impossible. New taxes were introduced on people and businesses. High earners could pay up to 97% of the income in the higher tax bands. The high profits tax on companies eliminated any incentive to invest. All investment in state industries was to be cut and even long term investment plans cancelled. Funding for Empire projects was to all intents and purposes eliminated.

That situation of misery was to continue throughout the remaining life of the government. But the cabinet was happy with it all, except for one item. It was obvious to Cripps that the country could not afford a completely free National Health Service. The thing was gobbling money at far too high a rate. So prescription charges were introduced. The charge made for each item was higher than the average cost of each item. The public soon learned that getting the doctor to prescribe everything was an expensive way of getting some medicines. They also learned that healthcare could never be entirely free at the point of delivery.

* * *

The Russian retaliation for Marshall Aid took the form of a blockade of all surface transport links into Berlin. The intention was to force Britain, America and France to leave that city. In recent years the Russian archives have proved that they thought about cutting off air links as well but they feared that that would lead to immediate war.

Russia took the first steps that would lead to the Berlin blockade in March 1948. They closed the road and rail links for a short time stating that urgent repairs were necessary, but in reality it was to test British and American reactions. After that they went on tightening things progressively until August when the blockade became total.

Even by June there was increasing desperation in the city. There was only enough food left for 36 days and only enough coal for the power stations to last 45 days.

From the Russian point of view things got a lot worse at the end of June when Britain and America introduced a new currency to the parts of Germany that they controlled including Berlin. On 23 June, despite communist street protests the Berlin City Assembly voted to accept the new currency in the western parts of the city and to leave the Soviet currency in the east.

Britain and America relieved the blockade by the operation of an airlift. The Russians had not anticipated that any such airlift would be capable of carrying anything like enough of basic commodities like coal, oil and food to sustain such a large city. They had expected that America and Britain would quickly be forced to leave the city. The airlift started on June 26th and lasted eleven months. Nearly 300,000 missions were flown. Some 600,000 tons of food were delivered as well as nearly 1.5 million tons of coal.

The start of that airlift proved to be a defining moment in the development of the cold war. Berlin became an isolated city on a real-time war footing for more than 40 years.

Another step was taken that intensified the cold war just a few months later. America and Britain had agreed to manage their two zones as a single economic unit. Initially this was done to reduce Britain's unsustainable financial commitment to Germany. But it was also done in recognition of the Marshall Plan that German industry should be revived and that

Germany should be structured so that it was clearly part of an Anglo-American alliance that could counter any threat from the Soviet Union.

From that moment on both America and the Soviet Union developed their armaments industries relentlessly in any ways possible to ensure that they were always able to counter any threat from the other.

Guy Burgess, by now working for the Foreign Secretary in London, was able to pass valuable information back to Moscow on almost a daily basis.

* * *

Independence for India and Pakistan was swiftly followed by Ceylon and Burma gaining their freedom as well. On each occasion there were large celebrations in the countries concerned and in London as well. Churchill was invited to them all but he declined all the invitations. He saw nothing to celebrate. He had desperately wanted to expand the Empire and he saw what was happening as a betrayal of the British people. He spent each of those Independence days with Alice.

He was now well into his 70's, keen to exercise power again but unlikely to do so and certainly not in any way that would enable him to fulfil his greatest remaining ambition which had been to lead the greatest empire the world had ever know through a period of peace and growth. He had accepted that if he was to become Prime Minister again it would only be for a short time while a successor emerged.

He had gone back to writing. His sessions with Alice were more about memories now. There was little, if anything that she could do to help him sort out his ideas about the future.

On the day of Indian and Pakistani independence in August 1947 their conversation was all about that dreadful meeting on *Prince of Wales*, and everything that it had led to. In retrospect he regarded that as the low point of his life. It was the point at which everything changed for him and everything changed for Britain. With each day that passed it became more and more obvious to him that Britain and America were not doing things together as he had suggested at Fulton. America was certainly providing help to Britain but it was not a shared relationship. It was much closer to a master/slave relationship. Britain had to do what it was told.

Alice often talked to him about that trip to Moscow at which he had offered that territorial deal to Stalin. Churchill had regrets about it as soon as he had been castigated by Roosevelt for it. But he maintained that at the time it was a worthwhile step forward in his plans to expand the Empire. But looking back at it now he could see that his attempt to get control of Turkey was every bit as bad as his attempt to control the Dardanelles waterway that was part of Turkey during the Great War. He would never admit publicly that he had ever had that conversation with Stalin, nor would be publicly admit that there had been any failings in what he had agreed or in the consequences. But he was well used to making historical judgments about people and had done so many times in the books that he had written. He had no doubts that future generations of historians would make judgments about him and they might be critical of that one.

* * *

By 1950 the main work of the Daily Express refugee charities was complete. George Patton had finished his work and had gone back to America.

Louise had had enough of spies and politicians and she was exhausted by all those years of running that huge relief operation. It had been very rewarding work but it had left her and everyone else associated with it in a complete state of exhaustion. She needed a complete change in her life. She had no idea what she wanted to do but she did know that it would have to mean that she would have lots of friends and that her life would have to be busy.

Her last trip to Germany with the charity was in May 1950. Over those five years she had been many times to numerous German cities and she had never ceased to be amazed at the sheer pace and energy of the German people as they sought to re-build their shattered land. Her last trip was to Hamburg and she went there to be honoured by that city for all the work that she had organised.

The ceremony took place in a small park down by the Alster Lake close to the city centre. When she had first been there the whole area had been devastated and had still been fire-scorched from those terrible bombing raids back in 1943. Now it was all green again and the young trees that had been planted a few years before were coming into bloom. All the rubble had been cleared long before and all along the Jungfernstieg buildings were being restored to their original glory. This time she did not sleep in an army tent. She stayed in the Vierjahrezeiten hotel which had re-opened a few weeks before.

In her speech in acceptance of the honour that she had been given she said that she was accepting it on behalf of the vast numbers of people who had worked for so long to try and return the families of many nations to a normal way of life, wherever that might be. It was an emotional time. She had made many friends in Hamburg and in many other European cities as well. She knew that when she left Hamburg she would be going into the unknown. It all seemed to be such a long time since she had first gone there when she was working with Achtgrenze.

She flew back to London the following morning on an RAF Dakota. They flew low over a Europe that was bathed in warm spring sunshine. It was a Europe that was slowly healing itself. From their cruising height of 5,000 feet that morning it looked brilliant. That was how she hoped the future would be for her.

More importantly she thought on that flight about what she was going to do next. It seemed to be the first time in years that she could have uninterrupted thoughts on anything. She perhaps came to an obvious conclusion. She would farm her large network of friends and contacts and through that she would attempt to find a completely new future within a year. She would certainly take time away from work. She might travel; she would certainly want to go back to Washington.

The following weekend she went back to Brighton with Max Beaverbrook. They stayed again at the Grand Hotel, but this time they did not just go for a single night. They went down on the Brighton Belle from Victoria station in London on the Friday afternoon. As before Max had his driver waiting for them at the station. It was only a few minutes drive to the hotel. It was a fine spring evening and they went for a long walk along the waterfront before dinner. While they walked they talked about her aspirations and hopes.

It was over dinner that Max told her that he had become a large investor in a new transport project. She had always remembered his enthusiasm for transport back in the 1930's and she was not surprised that he was still active in that area but this new one was something completely different. He talked about the gas turbine engine that had been invented by a British engineer called Frank Whittle. He explained how the engine worked and that it was now installed on a new generation of military aircraft. But what excited him was that a new application of that technology was being applied to the airliner market. He had invested heavily; indeed he was the single largest investor, in a project to build a new airliner called the Vickers Viscount. The aircraft had first flown a couple of years earlier and there were very promising results in the test flights. If she wanted it, he was in a position to guarantee her a job on that project. They talked about it for hours and she was very interested. He arranged for her to go and visit the factory and go on a test flight the following week.

She enjoyed the test flight. It was by far the smoothest and most comfortable aircraft on which she had ever flown. It was also very quiet. She was very impressed. She also liked the atmosphere of the factory. It seemed to be well run and the labour force seemed to be highly skilled and very committed to the success of the Viscount.

The following weekend she went to Chartwell to stay with Churchill. It was an enjoyable weekend and he was in very good form, but he had certainly lost some of his old fire. He told her that if and when he became Prime Minister again she could be the British Ambassador wherever she liked. It was a flattering offer but to her mind it would keep her too close to politicians. In any event there was no certainty that he would become PM ever again. But she did bear it in mind. If nothing better turned up she might find Washington or Germany to be very attractive.

The week after that she went to Washington. She went on the *Queen Mary* again. Washington was every bit as exciting as she had remembered it. Amongst numerous others she met up with Sally and George Patton. She met with Truman for the first time and he told her that her work had been very much appreciated and that she would always be welcome there. But she felt that Washington was all too political for her now.

* * *

She went back to Britain on the *Queen Elizabeth*. After it had docked at Southampton she rang Max to say that she wanted to talk. They met that evening but not at the Savoy this time. He had just bought a hotel out in the country at Henley-on-Thames. If she came to his office at five they would be driven out there. The hotel was called Ravenswood House.

It was that evening that she told him that she would like to work on the Viscount project. She wanted to be Sales and Marketing Director.

He arranged that for her and she started work the following week. Her work took her all over the world and she made many friends in the process. The Viscount went on to be the most successful British airliner project ever. She made sure that it was.

* * *

Two general elections took place in quick succession in 1950 and 1951. The failing Labour government lost an overall majority at the first and was kicked out of office at the second. Churchill was back as Prime Minister. He did contact Louise to offer her a diplomatic job but she said she was very happy where she was.

The first thing that Churchill did was abolish food rationing. It turned out that it had not been needed for some years. It was only the policies of Tom Williams that had kept it in place. It was the first genuinely popular social act that the Tories had done for many years.

* * *

In 1956 Britain still controlled major assets in the Middle East. In those days every part of the British Empire was still coloured red on maps of the world. On the map of Africa there was continuous red from Cape Town to the Mediterranean. One of the assets that Britain still controlled within that continuous line of red was the Suez Canal that separated Africa from Asia. It was definitely within the Middle East and it was owned by the British owned Suez Canal Company. It was protected, but not heavily, by British forces.

Gamal Abdul Nasser, the Egyptian President at that time, was seeking to secure American aid funding for the giant Aswan dam project which would have the twin benefits of improving irrigation in the Nile Valley and providing Egypt with vast amounts of cheap electricity. In the end America refused to provide that aid because Egypt was not a democracy and Nasser's response was to seek to punish foreign investors in Egypt by nationalising the Suez Canal. He knew that the loss of the canal to Britain would be a severe blow. It might therefore be an effective sanction just to threaten nationalisation.

Anthony Eden had succeeded Churchill as Prime Minister and Suez was his first big crisis. He was well aware of the importance to Britain of the canal but equally he knew that Britain alone was in no position to defend it if it was attacked in force.

He therefore telephoned President Eisenhower and set out the position for him and asked for American aid. Eisenhower was well aware of what had been previously agreed and had no hesitation in telling Eden that there was no way that America would contribute anything to a British colonial feud.

"You are on your own." He said.

Even in those circumstances Eden decided to invade Egypt to protect the canal from nationalisation. The whole exercise was a fiasco and he had to resign. He was succeeded by Harold Macmillan.

* * *

It had been an exceptionally fine summer in Britain in 1959. For a few years the economy had been improving well on all fronts. A light touch on economic controls by the Tory government had allowed all individuals and all businesses to make their own decisions about how they invested and about how they spent their money. Macmillan decided that that autumn would be a good time to consolidate his position with the electorate. He called a general election for October that year. The weather remained fine throughout the campaign and for Election Day itself. Macmillan campaigned under the slogan *"You have never had it so good"*. It proved to be a huge vote winner. The government got back with a parliamentary majority of more than 100.

After Macmillan's victory Eisenhower phoned him:

"Congratulations, Mac on a splendid win. My party is facing re-election in just a few weeks from now. Our opponent is John F. Kennedy. I am sure that you have read all about him. I am really ringing to tell you that he is a very tough democrat. He is also very much his father's son. As you know old Joseph was anti-Britain and did much to reinforce Roosevelt's own views on the subject. Over the last few years you and I have had many exchanges about the Anglo-American Alliance. Since Suez we have deliberately let things go quiet so that you could re-build national confidence. With your election, the Democrats, if they win, will see that Britain is getting stronger and they are certain to want to get Britain to speed up its implementation of the Alliance. I am certain that you will face some very tough talking with Kennedy. Just be careful, he is very tough and very determined.

* * *

In 1960 Harold Macmillan went to South Africa, then the most important African country in the Empire. When he arrived he made at speech on the dockside which expressed his view that Winds of Change were blowing over Africa. It was a policy statement that all British colonies in Africa were shortly to be given their independence. It was a deliberate statement of policy in advance of his first meeting with John F. Kennedy. The promise was to be fulfilled completely, with the only exception of Zimbabwe, within five years and only there because of local resistance by white settlers. Macmillan did not want disputes with America; he wanted a modus operandi and he wanted to take the initiative for achieving it.

But things were not to be that easy.

* * *

Macmillan met Kennedy several times. All of their meetings were portrayed as being friendly and positive. In reality they were nothing of the kind. Kennedy was determined to ensure that Britain had no effective voice on any significant issue that concerned America. Those meetings were characterised by their first meeting and then a later one in Bermuda.

The first one began with Kennedy speaking:

"I was very glad to read about that speech you made in Cape Town. It was realistic but long overdue. It would have been best if Churchill had gone there and made it when he became Prime Minister again in 1951. That would have proved to America that Britain was going to honour the spirit and the letter of the Atlantic Alliance. I know of all sorts of reasons why Churchill might have regretted what he agreed with Roosevelt but I can assure you that no one in any American government will ever forget what was agreed between the two of them. I can also assure you that every American government will want to enforce the terms of that agreement. That agreement made America a world power and there is huge pride in our country in what Roosevelt achieved.

"There are some steps that I will now insist that you take to complete it all. The first is that you must get rid of the rest of your Empire. Hong Kong, Singapore, Malaya, Yemen, and the Caribbean islands must all go. I will not use the word please. It is a long overdue treaty obligation that those states cease to be part of a governed empire. They must be completely free to determine their own futures.

"The next thing is that Britain must get rid of any British independent nuclear deterrent. I do not know why you are investing in such technology because America will never let you use it. What you can do is use nuclear weapons under our command. That means that your Blue Steel system must go and it must be replaced by our new Polaris system. You must therefore also cancel your TSR2 aircraft programme. Instead you must purchase and you must pay for Polaris and its associated submarines in full. It is your part of the war bargain."

The only thing that Macmillan was allowed to do unilaterally was to decide the date on which the British public were told about those decisions. In the event he fluffed any announcement and left it to the new Labour government that was elected in 1964. One of their first statements was about the cancellation of Blue Steel and TSR2.

* * *

In 1962 Nikita Khrushchev, who had been Zhukov's political minder through all the great campaigns in Russia, initiated the most confrontational event of the entire cold war. He was now the General Secretary of the Communist Party of the Soviet Union. He ordered the shipment to Cuba of several long range ballistic missiles that were clearly intended to reduce the warning time should any strike against America be contemplated or ordered. As a result of the inevitable confrontation with Kennedy the missiles were never landed on Cuba and they were returned to Russia.

* * *

There was a general election in Britain on 15th October, 1964. A Tory government was then in power and there was an expectation that it might be toppled by the Labour Party then led by Harold Wilson. The opinion polls indicated that there might be no clear result.

A few evenings before the election itself Harold Wilson went to have dinner with Clement Attlee, then 81 years old and long since retired from active politics. His main purpose was to seek advice from the last Labour Prime Minister about some of the problems that might lie ahead should he be elected as Prime Minister.

It was an amiable evening. Attlee talked at length about some of the issues he had had to face. That included the issue of a cabinet that would not face up to national issues and how to disguise to the public that policy issues were falling apart.

But right at the end of the evening just as Harold Wilson was about to leave Attlee said:

"Look, Harold. There is one issue on which you must get yourself briefed by the cabinet secretary just as soon as you can. It is the whole matter of the Atlantic Alliance that was drawn up by Churchill and Roosevelt. That agreement crippled my government and it will surely cripple yours. You must read it as one of the first things you do in Downing Street."

Wilson did win that election by a very narrow margin. During the weekend that followed he did read that agreement. He was deeply shocked by the implications of it all. Over the years that followed the pain that it had inflicted on Britain brutalised all economic policy in Britain. It caused the pound to be devalued and that in turn penalised Britain's economic performance for several decades.

Long after he had retired from politics Wilson completed his memoirs in 1986. They included the words:

"Lend/Lease also involved Britain's surrender of her rights and royalties in a series of British technological achievements. Although British performance in industrial techniques in the inter-war years had been marked by a period of more general decline, the achievements of our scientists and technologists had equalled the most remarkable eras of British inventive greatness. Radar, antibiotics, jet aircraft and advances in British nuclear research had created an industrial revolution all over the developed world. Under Lend/Lease these inventions were surrendered as part of the inter-Allied war effort, free of any royalty or other payments from the United States. Had Churchill been able to insist on adequate royalties for these inventions, both our wartime and post-war balance of payments would have been very different.

* * *

In 1982 when Argentina invaded the Falklands Islands the British Prime Minister, Margaret Thatcher, sought American assistance in evicting the invaders. President Reagan categorically told Thatcher that there would no American involvement because of the Atlantic Alliance. He said that specifically ruled out any American involvement in colonial issues.

* * *

The Berlin Wall was the last enduring symbol of the Iron Curtain that Winston Churchill had described at Fulton, Missouri in 1946. It stretched across the entire city and was designed to stop residents of East Germany escaping to the west. It was so badly built that it was eventually just pushed over by the angry citizens of East Berlin in 1989. Its collapse was to lead to the events that effectively brought some of the worst consequences of World War Two to an end.

* * *

In 1990 Iraq invaded Kuwait. America was disposed to go to war to evict Iraq from Kuwait. American President George Bush phoned Prime Minister Thatcher and demanded that Britain support America. He said it was America's call as specifically provided for by the Atlantic Alliance. Britain complied. The result was that Britain was committed to support America in Iraq for a decade and more.

* * *

In 2003 America decided to go to war with Iraq again, this time in order to depose President Saddam Hussein. I believe that President George "Dubya" Bush, son of President George Bush who ordered the Gulf War in 1990/91, phoned British Prime Minister Blair with a similar demand for British involvement. No one else knows exactly what they said but Britain did commit forces to Iraq then despite the largest ever peace demonstration in London and despite the overwhelming hostility of the British people to any such campaign. Again Britain was under orders, but this time in the face of a hostile British public. President Bush did exactly as President Roosevelt would have wanted him to do. Roosevelt would have turned proudly in his grave.

The British Prime Minister was accused of being an American puppet. His political popularity sagged and his entire leadership was brought into question.

The British public wanted to know the truth about why Britain went to war with Iraq. It was a major issue in the 2005 General Election. They were never given it by their government. But it was all in those documents drawn up on *Augusta* and *Prince of Wales* back in 1941

* * *

Between 1945 and 2004 there was a net reduction in the number of hospitals in Britain consistent with a closure rate of one every ten days. Political objectives still dominated the NHS in 2004.

In 2004 the railways were in a worse state of crisis than they had been in 1945. Political objectives still prevailed there, too.

Every nationalisation undertaken by that post-war Labour government except that of the National Health Service was reversed between 1983 and 1997. In all cases the state received less for the sale of the businesses than it had paid for them after full allowance was made for inflation. In all cases delivery standards improved after the privatisations.

* * *

The final end of that deal that Churchill had done with Stalin came in 2004 when many states that had become part of the Soviet sphere of influence joined the European Union. In all cases the decisions of those states to join the EU were made democratically. Roosevelt would have been thrilled.

* * *

Max Beaverbrook died in 1964. Louise went to his funeral. Winston Churchill died in 1966 and was given a full state funeral at St. Paul's Cathedral in London. Georgii Zhukov died in 1974 and was given a state funeral in Moscow which included a Red Square parade.

Louise died in 1995. Just before she died she was visited by her son. He was in his mid fifties. He said to her moments before she died: "Thank you, Mum, for everything." She never did tell him who his father was. It was a secret that she would take to the grave but she did truly love him.

Selected Bibliography

Barker, Ralph. *The Thousand Plan.* Pan Books, 1965
Beschloss, Michael. *The Conquerors.* Simon &Schuster 2002
Beevor, Anthony. *Stalingrad.* Penguin Group 1998
Bethell, Nicholas. *The War Hitler Won* Allen Lane The Penguin Group, 1972
Bullock, Alan. *Hitler and Stalin. Parallel Lives.* Fontana Press 1991
Chalfont, Alan. *Montgomery of Alamein.* Weidenfeld and Nicholson, 1976
Collins, Larry & Lapierre, Dominique. *Freedom at Midnight*, Collins, 1975
Cross, Robin. Citadel. *The Battle of Kursk.* Michael O'Mara Books Limited., 1993
Downing, David. *The Devil's Virtuosos.* New English Library, 1977
Duffy, Christopher. *Red Storm on the Reich.* Routledge 1991
Irving, David. *Hitler's War.* Hodder and Stoughton, 1977
Large, David Clay. *Between Two Fires.* WW Norton &Company, 1990
Lucas-Phillips, C.E. *Alamein.* Pan Books, 1962
Mee, Charles L. Jr. *Meeting at Potsdam.* Dell Publishing Co. Inc. 1975
Middlebrook, Martin. *Convoy,* 1976
Middlebrook, Martin. *The Battle of Hamburg.* Penguin Books, 1980
Moorehead, Alan. *The Desert War.* Sphere Books Limited, 1963
O'Donnell. James. P. *The Berlin Bunker.* Arrow Books 1979
Ryan, Cornelius. *A Bridge Too Far*. Hamish Hamilton, 1974
Schofield, B.B. *The Russian Convoys.* Pan Books, 1964
Seaton, Albert. *The Russo-German War 1941-45.* Presidio Press, 1971.
Shirer, William A. *The Rise and Fall of the Third Reich.* Secker and Warburg 1959